Praise for *The Intangible*

"*The Intangible* is about a rare condition known as phantom pregnancy. This fascinating story had me spellbound from the start. Washington writes with great humanity, and I found myself rooting for his deftly crafted characters, who show just what it means to love and to long and to pick yourself up from the wreckage of a failed life to stagger on to something more. Inspirational and beautifully written, this is a story I will not soon forget."

—Suzanne Redfearn, #1 Amazon bestselling author of *In an Instant*

"In this excellent and emotional debut, C. J. Washington creates highly intriguing portraits of two grieving women: one dealing with a psychological condition that tricks her body into thinking she's pregnant and the other hoping her brilliant math can find the string in the universe that will allow her to talk to the dead. Well grounded in research and full of twists, *The Intangible* is like the beautiful math equation it works to solve—complex, fascinating, with the answers to life's impossible mysteries within reach."

—Julia Heaberlin, bestselling author of *We Are All the Same in the Dark* and *Black-Eyed Susans*

THE
IN
TAN
GI
BLE

THE INTANGIBLE

A NOVEL

C. J. WASHINGTON

Little

Published by Little A, New York
www.apub.com

Amazon, the Amazon logo, and Little A are trademarks of Amazon.com, Inc., or its affiliates.

ISBN-13: 9781542032186 (hardcover)
ISBN-10: 1542032180 (hardcover)

ISBN-13: 9781542032193 (paperback)
ISBN-10: 1542032199 (paperback)

Cover design by Alex Merto

Printed in the United States of America

First edition

THE INTANGIBLE

CHAPTER 1

AMANDA

21 WEEKS PREGNANT

Mommy's voice is the predominant sound within the amniotic environment, and Baby has been listening for a few weeks. External sounds are reduced by half before they reach Baby's developing ears.

—Your Best Pregnancy

November 27, 2017

Amanda Jackson was eating avocado toast when her phone rang. It was her mother. She swiped the screen, sending the call to voice mail. The bread was warm, drizzled with olive oil, and perfectly browned, and her mother was—difficult. Derrick, Amanda's husband, a pharmaceutical sales rep, was out of town on business, and Amanda had two movies lined up for the night: a dark drama to match her mood and a romantic comedy that she hoped would put her in a good place to sleep. She wasn't optimistic about sleep.

Her phone chimed. A voice mail. And then it chimed again. A text message: 911. Received at 7:16 p.m.

She stared at the message as she chewed, the avocado creamy, the hint of lime ideal in its subtlety. 911. She felt queasy. Clearly, she had to call her mother. Now. She stood, phone in hand, and paced. More bad news. She couldn't do this sitting down. *7:18 p.m.* She made the call.

Her mother answered casually on the third ring.

"What's wrong?" Amanda asked.

"It's good to hear your voice also."

"You texted *911*," she said, annoyed, ironically, by her mother's lack of urgency.

"That's what the young people do. You know."

"I don't know." Amanda was thirty-five. "*911* means emergency to me."

"Well, I wanted you to call me back quickly. I have news. Meredith is getting married."

"To whom?" She hadn't known Meredith, her sister, was seeing anyone.

"Brian. A nice young man. She met him while she was backpacking in Peru."

"Have you met him?"

"No. He's still in Peru. He'll be here for Christmas."

"Is he Peruvian?"

"No, he's Black. That's the funny part. She went all the way to Peru and met a man from Greenville, South Carolina." Her mother and Meredith lived in Raleigh, North Carolina, a comfortable two states north of Amanda's home in Atlanta.

"She was in Peru for what, three weeks?" Amanda asked.

"She said you wouldn't approve. That's why she asked me to tell you."

That was a good call. Thirteen years separated the two of them. Meredith rarely sought Amanda's advice, and Amanda had a personal rule against offering unsolicited opinions. But at the least, Amanda would've had questions.

2

"You're okay with this?" she asked her mother.

"You know how Meredith is."

Yes, Amanda knew. And she knew her mother's double standards. Meredith did not respect social norms. She was brave and impulsive and unconventional. Amanda's opposite. Amanda would not have missed three weeks of class to go backpacking in Peru. If she had, their mother would have been furious. Their mother did not get angry at Meredith. Unlike Amanda, Meredith pushed back. Amanda had never learned how to counter their mother's aggression. Nor had she learned how to be a big sister to Meredith.

When Meredith told Amanda that she planned to major in anthropology, Amanda had pointed out that computing was changing the study and practice of every discipline. *If you study computer science, she'd told her, you can work in any field.* That piece of advice had earned Amanda months of silent treatment and a phone call from their mother: *Your path isn't the only valid path. You're making your sister feel as if it is.*

Amanda had a master's degree in computer science with a specialization in artificial intelligence. True, she'd wondered what one would do with a degree in anthropology, but her intent hadn't been to discourage Meredith from studying what she enjoyed. She just thought it smart to pair it with something practical like computer science. She hadn't defended herself.

If Amanda had chosen to study anthropology, their mother would have made her pay her own tuition. Besides, as much as Meredith lived by her own rules, it didn't stop her from judging Amanda. After Amanda and Derrick had endured three failed cycles of intrauterine insemination, Meredith lectured her on the selfishness of spending thousands of dollars on fertility treatments when there were children awaiting adoption.

"No judgment," Amanda said, pacing the living room now. "Tell her congratulations from me."

"Tell her yourself. Call her. Tonight. And sound like you mean it. You weren't very effusive just now."

"I'm busy tonight, but I'll talk to her soon."

"Plans with your gorgeous husband?"

"Hmm." She hoped that could pass for a yes. Her choice in husbands was one of the few things her mother didn't criticize. She couldn't tell her that she and Derrick didn't really make plans together anymore.

"Meredith and I," her mother said, and Amanda was relieved by the change in subject, "are coming to Atlanta this weekend. Clear your calendar for wedding dress shopping."

Amanda nearly dropped the phone. The heat of panic flared in her cheeks and raced down her neck. Her hands tingled. She took the stairs by twos as she asked, "Why Atlanta? Charlotte is right there."

"She wants to go to the shop where you bought your dress. Remember how fun it was?" Amanda didn't remember any fun. Meredith, fifteen years old with a fashion sense to match, had talked more than the consultant. Their mother had bullied Amanda out of her first choice. Amanda's best friend, Beverly, had complained that it should have been just the two of them. And Amanda hadn't thought to invite Derrick's mother, who'd acted as if she'd been excluded from the wedding.

Amanda flung open the bathroom door and looked at herself in the full-length mirror. She turned to inspect her reflection in profile, then slowly lifted the hem of her shirt. The stretch marks tracing her sienna skin seemed more pronounced than they had just yesterday. She looked pregnant. Baby bump would not be denied.

"I'm out of town this weekend," she lied, trying to keep the alarm out of her voice.

"Oh no. We'll reschedule. Maybe the weekend of the sixteenth?"

Would a baggy sweatshirt hide her bump? She hadn't told her mother she was pregnant. Nor had she told her about the miscarriage. There was no way she was going to tell her that—miscarriage be damned—she was still pregnant. Well, not actually pregnant. She'd had two ultrasounds, and there was no fetal heartbeat and no fetus.

But. Especially at night—and this was incontrovertible to Amanda—she felt the baby move. Amanda hadn't told her mother so many things that she didn't know where to start. She absolutely was not going to start with that.

CHAPTER 2

PATRICK

6 MONTHS AFTER THE ACCIDENT

November 28, 2017

Patrick's wife was onstage when he slipped into the auditorium. There were no vacant seats, so he stood against the back wall, next to the videographer. It didn't matter that he was late. Marissa was speaking on low-dimensional topology, and he had little hope of following anything she said. She paced as she spoke, pausing at the lectern occasionally to advance her slides. She gestured enthusiastically at an image of a knot as she emphasized some point that mesmerized the room. She looked like her old self up there. He closed his eyes, breathed in deep. He'd promised himself not to look for hints of the old Marissa.

A line formed to speak with her after the talk. He didn't want to draw attention to himself, so he stayed where he was, a failing strategy.

"Patrick." He looked up to see Frederick Peters, the dean of Halford University's math department. "What did you think?" Frederick extended his hand.

"I think my last-minute switch from low-dimensional topology to neuroscience was a wise one." He shook Frederick's hand. Courtesy cost him nothing.

Frederick laughed. Still holding Patrick's hand, brow furrowed with concern, he asked, "How have you been?"

"Surviving."

Frederick nodded. Patrick, unable to take it any longer, pulled his hand away.

"I was surprised to hear about your resignation."

"Well," Patrick said, "when the people you work for have the morals of fruit flies, resigning is the sensible action."

Frederick winced. Until three months ago, Patrick had been a tenure-track professor in the Department of Neuroscience at Halford. Now, he was unemployed. Frederick broke eye contact and turned to look at Marissa, who was speaking with an admirer, a young man in a bright-yellow sweater.

"I won't say she's happy," Frederick said, still looking at Marissa, "but I really can't overstate the importance of her work."

"Do you want to do this again? Here?" Patrick was embarrassed by the tremor in his voice. *Her "work." Her "project."* No one even had a proper name to describe it.

Frederick turned back to Patrick, his eyes contrite. "It's just, we all dream of contributing something groundbreaking. For most of us, it's nothing more than a dream."

"Maybe you should lose your mind, Professor, and then you can do your own groundbreaking work."

"I'm sorry," Frederick said softly. Then, with more confidence: "I have a friend in the biology department at Emory. They need a lecturer for the spring, a cell biology course. I know they'd be happy to have you."

If Frederick had a friend in Solna who was happy to appoint Patrick to the Nobel Prize selection committee, Patrick would have refused. "That's kind of you," Patrick said, "but if I decide to teach again, I'll have Marissa put in a call to get my old job back."

Frederick chuckled. "She does have a lot of clout. More than I, I'm afraid." His smile broadened when he saw Marissa approaching.

She didn't seem to notice as she took Patrick's arm and whispered, "Let's get out of here before anyone sees me leave. Take care, Frederick."

He waved.

∿

"Thank you for coming," she said. They walked arm in arm. They lived five minutes from campus, twenty-five by foot.

Patrick nodded. Walking with her was worth the encounter with Frederick Peters. They'd chosen their neighborhood on the outskirts of Atlanta for its proximity to campus. They both preferred to walk, weather permitting.

"Was I accessible?" She looked up at him, and her dark hair fell around her shoulders. Was she joking? He'd never known her to care about being accessible. And honestly, he hadn't listened to a word of her talk.

He feigned thoughtfulness. "I'm trying to decide if a man lacking my raw intellect would follow that business about the knots."

"That business about the knots?" She laughed. "Okay, I wasn't accessible."

He wanted to stop walking and kiss her, really kiss her, but he feared that would be too much. He couldn't remember the last time they'd kissed. Yes, he could. It was the night of the solar eclipse, three months ago. "Have you eaten?" he asked instead.

She shook her head. "I'm starving."

He waited for her to suggest stopping somewhere. They used to eat out all the time. Lately, she was busy. He'd been surprised when she'd told him she was giving the low-dimensional topology talk. She was on an unofficial sabbatical this semester and rarely left home. When she didn't suggest a restaurant, he said, "I got an email today from a woman who has pseudocyesis."

She looked at him blankly.

"Sorry. I'm not being accessible. Phantom pregnancy."

"That's a real thing?"

"Sure. It's extremely rare." He wondered if he was exploiting this woman's email.

"How does it work?" Marissa asked. "A woman believes she's pregnant, so she has the symptoms of pregnancy?"

"Causation isn't clear." Yes, he was making conversation, but it was more than that. He didn't want the evening to end. He wanted to captivate Marissa, to take her out for a meal. He wanted to feel married tonight. He couldn't let go of that glimpse he'd seen—the old Marissa. "A woman could be experiencing symptoms because she thinks she's pregnant, or she could think she's pregnant because she's experiencing symptoms."

"Chicken or the egg," Marissa said.

"Exactly. A classmate from grad school put us in touch because of my work with Capgras syndrome."

Marissa looked dubious. "I don't see the connection."

"Neither do I."

People with Capgras syndrome falsely believed a loved one had been replaced by an imposter. Patrick's thesis work, a model of Capgras syndrome, had resulted in his most (only) famous paper to date. Even now, a decade and a half later, colleagues at conferences approached him and said, *You did that model of Capgras, right?*

"Maybe he associates me with little-understood conditions of the mind."

"Does she want you to treat her?" Marissa asked.

"I hope not. I told her I don't practice medicine."

"Maybe you should."

Patrick didn't reply. He'd done an MD-PhD because he hadn't known if he wanted to practice medicine or do research. He'd decided on research during the third and final year of his psychiatry residency when a patient, Glenn, a young man he'd become fond of, killed himself. Glenn had received the best care medicine had to offer, and still, he'd died. And Patrick hadn't understood why. Dedicating his career to understanding the mind seemed to be the best thing he could do for Glenn and the countless others like him. After residency, he'd accepted an assistant professor position in the Department of Neuroscience at Halford.

"Are you going to meet with her?" Marissa asked.

He nodded. "I thought I wouldn't at first. I don't see how I can help her. But I'm curious." He didn't mention that he had nothing else going on. He'd finished transitioning his former graduate students to new advisers the week before, which meant he had absolutely nothing to do.

She was silent for a long while. "I don't need the damping constant."

"What?"

"The damping constant." Her voice rose with excitement. "It isn't necessary." She stopped walking and rummaged through her briefcase. He understood. She was thinking about one of her equations. He'd lost her. She pulled out a notebook, and as they stood on the sidewalk, she fingered through pages until she found what she was looking for. She tapped the page with her index finger and then scratched her forehead. She seemed startled when she turned and saw him standing there. "Sorry." She returned the notebook to her briefcase, and they walked for a while in silence.

"This woman with this extraordinarily rare condition contacted you for a reason," she finally said. "That reason is telling you to go back to research. Even if you don't treat her, you should study her condition. You're a neuroscientist. It's what you do."

No, he wanted to tell her. He was her husband. He was Laura's father. Only after that, only then, was he a neuroscientist. His voice trembled when he said, "You want to stop somewhere for dinner?"

She looked at him, her eyes unfocused. "Oh. Sorry. I really need to work." Her thoughts had already turned back to her equations. "Let's get takeout."

CHAPTER 3

AMANDA

21 WEEKS PREGNANT

November 30, 2017

The coffee shop was busy with young professionals stopping in after work. Amanda sat at a corner table and watched a Black woman in a beige pantsuit. She was near Amanda in age, probably loading up on caffeine for the commute home. She stood in line, eyes on her phone, and Amanda imagined she was texting her husband, checking in to see who would make it home first, who would assume responsibility for dinner. Amanda saw in the woman a life she barely remembered.

Of course, if the woman were to look closely at Amanda, she would see an expectant mother and might imagine that Amanda fell asleep at night reading baby books. If she could sense Amanda's nerves, she might assume that Amanda was awaiting the result of some prenatal test. She would never guess that Amanda was waiting for a stranger, a friend of a friend, a neuroscientist well acquainted with the bizarre.

"Amanda?"

She looked up. "Dr. Davis?" She stood and shook his hand. He smiled shyly, his eyes darting quickly to her stomach before returning to her face.

"Call me Patrick. I see you have a drink." He motioned to her coffee. "I'll just be a second. Do you want anything else?"

When Amanda declined, he joined the queue. She studied him, his polo shirt and khakis, his brown hair neatly combed back, the quintessential White college professor.

He returned with a coffee and two pastries and placed one in front of her.

"I'll gladly eat both, but that would be excessive." He patted his stomach. If he was carrying extra weight, she couldn't see it. She accepted the pastry.

"I apologize for the informality." He motioned to the bustle of the coffee shop.

"Steve," called a barista, nearly screaming, as if to punctuate Patrick's point. She watched as a chastened middle-aged man in a shirt and tie, presumably Steve, shoved his phone in his pocket and stumbled forward to claim his drink. Amanda appreciated the informality. She'd seen enough diploma-lined walls over the past couple of months.

"Is this your office?" she teased.

"Are you kidding? This table wouldn't fit in my office."

She laughed. The table couldn't properly fit three people. She sipped her coffee and grimaced. "Decaf. I can't get used to it."

He raised his eyebrows but didn't comment. "Full disclosure," he said. "I don't have an office. I'm actually between jobs. Did Charles tell you that?"

Charles was Beverly's brother. Beverly and Amanda had been friends since college. Amanda shook her head. "I can pay you for your time—"

"No." He put a hand up. "That's not what I meant. I just want to be clear that I'm not seeing you in the capacity of a physician or neuroscientist. I'm not currently conducting research, and I'm not affiliated with a university."

"You sound like a lawyer." She smiled.

"Sorry. It's just I don't want to mislead you."

"Thank you. Still, I can pay. I—"

"I don't have anything to sell."

"Okay. So you and Charles are good friends?"

"We worked in the same lab in graduate school. Before he called, I actually hadn't spoken to him in fifteen years."

She covered her face, embarrassed. "I'm sorry. Beverly gave me the impression that you two are good friends."

"Beverly?"

"You don't know his sister? She raved about how smart you are."

Patrick laughed. "Beverly is kind to say that."

"Oh God. You got a call from someone you barely know to meet someone you don't know."

"We're getting to know each other now. How can I help?"

She hesitated before retrieving her cell phone from her purse. "I haven't shown this to anyone, not even my husband." She pulled up the video that her obstetrician recorded before handing her off to the psychiatrist.

She passed him the phone, and as he watched the small screen, absently rubbing his close-shaved brown beard, she visualized what he was seeing: Her lying on an examination table, shirt pulled up to reveal her swollen belly. An IV dripped fluid into her arm. *Count backward from ten,* a woman, off camera, said. She made it to eight before trailing off. And then, as she lay unconscious, her belly flattened.

"They put me under general anesthesia," she explained when he glanced up, his expression neutral.

"Did your doctor say why anesthesia has this effect?"

She shook her head. "She doesn't know. Apparently, it's common with . . ."

"Pseudocyesis," he finished.

She scowled. "*Pseudocyesis* sounds like a parasite. *Phantom pregnancy* sounds like my uterus is haunted. *False pregnancy* sounds like something that happens with a defective test. Don't get me started on the implications of *hysterical pregnancy*. Can we call it my condition?"

He nodded and handed her phone back.

"I made videos of myself sleeping, but I'll spare you those. My bump doesn't disappear." Before he could respond, she asked, "Do you have children?"

He wore a wedding band. And she could only discuss her condition in small doses.

He hesitated, and she wondered if the question was out of bounds. He wasn't her doctor. He'd made that clear. Still, maybe she wasn't supposed to ask personal questions. Finally, reluctantly, he shook his head. "My wife is very focused on her career."

"What does she do?"

"Math. She's a professor at Halford." He smiled awkwardly. Amanda placed him in his midthirties. "Your husband, how is he coping with . . ."

"My condition?"

"Yes. How is he doing with it?"

"We don't talk about it. I don't know how he's doing."

Patrick nodded. "That must be lonely."

She bit her lip, and for a moment, she thought she might cry. "I want to know what's wrong with me," she blurted. "My doctors know nothing."

"I'm sorry to tell you this," he said, "but I know nothing."

"Charles said you developed a brilliant model of Capgras syndrome."

"It was the highlight of my career. I peaked early."

"Charles thinks you can help me."

And she wanted to believe Charles was right, because feeling like she was pregnant when pregnancy had been definitively ruled out was the most terrifying thing she'd ever experienced. She couldn't see a way back to her life. She didn't have a job, and despite the demand for data scientists, she was afraid to interview because she was showing. She didn't want to explain that. And even if she did explain it, how would she explain why her bump was getting bigger with each passing week? What if, a full year from now, five years from now, she was still wearing breast pads because leakage was an insidious, unpredictable threat? What if pregnant with no baby became her default state?

Patrick looked like a deer in headlights, and only this stopped her from begging him for help. He asked how it started, and she told him about the miscarriage. When she'd complained, a month later, that her body wasn't returning to normal, her OB had counseled patience. *It takes time.* She'd tried to be patient, but at night, alone in bed, tucked into darkness, she felt what could only be a baby moving. This insistence had earned Amanda a referral to a psychiatrist. It was isolating. Her mother and sister were visiting to go dress shopping, and every time Amanda thought about explaining her condition to her mother, she felt like her throat would close. Of the whole ordeal, what seemed to bother Patrick most was that she had no one to talk to.

"Did you get a referral to a therapist?"

She sighed. The therapist. Not her first. Her mother had forced her to see a therapist after her father died—a car accident. Amanda was thirteen, and therapy felt like punishment on top of tragedy. It was an awful time, and she'd just wanted her mother and everyone to leave her alone. Now, all these years later, Dr. Owens, the psychiatrist-recommended therapist, wanted to talk about her father's death. *I usually don't focus on childhood, but your feelings surrounding pregnancy must run deep, and we need to explore what shaped them. His death so shortly after your sister's birth must have made a profound impression.* Amanda, already medication noncompliant, acquiesced because she wanted to get better. Talking about her father reminded her of those horrid sessions of her adolescence. She was relieved when the therapist called time. Dr. Owens encouraged Amanda to continue the antidepressants. (Amanda had lied about taking them.) *The medication will make our work here easier.* And Amanda committed to never going back.

"The psychiatrist did two things: wrote a prescription for antidepressants and referred me to a therapist."

"Have the antidepressants helped?"

"I haven't filled the prescription. I know intellectually that there is no baby, but I have this fear that the antidepressants will harm her."

Patrick nodded. "And the therapist?"

"Will talking make this go away?"

"It might help."

"Do you have any theories about why this is happening to me?"

Patrick looked pained, like a parent refusing to indulge a child—long past the age of myths—with Santa Claus. "I'm not sure if anyone can tell you why this is happening. It seems reasonable to assume a blend of biological and psychological factors. As for the psychological factors, you miscarried, and that must have been traumatic. That might be a good place to start."

CHAPTER 4

AMANDA

12 WEEKS PREGNANT

Baby's nervous system is directing limb movements, though Baby is still too small for Mommy to feel.

—Your Best Pregnancy

September 28, 2017

Amanda's marriage was in critical condition when the bleeding began. Perhaps it was turning a corner. She was on the couch in her pajamas watching a daytime soap—the last vestige of an institution of broadcast television—when Derrick texted: a picture of a sad puppy, a fuzzy golden retriever with the caption: I miss you. They barely spoke when they were in the same room. She couldn't remember the last time he'd said something nice to her. Another text came through as she stared: I was going to send a selfie, but this guy sells it better than my mug ever could.

She smiled and typed: I miss you too. Her finger lingered over the send icon. Love would not get them through this. She hit send. Nothing would get them through this if they couldn't communicate. And she did miss him. She resented him, and she missed him.

He asked her to put on a dress and promised her homemade lasagna. He left work early and came home with grocery bags in both hands.

"Can I help with anything?" she asked.

"You can have a seat and try this drink." She sat at the kitchen table while he mixed pomegranate juice with ginger ale. He topped it with a fresh orange slice. "I found the recipe online," he said and placed the glass in front of her. He kissed her on the cheek, and she inhaled the familiar scent of him.

"I'm drinking alone?" she asked as he donned his *Breaking Bad* apron, a gag gift from her sister.

"You know I don't like fruity stuff."

She sipped her drink as he chopped an onion. He chatted about his day and then asked about hers.

"You like soap operas?" he teased when she told him how she'd spent the afternoon.

She smiled sheepishly. "Guilty." Early in her pregnancy, when fatigue struck, she'd fallen back into the habit of watching them. It reminded her of summer visits to her grandmother, the two of them sharing in the joys and outrages of the drama. Now that her energy was returning, she was hooked on multiple story lines. Derrick liked B horror movies, and he reminded Amanda that she'd once lectured him on the virtues of quality cinema.

Last night, he'd come through the front door and gone straight to their bedroom. If she hadn't caught a glimpse of him climbing the stairs, she might've thought they were being robbed. Tonight, he was charming. He was making her favorite meal. The change was jarring, but she didn't want to question it. She wanted to connect with him. They talked about everything except her pregnancy. She could still remember the man she'd fallen in love with, but for the first time in a long time, she didn't need memory. He was here, in her kitchen.

"Wow," she said appreciatively when she stepped into the dining room and saw what he'd been up to while the food was in the oven. "Fancy."

He'd used the nice tablecloth and candles. The lights were dim, and jazz played over hidden speakers.

"A beautiful arrangement for a beautiful woman."

She smiled. She wore the blue wrap dress he'd bought for her birthday. His lasagna was delicious as always. He served ice cream for dessert.

"Do you remember our song?"

"We have a song?" That was news to her.

She and Derrick agreed that the really good music—the best music—had been made when they were teenagers. But while she'd been in her bedroom singing along to Monica or TLC, oblivious to his existence, he'd been making mixtapes featuring Matchbox 20 and Savage Garden.

He played "Lady in Red," and she laughed.

Early in their relationship, they'd stayed at a cabin in the Blue Ridge Mountains. They'd each packed their favorite albums, but the CD player in the room had been jammed with a previous guest's *Into the Light* album. She'd lost count of the number of times they'd danced to "Lady in Red."

Now, all these years later, when they made love, it was like the old days. "I don't want to fight anymore," he said, his tone hushed and postcoital. "I'll do whatever it takes to make things right."

"Mm." She wanted to savor the moment, the feel of him, his arms wrapped around her. They could talk later about what it would mean to make things right. They would have to. But for now, she drifted into a deep, contented sleep.

~

She awoke, uneasy. Even before the cramping and blood and—terror. Through gritted teeth, she told Derrick that something was wrong. He sprang into action and helped her to the car, strong arms and comforting words. She wasn't comforted. She was losing the baby; there was no other explanation for what she was feeling.

"Will you put the phone away?" she hissed. They were stopped behind a car at a red light, and he was reading aloud from a pregnancy website. *Bleeding and cramps don't necessarily mean you're having a miscarriage.*

He put the phone away. "You and the baby are going to be fine."

~

She asked Derrick to sleep on the sofa bed that night. He didn't ask why. She was relieved because she didn't know how to articulate what she was feeling. She didn't want to give voice to it.

From their bed, she watched him gather his nightclothes. She'd never hated herself as much as she did at that moment. As he left, shoulders slumped, she started to tell him to turn off the light, but she couldn't ask anything more of him. She lay, eyes closed, exposed in the light of the lamp.

After she'd lost the baby, the doctor had performed a D&C to ensure that nothing was left behind. She felt empty. A day ago, there'd been a little life that was always with her. She was never alone. According to the website she visited, her baby was the size of a lime. Each week, she'd looked forward to learning which item of produce could stand in for the dimensions of her baby. She thought of the baby as a she. She hadn't learned the sex yet, but she wanted a girl. She'd chosen to be optimistic. No pressure on the baby. She would love a boy just as much.

Derrick had cried at the hospital. He'd held her hand and cried, which infuriated her. He hadn't wanted the baby. And being angry at him made her angry at herself. In the end, it didn't matter who she was most angry at. It didn't matter who deserved what percentage of what blame. In the end, she couldn't stand the sight of him. She couldn't stand the sight of herself.

CHAPTER 5

PATRICK

6 MONTHS AFTER THE ACCIDENT

December 1, 2017

Within their marriage, Patrick had two sacrosanct duties: securing their home before bed and brewing the morning coffee. When he and Marissa had lived in an apartment, locking the front door had completed his evening task. Once they'd moved into a house, the routine had expanded to checking windows, locking the back door, bolting the garage door, and activating the security system. He went to bed earlier than Marissa, but each night he fell asleep secure. And each morning, when Patrick wasn't traveling, as surely as the sun rose, Marissa awakened to the aroma of freshly brewed coffee.

He performed his duties well, but lately, the nuance was different. He secured their home from external threats, but as he drifted to sleep, he feared threats from within. And Marissa's sleep had become so erratic that she was just as likely to be awake when he measured the coffee grounds as she was to sleep until long after the coffee was cold, its air-suspended particulates settled to dust.

This morning, he awakened alone. Marissa hadn't moved out of their bedroom, but she often fell asleep in her office. Sometimes, she worked through the night and climbed into bed as he was stepping into slippers. On his way downstairs, he peeked inside her office. She was fully clothed, sprawled on the sofa. She might've fallen asleep twenty minutes ago. Or four hours ago. He spread a blanket over her before quietly pulling the door closed and continuing to the kitchen.

He put on coffee and prepared his usual breakfast: oatmeal with peanut butter. The day ahead looked bleak. Not wanting to think about it, he distracted himself with news articles on his phone as he ate.

He'd had grand plans when he quit his job: jog three days a week, learn about a new area of neuroscience, develop a brilliant idea for a start-up. Within a month, he'd realized that he didn't have the motivation to read a book, much less draw up a business plan. And after years of relative inactivity, running for more than ten minutes felt like self-mutilation.

It wasn't something he bragged about, but he had managed to binge-watch seven seasons of *The Walking Dead*.

He was finishing his oatmeal when Marissa, eyes bleary and hair disarranged, staggered into the kitchen. She poured a glass of orange juice and stood at the sink, gazing out the window as she drank. She was still wearing yesterday's clothes. When she finished the glass, she put it in the sink and turned to leave without a glance in his direction. He wondered then if she'd already decided that their marriage was over. He was afraid to ask.

"We haven't talked about her in months," he said to Marissa's back, surprising himself. He hadn't planned that.

She turned to him, a momentary look of confusion on her face. He saw it register, saw the darkness settle over her features. "Don't," she said, half plea, half command.

"If you want to talk." He could hear the apology in his voice.

She shook her head and left the kitchen.

He stared into his empty bowl, wishing he hadn't said anything. Whenever he acted, it turned out badly. Doing nothing was the rational strategy. He would have to learn to sit idly by while his life fell apart. That had to be better than manning the wrecking ball.

~

Being unemployed, Patrick had learned the rhythms of Piedmont Park. If he arrived before the sun, he would find himself dodging organized groups of runners and exercisers. Local track teams and boot campers claimed the early, dark hours. If he was lucky, he might spot the slow-moving outline of an opossum traveling between trees. With the sun came the dog walkers. If he wasn't distracted by the parade of purebreds and mixes and if he kept his gaze pointed upward, he very well could see a hawk, perched on a tree branch, watchful. On occasion, even when these birds of prey were far from his mind, one would intrude upon his consciousness as it swooped down upon an ill-fated chipmunk or pigeon.

Today, since he'd spent two hours watching television, a hostage to morning malaise, he'd arrived at the park shortly before noon. Mostly, the park was empty, giving free rein to ducks and squirrels, their foraging disrupted only occasionally by a straggler. He was climbing the stairs to the Legacy Fountains when his phone rang.

"Rob?" He braced for tragedy. It wasn't like his brother to call in the middle of the day.

"Patrick," Rob said cheerfully. Patrick relaxed. "How are you?"

"I'm good," Patrick answered reflexively.

"That, right there," Rob said, "is the problem. I don't believe you. What are you doing right now?"

"I'm walking in the park."

"Words, man. Paint a picture for me. Are you listening to music?"

"No, I'm just walking."

"Are you striding with purpose, elevating your heart rate, or are you shuffling along, shoulders slumped?"

Patrick considered it. "If there are only two options, I guess I'm shuffling, shoulders slumped. Why?"

"I'm worried about you."

"Why?"

"For one, you should be at work right now. I hate my wife too. That's why I have a career."

"I don't hate my wife."

"Right, you were just trying to get her attention. I get it. Are you two having sex?"

"And that's your business how?"

"Relax, Patrick. It's not like I'm asking for nude photos of your wife. It's a clinical question, and I'm a doctor. A real doctor." He was a transplant surgeon who specialized in livers. He didn't hold psychiatrists in high regard, and he had even less regard for those who did research. "Married couples typically have sex. I'm just trying to ascertain if you and Marissa are typical in that department."

"Let's move on."

"Fine. But if you do want to share nude photos of Marissa—"

"Um. No."

"Okay. I'm just saying. I would take a look."

"Did you call to ask for nude photos of my wife?"

"Of course not. I called to talk because I'm afraid you aren't talking to anyone. I spoke to Mom last night."

"How is she?"

"Dad is dead, and she's retired in Hawaii. I don't think she has a bad day. But she told me some things I didn't know."

"And now you're going to share them with me?"

"I don't have to. They're about you. She told me about Laura."

Patrick stopped walking. This morning, he'd wanted nothing more than to talk about Laura. With Marissa. Now, he could hardly bear the mention of her name.

"I had no idea," Rob said. "When she—"

Patrick braced himself for the words. But Rob didn't say them.

"I should've been there. Why didn't you tell me?"

"I don't know, Rob. I'm sorry."

"You are sorry. Every day I ask God why he sent me such a sorry little brother."

Patrick smirked and continued walking, past the botanical gardens. "Why didn't you tell me about your issues with the IRS? You almost went to prison."

"Believe me, I know I almost went to prison. Most surgeons have nightmares about uncontrolled bleeding or embolisms. I have nightmares about going to prison. I'll probably sleep poorly for the rest of my life. And I didn't tell you because I was embarrassed. I made bad decisions."

"I would've helped you with money," Patrick said.

"I make four times as much as you in a bad year. I'm supposed to come to you for a loan? Interesting question: Now that you're unemployed, what is the ratio of my salary to yours? How do you multiply zero?"

"Are we still trying to figure out why I don't talk to you about my problems?"

"Nah, we were raised that way. We don't talk about what's bothering us. And it made a certain amount of sense then. How many ways can you say, 'I'm afraid Dad is going to accidentally kill one of us the next time he loses his temper'? But we need to grow out of our silence. Have you been talking to anyone?"

"I tried to talk to Marissa this morning."

"I'm guessing that didn't go well. Mom mentioned you were thinking about visiting her without Marissa. She said you two might need a break."

"For someone who can't talk about her problems, Mom doesn't have any difficulty talking about mine."

"Someone has to tell me these things. Mom thinks you need to talk to someone. She said you wouldn't open up to her. Have you talked to any of your friends?"

"All my friends are neuroscientists. I—"

"That's your problem. You need friends who live in the real world. You guys spend so much time trying to understand the world that you don't learn how to do anything. You can't be blamed when life intrudes, demands some form of action, and you just sit there with a limp dick in your hand."

"Do I have any other problems you'd like to tell me about?"

"You're too sensitive. But that probably comes from thinking all the time. Do you still watch the news?"

"I do."

"And do you understand a goddamn thing that's happening in this country? I don't. Neither do you. But I still do my thing. Look at Ben Carson. He's one of the great neurosurgeons of our time, and he doesn't understand the basics of how the brain stores memories. That didn't stop him from opening people's skulls."

"I'm sure there's a point in there."

"I'm telling you your problems, and you're opening up to me. Why did you quit your job, Pat?"

"I'm not sure I can make you understand. I don't fully understand it myself."

"If you want to talk about anything," he said, "I'm here. I'm not good at saying it, but I care about what happens to you."

"I care about what happens to you also, Rob. I love you."

"Agh. Don't say that. Tell me you respect me. Tell me you admire me. Tell me I'm the greatest goddamn human you've ever had the pleasure of knowing. Any of that would be reasonable."

"I know that you love me too."

"Cut that out. I'm serious."

"Tell me, Rob. I want to hear you say it." The line clicked, and Rob was gone. As he slid his phone back into his pocket, he realized that he was smiling.

CHAPTER 6

AMANDA

21 WEEKS PREGNANT

December 2, 2017

Amanda opened her eyes slowly.

"Sorry to wake you," Derrick whispered. "I don't want this to get cold." He was standing over her. She squinted into the sun, unable to see what he held. She used an arm to shield her eyes, and as they adjusted, she made out the breakfast tray. And then she smelled pancakes.

"Is it my birthday?" she asked.

He grinned. "It's a brand-new day."

She propped herself against the headboard, and he settled the breakfast tray over her lap. He fetched his own tray from the hall. "May I?" He hadn't slept in their bed since the miscarriage.

"Of course."

He settled beside her. The breakfast trays, fashioned from dark wood, had been stowed in a corner of their basement for years. Amanda couldn't remember how they'd acquired them—a gift of some sort. This was their first use. "Maple syrup. The genuine article," he said with pride. "Heated for your culinary pleasure."

"Seriously," she asked, "what did I do to deserve this?" She drizzled syrup over the pancakes.

"I want you to know that everything is going to be okay."

The tears caught her off guard.

"What's wrong?" he asked.

She wiped her eyes. She didn't know where to start. "This is just very nice." She couldn't imagine anything being okay. She'd been angry with him for so long that she couldn't imagine not being angry with him. And maybe she was to blame for that. "And unexpected."

"So those are tears of joy?"

"Maybe." She lifted the fork to her mouth and felt a sudden wave of nausea. When she'd first smelled pancakes, her stomach had responded with hunger. Now, the aroma of syrup—how she'd once loved syrup—made her nauseous. That happened too often. She felt hungry and wanted to eat, but the aroma of food—formerly appetizing food—repulsed her. She hadn't told Derrick about it. They didn't talk about her condition. They didn't talk about anything. She forced herself to eat.

"Would you describe these pancakes as magnificent or exquisite?" he asked.

"Magnificent." More duplicity. But justified. They probably were magnificent. She was trying. "I'm going wedding dress shopping today." She filled him in on Meredith's surprise engagement.

"When is the wedding?"

"I didn't think to ask. Am I a horrible sister?"

"You have a lot going on." He fed her a strawberry. She chewed slowly, telling herself the nausea would pass, that she wouldn't throw up. "Things really are going to be okay."

She forced a smile. Right now, she just needed to make it through wedding dress shopping. "What do you think about Meredith marrying a man she met over a three-week vacation?" she asked.

Derrick sipped his juice. "I think that was some vacation."

Amanda laughed.

"Seriously, though, Justin lived with Lisa for six years before they got married." Justin was one of Derrick's divorced college friends. "Getting to know a person is no guarantee."

"True. But it has to be better than marrying a practical stranger."

"Sometimes it's about faith. Believing that something bigger than yourself is putting you where you need to be."

Amanda stared at him. Derrick was a thoughtful man, but never had he sounded like a Hallmark card.

"I want you to come to church with me."

"Church?" They'd never been to church together. Neither of them attended church.

"I know. If someone told me a year ago that God would change my life, I would've called him a liar."

"What are you talking about?"

He took her hand. She'd stopped eating. "I've been going to church. Have you wondered where I've been on Tuesday and Thursday evenings? And Sunday mornings."

She'd wondered vaguely if he was having an affair. For the past few weeks, he'd been coming in late without explanation. She hadn't asked. "Oh," was all she said.

"Come with me. Sunday service. I want you to meet Pastor Roberts. He's been helping me."

"How?"

"Guidance. Will you come tomorrow?"

"Have you been talking to him about us?"

Derrick nodded.

"Oh." What was he telling people? It struck her that she had no idea. Did she want to know?

She'd been perfectly happy not knowing what he did with his time. The door to his home office had been shut for the past few days. She'd barely noticed and had been surprised when he'd sheepishly mentioned that it was locked because he was remodeling—not because he was hiding something. It hadn't occurred to her to check.

She nodded now. She could go to church. For him. He was trying. If they both tried, maybe things would be okay. Maybe the two of them could move past this. Even if her body wouldn't move past it.

~

It was a warm, sunny afternoon. But it was December, so Amanda thought she could get away with wearing the loose-fitting gray sweater she'd bought for the occasion. She could see the bulge of her tummy, but she was looking for it. Her mother and Meredith had no reason to suspect she was pregnant and would probably be so focused on wedding dresses that they wouldn't notice. She hadn't seen them since February, so a little weight gain wouldn't be out of the question. She put on makeup for the first time in a long time, and she was surprised that she looked like her former self. She felt a hundred years older. The mirror didn't see it.

"You look great."

She turned. Derrick stood in the doorway.

"Sorry to startle you. But you do. Look great."

"Thank you." She almost asked if she looked pregnant, but she stopped herself. She'd explained her condition to him. And he'd read an article online. They hadn't discussed it further. That wasn't okay, but she couldn't worry about it now. Her mother and sister were almost here. She had to prepare.

"Wish me luck," she said.

Her cell phone rang. Derrick stepped away as she checked the screen: Beverly.

Amanda sat on the bed with the ringing phone. She'd ignored Beverly's last two calls. And right now, she just couldn't. She'd met

Beverly for dinner after having coffee with Patrick, and the evening had started with a fight over wine. Beverly wanted to share a bottle, but Amanda declined. She hadn't had a drink in weeks. "You're not pregnant," Beverly exclaimed in front of the waiter and anyone else who might have been listening. Amanda felt self-conscious for the rest of the night. Beverly had apologized by text the following morning, and Amanda had accepted her apology, by text. She knew Beverly meant well. But. She just couldn't. The doorbell rang as the call rolled to voice mail. Amanda was almost grateful for the distraction.

~

Meredith and Amanda didn't look like siblings. Amanda had brown skin and at five seven towered over her fair-complexioned sister. Amanda was curvy where Meredith was athletic.

"Congratulations." She took Meredith's hand and pulled her into the house. "I want to see pictures." She hoped she wasn't being overly cheerful, but she felt the need to distract them from her bump. "Where are the girls?" Three of Meredith's friends were joining them.

"If they're reasonable drivers," her mother answered, "they'll be here in about an hour. This one"—she pointed at Meredith—"drives like a maniac."

"Are you getting younger, Mom?" Derrick teased and hugged her.

"You need glasses, boy," her mother warned with a giggle. Amanda had inherited her father's height, but everything else was from her mother. Meredith was the inverse.

"Congratulations, Meredith," Derrick effused. They hugged.

Derrick gave Amanda a meaningful look. "We have an announcement," he said. Amanda had no idea what that could be.

Derrick took Amanda's hand. She wondered if he was going to announce their divorce. The word hadn't come up, but it had passed through her mind, and she imagined the thought wasn't foreign to him. Would he tell her like this in front of her mother and sister right before wedding dress shopping? Only if he hated her. He opened his mouth, and she braced for it: *We're separating.*

"We're pregnant!" he said.

CHAPTER 7

PATRICK

6 MONTHS AFTER THE ACCIDENT

December 5, 2017

Anxiety was like a blanket, opaque and heavy. Even when Patrick went to sleep feeling reasonably well, he awoke anxious. Getting out of bed in the mornings was a struggle, which was ironic because the anxiety—the symptoms, anyway—tended to subside once he was up and moving around. He typically spent a few minutes on his phone, catching up on news, before summoning the energy to throw off the blanket. This morning, he received a jolt in the form of an email from Amanda Jackson. The sight of her name lifted his spirits, added a sprinkle of unpredictability to his day. He decided to delay reading her message, at least until he made it down to the kitchen.

He peeked in on Marissa. She sat at her desk, wrapped in a blue robe, reading. "Did you sleep okay?" he asked.

She turned, startled. "I had strange dreams, but I feel like there was something important in one of them."

"Important for?"

Marissa laughed. "Is there anything else?"

At least she was aware of her obsession with work. "Do you want breakfast?"

"No. I ate a couple of hours ago."

Patrick nodded and shut the office door on his way out.

Sitting at the kitchen table, he paused before reading Amanda's email. What did he hope it would say? He'd been cautious when they'd talked, deliberate in his assertions that he didn't have solutions or answers for her. Frankly, after their meeting in the coffee shop, he hadn't expected to hear from her again. He hadn't realized that it mattered to him.

From: Amanda Jackson
To: Patrick Davis
Subject: Your Out Has Been Revoked

Hello Patrick Davis, not currently conducting research and not affiliated with a university:

I enjoyed talking to you last week, and I meant to send a thank you note. But I thought maybe you'd felt pressured into talking with me, and I wanted to give you a graceful out. But now, I want to revoke that out and ask if you'd like to meet today. No pressure. If you're busy, tell me. If you tell me enough, I promise to take the hint.

Amanda

Because Patrick lacked spontaneity, he put down his phone and turned on the news while he ate his oatmeal. He knew that he would see her. What else did he have to do? He was simply by nature incapable of committing to anything of import without thinking it through. Not that he hadn't already given this thought.

Since finishing medical school, he'd grown accustomed to fielding calls from friends and relatives about a lingering pain just behind the ribs or a child's recurring earache. He was happy to answer as well as he could.

Amanda was different. The best counsel he could give her was the advice she didn't want to hear: comply with treatment. She wasn't going to do that. Could informal discussions and advice do her more harm than good? He would take it step by step. And honestly, she was going to get information from him or misinformation from the internet. He was a much better option than the internet.

After finishing his coffee, he replied to her email.

> From: Patrick Davis
> To: Amanda Jackson
> Subject: RE: Your Out Has Been Revoked
>
> Hello Amanda,
>
> It's good to hear from you. Do you like to walk? I'm heading to Piedmont Park at 11 if that works for you. If not, we can figure something else out.
>
> Patrick

When he got out of the shower, he had a new email:

> From: Amanda Jackson
> To: Patrick Davis
> Subject: RE: Your Out Has Been Revoked
>
> Hello Patrick Davis, not currently conducting research and not affiliated with a university:

> I do like to walk and 11 at Piedmont Park works for
> me. Just tell me where to meet you.

Unlike yesterday and the day before that, he had something to look forward to.

~

They met inside the gate at Tenth Street near the *Free Nelson Mandela* sculpture, a declaration of injustice written in the language of granite, steel, and barbed wire. The day was warm and sunny, and Amanda wore black tights and a loose-fitting lavender shirt that bulged in front, the slight swell of pregnancy. Outside in the sunlight, she looked to Patrick like a healthy, exercise-ready mother-to-be. Her walking shoes were stylish, and her hair was pulled back in a ponytail.

"I should've said something earlier, but I have to take breaks when I walk long distances. My left calf cramps." She steadied herself against a tree to stretch. "I forgot about it until I was on my way here. Being pregnant is harder than I expected."

"Not a problem. There are benches everywhere. Would you rather grab coffee?"

"No. It's a nice day in December. We have to show gratitude that it isn't freezing."

They headed into the park, and Patrick pointed out Lake Clara Meer as they passed. "My brother insists it's a large pond, but I have it on good authority that it is a lake."

The water was pretty and stocked with fish. Occasionally, he'd glimpse a turtle swimming, its head breaking the surface. A variety of bird species congregated, along with what Patrick thought was a lone heron.

"I haven't been here in years," she told him. "Maybe fifteen. A brief experiment in in-line skating."

"What were the results? Of the experiment."

"A concussion. And a promise to myself to never again strap wheels to my feet."

He smiled. "There's something I need to say."

She glanced at him, face open.

"You asked me the other day if I had children. I had one. A daughter." He felt like he should say more, but he couldn't.

"Oh." She hesitated. "Do you want to talk about it?"

"No," he said quickly. And he knew it was awkward. He'd just needed to set things straight. She'd asked him if he had children, and he'd told her no, and he hadn't given it much thought until later that night, when his answer had come back to him, a sullen ghost. He didn't know if he'd lied, but if he didn't have children, that meant Laura didn't have a father. And Laura deserved to have a father. And even suggesting to someone who'd never heard of Laura, who would never meet Laura, that she didn't have a father caused him as much pain as he'd ever experienced. "I just wanted to say that."

"Okay." She seemed satisfied.

They walked, the silence uncomfortable. He racked his brain for something to say. She saved them.

"Does it make me a terrible person that I felt a teensy bit better about myself after reading about Capgras syndrome? It's just, I have this condition that I'd barely heard of, and reading about other conditions that I've never heard of makes me feel less . . . offbeat."

"I understand."

"What were the patients you worked with like? I'm not asking you to violate doctor-patient confidentiality, just—"

"It's fine," Patrick said. "Capgras syndrome is difficult to live with. I met a man in his midthirties, married with a five-year-old son. He suffered a brain injury in a car accident, and he made a full recovery except for his belief that his mother and cat were imposters. He acknowledged that the woman looked like his mother and the cat looked like his cat, but he insisted they weren't. He lived with the cat, so that was especially challenging. His wife had to leave him at home when she took their son to visit his mother."

"Can you imagine if he hadn't recognized his wife or son?" Amanda asked.

"That would've been uniquely challenging."

"Were you able to help him?"

Patrick shook his head. "We don't know how to fix brain damage."

She patted her belly. "Sounds familiar. When I need to feel better about myself, can I just email you? You can tell me about an unusual condition of the mind, and I can ask you questions when we talk."

"We would never run out of things to talk about," he said. They both fell quiet. It was as if he'd jinxed their conversation. He wished, as he always did when getting to know someone, that they could skip ahead to the comfort of not having to maintain constant chatter. "How did dress shopping go?" he asked, thankful that something had popped into his head.

"You have a good memory."

He shrugged. "It doesn't seem like it as I search for my keys every morning."

"Dress shopping was—I have to start when my mother and sister arrived. My husband shocked us all by announcing that I'm pregnant."

"Oh. Is he aware that—"

"I'm not pregnant?" she finished for him. "Yes. But apparently, he has a condition of his own. He has decided that I have a faith pregnancy."

"Faith pregnancy?"

"Don't bother to look it up in—what is that book you guys use? The *DSM*?"

"The *Diagnostic and Statistical Manual of Mental Disorders*."

"You probably won't find it there. You can't google it either. Apparently, I'm carrying a healthy fetus, but God is making it

39

undetectable to ultrasounds and physical exams. He's doing this so that I can find faith."

"Okay."

"Apparently, Derrick has found God."

"That must provide him comfort."

"I'm sure. But a faith pregnancy? He had the nerve to get mad at me for reneging on going to church with him."

Patrick considered turning left toward the bridge—the view of Lake Clara Meer was beautiful from there—but just beyond was a playground, and he generally avoided those. They continued straight until he steered her down a flight of stairs toward the dog park. He sometimes found the child-size barn and miniature benches at the education garden jolting, but he'd never seen kids there, so he considered it a safe space.

"The kicker," Amanda said, "is that he served me breakfast in bed that morning. He said it was a brand-new day. I thought we were making progress."

"I probably don't need to ask, but what do you think of his faith pregnancy theory?"

"I think he's fucking crazy."

Patrick laughed. And Amanda laughed. Patrick laughed harder until the laughter took him. He couldn't control it. He stopped walking and doubled over with hilarity right beside the beehives. Amanda stopped laughing. She stared at him.

"I'm sorry," he managed to say, barely. Still laughing. His abdominal muscles ached with the strain.

"Are you okay?"

He nodded, trying to bring it under control. His legs weak, he sat down on his butt on the pavement. He extended his legs and propped himself on his elbows. He let his head loll back and he laughed. Amanda sat down beside him, concerned. He had tears in his eyes when he was finally able to speak again.

"I'm sorry," he said. "It isn't funny."

"That's hard to tell from your reaction."

He managed to stop laughing. "No, really, I'm sorry. I have no idea why I reacted that way. I don't usually laugh at inappropriate moments. The thing is, I know how you feel."

"I doubt that," she said, peeved.

"My wife and I went through some awful things this year. Too much. For three weeks, I didn't know if she was going to survive. She cried, slept, and paced the house. She barely ate. She was like a ghost. I would wake up at three in the morning to find her staring out the kitchen window. At three that afternoon, she'd be asleep on the sofa. She barely spoke. I locked every knife and razor we owned in my desk drawer. I flushed every poisonous substance I could find down the toilet. Every time I walked into a room, I feared that I would find her hanging.

"Then, one morning, a little after two, I found her in her study writing equations on the wall. That isn't as odd as it sounds. The walls in her study are coated with dry-erase paint. There were lines and lines of equations. I didn't understand any of it, but I knew my wife was back. I asked her if she was working. She turned and smiled. Not a beaming smile, but more than I'd seen in weeks. 'It just came to me,' she said. I felt like weeping. I asked if I could watch, and she motioned to a chair. To me, in that moment, my wife scribbling equations on the wall was the most beautiful thing I'd ever seen. She was back. She was working. And she kept at it. Over the next few weeks, she worked at a pace I'd never seen. I returned the knives to their place in the kitchen. Things weren't normal, but she was no longer crying."

"What was she working on?" Amanda asked.

Patrick hesitated, his mouth suddenly dry. "She wouldn't tell me that for another month. She was working on a way to communicate with the dead."

CHAPTER 8

MARISSA

25 YEARS BEFORE THE ACCIDENT

Marissa Thomas grew up in Warren, Michigan, a city on the outskirts of Detroit. Her sister, Jen, four years older, excelled in gymnastics, and Marissa, a young ballerina, danced beautifully. They had a dog of indeterminate origin named Rigley who'd been born beneath their neighbor's porch on the same day as Marissa. Their father owned a small extermination business, and the family vacationed in Cape Cod every summer. Jen loved the beach, and Marissa was entranced by the history of Salem. Their mother, plagued by nightmares after her first and last visit to the Salem Witch Museum, was baffled by Marissa's fascination with the hunts and trials and left the task of accompanying Marissa to her father. Marissa bought a book about the Salem witch trials each year to read on the plane.

Their childhood was privileged and happy and left them singularly unprepared for the event that would define their youth: the disintegration of their family. The crumbling of the foundation of their upbringing happened outside the girls' sight, but its collapse, when it came, left nothing untouched.

Marissa was twelve when her father sold his business and moved with his mistress to New York to pursue their dream of writing children's books. She was the storyteller; he would illustrate. Their mother had possessed no inkling of the affair or her husband's ludicrous fantasies of a second career. She had a quiet breakdown that went mostly unnoticed. Then she commanded everyone's attention.

Her raised voice awakened Marissa at three in the morning. Marissa stepped softly through the dark hallway and paused outside her mother's bedroom door.

"You don't get to start over while I raise your children."

Marissa, who had wanted to hear what her mother was saying, had heard enough. She returned to her own bedroom and covered her mother's voice with the radio. She could only assume that her father called her mother's bluff, because after a month of haunting their house in her nightgown, her mother packed a suitcase. "When you talk to your father, tell him I'm with Charles."

The task of informing their father fell to Jen.

"Charles Wright?" their father asked, astonished. Charles had worked for their father for a decade. He'd shared Thanksgiving meals with their family. "And she's been gone for two weeks? Where is she?"

They didn't know. The message delivered, Jen didn't have much to say. He didn't have much to say either. He promised to send money.

Jen didn't return to high school for her junior year. Her seasonal sales job at a department store was extended to full-time work. Her father sent two modest checks, followed by a lengthy silence—during which he continued to pay the mortgage. Jen's paychecks handled the other bills. A year after their father's departure, Marissa won her first national mathematics competition and was honored with a trip to Princeton University.

CHAPTER 9

PATRICK

3 MONTHS AFTER THE ACCIDENT

August 25, 2017

Patrick was cleaning his breakfast dishes when the doorbell rang. It was eight sharp. He opened the door, expecting to find a delivery driver, but it was Frederick Peters, the dean of the math department at Halford.

"I hope I'm not too early," he said and brushed by Patrick.

"Too early for what?" Patrick was dressed for the office, khakis and a polo shirt. He closed the door and turned to Frederick, who was shifting his weight from foot to foot.

"To see Marissa. I've been calling."

Patrick couldn't imagine what was so urgent. "Are you okay?" Frederick was drawn and wired at once, like a man who'd spent the night popping amphetamines.

Patrick liked Frederick. Marissa thought highly of him, and after the accident, he'd stepped in and personally assumed her teaching duties.

"I couldn't sleep last night." Frederick's eyes darted around the foyer. "Marissa sent me some proofs she's been working on. I started looking at them yesterday afternoon, and I didn't make it to bed."

Patrick turned toward the living room and motioned for Frederick to follow. Patrick settled into the recliner, and Frederick sat on the couch. He fidgeted and then abandoned the couch to examine the pictures on the mantel.

"I've never seen her work this hard," Patrick said. "The intensity. I'm concerned that she's—"

"Brilliant," Frederick blurted.

Manic, Patrick thought.

"I've always known she was brilliant, but—" He turned to Patrick. "Do you have any idea what she's done?"

Patrick shook his head. He'd seen the equations on her office wall. He'd seen the scrawl in her notebooks. None of it meant anything to him.

"She's going to win the Fields Medal."

The Fields Medal?

"Is she here? Can I see her?"

"Are you saying her proofs make sense?" He'd assumed that her math was as misguided as her goal, the product of delusion.

"Do Mozart's compositions make sense?" Frederick asked. "Does the *Mona Lisa* make sense? You really have no idea."

"I know Marissa is troubled."

"Marissa," Frederick said, raising his voice, "is one of the greatest mathematicians of our time."

For the past two months, Marissa, practically a hermit, had been holed up in her office trying to communicate with the dead. He didn't know what mechanism she was employing, but he couldn't fathom how she was making math out of it. "Are you telling me she can communicate with the dead?"

"What?" Frederick stared at him blankly. "No. Of course not. I'm telling you that she's invented a new math, a novel system for high-dimensional geometry."

"She's trying to communicate with the dead."

45

Frederick looked sheepish, but only for a moment. "I know. She barely seems aware of the implications of her work."

"What about the implications for her mental health? She needs help."

"If I were accomplishing half of what she is," Frederick said, "I wouldn't want help. I wouldn't care where my inspiration comes from. I can hardly believe she's done this in two months."

"You're not suggesting I sit by while she tries to communicate with the dead?"

"That's precisely what I'm suggesting." The pictures on the mantel forgotten, Frederick was pacing.

"Would you sit?" Patrick scolded.

He sat.

"She's trying to communicate with the dead. How is she creating math?"

"I can't answer that fully," Frederick said. "Actually, I have no idea. If I knew, I would do it myself. But there is a clue in one of her proofs. Are you familiar with the many-worlds interpretation of quantum mechanics?"

Patrick shrugged. He'd heard of it. He knew nothing of the mathematics underpinning quantum mechanics, but he had an inkling of where this was going.

"It's the idea in theoretical physics that multiple universes exist," Frederick explained. "Every time a quantum particle changes state, every state it could possibly assume generates a new universe. In other words, everything that can possibly happen, happens. The differences play out in different universes."

"So there is a universe," Patrick said, "in which my wife isn't trying to communicate with the dead and you're not sitting in my living room telling me there are multiple universes?"

"Well, yes. But I'm not telling you there are multiple universes. I'm telling you that some physicists believe there are and that one of

Marissa's proofs seems to probe that possibility. My guess—and her mind is operating in ways that I can't understand—is that she wants to locate a universe in which—"

"Laura didn't die," Patrick finished for him. "Look, it isn't ethical for me to diagnose my wife, so I won't. But I'm telling you—whatever math she's producing—she needs to see a psychiatrist."

"I'm not a medical doctor, but as a mathematician, I know something about rational thought. Did you ever treat a rational psychotic? When you were a practitioner." The emphasis on this last point wasn't lost on Patrick.

He didn't respond. Most of his patients had been psychiatric emergencies—people in crisis. He wasn't comparing Marissa with them. She wasn't emergent—just manic.

Frederick checked his watch impatiently. "Can I talk to her?" He stood. "Is she upstairs? I don't have permission to share her work, and there's a physicist at Berkeley who needs to see it yesterday."

"She's asleep." Patrick stood and squared his shoulders. "You look like you need sleep too." He ushered Frederick to the door. The last thing Marissa needed right now was encouragement to do math.

CHAPTER 10

AMANDA

22 WEEKS PREGNANT

Baby is becoming more aware of the outside world—sounds, even the pressure of a hand rubbing Mommy's belly—as her senses mature.

—Your Best Pregnancy

December 8, 2017

For two and a half weeks, Amanda had esteemed her pregnancy pillow as a benediction. It was shaped like a doughnut, and she could lie comfortably on her side, the bottom of the pillow wedged between her knees. She even managed seven hours of uninterrupted sleep on a few occasions. Tonight, she couldn't find a satisfying position. She wasn't ready to toss the pillow, but her reverence was fading.

She unlocked her phone and played an audiobook. She'd been doing that lately when she couldn't sleep. She preferred fast-paced novels. The story, if it was interesting, distracted her from toxic middle-of-the-night thoughts, while the rhythmic cadence of narration carried on darkness pushed her toward sleep—if there was any mercy in the world.

She lay still, eyes closed, and tried to ignore the pain in her hip. She focused on the narrator's voice.

A flutter! She paused the audiobook. Waited. Again, another flutter. The baby . . . something . . . was active. Something. She couldn't dismiss it as gas or her imagination. It wasn't something she'd conjured up. It was surprising and unpredictable and . . . real.

The idea of a faith pregnancy was insane to her. And it infuriated her that Derrick's craziness shone a light on her own. But when she felt the baby move, the idea that she was pregnant didn't feel insane. It was incompatible with the ultrasounds but not insane. She felt pregnant, and how was that any less crazy than Derrick's faith pregnancy?

Patrick had told her something that struck her. *When the world is inexplicable, our explanations are apt to be creative.* Amanda wouldn't have been so generous in her phrasing, but it made sense. He'd been talking about his wife, but he could have been talking about Derrick. And now she wondered if he could have been talking about her. Her pregnancy, when it had come, wholly unexpected, had felt like a miracle, and it was inexplicable to her that a miracle could be lost. Was her condition her mind's way of explaining the inexplicable?

It wasn't a matter of belief. She didn't believe she was pregnant. Nor did she believe she wasn't pregnant. Her body was pregnant. Even when her OB showed her a video of her tummy flattening under general anesthesia, a sight incongruous with pregnancy, her body remained pregnant. Her pregnancy was a fact.

She got out of bed because her hip ached, and sleep was nowhere in the vicinity. She'd never kept a journal, but Patrick had suggested that she write everything down, anything that could have something to do with her condition. *Write without a filter,* he'd told her. *Of course, you don't have to tell me everything you write, but at least it will be there for you. And you might find that you remember things you've forgotten.*

As they'd sat together in the park, on a bench under a bridge, Amanda prying for answers, Patrick had agreed to help her uncover why this was happening. To try, anyway. *It could be purely biological,* he'd warned. Amanda had read online that false pregnancy was common in dogs. Following estrus, a dog's ovaries flooded her body with pregnancy hormones whether she was pregnant or not. Those hormones led to pregnancy symptoms, and their decline weeks later could end in false labor and nesting behaviors. Shots of testosterone could cure false pregnancy in dogs. Spaying could prevent it. Unfortunately, it was barely understood in humans. Amanda was like a lottery winner in her rarity.

She turned on the lamp beside her bed and sat down at the table she used as a desk. She booted up her computer, but instead of opening a blank document right away, she opened the browser. She'd never deleted the bookmark to her favorite pregnancy website. She navigated to it and clicked on the link for twenty-two weeks. *Your baby is the size of a papaya.* The last time she'd checked the site, she'd been twelve weeks pregnant, her baby the size of a lime. Patrick had suggested that she resume reading the blog. *I suspect,* he'd told her, *that your condition arises in part from a desire to be pregnant. Some part of your brain is creating the symptoms of pregnancy, and I want you to feed into that. Your doctors have tried to convince you that you aren't pregnant, and that doesn't seem to help.*

You want me to convince myself that I am pregnant? she'd asked.

I want you to reinforce the idea that you're progressing through pregnancy. I want your symptoms to progress to labor.

She continued to read the website. *Baby's somatosensory system is developing, and he's experiencing new sensations like sucking his thumb.*

It was too painful. She closed the website and finally opened the word processor. The cursor blinked at the start of an empty page, and she stared at it, unable to begin. There were things she needed to tell Patrick, things she dreaded talking about. She couldn't bring herself to record them. She closed the word processor and opened her email. She composed a message.

CHAPTER 11

PATRICK

6 MONTHS AFTER THE ACCIDENT

December 8, 2017

From: Amanda Jackson
To: Patrick Davis
Subject: Crazy Ideas

Hi Patrick,

Aren't you glad I have the good sense to email and not call at 3 a.m.? Still, I hesitated to email at this hour because I don't want to give you the impression that I'm crazy. Then I remembered that you know I'm crazy. In case you haven't guessed, insomnia here. But that's not why I'm emailing. When we were at the park, you said that people sometimes come up with crazy ideas to explain the inexplicable. Do you think I'm doing that?

Amanda

From: Patrick Davis
To: Amanda Jackson
Subject: RE: Crazy Ideas

Hi Amanda,

I hope you're getting some much-needed sleep as I write this. As for your question, I would be crazy to try to answer that in an email. Let me know if you're free later today. Maybe we can grab lunch.

Patrick

~

Patrick spent the morning scouring the literature for everything he could find on pseudocyesis. There wasn't much. And what he found was vague. *A strong desire for a child coupled with an intense fear of pregnancy* was an oft-cited cause. Patrick couldn't find data to back that up. It was frustrating, but it felt better than anything he'd done in months. He was feeling the first hints of bleariness when he shut down his computer. He had plans to meet Amanda for lunch.

She chose a Chinese restaurant in a strip mall, and he watched, impressed, as she ate fried rice with chopsticks. "You're better than I am with a fork."

"My husband lived in Tokyo for a year. He took me to a Vietnamese restaurant for our first date and almost blew it by insisting on teaching me how to use chopsticks. I found it annoying, but he persisted, and now it feels right."

They made small talk over their meal and sipped hot tea. Amanda had grown up in Raleigh but visited Atlanta every summer. "I was a teenager with a much-younger sister and a single mother. I resented my mother for needing my help. I'm not proud of that, but there it is. The three weeks in June when I visited my grandmother were my reprieve."

Patrick had grown up in New Jersey and come south for medical school. "You go to the best MD-PhD program you can get into," he told her. "For me, that was Emory." Neither of them had considered returning to their hometowns after school.

They were waiting for the bill when Amanda asked, "Do you think my condition is my crazy way of explaining the inexplicable to myself?"

Patrick considered his response. "I believe that one true objective reality exists. A full understanding of that reality is beyond our reach, however, so we construct narratives, approximations of reality. We collect rules, like 'Good guys always win,' and they become the framework for our narratives. Fiction genres, for example, have different rules. In an action story, a character can jump onto the roof of a speeding car and just hang out there until he debilitates the driver, shimmies his way behind the wheel, and coasts into the sunset. In a romance, that might kill our hero, but the same guy could make love all night without bathroom or water breaks. In our lives, we tend to assume that the rules are self-evident. But often, they aren't. And small shifts in rules can lead to large differences in narratives."

"Chaos theory," Amanda said. "The butterfly effect."

"Exactly. My mother believes that she can size up a person's character in a single meeting. I don't believe that I or anyone else can consistently do that. That small difference in belief can lead to very different narratives. And who's right? I can't say for certain that my mother is wrong. There are things I believed ten years ago that seem crazy to me now. But my change in perspective can be explained by small shifts in the rules I accept."

"Some narratives," Amanda said, "fit reality better than others."

"Presumably because the underlying rules are closer to reality. When I said that people can get creative in the face of the inexplicable, I meant that we're skilled at adopting new rules to expand our narrative structure. I don't believe in ghosts. If I see one, I can either add a rule that nullifies my senses, or I can add a rule that permits the supernatural. I may not know which is true, so I have to choose. I think people tend to be self-serving in those choices. We see the world as we want to see it."

"I wish I saw the world as I want to see it," Amanda said. "The morning I miscarried, I awoke with cramps. I was bleeding. Derrick took me to the hospital, and he kept telling me that everything would be okay. I didn't believe him. I knew I was losing the baby. When the doctor confirmed it, I wasn't surprised. She performed a D&C, and it never occurred to me that a mistake had been made. I left the hospital knowing that I would never have a child. And then"—she touched her belly—"this happened. I didn't wish myself into this."

"I believe you," Patrick told her. "Everything I've said is just a narrative to explain human behavior. Maybe not even a good one."

They argued over the bill until Amanda handed her check card to the waitress. "Next time choose the restaurant," she told Patrick, "and I'll let you pay."

~

The Chattahoochee River was five minutes from the restaurant, and the afternoon was gorgeous. Amanda suggested they take a walk.

"I should apologize again for my inappropriate laughter the other day," Patrick said. They strolled along a wide gravel trail, a thin row of pines separating them from the river, calm along these parts. And beautiful. "I don't know what happened."

Amanda smiled. "It is funny when you think about it. In an upside-down-world sort of way."

"How did your mother and sister take Derrick's faith pregnancy bombshell?"

"The faith pregnancy bombshell was just for me. He told them I'm pregnant. My mother was appalled, of course, that I hadn't told her. And excited at the prospect of a grandchild."

"Ouch. Did you tell her the truth?"

"I couldn't. I don't know how. I invented a complication involving the placenta and told her it's a high-risk pregnancy. The only way I made it through the day was by forbidding my mother from mentioning it. It was Meredith's day, after all. And strangely enough, I enjoyed dress shopping. Meredith insisted on a blush dress, and she looked beautiful in all of them, but my mother really wanted white. I enjoyed watching them spar."

"Who won?"

Amanda smiled. "Meredith chose a beautiful blush dress. We had a nice dinner, and I saw them off. Eventually, I'll have to pretend that I miscarried. Well, I won't be pretending, just moving the timeline. I should make Derrick call my mother to break that news."

"I'm not saying you should tell her about your condition," Patrick said, "but you shouldn't not tell her because you're ashamed. You have nothing to be ashamed of."

"If I tell them, my mother and Meredith, they'll use it against me one day. I can't give them this. Do you have anything like that with your family?"

Patrick hesitated before saying, "I quit my job to get Marissa's attention. My brother suspects as much, but I can't admit it because he'll turn it into a running joke."

"Really?"

"Yes, my brother can be downright vicious for the sake of humor."

"Did you really quit your job to get Marissa's attention?"

"Partly. I'd been thinking about leaving academia for a while. It requires so many things that have nothing to do with science, all while tenure is dangled over your head. I was fed up with the grind, but I wouldn't have quit without lining something else up. So yeah, I quit to get her attention.

"Halford University is very excited about Marissa's work. Apparently, it has implications for theoretical physics, something to do with parallel universes. Two Stanford physicists flew in to see her. The dean of Marissa's department brought them to our house, but I wouldn't let them in. Long story short, Marissa's dean called the president of the university, who called the dean of neuroscience." Patrick's anger rose as he told Amanda about his last day in the office.

~

Jack Spencer, the dean of neuroscience, stopped by Patrick's office unannounced. "You have a minute?" He closed the door and helped himself to a chair. Patrick liked Jack, despite his smile. Even at its best, it seemed insincere.

"Must be important," Patrick said.

Jack flashed an uneasy smile. "It warranted a call from Skip Robbins."

Patrick whistled. Skip was the president of Halford University.

"Look, Patrick, if I come across as an asshole here, it's only because this is awkward."

"You're making me nervous, Jack."

"It's about Marissa." Jack fidgeted in his seat. "The work she's doing is very important to Halford. Frederick Peters has spoken to Skip and expressed concerns that you may interfere with her work. It's important to Skip personally that you don't do that."

"What in the hell does that mean?"

Jack looked imploringly at him. "I didn't ask for details. Listen, I know you and Marissa have had a difficult time."

"A difficult time," Patrick said angrily, "is when your car breaks down on an icy bridge in the middle of the night."

"I know. I'll do anything I can to help. I just need for you to tell me that you won't interfere with Marissa's work."

Patrick stood abruptly. "Unbelievable. How about I tell you to go to hell, Jack?"

"Please. Sit down."

Patrick found the hesitance in Jack's voice satisfying. "I would tell you to get the fuck out of my office, but it isn't mine anymore."

"Patrick, don't do this. I'm truly sorry."

Patrick gathered his personal belongings. "I don't need your apologies, Jack. I needed you to tell Skip that my personal life is none of his damn business."

~

"They gave me an excuse to quit," Patrick told Amanda, "but at the core of it, I quit to get Marissa's attention."

"Did it?" Amanda asked. "Get her attention."

Patrick shook his head. "The only difference is that now I don't have a place to go during the day."

Amanda startled Patrick by taking his hand. When he looked into her eyes, he saw that it wasn't a flirtatious act but one fueled by genuine concern.

"Thank you for telling me that." They walked in silence, hand in hand. "I haven't been fair to my husband. We're not in a good place, but it isn't all his fault. I'm going to tell you something that I haven't told anyone, and it won't be easy for me."

He squeezed her hand.

"There was a time," she said, "and it seems far away now, when I thought my marriage was perfect."

They'd been married for two years, she told him, when they'd decided it was time. Amanda was thirty-two, and they thought getting pregnant would be easy, especially given the effort they'd put into not getting pregnant. She stopped taking the pill, and they waited. When that didn't work, they tracked her temperature and timed their lovemaking with her cycle. A year and a half later, they visited a fertility specialist. Even then, they were nonchalant. When asked for a semen sample, Derrick joked that he couldn't go three days without an orgasm, maybe two at the most. Amanda pointed out that they didn't have sex every two days and then committed herself to forgetting the implications of that. They had a good laugh. Everything checked out, and they started down the long path of fertility treatments. They did six cycles of Clomid, followed by three cycles of IUI. They paid for four cycles of IVF, but after the second cycle failed, she couldn't do it anymore.

She wasn't accustomed to giving up. From an early age, persistence had been her hallmark. She was ten when her father enrolled her in tae kwon do, the only girl in the class. Six months later, she distinguished herself by being the sole student to fail the yellow-belt test. The class moved on without her, and she committed to a practice schedule. By year's end, she was the sensei's star pupil.

When she fell in love with computer science during her first year in college, math phobia stood between her and the degree. She bought the textbook for every required math course and spent her summers working through them. She was shocked when her combinatorics professor told her she had a gift.

The moment she gave up on fertility treatments was one of the worst of her life. They'd been trying to conceive for three years. She dreaded sex. The anxiety that seized her before each pregnancy test felt almost debilitating. She wanted so desperately to be a mother, and every negative result was a wound that didn't heal.

Derrick was furious. She didn't know if he meant to, but he focused on the money. His hands balled into fists as he ranted over the $16,000 of unused IVF treatments. Nonrefundable.

The money was the least of it for her.

Without the fertility treatments, they had no reason to have sex. They'd become roommates who didn't particularly care for each other.

CHAPTER 12

AMANDA

Summer 2017

Amanda had read the Not Quite Human series as a child. When she was an undergraduate, memories of Chip, the humanoid robot, lured her to computer science. Her first artificial intelligence course was dispiriting. Modern AI was little more than the clever application of statistics to data. No one designed programs that were as intelligent as humans because no one knew where to start. Just defining intelligence was elusive.

Now, thirteen years later, she worked as a data scientist at BPI, a large business-intelligence firm. Her days were cyclical and routine. She met with clients to discuss their business needs. She collected and cleaned data. She built machine learning models to glean insights from the data. She reported back to the clients. And then she met with different clients to initiate a new cycle. She didn't dislike her work, and it paid well.

Just as she and Derrick were talking about having a baby, her profession became sexy, almost overnight. Deep learning, the use of complex neural networks, grew in popularity, and everyone was trying to apply machine learning to every problem. Recruiters from research labs, robotics manufacturers, and even a feature-film company reached out to Amanda. Thoughts of a more fulfilling job, meaningful work in the not-for-profit sector perhaps, crept into her daily grind. But she and Derrick had just bought a home, and she'd stopped taking the pill, so she stayed put. When the baby was born, she would take six months off before finding a more interesting job. A recruiter from a surgical-robots start-up asked Amanda to keep them in mind. And she did. But the baby never came, and her work at BPI began to feel something like drudgery.

As her marriage deteriorated, she spent more time at the office. There was never a shortage of work. But as far as she could tell, BPI only made her more miserable. She spent her days with wealthy people who wanted more wealth and her nights clinging to the edge of her bed in fear of inadvertently touching her husband. She was nearing the end of the cycle with a client when she received an invitation to an internal meeting called Project Iustitia.

~

Ralph Sturgess was an imposing figure, six feet two and broad shouldered, and ten minutes into his presentation, Amanda hadn't seen him smile. He was a technology director, a few rungs above Amanda in the corporate hierarchy, which meant she didn't know him personally. His project sounded interesting, and he was looking for a machine learning engineer.

"Our system," he explained, "will provide intelligence to lawyers in real time during voir dire. From her smartphone, a lawyer will be able to assess where a juror falls probabilistically on a host of issues, social and political. Our system will scour the web for public information on a juror: social media profiles, blog posts, news articles, political donations. The first version of Iustitia will focus on text data. The second version will analyze images and video. The data on each juror will be fed to a deep neural network, which will predict their social views on a range of topics. What the lawyer wants to know will depend on the case, so Iustitia needs to know everything. Put your hand up if you are a machine learning expert."

Amanda, along with roughly half of the twenty or so attendees, raised her hand.

"If your hand isn't up, you should get back to work." He paused, and several attendees looked at each other. "That wasn't a joke, people. If you aren't a machine learning expert, you're wasting your time and, more importantly, mine."

One person stood to leave, and others reluctantly followed.

"Good." He finally smiled. He had brown skin, a goatee, and movie star teeth. "If I'm lucky, I will be inviting one of you to spend the next six months working on Iustitia full-time. If there is any chance that you will decline, please leave now."

Amanda looked around. Everyone else did the same. One person rose to leave.

Ralph rubbed his hands together. "Let's start with some fundamentals. Open the notebook in front of you. You'll want to write these numbers down." Amanda opened her notebook. "I go to a doctor, and she tests me for a fatal disease called X. The test is ninety-eight percent accurate. One out of every one hundred thousand people in a given population is afflicted with X, and it is independently and identically distributed. My test comes back positive. How worried should I be?"

Amanda did the calculations on a blank sheet in her notebook.

He gave them a couple of minutes before saying, "Does anyone here think I should be worried about X?"

One brave hand shot up, an engineer named Wayne. Amanda worked with him on occasion. He was a smart guy.

"Explain," Ralph said to Wayne.

"The test is ninety-eight percent accurate. If one hundred people take the test, only two of them will have an inaccurate result. I don't like your odds."

"You're a machine learning expert?" Ralph asked.

Wayne nodded. "I am."

"Do you have a degree or any other evidence that you can do more than multiplication and subtraction?"

"I have a master's degree in computer science."

"And which illustrious university granted you this degree?"

"Halford."

Amanda shifted uncomfortably.

"And you can prove in a court of law that you were awarded this degree?"

"I could request an official transcript," Wayne replied.

"You do that. Do it immediately. You are going to sue Halford University for malpractice, and I am going to help you. They falsely led you to believe that you have even a basic grasp of statistics."

The room was silent. Amanda closed her eyes, embarrassed for him.

"Why are you still here?" Ralph asked.

Amanda stared at her notebook as Wayne stood and left the room. She wondered briefly if leaving made him the lucky one.

"Does anyone else think I should be worried?" Ralph asked.

Silence.

He walked around the room, checking answers. He glanced at Amanda's math and moved on without a word. There was less than a 1 percent chance that he had X, given a positive test. Given the rarity of the disease, his positive result was almost certain to be a false positive. One had only to apply Bayes's rule.

"I think you should leave," he said to a man sitting in the row behind Amanda. The man complied.

"Next question. I want you to write a program in two languages of your choice that recursively finds the edit distance between two strings."

The questions went on for an hour. Amanda and another woman were the only ones left.

Ralph looked at his watch. "I have a meeting. I'll be in touch with one of you." He walked out of the room.

Amanda sighed. She felt like she'd just finished the GRE. "I hope it's you," she told the woman, an engineer she'd never met. Ralph Sturgess would not be easy to work for.

~

Three days later, Zack Ames, Amanda's direct supervisor, informed her that she'd been requested to work on Project Iustitia.

"Do I have to?" she asked.

"No, but it sounds interesting."

"Will I get stress pay?"

Zack laughed. "Ralph is an acquired taste. You'll do fine. Besides, I'm still your manager. I can step in if you need me."

Amanda went home that evening feeling pretty sure she would decline, even with Zack's reassurance. She found Derrick in the living room watching television. She was going to talk to him about Iustitia, but then she noticed that he was eating a burger from Piney's on Piedmont.

Before buying their house, they'd practically lived next door to Piney's. It was her favorite destination for tavern food.

"Hey," he said robotically when he saw her.

"You went to Piney's?" she asked, though the bag on the coffee table answered her question.

He nodded and turned back to the television, a sitcom.

She didn't want to ask if he'd brought her anything. It would lead to a confrontation if he hadn't. She sat in a chair and waited for him to tell her that her food was in the kitchen. Instead, he said, "I called your cell, but it went straight to voice mail."

"I forgot my charger." She stood and went to the kitchen to make a sandwich. He knew that she liked the Impossible Burger with Tater

Tots. A year ago, he wouldn't have bothered to call. He would have surprised her. A year ago, she would have emailed to tell him she'd forgotten her charger.

She slathered the bread with peanut butter. This was typical of them lately. She would get angry at him, and then her own culpability would pop up and wave. He'd been annoyed that he couldn't get in touch with her, so he hadn't gotten her anything from Piney's. Now, she was annoyed that he hadn't gotten her anything from Piney's, so she wouldn't talk to him about Project Iustitia. As clearly as she saw the chain of effect, she couldn't break it. She didn't have the will to make nice with him tonight.

She ate her peanut butter and jelly sandwich at the kitchen table. The orange she had on the side was healthier than Tater Tots anyway. She kept telling herself that.

She missed their condo in the city. Now, just getting to the grocery store took fifteen minutes by car. And this house was too big for the two of them. Two of the bedrooms sat empty, waiting to be converted into nurseries. She felt trapped sometimes when she came home. She felt trapped sometimes when she was in the office. She needed a change, and if nothing else, Project Iustitia would present some interesting challenges.

As a graduate student, she'd worked in a computer-vision laboratory for one of the biggest jerks at Georgia Tech. The man cared only about his research and saw students as laborers who existed to do his bidding. He regularly belittled students who failed to meet his expectations, and Amanda had been his target at more than one lab meeting. She'd learned a lot working there. Not least that she could make it through anything. She could survive six months with Ralph Sturgess.

~

For the first time in a long time, Amanda enjoyed going into the office. She didn't resent taking work home with her. She met with Ralph daily, a fifteen-minute stand-up to discuss successes, obstacles, and direction. Every Friday, he took her out to lunch for a longer discussion. She thanked him the first time he picked up the tab. He explained that senior management was both excited about and skeptical of Project Iustitia. He didn't have many resources, but he did have the budget for a weekly lunch. Amanda had use of two junior data scientists to gather and clean data. She worked solo on the algorithms.

Ralph was always professional and complimentary of her work. A month into the project, he hadn't belittled her once. When she solved an especially complex problem or devised a clever trick to make the program faster, she actually looked forward to sharing it with him. Ralph was technical and had a deep appreciation of skillful design, even if he didn't understand the inner workings of machine learning algorithms. She'd tried to resist liking him at first, but she saw no hints of his earlier cruelty. Perhaps he'd been having an exceptionally bad day when he'd denigrated Wayne.

Piney's was a few miles from the office, but she talked Ralph into going one Friday afternoon. When they got into his Jaguar, he surprised her by talking about something other than work. "I bought my mother a cell phone, but I have the hardest time getting her to carry it when she leaves the house. Her mind isn't so sharp, so I worry. After months of ignoring my pleas, she finally took it with her this morning when she walked to the convenience store to buy that colored sugar in a straw. She's diabetic, but I can't tell her anything. Anyway, my phone rings at a quarter to ten, and Mom comes up on the display. But when I answer, it's a man.

"He says, 'Do you know how I got this phone?'

"I tell him I don't.

"He asks if I can hear him. I tell him I can.

"He asks if I'm sure that I can hear him.

"I'm already nervous and I have a meeting at ten, so I shout at him that I can hear him.

"He says, 'Okay, I want to make sure you hear me.'

"I'm signaling to my assistant because I want her to call 911, but she doesn't know what I want, and I'm trying to listen to this guy on the phone. I assure the guy I can hear him, and he asks me again if I know how he got the phone. My assistant is staring at me and I'm mouthing, 'Call 911,' but she can't read lips. I'm waiting for the guy to demand a ransom when he says, 'I found it in the grass. I've never used a phone like this before.' And then I guess my assistant understands because she picks up her phone. And the guy tells me that he's homeless and he'll return the phone; he just needs a few bucks."

Amanda laughed. "Your assistant called 911?"

"She did. That was embarrassing. I had to cancel my ten a.m. to check on my mother and pick up her phone."

"How much money did you give him?"

"I had eighty in cash on me, so I gave him that. He was ecstatic. He said, 'I'm not gonna lie. I'm gonna buy a beer.' I said, 'Hey, I'm gonna have a beer myself.' It's been an interesting morning."

He was strictly professional over lunch at Piney's, but Amanda felt more relaxed with him than usual on the ride back to the office. "Why were you so mean to Wayne?" she asked.

He glanced at her. "Who is Wayne?"

"You told him to sue Halford University."

"Oh," he intoned. "Wayne. I was trying to do him a favor."

"Some favor. What do you do when you're trying to humiliate someone?"

"My algorithms professor in college asked me to complete a simple proof by induction on the first day of class. I couldn't do it. He asked me what year of my studies I was in. When I told him I was a junior, he went on a rant. If I'd picked up so little in two years of schooling, it was doubtful I belonged in college, much less at Stanford, much less in his class. It felt like he went on for twenty minutes. I was the only Black student in the class, and I thought he singled me out for that reason. So I dropped the course. I was furious, and I couldn't let it go, so I went to his office hours. I wrote an inductive proof on his whiteboard and told him it took me fifteen minutes to understand it. I just needed a refresher.

"'Why haven't I seen you in class?' he asked me.

"I told him I dropped. He shook his head and said he was sorry he wasted his well-chosen words on me. By now, I was ready to go to the dean and report him for being a racist. And then he offered me a job in his lab. I was flabbergasted. When I asked him why, he said, 'You came here to show me induction. I suspect you'll never come to me unprepared again.' He became a mentor to me and helped me find my first job after graduation."

Amanda shook her head. "Men."

"What?" Ralph asked.

"That's a nice story, but only men need to be so brutal to make a point."

"It's a beautiful story. Unfortunately, I didn't get my point across to Wayne. I haven't heard a word from him. He saw me in the lobby and pretended to be on his phone to avoid riding the elevator with me."

"I don't blame him," Amanda said. "I hope I never fail to know something you think I should."

He smiled at her. "I hope you don't either."

~

Ralph was an attractive man, but Amanda didn't see him that way until it was too late. As Project Iustitia ramped up, they spent more time together. He came to her office every evening as her coworkers were heading home. He camped out and bounced ideas off her as she wrote code and performed experiments.

"Can I ask you a personal question?" she said late one evening. He nodded. "It's actually work related. How do you feel about Iustitia? I mean, it's a fascinating product, but its purpose is to help lawyers manipulate jurors."

"We're in the business of intelligence," he replied. "From my perspective, the sole purpose of providing intelligence is to make money."

"I'm well aware," Amanda said wryly. She'd always imagined that she would do useful work, something that benefited society. But she'd gotten comfortable at BPI. Complacent. "The justice system is already skewed toward the rich. We're helping people who can afford an expensive legal team gain an even bigger advantage than they already have."

"You don't think public defenders will use Iustitia?"

She searched his face for hints of sarcasm. He was deadpan. He laughed. "Okay. Public defenders won't have access to Iustitia. Everything is skewed toward the rich. You can't solve that here. But you can do other things. I teach a robotics class for underprivileged kids every summer."

Ralph was full of surprises. She never would have imagined that.

"Now," he said, "can I ask you a personal question?"

"It's only fair."

"When is the last time you went out dancing?"

She wasn't expecting that. And honestly, she didn't remember. It had been a long time since she and Derrick had been out anywhere.

"My niece is getting married. Her father isn't in the picture, so the first dance falls to me. I can't dance." He pulled out his cell phone. Amanda thought he was going to show her a picture of his niece, but "Always and Forever" filled the office. He extended his hand. "Help a brother out."

Amanda did not have sex outside her marriage. But even if she did, she would not sleep with her boss. But Ralph wasn't her boss. As Zack had pointed out, Zack was her boss, and Ralph wasn't in Zack's chain of command. Ralph directed Project Iustitia, but he'd have no say in her raises and promotions. She'd worked all of this out before he kissed her at the end of the song.

~

Amanda showered when she got home. Even so, Derrick would know. They'd been married for five and a half years, and she'd had sex with another man. How would he not know?

She fell asleep on the couch watching a movie. When she went to their bedroom, she expected the bed to be empty. She expected to find that Derrick had packed his things and moved out while she dozed. But there he was, snoring and oblivious. She climbed into bed beside him.

~

The feeling that she couldn't get away with her betrayal faded, and Amanda didn't know what to make of that. Having sex with Ralph got easier and easier. It was heady, working on Project Iustitia late into the night and then having sex with Ralph on the couch in his office. Mostly, it was the growing ease of it that bothered Amanda. She'd felt terrible after the first time, and as illogical as it was, the guilt had made her feel better. If she felt guilty, she couldn't be a bad person. But the guilt was fading. What happened when it was gone?

~

She wasn't thinking of Derrick when she got home that evening. She was on autopilot. She locked the garage door and placed her purse in the wicker basket beside the pantry. Her infidelity was at six weeks and running. When she saw him sitting at the table, his face in his hands, she knew that he knew.

"What's wrong?" she asked, her throat clenching around the words. She hadn't slept with Ralph tonight, but she had the night before. What would she say?

"Jeff died," he told her. "Heart attack. His wife just called."

"Jeff from college? He's our age."

Derrick nodded. They'd been close in college, and Jeff had been in their wedding. Jeff had moved to Seattle five years ago, and they'd drifted apart.

"I'm sorry." She sat down, and he reached across the table and took her hands. His touch felt almost foreign.

"I wish I'd been better about keeping in touch with him."

She squeezed his hands. "You both got busy, and we always think there's plenty of time."

She stood and pulled him into an embrace. He clung to her as any grief-stricken man would his wife, but she didn't feel comfortable in the role. Wives didn't sleep with other men.

"I don't want to stay in tonight," he said. "Can we go out for drinks?"

"Sure." She was tired and she had work to do, but she was still his wife. "Give me a minute to change."

~

They went to a pub, and Derrick told stories about Jeff, most of them from their college days. As a buzz settled over Amanda, she glimpsed the man she'd fallen in love with. He wasn't gone. She just couldn't always see him. When they arrived home, however, he barely glanced at her as they readied for bed.

As they lay together, she thought about her affair with Ralph. Where was it going? She didn't love him, and she had no reason to believe he loved her. At forty-five, he'd never married. She couldn't expect to change that. He hadn't asked her about leaving Derrick, and she'd never seriously considered it. Could she attend Jeff's funeral and stand at Derrick's side, the supportive wife, if she was still having this fling? People did it every day, but she couldn't imagine not feeling like a colossal phony.

~

Amanda had decided to end things with Ralph, but his desire pulled her in. She didn't find her voice until they were lying on his couch, undressed and spent. "We can't do this again."

"Do what?" Ralph asked, unfazed.

"This. I'm married."

"You were married last week. And the week before."

"My husband's close friend died yesterday. I had to comfort him, knowing I was doing this."

Ralph stood and pulled on his pants. "In all this time, you haven't mentioned your husband once."

"You haven't asked." She pulled on her dress.

"It's none of my business."

For some reason, that hurt. She didn't know why. "This was the last time," she told him, her tone sharper than intended.

Ralph shrugged. "Fine. Do you think this is the first time I've done this?"

CHAPTER 13

MARISSA

23 YEARS BEFORE THE ACCIDENT

When Marissa was four, she inherited Jen's Speak & Spell. She didn't take to it as Jen had, and this worried their mother. It was important to Donna Thomas that her children be smart. Her worries were assuaged when Marissa's father bought her a Speak & Math. Marissa loved it. *Greater or less than, level three,* she would repeat, imitating the robotic voice.

Marissa liked math class, but only nominally better than other subjects. She loved dance. It was her singular passion until she met John Wells at a neighborhood cookout. She was eleven years old, and John was a PhD candidate studying math at MIT. John was her neighbor's brother, visiting for two weeks.

All the faces were familiar as Marissa observed the segregation. The men gathered at the grill while the women chatted at the picnic table, spread with chips, sliced vegetables, and dips. The boys were throwing a football in the grass, and Jen led the girls in hopscotch on the patio. John stood apart, engrossed in a bed of sunflowers. Bored with hopscotch, Marissa wandered over until she stood beside him. Absorbed in his inspection of a single sunflower, he didn't seem to notice her presence. Just as she started to turn and leave, he said, "The arrangement of seeds follows the Fibonacci sequence."

Marissa had never heard of the Fibonacci sequence. She asked questions that led to more questions and explanations she didn't understand. When she asked what he studied at MIT, he showed her Fermat's last theorem, a proposition so simple that even Marissa could grasp it.

"I'm going to prove it," she told him, though she barely knew what a proof was. For two weeks, she saw John nearly every day, and he showed her more simple proofs. When he returned to Boston, Marissa had a new love: mathematics.

She was fourteen when John sent her Andrew Wiles's proof of Fermat's last theorem. It was one of the saddest and most exciting days of her life. She wouldn't be the first to prove it, but once she was able to fully understand his proof, she would have answers at last.

She hadn't heard from her mother in two years. Unlike her father, her mother hadn't looked back. Marissa hadn't seen her father, but she spoke to him on the phone once or twice a month. Jen spoke to him more frequently, and he sent money occasionally. Jen had been promoted to assistant manager at the department store. She swore Marissa to secrecy regarding their lack of parental supervision.

"I'm serious," Jen warned. "You know how everyone shares a secret with at least one other person? I'm that other person. You can't tell your best friend. You can't tell anyone."

Marissa didn't. When she wasn't at school, she studied math. She enrolled in a college correspondence course. That didn't leave money for dance, but Marissa didn't miss it. She missed her parents, a pain that became manageable with time. Like Jen said: *If they don't want us, why should we want them?* She had Jen. She had everything she needed.

~

"I can't imagine a birthday without him," Marissa told Jen. Rigley was sitting on the couch next to Marissa. He was a big dog, about fifty-five pounds, with a fluffy black coat that made him look even larger. He was a watchful guardian, fierce with strangers, and the reason that Marissa had never felt unsafe, even after her father left. They'd shared dual birthday parties for as long as she could remember. Even on those birthdays when the family had gone out for dinner, she'd insisted on takeout for Rigley. It was the one day of the year that he gorged himself on table food.

"I think he'll make it to November," Jen said. It was April. Marissa wasn't so sure. The arthritis in his hips was bad, and it was getting increasingly difficult for him to stand in the mornings. More and more often, Marissa had to lift his back end to get him moving. The medication had helped for a couple of years, but even increased dosages failed him now.

"It isn't fair," Marissa told Jen as she stroked Rigley. "We're both fourteen. I don't understand why dogs age so fast."

"Be grateful you're not a dog."

Marissa didn't reply. Watching Rigley age made her sadder than she'd ever been. She didn't know what to do with her grief.

"Do you want to see my prom dress?" Jen asked. She'd been dating Dan Foley for the past three months. He'd invited Jen to his senior prom, which would have been her senior prom had she not dropped out of school.

Marissa nodded. Then she began to cry.

"Marissa," Jen said and joined her on the couch. "It's okay. Rigley is a dog, and he understands that he's old. He doesn't cry about it."

"He won't have to celebrate his birthday alone."

Jen put her arm around Marissa's shoulder. "Rigley has had a good life, and he isn't gone yet. Enjoy him while he's here."

Marissa tried, but she couldn't. They used to take long walks. Sometimes on the weekends, Marissa would wake up early and they would walk for two hours, wandering her neighborhood and those adjacent. He could still do thirty-minute walks in the evenings, but Marissa couldn't shake the feeling that their time was short. She was losing him.

"I think I should take a college biology course," she told Jen one evening after her walk with Rigley. Jen was in the living room watching television. She'd been on her feet all day.

"Why is that?" She glanced up at Marissa and then turned back to the television.

"Why do you think Rigley is old?"

"What?" Jen was trying to listen to Marissa and the television.

"Can I turn this off?" Marissa asked. "It's important."

Jen sighed, but she turned the television off.

"Why do you think Rigley is old?"

Jen was thoughtful. "I have no idea. Fourteen is old for a big dog."

"It must have something to do with his genetics, right?"

Jen shrugged.

"What else could it be?"

"I don't know. Dogs are just made that way."

"Well, if humans can live for eighty years, dogs can live for eighty years. I just need to find where aging is encoded in the dog genome."

Jen stared at her for a long while. "Humans and dogs have been living together for what, a million years?"

Marissa laughed, not unkindly. "Humans haven't been on this planet for a million years. Maybe two hundred thousand."

"So you say. My point is, humans and dogs have lived together for thousands of years. Everyone has always accepted that dogs don't live long. I think you're the first person who wants to extend the lifespan of a dog to eighty years."

Rigley entered the room and lay at Marissa's feet. She scratched the back of his neck. "Maybe no human has ever loved a dog the way I love Rigley."

~

On the morning of Jen's prom, Rigley's hind legs stopped working. When Marissa tried to stand him up, he collapsed. He sat up and panted, seemingly unaffected by Marissa's panic. She ran into Jen's room, screaming.

By the time Jen, still groggy, made her way to Rigley, he'd wet the floor.

"We have to take him to the vet," Marissa said.

Jen looked stricken. "I have to tell you something," she whispered, as if she didn't want Rigley to hear. "The last time I took Rigley to the vet, he warned me this could happen. He thought Rigley might have spinal cord damage."

"We'll have the vet fix him."

Jen shook her head. "The vet can't fix him. He has to be put to sleep."

Marissa looked at Rigley. He looked fine. His hind legs just weren't working. "You said he would make it to November."

Jen hugged her. "I hoped he would."

"You didn't tell me about his spine."

"I didn't want to upset you."

"He's my dog," Marissa cried. "I'm upset."

"I know." Jen squeezed her. Rigley had always been Marissa's dog. They shared a birthday and a bond that left every other family member an outsider. "I'll take him to the vet. You stay here."

Marissa pulled away. "You're going to have him put to sleep?"

"We have to. Rigley is old. It's time."

Marissa lay on the floor next to him. "I love him."

"I know. That's why we have to put him to sleep. We don't want him to suffer."

"It isn't fair. He hates the car. Can the vet come here?"

Jen nodded and left the room. Marissa held Rigley and sobbed. She couldn't imagine a world without him. Jen returned, the cordless telephone in hand. "I'm sorry, Marissa. We can't afford a house call. I have to take Rigley in."

Marissa looked up at her. "The car scares him. He shouldn't spend his last moments on earth scared."

Jen began to cry. She lay down on the floor with Marissa and Rigley. "I'll call Dad," she said.

～

Marissa spent the morning on her bedroom floor with Rigley. She made him cheese eggs for breakfast. There was nothing wrong with his appetite, so she made him a hamburger for lunch. The vet came to the house at two thirty and administered shots that separated Marissa and Rigley for the first time in either of their lives. Marissa thought her world had come to an end.

～

It was early evening when the phone woke Marissa. She got up to answer, but Jen beat her to it.

"You're too late," Jen snapped after a polite hello. Marissa watched her sister, no idea who she could be talking to. "We don't need anything from you. We're fine. It's like you never left."

"Who is it?" Marissa mouthed. Their mother?

"Fine." Jen hung up.

"Who was that?" Marissa repeated. Jen didn't respond, so Marissa followed her to the kitchen.

"It was Dad," Jen finally said.

"Didn't he give you money for Rigley?"

"No, I couldn't reach him. I figured out another way."

"How?"

"It doesn't matter. Let's rent a movie from Blockbuster tonight. Your choice."

"What about the prom?" All Jen had talked about for the past month was the prom.

"I'm not going."

"Why?"

"Everyone there will judge me for dropping out. It doesn't matter that I make more money than any of them. I don't want to be judged."

Marissa didn't detect any cues that Jen was lying, but she knew her sister better than she knew any other human being. She knew her sister wasn't telling the truth. And then it occurred to her that she hadn't seen Jen's prom dress. Jen had mentioned showing it to her a couple of times, but she never had.

"I haven't seen your dress," Marissa said. "Can you show it to me?"

"I returned it," Jen told her. "I wasn't going, so what was the point?"

Marissa cried again and Jen hugged her.

"Movie night?" Jen asked.

Marissa nodded. "Movie night."

She let Jen believe that her tears were for Rigley. And in part they were. But these tears were mostly because Marissa knew where Jen got the money to pay the vet for a house call. And she knew that her sister wanted to go to the prom.

CHAPTER 14

PATRICK

6 MONTHS AFTER THE ACCIDENT

December 13, 2017

From: Patrick Davis
To: Amanda Jackson
Subject: RE: Unusual Conditions

Hemispatial neglect is an attentional disorder in which patients neglect (or are unaware of) one half of their visual field. A patient with damage to the right parietal lobe (typically caused by stroke) might be unaware of anything to their left. Men may only shave the right side of their face. Women may only put makeup on the right side of their face. They may only eat food on the right side of their plate. Their vision is normal, but their brain is unable to process anything to their left. If you tell them to look around a room, they might only look to their right.

~

Patrick was drinking coffee when Amanda called. She had two passes to the botanical gardens that expired tonight.

Patrick considered it. "That sounds like fun, but it's lawn-and-garbage day."

"Lawn-and-garbage day? Is that the male equivalent of washing your hair?"

"No, I think that's changing the oil in my car. But it really is lawn-and-garbage day. When I quit my job, I canceled garbage pickup and lawn service."

"Sounds exciting. Maybe next time."

"Yes, I appreciate the offer. Next time."

He finished his coffee and changed into an old pair of jeans and a T-shirt. He gassed up the lawn mower and pushed it to the front yard. He thought about Amanda, about holding hands with her at the Chattahoochee. It hadn't felt flirtatious, but was it weird?

For the past three months, lawn-and-garbage day had been the highlight of his week. Now, as he surveyed the yard, the job seemed staggering in scope. Loading trash into his car and driving to the dump seemed unendurable.

He pushed the lawn mower back into the garage and went upstairs to Marissa's office. She looked up from her notebook, acknowledged him with a smile, and then returned to her writing. That was all he was going to get.

"How do the botanical gardens sound?"

She blinked, confused. "Green and flowery. Fun if I wasn't so busy." She was already disengaging, her attention back on the notebook.

He called Amanda.

~

Amanda was waiting on a bench at the entrance when Patrick arrived. He thought she'd seen him coming, but she startled when he spoke.

"I'm sorry," she said. "I'm not sleeping well. My brain is foggy."

She handed him a pass, and they entered the gardens. The temperature was warm, upper fifties, the sky overcast and threatening rain.

"I'm sorry about the weather," she said.

He smiled. "You control that now?"

They wandered, Amanda leading the way. He hadn't visited the gardens in a decade, and nothing looked familiar. They lingered at the model-train exhibit. "Even before I gave up on getting pregnant," Amanda said, "I avoided places like this."

There were no kids around, but Patrick could imagine them crowding in on weekends, drawn by the miniature trains running on tiny tracks.

"I figured out pretty quickly that avoidance is futile. Kids and pregnant women are everywhere. Case in point." She splayed her arms and laughed.

Patrick was discovering the futility, but he hadn't yet capitulated.

"Do you mind if we sit?" she asked, motioning to a porch swing on the edge of the model-train exhibit. "I know we just got here, but—my calf."

They sat side by side, overlooking a courtyard with a blown glass sculpture. Minutes passed before Amanda broke the silence. "It's peaceful."

Patrick agreed. It felt like vacation.

"I feel lighter since talking to you about Ralph. It's the first real secret I kept from Beverly. But when you first declined to come, I thought maybe you didn't want to hang out with me because of it."

"What? No. I'm glad you told me. I appreciate your trust." He smiled at her, and she smiled back.

"I'm ready if you are," she said. Patrick stood and helped her out of the swing. "To the canopy walk."

~

They strolled along the walkway, high above the forest floor. Rain wasn't forecast for another two hours, but it came early, scattered sprinkles quickly upgrading to a steady drizzle. They spotted an awning in the distance beyond a beautiful man-made waterfall. They picked up their pace and made it to cover moments before the hard rains began. They sat on a bench and watched the droplets pelt the sparse trees.

"I have more things to tell you," she said. "It only gets worse."

CHAPTER 15

AMANDA

3 WEEKS PREGNANT

The first hints of Baby's nervous system are blossoming. In a week, the neural plate will develop into the neural tube. The neural tube will give rise to the brain.

—Your Best Pregnancy

July 24, 2017

The metallic taste was always there. If Amanda believed in the channeling of emotions through gustation, she would've called it the taste of guilt. But she didn't, so she called her dentist's office to make an appointment. The receptionist suggested that she try a different toothpaste. She did. Still, every time she ate, no matter what she ate, no matter what brand of paste she used to brush her teeth, she was left with a metallic aftertaste. Guilt.

Amanda was intimately familiar with her menstrual cycle. When her period was a week late—two weeks after the metallic taste had appeared—she noticed. The realization quickened her pulse. Of course she wasn't pregnant. She couldn't be pregnant. She hadn't had sex with Derrick in six months, their last desperate effort to conceive, a demeaning coupling. She'd initiated sex because she was supposedly fertile, but she hadn't wanted it. Something felt wrong when he entered her, and she suppressed an urge to violently defend herself against his onslaught. She closed her eyes and willed him to finish before she lost it and threw him off her. When he'd pulled out, she'd felt like a prostitute, slathered in bitterness, awaiting her pay. She never wanted to feel that way again.

Ending the affair with Ralph, she'd thought, was the act that would reclaim her marriage. She'd strayed, and there had to be a lesson in that. She'd driven home that night planning to seduce Derrick. When she arrived, he was sitting on the couch, reading, and when he looked up at her, she saw everything that was wrong with her plan. She'd just had sex with another man. Amazing sex. Would she compare sex with Derrick to that? And perhaps most scary of all, Ralph had been desperate to have her. What if Derrick's passion didn't measure up?

"How was your day?" she'd asked, not a hint of seduction in her voice. She would reclaim her marriage. She still believed that. She just had to ease into it.

That was three weeks ago. The magical reunion hadn't happened, and yet, she was pregnant. If the home pregnancy test could be trusted. As the panic bubbled up, she told herself that home pregnancy tests could be wrong. The thing was, she'd taken dozens of them over the years. And not once had one come up positive.

~

"I'm making dinner," she told Derrick over the phone. "Can you be home by six thirty?"

"What are you making?"

"It's a surprise. Be here."

"I will."

"I'll wear something special."

There was a beat of silence. "Amanda?"

She couldn't read anything in his tone, and she felt a pang of anxiety. What if he didn't want her to wear something special?

"Yes?"

"I've missed you."

She took a deep breath and pushed down the guilt. She didn't want to cry. "I've missed you too."

~

She made falafel, his favorite. She steered the conversation to the early days of their marriage, before they'd decided to have a child. She was unsettled, unsure how things would unfold. But the evening, their chemistry, felt right. She'd fallen in love with this man over three days in a cabin in the Blue Ridge Mountains. They'd been dating for eight months, and he'd taken her there to celebrate her birthday. As he'd maneuvered his little car out of the mountains, away from the cabin and the bliss of their weekend, she'd looked at him and known she wanted to marry him. That had been years ago, but neither of them was so different. They just needed to remember.

They made love that night, and she couldn't stop crying afterward. There had been nothing wrong with their lovemaking. Derrick wanted her, and even her tension was no match for his experience with her body. But she couldn't just pick up where they'd left off months ago. She couldn't pretend that she hadn't betrayed him, that she was carrying his child.

"Please," he said, rubbing her back, "talk to me."

They were both naked, Amanda lying on her stomach. She didn't want to talk to him. There was only one thing to say, and she didn't know how to say it.

"I love you," she said.

"I love you too. You know that."

"I'm afraid you won't."

"Amanda, you're scaring me. Tell me what's going on."

She hesitated, and then it came out in a rush. Ralph. She hadn't meant for it to happen. It wouldn't have happened, she told him, had they not been estranged for so long. It was an accident. She told him every cliché that came to mind.

"It was my fault?" Derrick asked icily. He was lying on his back now, still naked but no longer touching her.

"No, it was my fault. I'm just saying, it hadn't happened before."

"What was tonight about? Why did we do this before you told me that you fucked another man?"

She'd almost forgotten what tonight was about. She'd intended to pass Ralph's child off as Derrick's. A confession had not been part of the plan—until she imagined giving birth and raising the child with Derrick. The images came easily because she'd imagined it thousands of times before. With one difference. In every other imagining, the child had been Derrick's. Now she had to imagine the duplicity that would be required of her. She would have to lie to Derrick. She would have to lie to her child. She would never be free of the fear of being found out. She would fall asleep uneasily, terrified that she would talk in the night.

It was better to confess now. She told Derrick that she was pregnant. He didn't respond. He lay still and silent, and then he rose, dressed, and left the house. All she could do was cry.

~

She was waiting in the living room when he got home at 3:40 that morning. She smelled the alcohol before she heard the slur in his voice.

"Did you drive home?" she asked.

"Don't you dare question me," he said, oozing vitriol. "I didn't cheat on you." He took a few uneven steps toward her. "I never gave up on our marriage."

"I didn't give up on our marriage. I just . . ." What had she done? The idea of leaving Derrick for Ralph had never occurred to her. The affair had just happened.

"Does he still work at BPI?"

Amanda nodded, afraid that Derrick would ask who he was, demand a word with him.

"And you plan to go to work and see him tomorrow?"

"What do you want me to do?" she asked.

"I don't want you to go in tomorrow. I want you to quit." His tone left no room for discussion.

"Okay," she said without hesitation. As much as she loved working on Project Iustitia, she wanted her marriage more. She wanted to save it. "Will you stay so we can work things out?" This was the question she'd wanted to ask all night. If he said yes, she would be okay. It wouldn't be easy. But they needed a chance. She knew they could get through this if only they had a fighting chance.

"I don't know," he said. He turned and staggered up the stairs.

She slept on the couch, grateful for *I don't know* because it wasn't *No*.

CHAPTER 16

AMANDA

23 WEEKS PREGNANT

Baby drinks several ounces of amniotic fluid per day. Mommy's diet influences the taste of the fluid, shaping Baby's future food preferences.

—*Your Best Pregnancy*

December 13, 2017

"She's beautiful," Amanda said of the massive bust.

Patrick read the sign aloud: "Earth Goddess."

Amanda couldn't take her eyes off the flowing hair, the palm extended to fill the fountain. The rain shower had left their clothes damp and the air crisp. "I could stare at her all day." They sat on a bench facing her. "When I was failing to conceive, I wondered at the haphazard nature of fertility. I could have believed that this deity by her whim decided who got pregnant and who didn't. I would've felt comfortable talking to her, beseeching her." Amanda laughed self-consciously.

"I did so many little things to make myself pregnancy ready. They became habitual: healthy eating, exercise, decaf coffee, prenatal vitamins. And then I just stopped. When I realized I was pregnant, I was horrified that I hadn't had a folic acid supplement in six months. But it was easy to resume the routine. I'd done it for so long.

"Sometimes I could forget that the baby wasn't Derrick's. The day-dreams that once came so easily would creep in: Reading my favorite children's books with her, the three of us taking road trips to the beach, visiting the pumpkin patch in the fall. So many things. I don't think Derrick ever forgot," she mused. "Sorry, I'm talking a lot."

Patrick smiled. "Good thing you have a nice voice."

"We can go if you want. See the carnivorous plants." She stood. "Why do guys like carnivorous plants, anyway?"

"I didn't know it was a gender thing. Do women not admire insect-eating plants?"

"I won't speak for women everywhere, but I find the whole concept gross." She gave an exaggerated shudder. "I'm so coming back in the spring to see the Earth Goddess." According to the plaque, eighteen thousand live plants would cover the Earth Goddess in the spring. Her skin was silver now, her hair black. In the spring, her skin would be green, her hair red, purple, green, and yellow.

"It's a date," Patrick said, then smiled, embarrassed. "I mean, I'd like to see it too."

He worked so hard at propriety, and she found his discomfort amusing. She wanted to take his hand again, but she didn't. She'd done that at the river because she'd been so touched by his openness, the glimpse he'd offered into his wounded marriage. His despondency had brought her own feelings to the surface. There had been nothing roman-tic in it, just two troubled souls connecting. To do it now would be teasing him.

Besides, she would be happy to return in the spring with him. Most of her social life was composed of Derrick and his ever-growing network of friends. Derrick could make friends with a stranger over the course of a commuter flight. He enjoyed couples' dinners and business mixers, so Amanda had grown accustomed to the lightness of casual mingling, but it was something she could do without. She'd had four close friends at BPI, women who'd joined the firm the same year she had. Cecile and Sara were data scientists. Rani was a software engineer. And Jana was a project manager. She hadn't spoken to any of them since quitting. She felt bad about that. They'd all reached out to her, but what could she say? She'd been consumed with saving her marriage and then the miscarriage and now this. It was hard to imagine casual conversation.

Beverly was her oldest friend. She'd told Beverly everything until Ralph came along. Beverly's ex-husband cheated on her two years ago, and Amanda had been supportive of Beverly's righteous indignation, her decision to serve Cedric with divorce papers, do not pass go, do not collect $200. How could she talk to Beverly about Ralph? She found it difficult to talk to Beverly about anything these days. Last week, Amanda made the mistake of telling Beverly that she hadn't filled the prescription for antidepressants. Beverly had been so incensed that she'd threatened to tell Derrick. As if he were her father. Or worse, as if Amanda were no longer capable of making her own medical decisions.

What would Beverly think of Derrick's religious awakening, his dreamed-up faith pregnancy? She hadn't told Beverly about that, either, because somehow her affair seemed culpable. Derrick had been spending more time in his home office lately, wielding, by the sound of it, power tools. It was strange. Shortly after moving into their house, she'd come home to find one of their kitchen chairs sitting on the curb with the trash. *Loose leg,* he'd told her. She'd rescued the chair, purchased wood glue from the hardware store, and had the leg restored to new within twenty-four hours. He didn't fix things around the house. He called a guy. His use of power tools was as new as his fixation on religion. She'd knocked once, asked if she could look in on him, but he'd shooed her away, joking through the locked door that art couldn't be rushed. She'd just wanted to confirm that he wasn't at risk of maiming himself. She imagined him in there, an instructional video in one hand, a saw in the other.

"I've always wanted to garden," Patrick said, pulling her from her thoughts, "to shape nature into something beautiful. The closest I've gotten is mowing the lawn, and that was only after I quit my job."

Amanda could commiserate. Her thoughts of gardening had always been fleeting and unfruitful. Now, as they walked and she read the small plaques, she imagined growing plants for the beauty of their names as much as for their physical aesthetics: *Asarum splendens*, "Quicksilver"; *Musa velutina*, pink banana; *Hamamelis vernalis*, "Autumn Embers"; *Aucuba japonica*, spotted laurel; *Hydrangea quercifolia*, "Semmes Beauty."

She wanted to talk about beautiful things, but that wasn't the story she was telling. "I tried to fix things with Derrick," she continued. "I would have done almost anything for his forgiveness, to make things right. But he asked the one thing I couldn't give. He asked me to terminate the pregnancy. I was stunned. I mean, I couldn't blame him, but we tried for three years to have a child. Derrick wanted it as badly as I did. I was hoping . . . anyway, I did consider it, but I never got far. I played 'What if?' What if a screening found a congenital abnormality? A heart defect or spina bifida? Even then, unless it was life threatening, I didn't think I could terminate."

She fell silent and stopped walking. She leaned against a bench and covered her nose.

"What's wrong?" Patrick asked.

She pointed to a man ahead of them and whispered, "Too much cologne." She'd always been sensitive to perfumes, but now a strong whiff could spark a headache that lasted for hours.

"When people can smell your cologne outdoors," Patrick said, "it might be too much."

"Can you smell it? I thought it was my supersensitive nose."

"You don't need a sensitive nose to smell that guy." They waited until the man disappeared around the turn, then continued, more slowly than before.

"I asked Derrick to go to couples' counseling, but he couldn't. I'd humiliated him, and he couldn't bear to share that with a stranger. 'Just get an abortion,' he said. 'We deserve a fresh start.' But I couldn't. If I did that to save our marriage, I would've spent the rest of my life hating him for it. And there was something else, something I could never tell him: I wanted the baby more than I wanted him. As difficult as it was, I stopped trying to save our marriage. I gave him space to make a decision he could live with because I'd made the only decision I could live with. Maybe it was insensitive, but I wanted to be excited about the pregnancy. I understood his feelings, but sometimes I hated him for them. And I hated myself for that."

"Did he come around?" Patrick asked.

Amanda nodded. "He did. It took a while. I thought we were turning a corner."

"What happened?"

Amanda looked at the ground. "I miscarried."

CHAPTER 17

MARISSA

19 YEARS BEFORE THE ACCIDENT

When Marissa arrived at Princeton as a matriculating first-year student, John Wells was an associate professor in the mathematics department. They'd kept in touch over the years, and he'd provided a letter of reference for her application. She intended to double major in math and biology, but her first zoology course waylaid her plans. Biology was work, memorizing species and classes and phyla, information she wouldn't retain in five years. Math, on the other hand, was thought and logic.

She gravitated toward the mathematics community, her calendar booked with talks by famous professors. A long list of legends from Emmy Noether to Alan Turing to Kurt Gödel had spent time at Princeton. And then there was Albert Einstein. Mathematical energy was in the air, and Marissa had little patience for identifying obscure organs in a dissected frog.

"Everything is so different here," she told Jen over the phone. Most of her tuition was covered by scholarships, the rest by loans. She had a work-study job as a calculus tutor, and Jen sent her money each month. "Everything is math. It's all anyone talks about, and I want to be the best of them."

Jen laughed. "You will. I have no doubt about that."

~

Jen visited Princeton in February, during the second semester of Marissa's first year. Jen's twenty-third birthday would fall on a Saturday, and she wanted to spend it in New York with her sister. She arrived on Thursday afternoon, and Marissa gave her a tour of the campus before taking her to a talk on the Nielsen realization problem.

"I can explain it," Marissa told her as they walked out of Fine Hall, Jen having commented that she hadn't understood a thing.

"No, thank you," Jen said. "I think the bearded guy explained it enough."

Marissa was housed at Butler College in a single room. She shared a bathroom with a girl named Beth, a first-year student studying economics. Jen offered to sleep on the floor, but Marissa insisted they share the bed. "It hasn't been that long since we've shared a bed," Marissa said.

"You were seven," Jen told her. "And a wild sleeper, like you were doing acrobatics or wrestling a horse or something." Marissa had gone through a brief phase of not wanting to sleep alone. Over Jen's protests, their mother had given Marissa permission to sleep in Jen's bed. When they'd wake in the morning, the covers would be on the floor.

"Let's hope I've outgrown that," Marissa said.

They climbed into bed early but stayed up late talking. Jen told Marissa about a guy. They'd only had two dates, but she liked him. Marissa told Jen about a junior named Steven Shephard. He was a math major known for the unicycle he rode around campus.

"Why would he do that?" Jen asked.

Marissa shrugged. "To show that he can. Or maybe he likes it. I don't know. He's brilliant. And handsome," Marissa added shyly.

"Are you two involved?" Jen asked.

"I don't think he knows who I am."

~

A friend from Marissa's differential geometry course invited her out to dinner with a group that would include Steven Shephard.

"We can't say no to that," Jen said. They'd had plans to dine at an Indian restaurant near campus.

"I don't know him," Marissa warned, suddenly fidgety.

Jen grinned. "Your secret crush is safe with me."

~

The eight of them were seated at a large table at a Greek restaurant. Marissa and Jen ordered salads and an eggplant sandwich to split. The food was good, and mostly, Marissa and Jen listened to the others talk. Steven commanded the table. He'd lost $300 in a game of poker the night before, and he told the story with pride. Eventually he turned to them.

"You're Marissa, right?"

She blushed.

"I've heard you have a good grasp of number theory."

She shrugged. "I like it."

"She's good," Jen said.

Marissa glanced at her, annoyed. She doubted Jen knew what number theory was.

"Maybe I'll quiz you sometime," Steven said with a smile. "And you're Marissa's sister, but you don't go here?"

"That's right," Jen told him.

"Where do you go?" the boy sitting to Steven's right asked.

"I don't. I'm an assistant manager at a department store."

"Oh," the boy next to Steven said. "Where did you go?"

"I didn't," Jen said. She repeated her job title.

"What do your parents think of that?" Steven asked.

Jen hesitated, and Marissa said, "They're waiting for her to go back to school."

Jen stiffened. Marissa regretted her words, but she knew how some of her classmates could be. She wanted to head that off.

"Yes, our parents are very supportive," Jen said, her eyes on Marissa. "They were thrilled when Marissa was accepted to Princeton."

Marissa didn't know if their father was thrilled, but at least he knew where she was. She didn't know what their mother knew. Marissa wanted to take Jen's elbow and usher her to the restroom. She'd just been trying to move the conversation along. "Yes, they're very proud," she said warily.

Jen smiled and nodded. "Of course they are. Our parents are great. Wonderful people. I had breakfast with Mommy and Daddy yesterday morning. They drove me to the airport." She turned to Marissa. "Did you get the money they sent?"

Marissa nodded.

"What will you study when you go back to school?" Steven asked.

Jen glanced at Marissa, who was willing Jen not to answer. "Nuclear engineering," Jen said. "But first I'll have to get my GED."

No one said anything. Then Shelley, the girl who'd invited Marissa, said, "You didn't finish high school?"

Jen shook her head.

"Did you get pregnant?" Steven asked.

"Rude," a boy with red hair named Tom said. "It's none of your business if she got pregnant."

Marissa wanted to put this line of questioning to an end, but she didn't know how.

"I'm just making conversation," Steven said. "You can't get a real job with—"

"I have a real job," Jen snapped.

Steven shrugged.

Marissa looked down at her food.

"If you won't listen to me," Steven said, "you should listen to your parents."

"Yeah," Jen asked, "did yours tell you to get that stupid haircut?"

Tom laughed. He reached across the table and high-fived Jen.

"Testy," Steven replied with a smile. "I'm trying to compliment you. If you're Marissa's sister by blood, you must be smart enough to do something better than assist the manager of a department store."

Marissa felt Jen watching her, but she couldn't meet Jen's eye.

∽

They'd had plans to celebrate Jen's birthday in New York, but Steven invited Marissa to lunch at the house of Dr. Kazakov, a legendary number theorist who often hosted Saturday lunches for his brighter students.

"Go," Jen told her. "I'll be fine in the city by myself."

"Okay. Let's meet back here for dinner," Marissa said. "I still want to take you to the Indian restaurant."

∽

Marissa was at her desk studying when Jen returned. It was almost 9:00 p.m.

"Ready to eat?" Marissa asked. She hadn't eaten since lunch.

Jen held up one of the several bags she was carrying. "I brought you food. I found an Indian restaurant in New York."

"Oh," Marissa said. "What else did you get?"

"Just some birthday presents for me."

The bags were mostly from clothing stores. Marissa took her food to the microwave. While it heated, she retrieved a wrapped package from the closet. "Happy birthday," she said and handed it to Jen.

"Thank you." It was a mystery novel by an author Jen enjoyed. "I'll read it on the plane. Speaking of which, I switched my flight to tomorrow morning. I got a good deal."

Marissa stared at her, incredulous. "You got a good deal? What does that mean?"

"A deal," Jen repeated. "I save money if I go back early." She was supposed to fly out Monday morning.

"What time?" Marissa asked.

"Five."

Marissa looked at the clock. "Why, when you lie to me, do you tell me stupid lies?"

"Maybe the lies aren't stupid to me. Maybe they're just stupid to you because you're a Princeton student."

"That's not what I meant."

"Isn't it? Your friends barely stopped short of calling me stupid. I would never let my friends talk about you that way."

"They aren't my friends."

"I spent my birthday alone in New York. And you spent it with people who aren't your friends?"

"You said I should go."

"And you went. Just eat your food." The microwave had beeped moments before. "I'm going to bed because I have to get up at three."

"Don't," Marissa said. "Not like this. I thought we would have another day together."

Jen's expression didn't soften. "I would leave right now if I could."

Marissa ate the food Jen brought her. It was good. Very good. But Marissa couldn't enjoy it.

"I'm sorry," she told Jen before they went to bed.

"I am too."

~

Jen gave Marissa fifty dollars before she boarded the flight. It was 4:45 a.m. Jen hugged her. "Let me know if you need anything."

Marissa fought back tears. There was so much she wanted to tell Jen. She wanted to tell her that she regretted not standing up for her. She wanted to tell her why she hadn't. Jen was her big sister. She'd never had to stand up for Jen. She'd never known that she could. Jen did the standing up. Jen was the protector. She cried. Jen cried too.

"Listen to me, Marissa. If you need me, I'm here for you. I'll see you in a couple of months for spring break. Study hard."

Marissa nodded. "I'm sorry," she repeated.

"I know." Jen picked up her carry-on, presented her ticket to the gate agent, and boarded the plane.

CHAPTER 18

PATRICK

6 MONTHS AFTER THE ACCIDENT

December 19, 2017

"Something is different," Marissa said.

Patrick looked up. He was sitting at the dining room table, articles and notes spread haphazardly. Used for work more often than meals, the area was occasionally commandeered when he needed space. Marissa, when she wasn't using her home office, preferred the kitchen table. She coveted windows, and their dining room had none.

She took a seat in the chair across from him. "You're working?"

"In a sense. The woman I told you about with pseudocyesis—I'm trying to help her." He'd made handwritten notes based on his conversations with Amanda. He was reading everything he could find in the literature.

"How is that going?" Marissa asked.

Patrick could tell she was pleased. She'd never criticized him for quitting his job, but he knew her well enough to know that she didn't— couldn't—understand it.

"Amanda doesn't fit the profile," he told her.

Pseudocyesis was most common in developing countries, in cultures where women were valued primarily for fertility, in women who were uneducated and lacked social opportunities beyond maternity. None of that fit Amanda. Difficulty conceiving or carrying a pregnancy to term was a risk factor, but so was lack of prenatal care. Some women with pseudocyesis didn't seek medical care until they believed themselves to be in labor.

"She's very logical and rational. She's a data scientist."

"What does she make of the data," Marissa asked, "the medical test results?"

"She doesn't confront them directly. She lives in a gray area between the objective science and her intuition. I've been reading case studies. One woman believed that her jealous mother-in-law put a curse on the medical tests. Amanda seems incapable of constructing those types of defenses, and yet she has pseudocyesis."

"Do you have any ideas to help her?"

"Nothing satisfying. She wants to know why it's happening, how to make it stop. I want to know that too. Do you remember when you were starting out, learning the basics? There was a lot to know, but it was tidy, just waiting to be unwrapped." He met her eyes. "It's harder when you have to discover the unknown."

"Amen," Marissa said, a kindred spark in her eyes.

He looked down at the table and the dozens of pages of handwritten notes.

"False pregnancy seems to serve a psychological purpose for these women. They don't have Amanda's resources, so adoption or donor eggs aren't an option for them. But it follows that Amanda, too, needs this experience for some reason. I'm encouraging her to lean into it, to progress through her symptoms. To false labor."

"That sounds excruciating."

"All of these stories are."

He told her about an eighteen-year-old Haitian woman known as LK in the literature. Her mother was one of two wives in a polygamous household, and her father had died when she was young. Her mother had worked as a maid until a debilitating spinal disorder meant that she couldn't. LK worked at a food stall before she moved to Port-au-Prince for a factory job. It was a difficult life of long hours in harsh conditions, but things changed when she fell in love with a twenty-five-year-old bodyguard. In time, she moved in with him and stopped working at the textile factory. She planned to marry him. And then he met another woman.

Arguments began to plague the young couple. The boyfriend would sometimes leave her alone in the house with no money or food. He became violent and threatened to break up with her. And then she missed her period.

When she sought prenatal care, the physician doubted pregnancy. A follow-up appointment was made for an ultrasound, but LK did not show. She experienced morning sickness and slept excessively. Her appetite grew fickle. Her boyfriend was unmoved.

LK's brother tried to persuade LK to move back to their village, but she refused. Who would support her child? LK believed that the child would fix her relationship.

LK's boyfriend assaulted her shortly before the labor pains began. It had been eight months since her menstruation had ceased. She went to the hospital. An ultrasound revealed that there was no baby. LK was furious. She wept. The doctor prescribed her medication for anxiety.

"That's it?" Marissa asked. "What happened to LK?"

Patrick shrugged. "She discharged herself from the hospital."

"You're an awful storyteller."

Patrick laughed. "I'm just telling you what happened."

Marissa's smile made him both sad and hopeful at once. She hadn't teased him in a long time. "You didn't tell me what happened. But honestly, I don't think I want to know. If she was lucky, she got her job back at the factory. I doubt she could hope for better. So fundamentally, she's unlucky." Marissa shook her head. "This world."

"This world," Patrick agreed and admired his wife. The moment seemed so normal that he could almost imagine them stepping into their old life. He wondered, not for the first time, if he was selfish for wanting that. Marissa was sick. Of that he had no doubt. But if Frederick Peters could be believed, she was also accomplishing her life-long ambition. Who was he to take that from her?

He thought to ask her to lunch, but he hesitated. She stood to leave. Probably for the best. He had more reading to do.

CHAPTER 19

PATRICK

6 MONTHS AFTER THE ACCIDENT

December 24, 2017

"I have a houseful of guests coming, and I haven't bought a single Christmas present," Amanda told Patrick. He was sitting at the kitchen table talking to her on the phone. "Do you know what that means?"

"You're screwed?" It was a few minutes after 10:00 a.m.

"Well, yeah, but there's still hope. The mall."

"The mall? Perhaps you can make gifts this year."

"Make gifts out of what? No, I'm going to the mall. And at the moment, you're my only friend, so you're coming with me."

"Say what?"

"It's in the friendship handbook. Meet me in an hour."

"What about Beverly? This is a great opportunity for reconciliation."

"My in-laws, my mother, my sister, and her fiancé are all on their way here. My mother usually has Christmas at her house, but not this year because I'm pregnant. This is not a good day for reconciliation. Anyway, if you don't come shopping with me, what are you going to do today?"

"That's cold, Amanda. See you in an hour."

~

"Clearly," Patrick said, "I'm out of touch." The mall was crowded but not overflowing. They met on the upper level. "I expected stampedes and brawls over iPhones."

"That's Black Friday."

"When I was a kid, people would've been walking on top of each other."

"The internet snuck up on you. Remember before the dot-com crash, when people were saying that grocery stores and malls would disappear?"

Patrick nodded.

"They weren't right, but we'll have to wait to see if they were wrong. Food court and then shopping. Does that work?"

Patrick agreed, and they headed to the escalator. They'd met for lunch three times since their visit to the botanical gardens. She'd introduced him to two new restaurants.

"There was a movie theater here," Amanda said as they descended. "In the days when movie theaters were small. My grandmother used to bring me."

Finding a table was a challenge, but luck awaited in a secluded corner where a couple was packing up. They settled with their food, Chinese for him, Tex-Mex for her.

Amanda coughed softly, a tell that preceded the sharing of personal information. Patrick wasn't sure when he'd first picked up on it. "You asked me the other day why I was so hurt by the argument Derrick and I had over quitting IVF."

Patrick nodded.

Amanda was thoughtful. "His focus on the money, those damn prepaid treatments, made it all feel so transactional and like my body was part of the transaction. We paid for a child, and my body needed to deliver."

"Do you think he felt that way?"

"No. But maybe I did. I felt like I'd failed."

"Even though it takes both of you to get pregnant?"

"It didn't feel that way. We were charting my cycles and taking my temperature and pumping me full of drugs, and I think my grand-mother screwed me up."

"Your grandmother?"

"She was like a mother to me. I was thirteen when my father died. Meredith was an infant. My mom was suddenly a single mother, and my grandmother filled the void. I was in graduate school when she was diagnosed with lung cancer. She was proud of me, but she worried that I was too focused on my career, that I wasn't leaving room for a family. The last time I spoke to her—I knew it would be the last—I told her I was going to have it all. I would be a computer scientist and a mother, and I would raise my children on stories of her. She couldn't speak, but she squeezed my hand." Amanda paused as if lost in the pain of that memory. "When I gave up on IVF, I felt inadequate as a human being and as a woman, and he was upset about the money. I don't think I'll ever forgive him for that."

Patrick reached across the table and took her hand. "Look at me." She met his eyes. "I've known inadequate human beings, and you are not one of them. I'm lucky to know you."

She smiled. He released her hand and they finished eating. He could still feel the warmth of her touch.

She was the first to break the silence. "What did you get Marissa for Christmas?"

Patrick hesitated. "A locket." He didn't know how to explain the significance. He didn't know if Marissa was ready. "For pictures," he added.

Amanda nodded. "Sounds nice."

~

"Backup plan for everyone," Amanda said as they passed a shop that sold handmade cosmetics.

"And the men in your life?"

"Handmade bar soap. Men bathe too. I was tempted to tell Derrick to pick out his parents' gifts. I've been doing it since we married, but I'm not feeling it this year."

"Do you get along with them?"

"I get along with his dad. Probably because he doesn't say much. But Derrick's mother more than makes up for that. My relationship with her is odd. Derrick insists she likes me, but every time I see her, she makes a remark about how dangerous artificial intelligence is. You would think I work on Skynet."

"Skynet?"

"*The Terminator*. Extremely violent, and yet a deeply philosophical film."

"Right, the computer that tries to destroy humanity."

"It isn't just a movie to Derrick's mother. She's waiting. The last time she was in town, she loaned me a book about AI and human extinction. It wasn't even written by a computer scientist. When I see her today, she's going to ask if I've read it."

"I assume you haven't."

"No. She wasn't even interested in artificial intelligence before she met me. She's barely interested in computers. Derrick says she feels threatened by my career. His mother is a homemaker. Henry is an investment banker."

"What are you getting them?"

Amanda smirked. "I'll get her *Ex Machina* if I can find it on DVD. Just to mess with her."

"Otherwise, soap," Patrick said.

"You're paying attention. His father loves chocolate, so we can stop by the candy store."

As they walked, Patrick noticed that some stores were throngs of activity, while in others, bored employees busied themselves arranging shelves. "It's like academic funding," he told her. "What other gifts do you have? Your sister and mother?"

"Meredith is easy. I was thinking a digital picture frame for her and the fiancé to commemorate their Peru trip. Do you think it's okay to buy them a joint gift?"

"I think that's a nice way to welcome him to the family."

"Yes," Amanda agreed. "Even though they barely know each other. Sorry. I have to get this stuff out of my system before they come."

Patrick laughed. "Anything you need to say about your mother?"

"We'd be here all day, and I'd never finish shopping. I could spend years in therapy talking about my mother. Not that I would."

"What are you getting her?"

"That's a good question."

"What does she like to do?"

"She likes to criticize me. And make me feel guilty for not calling and visiting more. I don't think she's ever forgiven me for my closeness with her mother. The two of them never got along. There are so many things I've never forgiven her for. I'll buy her a coffee maker, and I'll suppress my resentment, and we can continue as we have. That's what family does, right?"

"We don't talk about our feelings in my family," Patrick said, "but we communicate effectively through sarcasm and cruel humor. By the time my brother was a senior in high school, he'd been trying to get our mother to leave our dad for a few years. For Halloween he wrapped his head in a bloody bandage, painted on a black eye, and wore a sling on his arm. My mother thought it was great. She asked him who he was, and he said, 'Todd Davis's son.'"

Amanda lifted an eyebrow.

"Todd was my father."

"I got that."

"That's my family. We don't talk openly, but we know what the other is thinking."

"Is your brother anything like your father? Is he—"

"Violent?" Patrick finished. Amanda hadn't known that boys raised by violent men could grow up to be nurturing. She'd found it hard to believe when he'd first told her about his father. Patrick shook his head. "Rob has a temper, but he isn't violent. Neither of us came out unscathed. But we don't hit our wives."

Amanda led him to a candy store. She purchased fancy chocolates for her father-in-law and peanut brittle to share with Patrick. "It's the pregnancy," she said.

"What's my excuse?" He bit into the hard candy.

Amanda shrugged. "I should get Derrick a nice Bible. That's what a supportive wife would do. The thing is, his religious beliefs piss me off. He didn't want me to have the baby. And then when I miscarried, he couldn't handle it. He invented a faith pregnancy. To be fair, his faith pregnancy is no more outlandish than my false pregnancy. But I'm supposed to be the sick one. It's almost as if he's competing with me. Anyway, he's been talking about taking up golf for years. I'll buy him some golf balls and a golf outfit. A nudge. Because even though he goes to church three times a week, I want him out of the house more. I want him out of the house as much as possible."

As she shopped, Patrick carried the bags, citing her condition. He willfully did not look at the kids lined up to see Santa, just as one level above, he'd averted his eyes from the children waiting to ride Macy's Pink Pig.

"I'm sorry, Patrick. I'm trying to get into the Christmas spirit." She huffed. "I'm just angry. I've been listening to myself talk, and I only have one question: Why am I spending Christmas with these people?"

"They're coming to your house," he answered. "You have nowhere to hide."

CHAPTER 20

MARISSA

17 YEARS BEFORE THE ACCIDENT

Marissa dreaded telling Jen that she was staying at Princeton for the summer. Jen had moved to Atlanta the month before, and every time they spoke, she told Marissa about a new place she wanted to show her. Hiking at Kennesaw Mountain. Shopping at Lenox Square. The parent company of Jen's employer in Detroit was opening a new line of stores that specialized in women's fitness apparel. Jen was managing the flagship location. Marissa wanted to travel south to see Jen's new life, but John Wells had offered Marissa the opportunity to do research over the summer. She couldn't pass that up.

"You're kidding," Jen said when Marissa told her. "You don't work hard enough during the school year?"

"I do, but I have to establish my reputation."

Marissa was nineteen years old, a rising junior entering her prime as a mathematician. John Nash had completed much of his Nobel Prize–winning work by the time he was twenty-two. Claude Shannon had established his genius with his master's thesis. And Maryam Mirzakhani's doctoral work was amazing. There would be time, once she'd made her mark, to hang out with Jen. She would have the rest of their lives. For now, she needed to focus.

And she did. She didn't party. She didn't date. She read, she contemplated math, she worked on proofs, and she attended talks. She enjoyed the singularity of her efforts. She was exploring uncharted regions, ocean depths untouched by sunlight. She was hunting for something staggering, and she would come up for air only after she'd found it.

She spent Christmas and New Year's in Atlanta but stayed at Princeton again the following summer. She was asleep in her dorm room when the phone rang at 11:30 a.m. Until four that morning, she'd been working. Most of her friends kept a similar schedule.

"What in the hell is going on with Jen?" It was her father.

"Jen?" she asked, her mind still cloudy with dreams.

"She was arrested this morning. She and some man, Melvin something, were caught burgling a house."

"What?" Marissa was awake now. Melvin Young was Jen's boyfriend. Marissa hadn't met him, but she'd heard plenty from Jen. He was a bartender, and they'd met on I-285 when he'd stopped to help Jen change a flat tire.

"Is this a complete surprise to you?" her father asked, accusation heavy in his tone.

"There must be a misunderstanding. Jen wouldn't burgle someone's house."

But she had. They'd broken into Melvin's boss's house shortly after midnight. Jen had been holding a jewelry box when its owner had woken up and pulled a firearm from beneath the bed. Melvin's boss had held them at gunpoint until the police arrived.

Their father arranged for bail, and Marissa flew to Atlanta. Jen didn't have anything to say about it. Melvin lived with her and no longer had a job, so Marissa had to get Jen out of the apartment to talk in private.

"Did his boss fire him before or after the police cuffed him?" Marissa asked. They were in a sandwich shop, two subs on the table between them. Jen didn't smile. "You need to talk to me. What's happened to you?"

"What's happened to you?" Jen shot back.

"I wasn't arrested for breaking and entering," Marissa said through clenched teeth.

"Of course you weren't. You have scholarships. And when you need money, you come to me. You've never had any responsibility."

"Is breaking into houses responsible? Just tell me why you did it."

"Melvin needed money."

"For what?"

Jen didn't answer.

"How is he doing for money now?"

"Ha. Funny."

"Melvin isn't good for you."

"Really? You know what's good for me? What else do they teach you at Princeton?"

∼

Marissa didn't like Melvin. He rarely spoke, which she appreciated, and he monopolized the television, which she didn't care to watch anyway. He watched court shows in the afternoon and sitcoms in the evening. He was watching *The Jerry Springer Show* when Marissa made her first and last overture. "What do you like to do when you aren't watching television?" she asked him.

"I like to have sex."

She left Jen's apartment. She took MARTA downtown and walked to Centennial Park. She was afraid to be alone with him.

∼

"Dump him," she told Jen. They were sitting in the lobby of Jen's apartment building because Melvin was stretched out on the couch watching a washed-up rock star have dinner with his family.

"What?" Jen asked.

"You're obviously committed to this. You've been to jail for him, but you need to get out now. This guy has nothing to offer you."

"What do you know about him or me? I've been living in Atlanta for a year, and this is the second time you've visited. I didn't even invite you."

"I'm here because you got arrested. And I won't be back if you don't get rid of this guy."

Jen laughed. "Oh, really? You won't be back? My life will be so different without you. I think you should go back to Princeton."

~

Marissa applied to graduate programs in the fall: Princeton, MIT, Harvard, and UC Berkeley. Dr. Kazakov told her not to bother with a safe school. Her first acceptance letter arrived in mid-March, from MIT. Three days later, she received a middle-of-the-night phone call. Jen was in the hospital with three broken ribs, a dislocated shoulder, a fractured eye socket, and a probable concussion.

CHAPTER 21

AMANDA

24 WEEKS PREGNANT

Mommy may be feeling a little off balance these days, but Baby's inner ear is functional, letting him know when he's upside down.

—Your Best Pregnancy

December 24, 2017

It had been a mistake, Amanda realized, to buy such a large home. They could comfortably accommodate Derrick's parents, her mother, her sister, and her soon-to-be brother-in-law—and here they all were, sitting in her living room.

She and Derrick had planned on having two, maybe three, kids, so a four-bedroom home had felt right. This holiday, it wasn't working out so well. Derrick's parents had arrived first, and he'd shown them to one of the unfurnished bedrooms. They had two spare rooms, as bare as the day they'd moved in, because they were meant for babies and furnishing either with anything besides a crib would have felt like giving up. Derrick had bought a couple of air mattresses in anticipation of their guests.

Amanda had been surprised when her mother insisted that Meredith and Brian, not yet married, take the other spare room. That left her mother with the sofa bed in the living room—where Derrick had been sleeping. They hadn't discussed it, but clearly Derrick would return to their bed while they hosted guests. She still hadn't seen his home office, but she'd smelled paint in the hall the other night and assumed it wasn't habitable.

"My church is having a Christmas Eve service," Derrick said during a lull in chatter. "You're all invited."

Amanda was clearing her throat to decline when her mother said, "What a wonderful idea."

Brian, Meredith's fiancé, nodded enthusiastically. And of course, Derrick's parents were all nods and smiles. The decision was made, and Amanda hadn't uttered a word.

~

Amanda had not been to church in over a decade. That was for a wedding. She wasn't opposed to attending church in theory, but this particular hallowed institution had inspired the faith pregnancy. As she looked through the maternity dresses in her closet, she decided to give herself an early Christmas present.

She found Derrick in the bathroom brushing his teeth.

"I don't feel well," she said. Her back did hurt, but she invented a headache for good measure. "It feels almost like a migraine."

"Did you take anything?" Derrick asked, concerned.

"Thirty minutes ago. It doesn't seem to be helping."

"You should lie down. I'll stay with you."

"No," she said, a bit too quickly, in fear of losing her alone time. "Everyone is excited about church. You go. I just need some sleep."

She changed into her nightgown, anticipating the peace of an empty house. She didn't realize how tired she was until she laid her head on the pillow.

~

When she awoke to the sound of voices downstairs, she thought, *Finally, they're leaving.* And then the passage of time caught up with her. She checked her phone: 9:30 p.m. She'd slept for three hours. She changed into a T-shirt and yoga pants and joined her family downstairs.

"How are you feeling?" Meredith asked.

"Better. How was church?"

"Loud," Derrick's father said. "A lot of electric guitar."

But they hadn't had enough music, apparently, because Amanda's mother suggested they sing Christmas carols. Derrick fetched a bottle of rum for the eggnog while Brian loaded online Christmas karaoke. Derrick enlisted Meredith's help in passing out drinks, and when Amanda sipped hers, she was both relieved and annoyed not to taste alcohol. If asked, she would have told Derrick to make it virgin, but he hadn't asked. He was acting unilaterally to protect their faith fetus.

Brian cued up "Hark! The Herald Angels Sing," and as they harmonized, Amanda thought she might cry. Had the song been this sad last year? "The Twelve Days of Christmas" provided an emotional respite, but she knew she was in trouble when her mother said that "Give Love on Christmas Day" was her favorite. Following a brief debate on the merits of the Jackson 5 versus the Johnny Gill rendition, Brian played the karaoke instrumental. Meredith bowed out to use the bathroom. Amanda slipped away before the song was finished. She pulled on a coat and stepped into the chilled night. She just needed a moment.

She and Derrick had moved to the suburbs in anticipation of children that had never come. She missed a lot about the city, particularly the proximity of everything, but she didn't miss the ceaseless light. The condo she'd shared with Derrick had never gotten dark. She'd meant to buy blackout curtains, but then they'd moved, and she no longer needed them. In the suburbs, she could see stars.

She glanced back at the house. It was warm inside, filled with music and light, but not inviting. She didn't like who she was out here—hiding, moping—but she preferred it to the person she had to be in there.

She wandered before halting suddenly. "You scared me." She could just make out Meredith's silhouette, sitting in a chair beside Derrick's toolshed. "I thought you were in the bathroom."

Meredith shrugged and lifted the joint, its tip glowing, to her lips.

"I thought I smelled something. Give me a hit of that." She reached for the joint.

"Fuck you." Meredith pulled her hand away. "You're pregnant. Have you even smoked before?"

Amanda ignored the question, opting not to cement her position as the uncool older sister. She sat in the empty chair next to Meredith.

"I've heard it's good for morning sickness," Meredith said. "But I also heard it isn't safe." She put out the joint.

"I didn't have morning sickness. Lucky, I guess." Amanda hesitated. She was just so sick of pretending. "Can I tell you something?" If she didn't tell Meredith now, she feared she would have a breakdown and tell everyone later.

"If you must," Meredith said, and Amanda knew she was expecting a lecture. In better times, Amanda would have given her one. Marijuana wasn't legal in Georgia without a prescription. And presumably, Meredith had carried it across two state lines. Amanda didn't like to think of her mother and sister, two Black women, incarcerated in some small-town jail.

"You have to promise not to tell anyone. Especially Mom."

Meredith leaned forward with interest. "Sure."

"I'm not pregnant."

Meredith glanced at her belly, as if she could see in the dark. "You're in denial. If I remember one thing from sex ed, and I only remember one, it's that you can't be a little bit pregnant."

"I'm not saying I'm a little bit pregnant. I'm telling you I'm not pregnant."

Meredith was the last person Amanda could imagine sharing this with. She had no idea why she'd chosen Meredith, but since she'd taken the plunge, she went for the deep dive. She told Meredith everything. The fights with Derrick over quitting IVF. Ralph. The positive pregnancy test. The miscarriage. Feeling the baby move. Derrick's faith pregnancy pronouncement. Meredith listened without interrupting. "I don't even think I'd heard of this until it happened to me," Amanda finished.

Meredith surprised Amanda by not speaking. She stood, took Amanda's hand, and pulled her to her feet. Meredith hugged her.

CHAPTER 22

MARISSA

16 YEARS BEFORE THE ACCIDENT

John Wells took Marissa to lunch, an Italian restaurant near campus. She wondered what she would be doing right now if she hadn't met John at her neighbor's cookout ten years ago, if he hadn't introduced her to Fermat's last theorem. She found it unsettling, the role chance encounters played in one's life. A career in mathematics felt inevitable to her now. But if she thought back to the time before she'd met John, it didn't seem certain at all.

Marissa was tired. She'd only been back in Princeton for three days. Acceptance letters from UC Berkeley and Princeton had been waiting in her mailbox. Harvard alone had yet to respond.

"Congratulations are in order," John said. He was in his late thirties now, and the black beard he'd worn when she'd first met him was speckled with white.

Marissa forced a smile. "I wish I felt more celebratory. I don't know what to do."

Over pasta, oil-dipped bread, and a single glass of wine, Marissa told him about her trip to Atlanta. It had been one of the scariest experiences of her life. The woman who'd called from the hospital had been circumspect. Three times Marissa asked if there was a chance Jen would die. "That's unlikely," the woman finally said, "but a family member should be here." She said it as if Marissa were trying to get out of coming. She was on a flight that afternoon. Jen confirmed that she'd had an argument with Melvin. It had turned violent, and Jen didn't remember the details. What shocked Marissa—and she was still trying to make sense of it—was that Jen was being treated, along with her injuries, for heroin withdrawal. She wondered, as she confided all of this to John, where her sister would be if Marissa had never met him. Would Marissa have left home if she hadn't heard of Fermat's last theorem? Unlikely. Would Jen be involved with Melvin if she hadn't been lonely? Doubtful. Would Jen be a heroin addict if Marissa had been there with her? Absolutely not.

"I'm sorry," John said. "This should be one of the happiest times of your life. Can your parents help with Jen?"

"I wouldn't ask. Even if they could, she's my responsibility. She's been taking care of me for a long time. I need to take care of her."

"Maybe you can take her with you, wherever you decide to go," he suggested.

"I don't think so. Her caseworker got her into a state-funded drug treatment program. And apparently, she'll still have her job if she completes treatment."

John nodded.

"Halford University is there," she said. "It's not Princeton. What should I do?"

"I can't tell you what to do," John told her. "I can tell you something I wish someone had told me when I was your age. To a young mathematician, nothing is as important as math. But when you get older, you begin to see other things. You learn how important your health is. You learn that your health is less important than the health of your loved ones. What I'm saying in my roundabout way is that you learn that people are more important than math."

She couldn't imagine not going to Princeton or MIT or Harvard or UC Berkeley. For years, she'd been singularly focused on gaining access to the world's greatest mathematicians. She wanted to be one of them. That was all she'd ever wanted. "Do you think I can learn as much at Halford?"

"You can learn math anywhere. Look at Ramanujan. Every person in every one of your classes has more formal mathematical training than he did when he began his important work."

Marissa nodded. The brilliance of Ramanujan's contributions was indisputable. "If I get a degree from Halford, do you think I could get a tenure-track position at Princeton?"

John smiled. "Honestly, it would be difficult." He wasn't telling Marissa anything she didn't know. "You would have to publish something groundbreaking, and more importantly, your contribution would need to be recognized." Marissa knew this too. It wasn't enough to do great work. You had to convince others that you'd done great work. Ramanujan, after all, hadn't been taken seriously by British mathematicians until he'd connected with G. H. Hardy. And when you were a tier-one mathematical institution like Princeton, nothing existed outside your tier. "If you do choose to study at Halford, I want you to show all of us. Show us that your work can't be ignored."

"Because I won't be one of you," she said.

"You'll always be one of us."

But she knew that wasn't true. She knew her classmates.

～

Marissa had missed Halford's application deadline by three months. John Wells made a phone call on her behalf, and she was provided instructions for submitting a late application. Her friends had long since committed to schools when Marissa's acceptance from Halford arrived. She was five for five. She'd been accepted everywhere she'd applied. And she accepted the one offer she didn't want. It felt unreal, as if she'd been overtaken by a catastrophic act of nature. She'd been on a well-lit road, speeding enthusiastically toward her destination. Now, she was adrift on a life raft, wondering where all the water had come from.

~

Marissa was in court for Melvin's sentencing. He'd pleaded guilty, and the prosecution recommended time served, probation, and court-ordered drug treatment. The judge accepted the recommendation as Marissa fumed. She didn't blame Jen for not showing. Jen was doing better, though not quite pain-free. Jen hadn't spoken to Melvin since the fight, and Marissa intended to keep it that way. Marissa left the courtroom, furious that Melvin would be going home. But it wasn't over. Three months in county lockup was not enough punishment for what he'd done to her sister. Now, he would have to deal with Marissa.

CHAPTER 23

PATRICK

6 MONTHS AFTER THE ACCIDENT

December 24, 2017

"I'm in the bathroom," Amanda said.

"Is everything okay? Why are you whispering?" Patrick was in his living room watching television.

"No." Amanda sighed. "Nothing is okay. But I'm glad you answered. I just wanted to talk for a few minutes."

"Okay." He muted the television to give her his undivided attention.

"When I was a kid, Christmas Eve was magical. I imagined this man in the North Pole packing up toys. My mother told me he was Black. All of the White Santas were his helpers."

Patrick laughed. "I learned that Santa was White."

"Of course you did. Do you remember the Santa Tracker on the evening news? I was glued to that. When my mother wanted me to go to bed, she would say, 'Oh my, I think I hear reindeer bells.' I would run up the stairs, and it was so hard to sleep. But somehow, I did. And those moments between waking up and getting downstairs to my toys . . ." She sounded wistful. "Was Christmas Eve like that for you?"

He nodded and then realized she couldn't see him. "I have good memories of Christmas."

"I thought that Christmas Eve would always be magical. How has your evening been?"

"Quiet. Marissa is working. I'm watching movies."

"I wish I were there," she said. "I'd better go. Being pregnant buys me extra time, but there are limits. It also brings more scrutiny."

He didn't get to tell her that he, too, wished she were here.

~

Patrick awoke with anxiety, the vague sense that he faced something frightening, a monster to slay. Then he remembered what day it was. Marissa was in bed beside him, a rarity. He enjoyed her presence as he scrolled through news articles on his phone.

"Merry Christmas," he said when she stirred.

She turned to him, groggy. "Are you serious?"

"It's December twenty-fifth."

"Oh no." She covered her eyes with her arm. "I didn't get you anything. No one told me it was Christmas."

"Have you spoken to anyone lately?"

"You."

Patrick laughed. "I assumed you knew."

"We don't have a tree."

"I couldn't do a tree this year." He didn't want reminders of last year.

"I didn't even get you a card."

He rolled over and pulled her close. "Waking up next to you is gift enough."

She groaned. "You're making me feel worse."

And with that, the lightness of the morning was gone. Flirting with her, even today, felt impossible.

~

"Smells good," Marissa said when she joined him in the kitchen.

"Waffles," he told her. "And then gifts."

"But I didn't get you anything."

"Give me the joy of watching you open your present. Now sit down and savor Christmas breakfast." He placed a bowl of cut fruit on the table.

"I'm broken, Patrick."

He hesitated before retrieving maple syrup from the pantry and sitting down at the table across from her.

"I'm broken too," he said. He searched her face for something. What, he didn't know. He put a waffle on her plate and then fixed his own.

"I haven't been much of a wife since . . ."

He waited, braced himself. But she couldn't say it. "We have the rest of our lives," he told her.

She drizzled syrup over her waffle and then took a bite. They ate in silence. But they were together. They could take a walk later, maybe watch Christmas movies in the afternoon.

He was finishing his orange juice when she pushed away from the table. "I have work."

"It's Christmas."

She looked at him imploringly. He understood. Mathematics was her solace. She was asking him to let her go without complaint, without guilt. And he would because she would go regardless. "Okay, but first, open your gift." He rose to get it.

"I'm distracted," she said. "Let me make some progress. When I reach a stopping point, I'll open it."

~

He walked in Piedmont Park that morning, thoughts of Amanda creeping in as he passed the Active Oval. He thought about her often, but not as a curiosity anymore. He missed her when she wasn't with him, and again, he regretted not taking the opportunity to tell her that last night. He took out his cell phone to make the obligatory Christmas calls and then decided to send text messages. He wasn't up for cheery conversation.

~

Marissa was in her office writing in a notebook when he got home.

"How is it coming?" he asked.

She looked up and smiled. "It's been a good day."

"I'll be downstairs when you're ready to open your gift."

"Okay. I'll be down soon."

A Christmas Story was ten minutes in when he settled on the couch. He needed to laugh. Marissa's words replayed in his mind: *It's been a good day.*

Fuck you, he wanted to tell her. But wasn't this what he'd signed up for? Marissa had always been . . . Marissa. Now, she was more so.

They'd been seeing each other for two years when they'd taken a weekend trip to Savannah. They got on the road by 4:00 a.m. and arrived in time for a leisurely breakfast before heading to the beach. They swam in the ocean and took a long walk along the shoreline. They rented an umbrella and chairs and talked as they lounged. When they checked into their bed-and-breakfast, Marissa joked, "Who knew vacation could be so tiring?" They took a shower, made love, and napped.

When Marissa leaped out of bed with an exclamation, Patrick thought something was wrong.

"What is it?" he asked, dazed.

"I see it now." She pulled out one of the notebooks she carried everywhere and sat with it at the antique desk.

"Glad you see it," Patrick teased. He just wished she could see it after their trip.

She didn't respond.

She sat for hours, filling pages with mathematical scrawl, punctuated by fits of pacing and infrequent trips to the bathroom. He went out to get them lunch, and she wouldn't stop working even to eat, nibbling at the food as she scribbled in her notebook.

"Should I cancel our dinner reservation?" he asked.

She offered an obligatory apology, and he walked across the street for sandwiches. Instead of fuming over the stealth intruder, the third vertex in their love triangle, he focused on the morning and early afternoon they'd shared. She got a publication out of the work.

CHAPTER 24

PATRICK

12 YEARS BEFORE THE ACCIDENT

It was a game, finding new places to work on his dissertation. Patrick didn't particularly enjoy writing. Discovery excited him, and writing felt like treading over trails he'd already walked. He preferred to read and could do that anywhere. Writing required novel surroundings and a flow of strangers. He was a people watcher. He would write a few paragraphs, reread them for clarity, and then survey his surroundings. He never spoke to anyone or flirted with a stranger—he hadn't mastered that social grace. He preferred admiration from afar. He was good at it, at quick, oblique glances, careful not to make eye contact. That was enough for him. Until it wasn't. And when that happened, he had no idea what to say.

"Excuse me." He was in a bistro on North Decatur Road when he found himself interrupting a woman one table over. She looked up from a notebook, the tip of her pencil at rest on the page. This was as far as he'd planned. He'd only wanted to speak before he lost his nerve. And he'd succeeded.

"Did you say something?" the woman asked.

She'd seemed more approachable when she'd been scribbling in the notebook, her eyes not on him.

"Me? No."

She frowned before turning away. He didn't know why he'd bothered. Sure, she was pretty, beautiful, actually, but he saw beautiful women all the time. Why had he felt compelled to speak to her? And why the nagging sense that an opportunity was slipping away?

"But since you mentioned it, I was wondering. How is that?" He motioned to the portobello mushroom wrap on her plate. "I was torn between that and the eggplant."

She shrugged. "It's fine."

He smiled. "Not great? So I made the right choice?"

"I don't know what you like."

I'd like to be the chair you sit upon. Fortunately, he didn't blurt the first words that came to mind. Unfortunately, it was his turn to say something. It wasn't that he was inept with women. He'd been involved in the past. He just wasn't good at small talk. He needed a shared interest beyond sandwiches.

"Fair enough. Would you like to get coffee sometime?" He cringed inwardly. Had he jumped the gun? Was more small talk called for?

"No, thank you." She said this as if he'd offered her a flyer for a discount car wash. She resumed writing in her notebook.

He returned his attention to his laptop screen. *The right limbic and temporal regions are implicated . . .*

Implicated in what? He couldn't remember. And now, with the burn of embarrassment in his gut, there was no hope of regaining concentration. That was why he didn't talk to strange women in public. He looked furtively in her direction. She was in her twenties, dressed in faded jeans and a white blouse. Occasionally, she used her left hand to brush dark hair out of her face. Otherwise, she focused on her notebook, seemingly oblivious to his existence. Again, why was he fixating on her? Did she remind him of someone from his past, some boyhood crush on an older woman? She looked at her watch and then hurriedly gathered her notebook and papers. She left half of her sandwich and a pickle behind.

He was relieved. If she had lingered much longer, he would have had to leave. And how would that look? Like he was fleeing the scene of his humiliation. No chance of a graceful exit. Now, perhaps, he could get some writing done.

He stared at the food she'd left behind. He was still hungry, and she hadn't touched half of her sandwich. He glanced around, satisfied himself that no one was watching, and, as if it were the most natural thing in the world, leaned over and grabbed her sandwich.

No, he had not made the right decision. The eggplant was good; the portobello was delicious. The next time he was here, he would . . .

He felt eyes on him. He looked up. The woman was standing there. "Are you eating my sandwich?"

"Um." He wiped his mouth and put the sandwich down. "No."

She looked back at the table she'd vacated, a pickle sitting on an otherwise-empty plate.

"Okay, yes. The way you described the sandwich, I couldn't resist—"

"I said it was fine." The corners of her lips were subtly turned, hinting at amusement.

"It's the way you said it. Listen, I know I bothered you earlier. The truth is I'm not good at this. I don't even know why I bothered you. You're pretty, yes, but if that's all it was . . . I'm a neuroscientist, and I don't believe anything random happens in the mind, so when I have an impulse . . ." Where was he going with this? "Never mind. Clearly"—he motioned to the half-eaten half of a sandwich—"I owe you a meal. We can meet here. I can buy you lunch."

She regarded him curiously, and he felt hope. He wanted to say more, but he had nothing. She turned to her table and picked up her pencil. "I love these," she said and showed it to him. It looked like a mechanical pencil. "I came back to get it."

"What's your name?"

"Marissa."

"I'm Patrick." He extended his hand, and she shook it.

"You're a neuroscientist?"

"I'm a graduate student."

She smiled. "You know how when you're trying to solve a problem, you can mull over it for days with no progress, and then suddenly, even though you haven't learned anything new, the answer comes to you?"

He nodded. "Insight."

"Exactly. Insight. How does the brain do that?"

He stared at her for a long while. She stared back, as if they were both waiting for insight to find him.

"I have no idea," he said finally, feeling like a failure.

"I'll be here at two next Wednesday," she said. "I have a meeting with my adviser. Bye."

And then she was gone. Two o'clock next Wednesday. One week away.

~

He barely worked on his dissertation. He spent the week researching insight. He practically prepared a lecture on the topic. He paced his bedroom as he practiced the words he would use.

"According to the associative network model, related memories are stored proximately and can activate each other. If I say waffles, breakfast may be activated in your mind because the concept of breakfast is stored near the concept of waffles. In the brain's left hemisphere, fine semantic coding is used, meaning that a memory only activates nearby memories. The right hemisphere uses coarse semantic coding, meaning that a memory weakly activates more distant memories. If I say waffles, your right hemisphere might activate covered wagons because you once watched an episode of *Little House on the Prairie* while you were eating breakfast. Interrupt me when you see what this has to do with insight.

"You specifically mentioned failing to solve a problem. You think about it, but the correct solution doesn't come. And then suddenly, without receiving any new information, you have the answer. This implies that the answer was somewhere in your mind all along. You're probably familiar with the concept of the subconscious mind. Take the visual system. Your eyes pass information to your brain, and your subconscious processes lines and colors and shadows without any awareness on your part. Your conscious mind just receives a picture, wholly formed. Something similar is happening here with problem-solving. Your subconscious mind is working on the problem without the awareness of your conscious mind. When the answer is presented, it feels sudden.

"Let's return to the right hemisphere and coarse semantic coding. Your subconscious is working on the problem. Your left hemisphere is strongly activating nearby memories. These might be the obvious solutions, which aren't working. Your right hemisphere, meanwhile, is weakly activating memories with less relevance. And suddenly, it hits on a nonobvious solution to the problem. This is your insight. The answer was in your mind all along, but it wasn't activated immediately because it isn't stored near any concepts in your problem. The really cool thing is that people who tend to solve problems by insight have more widespread activation in the right hemisphere, even at rest. So if you really want to be good at solving problems with insight, your right hemisphere should have broad activation. I can't tell you how to make that happen, but there it is."

When he wasn't studying insight, he turned inward, trying to peer into his own subconscious to understand why this woman he didn't know was so important to him.

When the big day arrived, he wore jeans with a lavender polo shirt. He'd received compliments on the shirt, so really, it was the only choice. He entered the bistro at ten before two. She'd yet to arrive, so he ordered a tea and sat at the table she'd occupied the week before.

At two thirty, he booted his laptop and opened his dissertation. He hadn't looked at it in days, and the prospect of finishing it wasn't improving.

By three thirty, he'd fallen back into the groove of writing. And he had to acknowledge that he'd been stood up. Of all the scenarios he'd invented over the past week, sitting in the bistro by himself and working, productively at that, wasn't one of them. Another reason not to approach strange women in public.

"Did you pay for that?"

He looked up, and there she was.

"I did," he said, elated despite himself. "I didn't think you were coming."

"Were you waiting for me?"

He studied her. They'd made plans to meet here, and she asked this as if another possibility might exist. "Well." He shrugged, bemused.

She deposited her backpack in a chair and sat across from him. "I wasn't here at two because I was running late for my meeting. I wouldn't have come at all except my sister called and asked how things went with you. She said I was mean not to show, and I told her it wasn't like that. I wasn't going to finish the sandwich anyway, so you don't owe me anything. She insisted that your offer to buy me a sandwich was an excuse to see me again."

He didn't know what to say. He opened his mouth and the truth came out. "It was an excuse to see you again."

She flipped her cell phone open.

"What are you doing?"

"My sister asked if you were cute. I told her I couldn't remember."

Heat rose to his face. "Did you just text her?"

She put her phone away.

"What did you say?" he asked.

She smiled and broke eye contact. They sat in silence for a beat.

"Why did you want to see me again?"

Was it always this difficult? He didn't have much experience. "I don't know. I don't know you, but I have the feeling that good things will happen if I get to know you." He suppressed a wince. Was that covertly sexual?

"Why didn't you ask me out on a date?"

"I did."

"You asked if I wanted to get coffee. I don't drink coffee."

"I wouldn't have forced you to drink coffee. You could've had tea or orange juice or a muffin."

She considered that and nodded. "But getting coffee isn't a date. A professor could ask if I want to get coffee, and I'd never think that was a date."

"I'm not your professor. And I said you're pretty. That made my intentions clear."

"I don't remember that."

"I said it."

She paused to think. "You told me you're a neuroscientist. I asked you about insight problem-solving."

"And I said you're pretty." He loved saying it. She was pretty. He wanted to tell her over and over.

"Did you record the conversation?"

"What? No. Why would I do that?"

"Your faulty memory."

He laughed.

She laughed.

"Well, you are pretty."

She blushed. "I told my sister you're cute."

"Have I told you that I love your sister? What is her name?"

"Jennifer. And you don't know her."

"I know enough. I'll christen my firstborn daughter Jennifer."

"So are you going to ask me out on a date?"

"Yes. Will you have dinner with me?"

"When?"

"This Friday."

"And a movie?" she asked.

CHAPTER 25

AMANDA

25 WEEKS PREGNANT

*If Baby's eyelids are open, she might blink when startled—
the blink-startle reflex. This tends to happen a bit earlier in
females.*

—Your Best Pregnancy

December 25, 2017

Amanda woke early on Christmas to make pumpkin bread. She enjoyed the quiet of morning, especially given the tumult that would be her kitchen in a few hours. She felt a pang, noting that it wouldn't be the type of chaos she'd always imagined.

She wondered how many children were lying awake, waiting with preternatural patience for an hour decent enough to rouse their parents. She wondered if a little voice would ever wake her on Christmas morning. *Mom, is it time to get up?*

She had to abolish those thoughts. They would only lead her deeper into despair, and already, she was below the surface. She hoped that making pumpkin bread would rally her Christmas spirit, that the smell of warm cinnamon would conjure well-being. She placed the batter in the oven and waited.

"You're up early."

Amanda looked up from her phone. Her mother, wearing a pink bathrobe, surveyed the kitchen.

"I'm usually good at falling asleep but not so much at staying that way."

"Smells good." Her mother poured a glass of water and joined her at the table. "Is Beverly coming by? Is she in town?"

Amanda closed her eyes. Secrets spawned more secrets. And lies. "She's with her brother's family." Amanda felt especially bad about this lie because it reminded her that Beverly had spent last Christmas with her and Derrick. She hadn't even sent Beverly a Christmas card this year. After ignoring several of Beverly's calls and text messages, Amanda had emailed her that she would be in touch when she was ready. Subtext: *Don't call me. I'll call you.* Did one send a Christmas card after such an email?

"You seem troubled," her mother said.

Amanda forced a smile. "Who isn't?"

"I mean it. You might not think I know you. But I do. You're my baby, and you'll learn what that means soon. Are you worried about the pregnancy?"

Amanda shook her head. "I don't know." She wanted to give her mother something more, but she couldn't. Confiding in Meredith the night before had just happened. Amanda didn't know why. If she'd stumbled upon Meredith five minutes earlier or five minutes later, perhaps it wouldn't have.

"You've done everything you can," her mother said. "You follow your doctor's orders. You stopped working."

Amanda's vision blurred. Before she could take preventative measures, she was crying.

"Oh, honey." Her mother took her hand. "You'll be fine. I'm going to tell you something I never have before. And you'll understand it when you're a mother. Even during the worst arguments we've had, I've never, even for a second, loved you less than the day you were born. I'm proud of you even if I don't always know how to show it. Now stop crying before you make me cry."

Amanda laughed and wiped her eyes. "I love you, Mom." And still, she couldn't tell her. Maybe she would tomorrow, but right now, she couldn't.

~

Meredith and Brian were going to Centennial Park to ice-skate. "Are you sure you don't want to come?" Meredith asked Amanda. "You can drink hot chocolate and watch Brian embarrass himself."

"Sounds fun, but I'm sure." Hemorrhoids. She spared them an explanation. She staked out a spot on the couch to watch Christmas movies. Her mother and Derrick joined her.

They'd opened presents in front of the tree that morning. Amanda's mother had given her a third-trimester kit. Except for the baby book, it had some useful items: a foot soak and a wood massager. Derrick's parents had given her a deluxe body pillow, and Derrick had shocked her with a tennis bracelet. Meredith had sheepishly whispered that her gift was no longer appropriate, and Amanda had nodded, understanding.

"Are you sure I can't help your parents?" Amanda's mother asked Derrick. "I feel bad doing nothing." His parents were preparing Christmas dinner. They'd refused all offers of help.

"Cooking together is their thing," Derrick said. "They're a well-oiled machine."

Amanda settled on *National Lampoon's Christmas Vacation*. She wouldn't be watching anyway. Her mother would talk through the entire thing.

"Did I tell you how scared I was when I found out I was pregnant with you?" her mother asked.

"Yes."

"It was two weeks before I was to start nursing school. Your father was in his junior year of college. We had no money. I called my mother and told her I had to choose between going to school and having you. She didn't hesitate. She insisted I move back home. She paid for a babysitter to watch you while I was in class, and then she watched you in the evenings so I could study."

"Have you heard this story?" Amanda asked Derrick.

He smiled and nodded politely.

"There's a part of this story," her mother said, "that you haven't heard. I was shocked by my mother's reaction. I expected her to tell me to get an abortion. And I wanted her to. I wanted to tell myself that I was willing to step up and become a mom but that my mother didn't support me. I wanted to blame her. She never approved of anything I did, and I didn't imagine she would help me with you. But she did. She was the reason I was able to have you and become a nurse. I want you to know that people, even the ones you think you know best, can surprise you."

"I miss her," Amanda said.

"I do too," her mother said.

~

Food was arranged appetizingly on the dining room table. Derrick asked everyone to bow their heads and proceeded to pray for everything but a hastening of the Second Coming. "Let's eat," he then said with a flourish.

"When is the baby shower?" Derrick's mother asked, helping herself to sweet potatoes and passing the bowl.

"There's plenty of time for that," Amanda replied, a little too sharply.

"It would help to know if we're having a boy or a girl," Derrick said with a pointed look at Amanda.

Might be hard to tell the sex, she wanted to scream at him, *given that it's invisible.* "Can we talk about something else?"

They ate in silence.

"I read a biography of Stephen Hawking," Derrick's mother said. "He was a smart one. He believed that artificial intelligence will lead to human extinction."

"Stephen Hawking was a physicist," Amanda told her.

"A brilliant one," Derrick's mother countered. "We're destroying ourselves, and we don't even know it."

"You and Stephen Hawking know it," Amanda snapped.

"I just don't understand why anyone would want to create super-intelligent computers. Look at how we treat beings less intelligent than ourselves. What if the computers treat us that way?"

"I was glad to have everyone at church last night," Derrick said. "We missed you," he told Amanda. "But you have an open invitation."

Amanda forced a smile. She noticed Meredith watching her.

"Were you religious when you got married?" Meredith asked Derrick.

"We raised him in the church," Derrick's mother said.

"But he had the good sense to stop going."

"Meredith Lynne," Amanda's mother rebuked.

"It's okay, Glenda." Derrick smiled. "My parents did raise me in the church. And I did stray. But I'll tell you, it's good to be back."

"It's good to see you back," his father said.

"Right," Meredith said. "I guess there's nothing wrong with one of you going off and joining a church. Assuming the church is reasonable."

"Reasonable?" Derrick asked.

"Yeah," Meredith said, "reasonable. Women are allowed to have opinions. Gays aren't condemned to conversion therapy. I don't know where your church stands on those things, but the idea that diabetes is caused by demons isn't encouraging."

"That probably wasn't literal," Amanda's mother said.

"The prayer warrior on stage," Meredith countered, "literally commanded the demons in Sister Jocelyn's foot to return to hell. No one said anything about her pancreas. But I digress. If neither of you were religious when you married and then one of you became a Methodist, that's a bridge that could be crossed. But when one of you becomes a snake handler—"

"We don't handle snakes," Derrick interrupted.

"I didn't mean that literally."

"You're being rude," Amanda's mother told her.

"I can't wait until you meet my family," Brian said, grinning. He squeezed her hand. "She says what she's thinking."

Meredith smiled at him. "Thank you, honey. But I'm afraid I have been holding my tongue. Derrick"—Meredith looked him in the eyes—"if you want to attend church, that's fine, but the church you chose is plain crazy. Amanda didn't sign up for that, and it isn't fair to her."

For a moment, Derrick looked shocked as Amanda suppressed a smile, but he recovered quickly and beamed. "You know what?" He clapped his hands together. "I know everyone is enjoying the food, but at the risk of letting it get cold, I want to share a surprise."

He stood, everyone watching him. "Amanda, I hope you didn't think the bracelet was your only gift." He gestured for everyone to follow him.

"It's beautiful," Amanda said and then stood along with everyone else. "More than enough."

He led them upstairs and paused in front of the closed door to his home office. He turned to them. "I've been busy." He retrieved a key from his pocket and held it up with a flourish. "Amanda, will you humor me and close your eyes?"

She didn't have a good feeling about this. Those weeks, the power tools. What had he been building? A life-size manger scene? She humored him.

She heard the key in the lock and then the soft creak of the door opening. He took her elbow and led her inside. The room smelled of paint and something else—newness. "Stand right here."

She gamely kept her eyes closed but registered a light coming on. Someone gasped. She opened her eyes.

CHAPTER 26

PATRICK

12 YEARS BEFORE THE ACCIDENT

Marissa, Patrick thought, was a mathematician to her core. That was his early impression of her, anyway. He imagined opening her like a Russian doll and finding a smaller mathematician that he could open to find an even smaller mathematician. If he continued, he would find a mathematical equation, perhaps one that unified her consciousness. His view of her had changed slowly, so inconspicuously that he couldn't pinpoint the moment of revelation. Even her face began to look different to him, softer.

The first crack in his early impression appeared when he met her sister. They'd been dating for four months. The three of them had breakfast together, and the night before, Marissa had filled him in on Jen's struggles with addiction.

"What does she use?" he'd asked. They were sitting on Marissa's balcony watching the sun set.

Marissa shrugged. "Mostly heroin, but I don't think she's picky. She's been arrested with cocaine and ecstasy, not at the same time. She tells me that she won't try crystal meth. I'm glad, but I don't know how that line was drawn. I think she's been clean for a few weeks, but

I'm hiding the mouthwash when she comes. If you have any cash, you should keep it close."

"She steals from you?" he asked, mildly surprised.

She looked at him. "You don't know any drug addicts." It was a statement, not a question.

He didn't.

"You will when you do your residency."

He planned on a residency in psychiatry.

He'd seen pictures of Marissa and Jen when they were younger. The Jen he met was a harsher version of the girl in the pictures, more angular. She smiled easily, but the light in her eyes had dimmed. The four years between them had also stretched; Jen looked a decade older than Marissa.

Meeting Jen opened new vistas onto Marissa's inner life. It freed them to talk more openly. She told him she'd struggled with her decision to study at Halford University. She still struggled with it. She told him she blamed herself for Jen's addiction. She blamed mathematics and her obsession with it.

He took her and Jen to an Italian restaurant to celebrate Marissa's birthday. Jen told Patrick about Rigley, and Marissa choked up with grief that implied Rigley had died one, not eleven, years ago. Jen seemed to accept this as normal, and Patrick was touched by that. "If Rigley were still alive," Marissa said, "he would be twenty-five." Her next pet, she told them, would be a sea turtle. "It will outlive me."

"No more dogs?" Patrick asked. He was new to the family.

Marissa turned serious. "I loved Rigley for as long as I can remember. When I fell in love with him, I had no idea that he wouldn't always be with me."

In time, he came to see that if he could open Marissa like a Russian doll, he would find a mathematician. Inside of that, he would find a woman who loved with a ferocity that nature had never intended. He would find a woman who thought mathematical mysteries to be the redemption of a cold, uncaring universe. He would find a woman who hated mathematics and felt guilt for the pleasure she derived from it. He would find a woman of intense feeling and unexplored complexities. And he would find hope for himself. Hope that he could mean something to her.

~

"Melvin Young's birthday is coming up," Marissa said. They were in bed, reading academic papers.

"That sounds like a joyous occasion worthy of celebration. Who is Melvin Young?"

"Did I tell you about the guy who put my sister in the hospital for five days?"

Patrick sat up. "No."

"He was her boyfriend. He pleaded guilty to felony assault and was sentenced to probation and court-ordered drug treatment. I do something special for him every year on his birthday."

"Why does that make me nervous?" Patrick asked.

"I don't know. I'm very careful. This is year number five, and it will probably be the last. Time to move on. The first year, on his birthday, I used Jen's key to enter his apartment. I stopped up his bathtub, kitchen sink, and bathroom sink and left them all running." She smiled. "Don't look at me that way. He lives on the ground floor."

"You're not joking?" Patrick asked.

"Did I mention that I put his television, computer, and printer in the bathtub?"

Patrick laughed. "Remind me never to make you angry."

"He put my sister in the hospital and got a slap on the wrist. I'm beyond angry. For his second birthday, I broke into his car and set off six bug bombs. I only wish I'd had the nerve to stay and watch him find that."

"You're a wicked woman."

"I can be. I was worried that I did him a favor with the bug bombs. You know, what if his car had roaches? To make up for that, I sent him a clock radio for his next birthday."

"With roach eggs in it?"

She smiled. "Better. I tutored a guy whose mother trains bed-bug-detection dogs. Did you even know there was such a thing? He gave me a hundred live baby bedbugs. I took the radio apart and put the bedbugs inside, wrapped in cloth."

Patrick laughed. "You are seriously twisted."

"Melvin brings out the worst in me."

"What did you do last year?"

"Last year was a big risk. But I was very careful. I cut letters out of a magazine to write him a note. I didn't handle anything without gloves. I even wore a hairnet."

"What did you write?"

She grinned. "*I know what you eat and I'm going to poison you. When you feel sick, head straight to the ER. You won't have long.*"

"Marissa Thomas, I don't believe you."

"It was either that or mail him white powder. I figured the authorities would take white powder more seriously."

"He's never suspected you?"

Marissa shrugged. "I don't know what he suspects. I doubt Jen is his only victim."

"You're very sexy," Patrick said, clearing the bed of academic papers. "Your tales of mayhem have turned me on."

"First," Marissa said, extending a hand to stop him, "we have to plan his fifth and final punishment."

"We?" Patrick asked.

"Yes," Marissa said. "We."

CHAPTER 27

PATRICK

7 MONTHS AFTER THE ACCIDENT

December 25, 2017

Patrick was dozing on the sofa when his phone rang.

"Merry Christmas," Amanda said.

She didn't sound merry.

"Merry Christmas. How was your day?" It was a little after 9:00 p.m.

"Derrick built a nursery for our baby."

"In your home?"

"Well, yeah. He so wanted to surprise me that he converted his office instead of one of the empty bedrooms. I thought he was building a man cave or something."

"Oh." Patrick didn't know what to say.

"That's what I said. I want to find a crowbar and destroy the fucking thing."

Patrick couldn't tell if she was laughing or crying. "Are you okay?"

"No. I'm not okay. I cannot ever step foot in that room again. I don't want to be in this house."

"What will you do?" He couldn't think of any words of comfort, any advice that might help.

"I feel like things are spiraling out of control. But I felt that way last week. And the week before that. I didn't need this surprise."

"Surprise," Patrick said, careful with his words, "is an understatement. Given what you're going through, having a nursery constructed in your home is—" How to articulate it? *The worst thing imaginable.*

"Tell me about your day," she said.

Patrick hesitated. He felt like he should say more. But what? What could he say?

"My day was typical. I made breakfast, and then Marissa disappeared into her study." He glanced at the wrapped package sitting on the coffee table. He was tempted to throw it in the trash. If he did, Marissa would probably forget that it had ever existed.

"What did you do with yourself?"

Her words were sluggish, and Patrick wasn't sure that she really cared to hear about his day.

"I went to Piedmont Park. I watched *A Christmas Story*. Twice. I saw two versions of *A Christmas Carol*, and I fell asleep during *It's a Wonderful Life.*"

"I'm sorry you were alone," she said with sincere sympathy. "I'm sorry I was surrounded. I don't want to be here, and I don't know what that means for my future. My marriage. I wish I could see you."

She sounded distraught, and yet, her words buoyed him. He didn't know what to make of that. He didn't know how to respond. He eyed the wrapped gift on the coffee table. "Are you free on Wednesday? There's something I need to return to the mall."

~

He went to bed shortly after hanging up with Amanda, still clinging to her words. He didn't know what they meant, but he felt a warm glow as he undressed. *I wish I could see you.* He thought of Amanda as he pulled back the cool sheets and lay down beneath them. For the first time, he allowed himself to imagine what it would be like to make love to her. He thought about touching her body, and as he slipped deeper into the fantasy, he felt himself cross a line. He would feel guilty about this later, but for now, he imagined her in bed with him, beneath him, on top of him. He allowed himself to whisper her name.

CHAPTER 28

PATRICK

12 YEARS BEFORE THE ACCIDENT

For the past few weeks, Patrick and Marissa had been hunkered down working on their theses. Marissa was defending in a month, Patrick in six weeks. It was midmorning, and he found her where he knew he would: at the desk in her bedroom.

She looked up. "What's wrong?" she asked as if she could sense his distress.

Patrick was still holding the phone. "My father has cancer."

"Oh my God," Marissa whispered. "What kind?"

"Pancreatic. The good news is that the doctor gave him six months to live."

She frowned. "What's the bad news?"

"That was four months ago."

"He said that?"

"He hasn't lost his sense of humor."

"Are you okay?"

He sat on her bed. "It was weird to hear from him. Even weirder to know that he's dying. Soon."

She joined him and put an arm around his waist. He hadn't spoken to his father in seven years. Throughout high school, he and Rob had begged their mother to leave him. She finally had when Patrick left for college, and Patrick hadn't spoken to him since.

The only thing that shocked Patrick more than the news of his father's imminent death was the gaping hole it left in his gut. "Apparently, he tried to call Rob, but Rob isn't returning his calls."

"Are you going to see him?" Marissa asked.

"I don't know." Patrick lay down. He should have been working on his own thesis.

Marissa curled up beside him. "I'm sorry this is happening."

He squeezed her hand. They lay in silence for a long while until they both drifted to sleep.

~

By evening, Patrick thought he was okay. He'd adjusted long ago to the idea of not having a father. This wouldn't change his life. He went to bed at eleven, his typical time, and woke with a start at 3:00 a.m. Marissa was asleep beside him, snoring softly. He didn't know what had woken him. He had no memory of a dream. He felt wired, too awake to stay in bed. It was his first experience with middle-of-the-night anxiety, and he didn't recognize it.

He called Rob, who answered midway through the second ring.

"Hey," Patrick said, "I didn't think you would be up."

"I wasn't. I get woken up so often that I never sound like I'm sleeping. Why in the hell did you call if you didn't think I would be up?" Rob was in his third year of a general-surgery residency.

"Dad is dying."

"That's why he's been calling? I thought he wanted his Marvin Gaye records back."

"He has pancreatic cancer."

"That's not the cancer you want."

"Does Mom know?" Patrick asked.

"How would I know? I didn't know until you told me."

"Should I call her?"

"Not now. She's probably sleeping."

"Are you going to call Dad?"

"No."

"So that's it?" Patrick asked.

"I lost a patient tonight. Car accident. Male, early forties. I had to tell his wife and kids. Those kids never expected to lose their father so early. When I was their age, I prayed that Dad would die. Figure that one out. Do you mind if I get some sleep? I have rounds in three hours."

Marissa didn't have a television, so Patrick tried to read, an academic paper first and then one of Marissa's science fiction novels. His concentration was shot. He returned to bed and tried to focus on the contours of Marissa's face. His mind, however, whenever he dropped his vigilance, returned to his childhood, a ruined landscape bereft of solace. His father, in his memories, took the form of a monster, and somehow, as Patrick had grown toward manhood, a piece of that monster had been assimilated into him. It used to haunt him. It had affected his relationships with women. Not anymore, thank God. Not once since he'd met Marissa had he heard his father's voice come out of his mouth. He felt flashes of temper, but they didn't control him. He didn't know if it was his mindfulness or maturity or both. He thought about Kim. He wondered if she'd found someone who made her happy. And he felt a pang of guilt for failing her.

~

Patrick met Kim in the summer before he started medical school. A year later, he was in a bar near the hospital where Rob was doing his internship. Patrick, on his second beer, was monitoring his internal state closely. If he had too much to drink and cried, Rob would have a story to repeat up to and on one of their deathbeds. He wasn't sure that he and Kim had broken up, but it felt like it. Neither of them had said the words. It was the unsaid that spelled their ruin. She'd told him he didn't love her the way she loved him. And he had no response. It hurt. But he had no response.

"Buy her flowers," Rob said, nursing a whiskey. He looked tired, as usual. Patrick was not looking forward to residency.

"Flowers are a Band-Aid."

"Nonsense. They're a grand gesture. She needs to know you appreciate her."

"She needs a better man," Patrick said. "I want to be a better man."

"What does that even mean? You're barely a man now. That's like me saying I want to be a better CIA agent."

"Hilarious. It's good to see you got more from Dad than that ugly face."

"Dad was a funny man," Rob agreed. Rob looked like their father. It was always a point of pride for Patrick that he looked like their mother.

"Yeah. Do you remember that time he shoved you and you hit your head on the coffee table?" Patrick asked. "He stitched you up himself because he wouldn't let Mom take you to the hospital. I almost passed out laughing over that one."

"I didn't say he was a nice guy. I said he was funny."

Patrick grimaced. "His humor was mean. Always at someone's expense. Never self-effacing."

"You've always been sensitive," Rob said.

"I think our childhood has affected my relationships with women. How are you with Sandra?" Rob had met Sandra earlier that year. She was the first woman he'd introduced to their mother since high school.

"I don't break her prized possessions when I get angry," he said. "What do you mean?"

"When I'm in a bad mood and Kim asks me something innocent like, 'Do you have any tests coming up?' Without even thinking, I'll say, 'Do you need me to do something?' And the thing is, I hear Dad's voice when I say it. It's like I'm channeling him."

"Have you pulled a gun and pointed it at her head?"

"I don't have a gun," Patrick said.

"Then you're doing a poor job of channeling Dad."

"I'm not violent. But I don't like myself when I'm moody or annoyed, because I sound like him. Do you ever hear his voice come out of your mouth?"

"I'm an asshole," Rob said. "A lot of great surgeons are assholes. I can embrace it because I don't beat people up. I save lives. Except for his uncommon wit and rugged good looks, Dad and I have nothing in common."

"Six months ago, Kim told me she'd been in two abusive relationships. She was so glad I wasn't like the other guys. I was thinking, 'This woman has no clue why she's attracted to me.'"

"I've never understood why any woman is attracted to you, little bro."

"I think Kim was drawn to me because I'm abusive. And she doesn't even realize that I'm abusive."

"Why do you say you're abusive? Because you snap at her? Do you do it all the time?"

"I do it enough."

If it bothered Kim, she never mentioned it. But it bothered him. He'd tried to stop after she'd told him about her previous boyfriends, but it always happened so quickly. He didn't know it was happening until he heard his father's voice.

"It sounds like she's better off with you," Rob said. "If she fishes in the lake of abusive men, she could catch someone worse. You can be moody, but you don't terrorize her. And she'll never have to worry about you cheating because, well, look at you."

Patrick didn't believe that. Kim deserved someone who treated her with respect, period. When he didn't respond, Rob said, "Let's recap.

You're here drinking with me and not fighting for her because you get snippy when you're in a bad mood."

Rob didn't understand. Patrick could forgive himself for being snippy. He couldn't forgive himself for giving voice to his father. He changed the subject. "We can be grateful that Dad didn't take drinking away from us." He held up his mug. In every story of domestic violence Patrick had heard, alcohol or some chemical substance was involved. Not with their father. Their father had done it all sober. He'd only seen his father drink a beer on one occasion. He was an asshole even with his inhibitions intact.

"I hate it, bro, but I have some bad news for you."

Patrick inhaled deeply.

"You inherited Dad's sense of humor too. That comeback about my ugly face. That was classic Dad."

Maybe Rob was right. But when Patrick was sarcastic, he didn't hear his father's voice. He heard only his own. And he could live with that.

~

Now, as he watched Marissa sleep, he wondered why he couldn't stop thinking about the death of a man he despised. He drifted to sleep just as Rob was starting rounds.

~

The early-morning call to Rob was downright jovial compared to the midafternoon call to his mother. She hadn't heard that her ex-husband was dying, and she didn't understand why Patrick was disrupting her day with the information. Why had Patrick even spoken to the man? Hadn't Patrick begged her to leave him? Now they were fast friends?

Marissa took him to a carnival to cheer him up. He won her a giant stuffed panda by tossing three balls into a tilted basket. The panda was so large that they returned to his car to leave it in the trunk. They ate soft pretzels and vinegar french fries and cotton candy. They rode the Ferris wheel, and he kissed her at the top. He knew she wanted to be home working on her dissertation, and he also knew that he would be having a miserable evening if she were.

He was surprised by the vehemence with which she insisted that he do what was best for himself. She didn't tell him he should see his father, but she did say that Rob and his mother shouldn't factor into the decision. He tried to explain that the territory of his childhood was delineated by uncrossable lines and ruled by rigid hierarchies. Fraternizing with his father was not only dangerous but treacherous. His mother was their first line of defense and so was accorded with battle-won reverence. Rob had his first adolescent growth spurt before Patrick entered puberty, and all hopes rested on his race toward manhood. Patrick never called the shots. He looked to his mother and Rob for everything.

"You'll have to live with what you decide," Marissa told him. "I'll be here for you no matter what, but you'll have to live with it."

CHAPTER 29

AMANDA

25 WEEKS PREGNANT

December 27, 2017

If Derrick's mother mentioned the nursery one more time, Amanda was going to scream. The detail with which she described it made Amanda wonder if she and Derrick had consulted on it long before. *The aqua walls with citrus-yellow accents are perfectly unisex,* she'd gushed. She had a way of transporting Amanda back to the moment when she'd first opened her eyes. The shock, her knees going weak, wondering if she would collapse. The expectant grandparents in awe of Derrick's handiwork and tastes: the white crib with a yellow-striped mattress, the recliner in the same shade of citrus.

"You did all of this without Amanda knowing?" her mother had asked, impressed.

Irrationally, Amanda had felt betrayed by her mother. Shouldn't she be on Amanda's side?

Derrick had beamed with pride. "It wasn't easy. I had to wait for Amanda to leave the house to move stuff in."

Had Amanda been out of the house that much? Had she really been so oblivious?

Only Meredith had seemed to realize that Amanda's silence was not indicative of giddy astonishment. "Are you feeling okay, Amanda?" she'd asked. "You barely had a chance to eat."

It had taken Amanda a moment to recognize the out Meredith offered. She'd nodded. "I didn't have much lunch."

And with that, they'd all returned to the dining room table, still chattering about the beautiful nursery. "We still need dresser drawers and a changing table," Derrick had mentioned as Amanda forced down the nourishment she'd supposedly needed.

Now, Amanda hugged her in-laws with relief, their suitcases by the front door awaiting departure. Derrick drove them to the airport while Amanda had a leisurely breakfast with Meredith, her mother, and Brian.

"Spring is a nice time to have a baby," her mother said. "Do you remember the winter Meredith was born? One of the coldest on record."

"Mom," Meredith said, "can you talk about anything else?"

Her mother glanced knowingly at Amanda. "Someone is jealous of her big sister."

"She's right," Amanda said. "Meredith will be graduating and getting married next year."

Her mother sighed. "My girls are growing up."

~

While Brian arranged their suitcases in the trunk, Amanda took Meredith's hand and led her down the driveway. "Thank you for everything." They stopped at the street.

"I have your back," Meredith said earnestly. "You should know that."

"I know it. And I love you. I'm glad to see you're happy with Brian."

Meredith smiled. "Thanks. But I've been thinking. Maybe you should come with us, stay in Charlotte for a while. I don't think you should be here. Alone."

"I'm not alone. I—"

"Right," Meredith interrupted. "But that's the thing. He's giving me a bad vibe."

"Derrick?"

"Don't tell me you can't see it. Something is off. It's more than just joining a church and—"

"We've been through—" She paused. "We're going through a lot. It isn't all his fault."

"You've said." Meredith waved a hand dismissively.

"I wanted to tell Mom, about . . ." She placed a hand on her stomach. "I just couldn't. Can you imagine me staying there and her not knowing?"

"I can stay here with you for a few weeks. Let's do that."

"Don't be silly. You have a wedding to plan. You need to spend time with your fiancé."

"I can plan the wedding from here. The nursery. It's creepy."

Amanda couldn't disagree. "You have big things coming up in your life. I'm glad we've talked, and I want us to keep talking. Call me when you get back. Check in with me. I want us to stay in touch more."

CHAPTER 30

MARISSA

12 YEARS BEFORE THE ACCIDENT

Marissa knew that Patrick wanted to see his father, even if he couldn't admit it to himself. He was letting his mother's influence paralyze him, and that was a mistake. *Am I making a mistake?* If so, she was committed. She'd told Patrick she was attending a math conference in Asheville. A lie. She was on her way to Alexandria, Virginia.

The monotony of I-95 was hypnotic, and her right foot was numb, but she pushed forward. She'd left early that morning and wanted to finish the nine-hour drive by early afternoon. She sang along with the radio to stay alert.

She and Patrick had been seeing each other for eight months. She was still surprised by the speed and intensity of it all. She'd always seen herself as a focused career woman, unencumbered by the silliness of romance. She'd expected to have a family one day, but her existence wouldn't revolve around that. Her husband would complement her professional life, and she would treat their children as young professionals in training.

Patrick was her first serious boyfriend, and the rush of feelings that accompanied that was startling. He was smart and sweet and handsome, and a part of her wouldn't mind taking off a year after graduation to backpack through Europe with him. That part of her held conversations with him in her head when she was supposed to be working on her thesis. That part of her went to sleep thinking about him and whispered his name first thing upon waking. He made her feel safe, and probably, that was why she found herself with her guard down.

She'd never liked the idea of romance because it meant that your happiness depended on another person. People, in her experience, were anything but dependable. But Patrick was unabashed in his affection for her. He was devoted and she needed that. And she needed fun, even if she hadn't known it. Her days consisted of watching over Jen and performing her doctoral duties. It was a grind, and she needed the frivolous element Patrick brought to her life. There was a part of her that wanted to proclaim that she was his. She resisted that part of herself. When that part of her threatened to take over, she reminded herself, an affirmation, that she was a mathematician, destined for greatness. Once she made history, she could indulge endlessly in him. Until then, math was her god.

~

She checked the address against the one jotted in her notepad. It was a small yellow house in a neighborhood of picturesque, distinct homes. She sat in the car for a moment, steeling her nerves. As she approached the house, legs stiff, heart racing, she silently rehearsed her prepared speech. One deep breath, and she rang the doorbell.

A fit woman in her midfifties answered. "Ms. Davis?" Marissa asked, her voice tremulous, a throwback to her first semester of graduate school, before she'd grown accustomed to making public presentations.

"Yes," Patrick's mother said warily. Marissa saw recognition and then confusion in the woman's eyes.

"I'm Marissa Thomas."

Ms. Davis smiled and glanced over Marissa's shoulder.

"Patrick isn't here," Marissa said quickly.

"Well, come in," Ms. Davis said. "I thought I recognized you from the pictures. I just wasn't expecting you." She led Marissa through a hallway to the kitchen. The house was well worn but clean.

"I'm sorry for stopping by unannounced."

"Is Patrick okay?"

"He's fine."

Ms. Davis offered Marissa something to drink. The two of them sat at the kitchen table with two glasses of orange juice.

"It's great to meet you," Ms. Davis said. "I've heard a lot about you."

"Likewise. You're probably wondering why I'm here."

Patrick's mother nodded. Now that the moment was at hand, Marissa wasn't certain she could follow through.

"I haven't known Patrick long, but he's become my family, and I don't have much of that." Her prepared speech sounded wooden to her ears. "I want to help him."

Ms. Davis looked stricken. "Is he abusive?"

"No," Marissa said quickly and laughed. "He's the farthest thing from abusive."

Ms. Davis sighed with relief.

"It's about his father." The older woman stiffened. "One of my biggest fears," Marissa said before she could lose her nerve again, "is that I will get a call that one of my parents died. I haven't spoken to my mother in thirteen years. I haven't seen my father in that long. He left our family and broke my mother's heart. So she left. I don't even know where she is. If you ask me on a typical day what I think about my parents, I would say that I don't. If I'm feeling less charitable, I might say that I hate them but not on my behalf. My sister raised me, but no one raised her, and she feels the effects of that every day. But my hatred isn't the whole story, because I fear my parents' deaths. I don't know why we love our parents even when we have every reason not to. Maybe the bonds formed during infancy stretch into adulthood. Or maybe we've all watched too many Disney movies. I'm not sure I want a reunion with my parents, and if I did, I have no clue how to go about that. I very well may not get the opportunity that Patrick has with his father. I don't know what it will be like for me when my parents die, especially if I don't get to say goodbye, but whatever it is, I'll have to live with it for the rest of my life.

"Patrick doesn't want to absolve his father of the pain he's caused. He wants to say goodbye to a man he loves even though he shouldn't. He wants closure, and he won't get that without your blessing. For all Patrick's father has done, and I don't want to minimize any of it, he can't do anything else to you. I'm asking you to give Patrick this thing. Give him your blessing."

"Did Patrick ask you to talk to me?"

Marissa braced herself. "He doesn't know I'm here."

CHAPTER 31

AMANDA

25 WEEKS PREGNANT

December 27, 2017

"Perfect timing," Derrick said as Amanda entered the kitchen. "I'm heating leftovers. You hungry?"

The remains of Christmas dinner, packaged neatly in Tupperware containers, lined the countertop.

She placed her purse and keys in the wicker basket beside the pantry. "Not yet. I might have something later."

She was on her way to the living room when Derrick said, "Did you eat at the mall?"

She halted, turned to look at him. He was absorbed in fixing a plate. "I did," she said hesitantly. She hadn't told him she was going to the mall. In fact, they hadn't spoken after he'd returned from dropping his parents off at the airport. Their guests gone, the house quiet, he'd watched television in the living room while she'd retreated to the bedroom. They'd fallen out of the habit of sharing their comings and goings.

"Did you have a cinnamon-sugar pretzel?" he asked casually. When he looked up from the plate, he smiled, nonchalant.

"No." Indulging in a cinnamon-sugar pretzel was synonymous with outings to the mall, but she hadn't been tempted since getting pregnant. She almost didn't ask. But it would bother her. "How did you know I was at the mall?"

He retrieved his cell phone from his pocket and held it up. "Apparently, we can track each other's locations. Family Sharing. I wasn't spying. I just wanted to see how it works. As your due date gets closer, it might come in handy. You can locate me also."

"Or I could just call you." The anger rising within her was at odds with his composure. And her guilt. Did she want to hide her whereabouts from him, hide Patrick? She'd accompanied him to return Marissa's gift. Should that be a secret?

"I was just testing it. I didn't need anything. Were you there by yourself?"

As if to answer her own question, she nodded. And then she turned and continued to the bedroom.

CHAPTER 32

PATRICK

7 YEARS BEFORE THE ACCIDENT

Patrick wanted to do something special for Marissa's thirtieth birthday. Marissa was not taking the advent of her third decade well. They negotiated.

Patrick: *Let's fly to Venice for an evening gondola ride.*

Marissa: *How about lunch in the faculty dining hall?*

Patrick: *A bed-and-breakfast in the mountains of Asheville.*

Marissa: *A picnic lunch on the quad.*

Patrick: *Dinner at the Sun Dial, followed by a night of dancing.*

Marissa: *Dinner at home. Spaghetti.*

Patrick: *Why are you ruining your birthday for me?*

They settled on dinner at her favorite Indian restaurant, where she morosely picked at chickpea vindaloo.

"I'm just really disappointed in my career," she said at his prodding.

"You're going to make tenure next year."

She shook her head. "It isn't about tenure."

He knew that. They'd been together for five years, married for two. She was thirty years old and hadn't accomplished anything great. A PhD in math and tenure at a prestigious university didn't qualify. "You're just getting started," he told her.

"No," she said, "you're just getting started." He was in the first year of a psychiatry residency. "Your field requires tons of specialized knowledge. It isn't so for math. I don't need more knowledge. I need insight and creativity. If anything, my mind is becoming more ingrained in familiar patterns."

There was something else. She wasn't saying it, but he knew she was thinking it. If she were truly a great mathematician, she should've shown it by now.

"Should I put you out to pasture?" he teased.

"What? No." She laughed. "I don't feel old. I don't feel any different than I did when I was twenty." She whispered: "Except for morning sex. My flexibility isn't what it once was."

He took her hand and squeezed it. "You haven't heard me complain."

She smirked.

"You're going to make a groundbreaking mathematical contribution," he told her. "And you don't have to put your life on hold to do it."

"What does that mean?" Marissa took her hand back.

He hesitated. He really wanted to say this, but he needed to tread carefully. He knew she wasn't ready. "You should stop taking the pill."

She looked down at her plate.

"I know," Patrick said. "You want to focus on your career. Have you ever considered that having a child could enhance your career?"

Marissa laughed. "How does that work? I'm not a man."

"Believe me, I've never mistaken you for a man. A new perspective on life could give you a new perspective on math."

"Yeah, throw in sleep deprivation, and you might have the formula for success. When I become a mother, I want to be present. I don't want to begrudge our child my attention."

"I'll help, you know."

She laughed, unconvinced. "You work sixty-hour weeks." Rob ridiculed the light hours of a psych residency. "Give me time. You said yourself that I'm going to make a breakthrough. Once I do, we can talk about children. Okay?"

It was her birthday, and he shouldn't have brought up children. He took her hand again and smiled. "Okay."

But it wasn't okay. He could imagine them sitting here in ten years having the same conversation. He wondered, not for the first time, if marrying her had been a mistake. He didn't love her any less as he contemplated his doubts. The doubts had always been there. Before he'd proposed, he'd visited his mother in Virginia to get her advice.

~

"I have a confession to make," his mother had told him. They were in her vegetable garden. He was helping her weed.

Patrick sighed and sat in the dirt. "You don't like her."

"Your father's funeral was not the first time I met her."

"What?"

"I promised her I wouldn't tell you. Marissa came to see me a couple of months before your father died."

"Here?"

His mother nodded. Patrick didn't recall Marissa traveling to Alexandria. "She spent the night with me."

"I think you're confused, Mom." The heat was certainly getting to him.

"She showed up out of the blue and asked me to give you my blessing to see your father." His mother paused, giving him time to process that.

His mother had softened seemingly overnight. One day she'd been angry at the mention of him visiting his father; the next day she'd encouraged it. When his father passed, he asked his mother and Rob to attend the funeral. Rob declined, but to his surprise, his mother agreed.

It was a small affair, just a handful of people. His mother wiped away tears as Marissa held her hand. He'd found that odd, even then. Marissa was not an outgoing person. Warmth was reserved for people she knew well.

"I was so impressed with her," his mother said. "We stayed up late talking, and by the time she left in the morning, she felt like the daughter I never had. I hoped that you would fall in love with her and that things would work out for you two."

"And neither of you ever told me," he said, astonished, angered.

"Don't tell her I told you. She isn't perfect. But you love her. And she loves you. I've loved her since the night I met her. You can never know if a marriage is going to last forever. The best you can do is marry someone who has your back. Marissa has your back."

~

"I'm holding you to it," he told Marissa now in the Indian restaurant. "The day you become famous for solving some five-hundred-year-old math problem, we're throwing your birth control away."

She laughed. "We'll talk about it."

CHAPTER 33

DERRICK

13 WEEKS AFTER THE MISCARRIAGE

December 27, 2017

Everything, Pastor Roberts once told Derrick, *is a battle of wills. Good versus evil. God versus Satan. You were married before God, and it is His will that your marriage flourish. You must trust in God. But you must also remain vigilant against Satan. If your marriage falters, it is Satan's victory.*

God's will was on Derrick's mind as he booted Amanda's computer. He was striving for perfect faith. His marriage, his future—he placed it all in God's hands. And still, he agonized, an insult to God, as if his and Amanda's problems were too big for Him. Worry was Derrick's chief sin. Worry was not vigilance against Satan. Vigilance against Satan required action backed by the knowledge that God ordained victory.

Worry was like an encroaching virus, seeking and destroying joy. Derrick was in the running for regional sales manager—the culmination of twelve years of meticulously building sales contacts and expanding his territory—and it hardly seemed important. Georgia football at its finest could bring tears to his eyes. They were in the playoffs this year, and he doubted he'd watch. Amanda consumed his thoughts.

Derrick didn't know how he'd lost control of his life. He'd had everything. He'd always had everything. When he was a child, divorce among his friends' parents had been epidemic. And through it all, his home remained intact. Friday was family night. They'd go out to dinner and then to a movie or bowling. His parents had a date night every other Saturday, and he and his brother, Stephen, one year his junior, would play video games with the sitter. He played baseball in high school and excelled on the debate team. He went to the University of Georgia, his first choice, and majored in marketing. He spent a year in Japan after college teaching English. Stephen followed him, married a Japanese woman, and never left. Derrick met Amanda at a friend's wedding, and he knew when he shook her hand that he was ready to settle down. He wanted what his parents had.

He fell hard for her. She was funny and beautiful, and they never ran out of things to talk about. She was his best friend. Their children, he imagined, would have the best of them both—Amanda's intelligence and his charisma.

Their inability to conceive was the first major difficulty in his life. And he handled it in the same way that he handled minor difficulties. He threw money and effort at it. He persisted. They did it together. Until it was just him. Until she quit. And even then, he didn't consider it finished. Even when their marriage was awkward and sexless, he gave her space and waited for her to rally. And then she'd gotten pregnant.

Action, Pastor Roberts said, was the strongest weapon against doubt.

He opened the browser on her laptop and searched for Gmail.

He'd been certain that the nursery, perfectly equipped for the family he envisioned, would bring them together, but Amanda only seemed more distant. She didn't share anything with him. He had no idea what she was thinking or feeling or doing.

"Come on," he muttered to the computer as her Gmail home page loaded. Yes. God had his back. He was in her account. If she'd logged out, he wouldn't have had a prayer of guessing her password. She was too sophisticated for $DrugPeddler3000—his password for everything. Her Windows password was a random string of characters she'd memorized. Luckily, she'd written it down for him when his computer had been on the fritz.

"What are you up to?" he mumbled to himself and clicked on her inbox.

He scanned subject lines, tons of data science job alerts. He hadn't known she was looking for a job. If she'd spoken to him, he would have suggested she wait until after the baby came.

There were emails from LinkedIn, Emory Alumni Association, and Georgia Tech Alumni Association, as well as several from a name he didn't recognize. Patrick Davis. He started with the oldest Patrick Davis thread he could find. Four weeks ago. He opened the email.

CHAPTER 34

PATRICK

6 MONTHS BEFORE THE ACCIDENT

November 2016

Patrick didn't want to be a downer at the birth of a baby, so he didn't accompany Marissa to the hospital when Jen went into labor. He liked Jen. She loved Marissa and could talk incessantly about their childhood. Marissa rarely talked about it, so Patrick hung on Jen's every word. She had a lot of good qualities, but he couldn't imagine that she would be a good mother.

He'd known Jen to be clean but never for longer than a few months. She'd once been a talented saleswoman, according to Marissa, but those days were behind her. She worked odd jobs now and relied on Marissa's financial help. And the father? Jen didn't know who that was, not even a guess. It didn't matter. None of the candidates would be good fathers, not to her baby anyway. This birth was not a joyous occasion.

I wonder if this could be what Jen needs, Marissa had said to him after Jen revealed her pregnancy.

Patrick hadn't responded. He thought that an unreasonable responsibility for a baby, to fix adult problems. And what about the baby's needs? Did this kid have a shot?

Patrick had been surprised when Marissa threw a baby shower and invited the female employees and wives of male employees from the math department. None of them knew Jen, but many attended. Marissa was well liked. And Jen got much-needed supplies. Marissa bought her a crib, a stroller, and a bouncy seat. Patrick dutifully assembled the baby gear and kept the negativity to himself.

Laura Thomas was born on November 20 at 7:13 p.m. Marissa sent pictures and asked Patrick to come to the hospital. He declined. Marissa spent two nights in the hospital with Jen, and then they took Laura home to Jen's apartment. Marissa took a week off from work to help them get settled.

The three of them had been at Jen's apartment for two days when Marissa called Patrick, Laura wailing in the background. It was nearly 9:00 p.m.

"Jen went out to get a pizza," Marissa told him.

"Okay."

"Three hours ago. She isn't answering her phone, and Laura is hungry. Obviously, I can't feed her."

"I hope Jen is okay," Patrick said.

"She isn't okay," Marissa yelled over Laura's cries. "She took my car. It was a twenty-minute errand, tops. There is no scenario in which she's okay."

Patrick agreed. "What can I do?" he asked.

"Can you pick up some infant formula and bring it over? It will have to do."

~

At midnight, Patrick stretched out and went to sleep on Jen's sofa. When he was shaken awake, he thought Jen was back.

"She's trembling," Marissa said.

"Jen?" he asked, disoriented. Laura was in the bedroom screaming.

"Laura is trembling. Jen hasn't come home. I think it's the formula."

Patrick got up and checked on Laura. She was in her crib, crying and shaking. He'd seen this as an intern. But that was a long time ago, and he hoped he was wrong. "Neonatal abstinence syndrome."

"English, Doctor." Marissa was exhausted. She pulled at her hair.

"Withdrawal. We should get her to an ER."

"Is she okay?"

Patrick turned. Jen was standing in the doorway, her clothes rumpled. She looked like she hadn't slept in days.

"Where have you been?" Marissa snapped.

"I just needed a few minutes."

"A few minutes?" Marissa looked at her watch. "You've been gone for nine fucking hours."

"Oh."

"Don't tell me where you've been," Marissa said, "but I need to know the truth. Did you use while you were pregnant?"

Jen opened her mouth. For a moment, nothing came out. And then: "No. Of course not."

"Laura is not going through withdrawal?" Marissa looked at Patrick. He wasn't sure. Perhaps he was jumping to conclusions because of Jen's history.

"No," Jen said, "I don't think so."

"I don't want you to think. I want you to tell me if you used while you were pregnant."

Jen didn't respond.

"It's important," Patrick said gently.

"If I did, could that hurt her?" she asked Patrick.

"Are you fucking kidding me?" Marissa said. "Let's go." She moved to pick up Laura. Jen stepped forward to block her.

"I wouldn't intentionally hurt her."

"Did you use while you were pregnant?" Marissa repeated.

"I might have. A little."

174

"Fuck!" Marissa said.

Patrick picked up the screaming baby.

"I'm sorry."

"Tell that to her," Marissa said coldly and followed Patrick out the door.

~

"She's never judged me before," Jen said.

Patrick looked up. Being at the hospital in the middle of the night conjured unpleasant memories from his residency. Jen sat down next to him. They were in the lobby. Marissa had gone in search of a restroom.

"She's upset," Patrick said.

"Maybe she's right." Jen ran a hand through her hair. "I told the nurse everything."

"That's good." He'd explained on the way to the ER how important it was for Jen to be honest. "That's the best thing you can do for Laura right now."

The hospital was admitting Laura for neonatal abstinence syndrome.

Jen stood suddenly. "I'm getting out of here."

"What? Laura needs you."

"I'm the reason she's here. Everyone knows it."

He thought about grabbing her arm, physically restraining her, at least until Marissa came back. But in the time he considered it, Jen had made it to the door. He called after her, but she didn't turn back. He sat down and sighed.

"Jen left," he said when Marissa returned.

"Where did she go?"

"I don't know. I don't think she's coming back."

"She'll be back. I know Jen. Underneath it all, she's loyal. She won't leave Laura here by herself."

"She isn't by herself."

"I can't go in there," Marissa said.

"You can." Patrick took her hand. "We'll both go."

"I can't," she insisted. "I can't see Laura this way. I can't see what Jen has done to her. She's lied to me and stolen from me, but I have to believe the sister I grew up with is still in there. I don't want to hate her."

Patrick put an arm around her shoulder. "You're exhausted. Go home and get some sleep. I'll stay with Laura."

She kissed him on the lips. "Thank you. I'm sorry about this, Patrick. But Jen will be back. My sister is still in there."

~

Laura screeched in pain. Her arms and legs shook. She clenched her fists. Patrick lost all sense of time. He sat for hours, his shirt unbuttoned, holding Laura against his skin. She was running a fever, but the nurse had assured him that physical contact helped. Patrick couldn't tell. Laura was so angry. She got angrier when he put her down, so he held her. The room was dark. The door was shut to keep out noise. Multiple nurses inquired about Jen. Breastfeeding would help, they said. Patrick had no idea where Jen was.

Days passed. Marissa stopped by in the mornings and evenings, but she hadn't heard from Jen either. He and Marissa ate in the cafeteria, the only breaks Patrick took. He felt fidgety during those brief meals. Laura was in pain, her suffering almost palpable, but he believed that he was helping. He didn't like being away from her.

The methadone seemed to help, too, but not enough. He fell asleep with Laura in his arms and dreamed that she'd stopped breathing. He awoke with a start. She was breathing, but it was labored. He measured time by Marissa's visits. Every morning, she asked if Jen had come by. Every evening, she stopped by Jen's uninhabited apartment on the way to the hospital.

Laura seemed to be improving, her screams a little less angry, and then the diarrhea started. The medical team battled dehydration through her IV. Patrick fought diaper rash with frequent changes and ointment. He woke up crying and couldn't stop. A nurse came in to check Laura's weight, but she didn't mention his sobs. She spoke to him as if he were okay, and that made him feel like maybe he was. He took a shower, but the only thing that gave him comfort was holding Laura.

His world shrank. He rarely thought about his research or his graduate students. He imagined the day when Laura beat this, her pain dried up. He imagined protecting her, wrapping her in a bubble where pain could never reach her again. He didn't know what that would look like, but those were his thoughts now, fuzzy and ill formed.

"You look exhausted," Marissa told him. "Jack sends his best. He found someone to cover your classes." He knew it was breakfast because they were eating muffins. "I think you should come home tonight and get some sleep."

He shook his head. He couldn't think of anything worse than leaving Laura. He didn't know how to tell Marissa that. "How long has it been?" he asked.

"Thirteen days."

CHAPTER 35

PATRICK

7 MONTHS AFTER THE ACCIDENT

December 30, 2017

From: Patrick Davis
To: Amanda Jackson
Subject: RE: Unusual Conditions

People with developmental topographical disori-
entation are unable to form mental maps of their
environment. Some patients get lost in their own
homes. I read about a woman who would find the
nursery by following her son's cries. They're cog-
nitively normal in every way except that they can't
find their way around.

~

Patrick and his mother worked for three days on a thousand-piece jigsaw puzzle before his father wrecked it. "If it was worth a damn," his
father said, "it couldn't be undone so easily." His father, who enjoyed

watching sports and bullying children, thought puzzles a waste of time. Following that, Patrick and his mother worked on puzzles during the day and covered their partial solution with a tablecloth before his father came home.

Patrick's love of puzzles could not be suppressed. Science reminded him of puzzles, only the pieces were abstractions, ideas drifting in the universe, waiting to be put together.

Now, as he sat at the dining room table, puzzle pieces scattered in front of him, the doorbell rang. It was Saturday, early evening. It had to be Frederick Peters.

Why did that guy think he could just show up whenever he wanted? Patrick's anger built as he walked through the living room. He pulled the front door open, prepared to say, *She isn't here,* which was true. Marissa had gone for a walk. But before he could speak, he realized that a stranger was standing in front of him. He hesitated a beat.

"Patrick Davis?" the man asked.

"Yes."

"I'm Derrick Jackson. Amanda's husband. Can we talk?"

"Is she okay?" Patrick asked, a sense of panic just beneath the surface.

"She's fine. I just want to talk to you."

Patrick considered slamming and locking the door, but that reaction seemed ludicrous. Patrick wasn't a man who had affairs with other men's wives, and there was nothing threatening in Derrick's demeanor.

Did Patrick feel guilty?

He stepped back and motioned for Derrick to come in. He led him to the kitchen. "Can I get you something to drink?"

"No, thank you." Derrick took a seat at the kitchen table. He was of medium build and average height. Patrick had possessed a fuzzy mental picture of him, something he imagined when Amanda talked about her husband. The intelligent eyes that surveyed his kitchen, surveyed

Patrick, didn't match. He was suddenly real to Patrick in a way that he hadn't been before.

Patrick sat across from him. Perhaps Amanda had sent him so that Patrick could explain pseudocyesis. But wouldn't she have told Patrick beforehand?

Neither of them spoke.

"How can I help you, Derrick?" Patrick finally asked.

"Are you sleeping with my wife?" His voice was level. Just a man with a question.

"No," Patrick said quickly. He considered explaining himself but feared he would ramble. He wasn't sleeping with Amanda. He left it at that.

"You've been spending time with her," Derrick said, not quite a question.

Patrick nodded, aware of the force of his own heartbeat. "I think this is a conversation you should be having with Amanda."

"I agree, Patrick. And in an ideal world, I would. But when I talk to my wife, I hear your words come out of her mouth."

Patrick wasn't sure what that meant. "I'm not comfortable—"

"I'm not comfortable, Patrick." He raised his voice, but only slightly. "I didn't know you existed until I accidentally opened my wife's email. Please stop spending time with my wife. I'm asking nicely." He didn't wait for a response before showing himself out.

Patrick was still sitting at the kitchen table, unmoving and shaken, when Marissa walked through the back door. She didn't seem to notice. She took one look at him and said, "I'm so sorry. I forgot to open your Christmas present."

CHAPTER 36

MARISSA

5 MONTHS BEFORE THE ACCIDENT

December 2016

"Long time no see," Marissa said. She hadn't expected Jen to answer. She hadn't expected Jen to be home. Jen moved aside to let Marissa in.

Over the years, the frills had disappeared from Jen's apartment. Marissa had bought her a television for her last birthday, but it was nowhere to be seen. Marissa never asked about it. She understood. Sold to buy drugs or pay rent because the rent money had bought drugs.

Marissa sat on the worn couch.

"How is she?" Jen asked.

"Patrick tells me she's getting better. He hasn't left the hospital."

"They all blame me. I can't—"

"No need to explain," Marissa told her. "Sit down. Let's talk."

Jen didn't move. "I'm sorry."

"I know. Please sit."

Jen sat reluctantly in a chair across from Marissa. Marissa reached into her briefcase and pulled out papers she'd been carrying for the past five days. "I want you to grant temporary guardianship of Laura to Patrick and me."

"You don't think I can take care of her?"

Marissa shook her head. Patrick had told Marissa to ask for permanent guardianship, but he was cantankerous, and Marissa couldn't do that to Jen. This whole affair proved something Marissa had always suspected: Patrick was meant to be a parent and Marissa was not. She felt guilty about it, but there it was.

"I can take care of her. I know it. I just need a chance."

"I don't want to argue."

"You think you're just going to take my child?"

"Don't make me the bad guy."

"You're doing that all on your own."

"I didn't make you do this," Marissa said quietly, forgetting the promise she'd made herself, that she wouldn't let this turn into a fight. "If you don't sign these"—Marissa held up the papers—"you won't get another cent from me."

Jen's mouth fell open. Marissa gave Jen an allowance each week. She knew Jen used the money to buy drugs sometimes, but Marissa preferred that to prostitution or any other host of ways Jen might acquire drugs. The rock-bottom thing was a myth. The streets were full of people who'd hit rock bottom. There were no miracles waiting there.

"I took care of you when—"

"Stop it, Jen. When Mom left, I wanted to get a job. Do you remember that?"

"You wanted to clean our neighbors' homes."

"I was twelve. It was the only thing I could think of. And you told me I had a good brain and that I should concentrate on school. What I'm doing now, I'm not doing to you. I'm doing it for my sixteen-year-old sister who took care of me. If I could go back in time and tell that sixteen-year-old what is happening, she would beg me to do this."

Jen put her face in her hands and cried. Marissa couldn't hold back her own tears.

"I want to be that girl again. I want that more than anything in the world."

"I know," Marissa said. "This isn't your fault. You're sick."

"The first time I—it never occurred to me that—if I had known, I never would have—"

"It isn't over. I'm not giving up on you. You can see Laura whenever you want. We just have to do this." She placed the papers in Jen's lap. "Let us take care of her."

Jen looked at the papers. "Who will watch her while you and Patrick work?"

"We'll hire a nanny."

"I'm going to make it back," Jen said.

"I know you will." She knew Jen meant it. And she knew that it wasn't enough for Jen to mean it now. She had to mean it in those early hours when she was alone with craving, when even in a roomful of people, she could be alone for her hunger. "I know you will," Marissa repeated because Jen needed one person who believed in her, who took her side, who had her back, no matter what.

"She's my ticket back," Jen said.

CHAPTER 37

AMANDA

25 WEEKS PREGNANT

December 30, 2017

Amanda changed the passwords on her laptop and email. She turned off location sharing on her phone. Derrick had crossed a line, and she was fuming. She could leave him. She was that angry.

Her fury was simple, but the mechanics of leaving were not. She hadn't worked in four months. She could find a job, but there was her condition. And her skills. Even an experienced data scientist would be asked to jump through hoops during a technical interview, to demonstrate her algorithmic prowess. Her skills couldn't be rusty.

More for a distraction than for practical preparation for an interview, she visited a website that hosted coding challenges. She hadn't used it for years and was pleased that it still existed. She selected Python for the programming language and "advanced" for the skill level.

When she heard Derrick come in, nearly an hour later, she didn't go out to confront him as she'd planned. Either the logic of programming had soothed her and her desire to fully crack this challenge was strong, or cowardice held her in place. She preferred to believe the former but couldn't discount the latter.

She was surprised when the bedroom door opened without a knock. A formality had emerged between them of late, and barging into her space was a violation of the new norms.

"I have a confession," Derrick said. He stood in the doorway, nervous. She hadn't seen him like this since he'd proposed, and the memory of that night was jarring.

Now, almost seven years later, everything between them changed, he had a confession. She waited. She watched him fidget in the doorway from where she sat in front of her computer, and she waited for him to tell her that he'd had an affair to even the score. How did she feel about that? Nothing. She felt nothing as she waited to hear about her husband's affair. "You don't have to tell—"

"I read your email," he blurted. "I didn't do it on purpose. I was trying to check my email on your computer, and your email came up."

She nodded, waited. When Patrick called, he'd told her that Derrick had mentioned their email exchanges.

"Who is Patrick Davis?"

"I think you know," she said coolly.

He stepped into the bedroom, placed a hand on the dresser as if to steady himself. "I should have talked to you before I went to his house."

"Why didn't you?"

He ran a hand through his sandy-blond hair. "I needed to see him. You would have talked me out of it. You would have told me you weren't having an affair, and then I would've looked like I didn't trust you by going to see him."

She almost laughed, amused in a twisted sort of way. "At least you trust me," she said.

"Do you blame me?"

He said it bluntly and it stung. Her face felt hot, and she looked away from him, to the cool logic of symbols and operators on her monitor.

"You emailed him at three in the morning. You barely talk to me." His voice tremored, a plea.

"What do you want to talk about, Derrick?" Shame compounded her anger.

"Are you sleeping with Patrick?"

He stared at her, and she wondered if this could be her out. The holidays had been miserable. Not only had she wanted to spend Christmas with Patrick; she'd actually said it. Aloud. To Patrick. She hadn't meant to. It had just come out. She'd seriously thought about leaving Derrick then. She'd been thinking about it since. The weight of the decision felt so heavy. And the upside was unclear. Leaving him didn't mean she would spend next Christmas with Patrick. Patrick was married. Patrick loved his wife.

No, Patrick couldn't be her out. They weren't having an affair, and she wouldn't scapegoat their friendship. There had been enough lies. She wouldn't end her marriage in a lie.

"No," she said, the force of truth behind that word.

His shoulders relaxed, and she felt pity for him. She didn't want to hurt him. He sat on the edge of their bed, and she turned her chair to face him.

"Why don't you talk to me?" he asked.

She sighed. "I can't talk to you. You told my mother I'm pregnant. I don't want to hear about faith pregnancies. I don't want a nursery."

He threw up his hands. "When you give birth to a healthy baby—"

"It won't be yours."

He looked stricken. She closed her eyes and bit her lip. Why had she said that? She touched her swollen belly.

"I'm sorry," she said.

The look on his face.

"I love you," Derrick told her. "I want you. I want our child. I didn't always see that."

She remembered the way he'd said *abortion*, as if it were nothing. As if she could walk into a clinic and walk out good as new. As if she owed him that.

"Who is Patrick to you?" Derrick asked, and she could see the vulnerability in his eyes.

"He's a doctor," she said. "A psychiatrist."

"Your doctor?"

She didn't want to be interrogated, but she owed him this. *It won't be yours.* Where had that cruelty come from?

"No. A friend introduced us. He's helping me to understand my condition."

"He's sowing doubt?"

She hesitated. "Yes, I guess you would say that."

"What do you two do together?"

"We talk," she told him, wanting nothing more than to steer the conversation away from them and their marriage—even if it meant talking about Patrick. "He's trying to save his marriage. His wife is a brilliant mathematician, but she's having a nervous breakdown. She spends her days trying to communicate with the dead through math."

"People have been trying to communicate with the dead for as long as people have been dying."

"This is different. The math she's doing is real. It's inventive and brilliant. But she's confused." *Like you,* Amanda wanted to add. *Like me.*

Derrick stood and took her hand. She stood because she didn't know what else to do. He hugged her. "Let's go to Blue Ridge in March. I'll make reservations."

Amanda nodded. Getting away sounded wonderful. She wanted to forget everything, if only for a few days. But when she saw herself relaxing, a beverage in hand, Derrick wasn't there. She was with Patrick. She wondered if that feeling was the same as having an affair.

CHAPTER 38

PATRICK

7 MONTHS AFTER THE ACCIDENT

January 19, 2018

Prior to Derrick's visit, it hadn't occurred to Patrick that he could be a complication in Amanda's marriage. He didn't want to cause trouble, and yet, he couldn't follow his misgivings to their logical conclusion: *Maybe we should stop spending time together.* He couldn't bring himself to say those words aloud. Not to himself and not to Amanda.

He needed to say them. She needed to hear them. She needed to know that she could walk away with his blessing. And yet, the thought of not seeing her felt indescribably lonely. A future without their talks seemed hopelessly bleak. Craven, selfish, he felt guilty on both counts.

"Since you've met Derrick," Amanda said, "I feel like I should meet your wife." They were walking along the BeltLine behind Piedmont Park.

"You don't want to meet her now," Patrick said. "She's in a foul mood. The math has dried up, and it's made her miserable."

"What does she do when she can't do math?"

"She goes for walks. Listens to music. Basically, she tries to do math. How has Derrick been?" Three weeks had passed since Derrick had shown up at his house, one since he'd seen Amanda. When she'd texted him out of the blue, he hadn't been proud of the relief he felt. They'd met at a food truck park for lunch.

"Quiet. We haven't spoken much. Probably for the best. I've been thinking. What if our marriage was over before I had the affair? Maybe I knew it and that's why I did it. Maybe Ralph was my way out, and I just got scared to take it. Maybe breaking off the affair was my unwillingness to let go."

Patrick didn't reply. Claiming objectivity on her marriage would be farcical. He was the last person who should be giving her marital advice.

"I just don't see how we make it back," she continued.

Patrick waited a beat to see if she would say more. He didn't want to comment on her marital prospects. When she remained quiet, he said, "Marissa realized that she forgot to open her Christmas present. Five days after Christmas."

"The present you returned? Awkward," Amanda intoned.

"I told her it was perishable and that I ate it."

"Clever."

Amanda nodded at an elderly woman passing in the opposite direction. "She reminds me of my grandmother," she told Patrick. "It's not that I ever forget she's gone, but sometimes, it's a jolt. I guess that will never go away."

"I never knew my grandparents," Patrick said. "My father's parents weren't in the picture, and my mother's parents died when I was young. I wonder what it would have been like."

Amanda smiled. "For me, it was essential. My grandmother loved movies. She had one for every occasion."

"What was her favorite?"

"There were many. She and I enjoyed watching *An Affair to Remember*."

"I haven't seen that."

Amanda stopped walking. "You've never seen *An Affair to Remember?*"

Patrick smiled. "No."

"I'll fix that." They continued walking. "To let you go through life without seeing *An Affair to Remember* would dishonor my grandmother's memory. And my grandmother's memory is sacred to me."

CHAPTER 39

MARISSA

7 MONTHS AFTER THE ACCIDENT

January 19, 2018

Marissa chose to have faith that the math would return. Really, faith was all she had. She couldn't go looking for the math because she had no idea where it came from. Patrick, being a neuroscientist, would posit that it arose through cooperation of the default mode, salient, and executive control networks of her brain. That could be, but the math she sought was ethereal, and those networks were nothing more than collections of interconnected nerve cells. She liked to believe that math existed in the universe, independent of discovery by her or any other mathematician. But if so, what were they discovering? Truth. That was the simple answer. But that truth had to be packaged in language. And that language was mathematics. And when the math came, she felt as if she were scooping it from unvisitable regions of the cosmos, like water from the sea. She could drink and drink and never be sated. The magic was in the intangibility of it.

The magic, Patrick would say, *is in the unconscious processing. You are your brain, and yet, so much of what it does happens beyond your awareness.*

It does its work unbeknownst to you and then passes you the fruits of its labor. That's magic.

Lately, she had more conversations with Patrick in her head than they had in real life. That bothered her, but as much as she missed him, she just never felt like talking. He always wanted to talk. He was talking now. To Amanda. They were on the BeltLine behind the dog park. Marissa kept a safe distance, probably more than she needed, given their nonchalance. They walked easily, unhurried. If they were concerned about being spotted, they didn't show it. She'd watched them picnic on the hilly lawn next to Tenth Street. She hadn't gotten close enough to see what they were eating, but she'd recognized their ease.

This section of the BeltLine, new to Marissa, felt like a nature trail. Thick shrubbery lined the gravel path and created an illusion of seclusion. It would be a nice place to walk if she weren't covertly following her husband. She stopped walking and watched as Patrick and Amanda lazily turned a corner and passed from her sight. She started back the way she'd come.

CHAPTER 40

MARISSA

5 MONTHS BEFORE THE ACCIDENT

December 2016

Marissa revered her birth control pills. She took them at 9:00 p.m. sharp, nightly, even when she was down to the placebos at the end of the pack. She considered them one of the most important inventions in human history. The ability to have sex with her husband while controlling her fertility was priceless.

She didn't know if she wanted to be a mother. On the rare occasions when she imagined having children, she was comfortable in her career and the children were older. They were interested in math and science, and she carefully guided their intellectual development. She wondered if her apathy toward motherhood signaled emotional damage. Of course, emotional damage could present itself in many forms.

She thought of Patrick and the time he'd ordered a case of vegan ice cream. She hadn't known it was coming until a courier showed up at their door. There was so much ice cream that she couldn't fit it in the freezer and ended up giving the surplus to neighbors. When she asked him why he'd ordered an entire case, he said:

I saw the founder of the company on television. He isn't vegan, but his twelve-year-old son adopted a vegan diet after visiting a petting zoo. The boy loved ice cream. It was the eighties, so that kind of thing wasn't readily available. The father spent six months developing and perfecting a vegan ice cream recipe. He served it to his son on his fourteenth birthday. Patrick choked up as he told the story, and Marissa was afraid he would cry. *If I'd come home from a petting zoo and told my father I was vegan, he would've petted me with his fists and restricted my diet to hamburgers and chicken nuggets for a month.*

Patrick had spoken seriously for the first time about having children. He wanted to emulate that vegan boy's father. He was damaged and wanted to see what his life might have been like had he had different parents.

And now, Marissa was shopping for baby supplies: diapers and formula and wet wipes and baby body wash. Patrick was at home, the first time she'd seen him outside the hospital in sixteen days. Laura was still there, but only for a few more hours. Patrick had returned ahead of her to help ready the nursery.

"Has our room always been so big?" he'd asked. "And bright?"

He would return to work in two days, and Marissa was taking off two weeks to stay home with Laura. She was terrified. And maybe a little thrilled. She loved Laura and she loved Jen. She could do this. For Jen.

She would never give up on Jen's recovery, and she liked to imagine the day when a drug-free Jen would pick up a happy and well-adjusted Laura and they could be together, mother and daughter. And forever, Marissa would know she'd played a role in that. This felt as important to her as math, and for her, that was a rarity.

CHAPTER 41

AMANDA

29 WEEKS PREGNANT

Reflex smiling has arrived. Baby is preparing for selfies.

—Your Best Pregnancy

January 22, 2018

Amanda was dressing when the doorbell rang. Derrick had left for work moments before, and she wondered if he'd locked himself out of the house. She pulled on a pair of black tights and a gray sweater and walked downstairs to the front door. She glanced out the sidelight and met Ralph's eyes. She reflexively pulled back, but it was too late. He'd seen her. She reluctantly opened the door.

"You didn't return my calls," he said. And then his eyes settled on her belly. His mouth opened as if he were going to speak, but he just stared.

"I've been busy," she said, wanting to distract him. As if she had a prayer of that.

"I'll say. Did you listen to my voice mails?"

She shook her head. He'd called three times over the past week, but she hadn't listened to the messages. She just wanted to leave the entire mess behind her. "I documented everything I did on Project Iustitia."

"I wasn't calling about work. Can I come in?" He wore slacks and a dress shirt, no tie, his typical office attire. She assumed that was his next stop.

Instead of letting him in, she stepped forward onto the porch and closed the door. Ralph always took control. She wasn't going to let him do that now.

"You just left."

She nodded. "My husband. I told him about us."

Ralph looked surprised. "He made you quit?"

Amanda folded her arms. "Do you blame him?"

Ralph shrugged. "I had no idea why you left. Zack emailed that you were resigning effective immediately for personal reasons. He forwarded your documentation on the project. I thought—"

"What? That I was heartbroken?" They'd continued to work together for three weeks after she'd ended the affair. He'd been icy but professional.

"I didn't know what to think. What was I supposed to think?"

She looked at him. She didn't know what to say.

"I never said it, but I had feelings for you. I tried not to admit it, even to myself—"

She scoffed. "It wasn't the first time you did it."

He sighed. "I wish I hadn't said that. I'm sorry. I was hurt." He paused. "I love you, Amanda."

She laughed before she realized the cruelty in it. She stopped. "Why didn't you tell me this when we—"

"I should have. Would it have mattered?"

She didn't know. It had never occurred to her that he felt anything for her, so she'd never entertained the idea of them having something serious. Sex with Ralph had been about feeling and not feeling, all at once. She'd felt sexual with him, desire and desired, and that had allowed her to feel the dissolution of her marriage less. It had extinguished, if only momentarily, her feeling of aloneness.

"I'm telling you now. Does it matter?"

She felt trapped, claustrophobic. She wanted him to leave.

"Is that our . . ." He nodded to her swollen belly.

"I'm trying to put my marriage back together." The words sounded ridiculous even to her. She didn't know the first thing about putting her marriage back together. She was trying to survive.

"Why did you tell him about us? Is it because you're pregnant?"

She could hear the pulse in her temple, the racing blood. "I want you to leave."

"Is that my child?" There was hope in his voice.

She shook her head. "I'm not pregnant. I miscarried."

His face collapsed. "I'm so sorry. When?"

She paused as if to think. "Sixteen weeks ago."

He stared at her in disbelief. "Fuck you."

She turned to go back inside. "Please leave."

"If you're having my child," he hissed, "I have rights."

"I'm not having your child. I'm not pregnant."

"I don't know what you told your husband, but if that child is mine, I'm doing what's right. I want to raise our child with you. I'll talk to your husband myself if I have to." He stepped down from the porch. "We never had a chance, but maybe we should have." He turned and walked to his Jaguar, parked on the curb in front of her house.

She felt relief as she watched him drive away. But it was short lived. She had no idea what he would do next.

CHAPTER 42

PATRICK

7 MONTHS AFTER THE ACCIDENT

January 22, 2018

From: Patrick Davis
To: Amanda Jackson
Subject: RE: Unusual Conditions

Korsakoff syndrome is a memory disorder and it's often accompanied by confabulation, which means that the patient fills memory gaps with invented stories. The patient is unaware of the confabulation. They're convinced that their invented stories are real memories. Korsakoff syndrome is caused by a thiamine deficiency often from chronic alcohol abuse.

~

"You're finally fixing that?" Marissa asked. Patrick was squatting beside the toilet in their downstairs bathroom, replacing one of the missing nuts that secured the seat. If they weren't careful, the toilet seat would slip out of place when they sat down.

"We'll see," he replied.

"I believe in you," she said, though her smile suggested differently. His DIY track record was spotty. He'd managed to unclog the bathroom sink, which required disassembling and reassembling the pipes, but his attempts to replace the brake light on Marissa's car had ended with a trip to the dealership. "And it's okay if you don't. I've learned to balance on the seat. I'm off to get some fresh air."

He looked up. "Want company? I'm almost finished."

"No," she said. "I don't even know where I'm going. I'll take a walk somewhere, maybe grab lunch."

"I have legs and a stomach."

She laughed. "I know. I just need to think. I'll be back in a few hours," she said with a note of finality.

He didn't respond. He was resigned to not seeing her when she was busy with math. But she wasn't doing math. She was blocked, and still, she couldn't be bothered to spend a few hours with him.

He tightened the nut, and the toilet seat seemed secure, but he would wait a week before claiming victory. He offered no guarantees on his workmanship.

He thought about texting Amanda to invite her to lunch, but he worried that would be too soon. They'd met at Piedmont Park the day before and had plans for tomorrow. He sat down at the dining room table to finish the jigsaw puzzle, which reminded him of the visit from Amanda's husband. He tried not to think about that. He felt bad for the man, but he couldn't stop seeing Amanda. He felt so lonely sometimes that thoughts of her were the only thing that kept him from drowning in it.

When he turned to Marissa, there was nothing there. They hadn't shared anything real since the solar eclipse. That had been five months ago. His mind drifted back to that day as he searched for the next puzzle piece.

~

"What time is it?" he asked. It was early morning, pitch dark, and Marissa was shaking him.

"Four fifteen. If we don't leave soon, we'll get stuck in traffic."

"Leave?"

"For Anderson," she told him. "The eclipse is in ten hours."

"Eclipse?"

Marissa had been waiting for the 2017 solar eclipse since Patrick met her in 2005. Anderson, South Carolina, two and a half hours north of Atlanta, was in the path of totality. She'd booked a hotel room and ordered viewing glasses in late 2016. But she hadn't mentioned anything about the eclipse to him in months.

"I thought you forgot about it," he said. She didn't respond. "I mean, I'm glad you didn't forget. I just didn't know we were still going." She'd been consumed with math and communicating with the dead.

"I didn't know until now," she told him. "I didn't think I could do it, but I can't not do it." She was excited.

"Turn on the light," he told her. "I'll take a shower, and we can hit the road."

~

The road was dark, and Marissa chattered about astronomy as Patrick drove. She explained the new moon and the ecliptic plane and why total eclipses were rare in any particular location. "We'll stand in the moon's shadow," she said breathlessly. She told him things he didn't know about the moon. "It moves farther from the earth each year, a little more than three centimeters." She told him that when the moon formed four and a half billion years ago, days on earth had been just five hours long. "The moon has been slowing the earth's rotation since, making our days longer."

"Someone should tell the moon I need an extra six hours in every day," he quipped.

The sun was rising when they arrived in Anderson. They stopped for pancakes and coffee, and as they ate, Marissa fretted over the weather. "I chose Anderson because Stella lives here." Stella was a former graduate student of Marissa's. "I didn't bother to calculate the probability of cloud cover," she said apologetically.

"I think we'll be fine."

"Can you imagine," she asked, "what it would feel like to know that an eclipse is happening right behind the clouds blocking your view?"

~

They stood on Stella's back porch with her friends and family and watched through solar viewers as the edge of the moon passed over the edge of the sun. "It's happening," Marissa said, her voice humming.

It was Patrick's first solar eclipse. He'd put on his glasses and seen only darkness. When he'd looked up, the sun had been a lone, glowing orb in the sky. Beautiful.

Totality was several minutes away, and guests moved between the kitchen and the porch, carrying plates of food Stella had prepared for the event. A boy and girl sat on the steps, working against time to build a pinhole camera.

"I can't believe it's finally here," Marissa whispered.

The moon worked its way across the sun, and conversation quieted as its shadow swallowed all but a sliver of sunlight. Crickets began to chirp, and Patrick shivered in anticipation. Marissa took his hand. He watched through his solar viewers until suddenly the darkness was complete. He removed his glasses, and his mouth fell open at the sight of the full moon surrounded by the silvery corona of the sun. Marissa gasped, and he took his eyes off the sky to look at her. Wonder bathed her face as she stared skyward, unblinking. She was beautiful. He clutched

Marissa's hand tighter as he returned his eyes to the majesty of the eclipse. He felt small, insignificant. In the face of this most awesome of nature's displays, he felt as if he knew nothing and understood less. The mere existence of these grand bodies, the sun and the moon, made anything seem possible. He glanced at Marissa again. She was transfixed. He was in awe of this woman who'd led him here, into the shadow of the moon. She wasn't just smart. She was the most brilliant person he knew, and he knew the greatest living neuroscientists. She was creative and disciplined, and if consciousness continued to exist after the death of the body, and if there was any way for the living to access that consciousness, then Marissa, he believed, could do it. Even before he'd gotten to know her, really know her, he'd known that she was special, destined for greatness. Perhaps now, he just needed to open his mind and let her lead the way.

The total eclipse lasted for 150 seconds, and yet, Patrick felt as if he'd experienced a lifetime of insight. As the moon moved past the sun, Marissa turned to him and laughed. "You're crying," she said.

He wiped his cheeks. "I'm just cleaning my face."

She embraced him. "I love you." When she pulled away, she was crying also.

∼

They didn't make it to their dinner reservation in Greenville. When they stopped at the hotel to check in, the sight of their bed was too much for Patrick. They hadn't made love in two months, and the rituals of a fine meal seemed interminable.

"I want you to think about this over dinner," Marissa said playfully as he unbuttoned her shirt. He kissed her neck until they were on the same page.

∼

"Do hotels have the best kitchens in the world?" Marissa asked. "Or is room service so good because it's delivered to your door?"

~

Patrick stood and left the puzzle unsolved for now. He turned on the television just to kill the silence. After the solar eclipse, he'd thought that Marissa was on her way back to normal. He'd been wrong. Upon their return home, she'd disappeared into math. And now, even when she had no math to hide in, she was still unreachable.

His own memory of the eclipse had been darkened by disillusionment. The celestial display had triggered something akin to a spiritual experience in him. For a moment, he'd believed that Marissa's goals transcended the bargaining of grief. He would be exercising his own form of denial to believe that the sight of the eclipse had gifted him with insight. Spirituality, he knew, was mediated by the temporal lobe. No divinity required. Epilepsy could lead to hallucinations that were experienced as holy.

He'd met people at dinner parties who turned hostile when they learned that he was a neuroscientist. He understood why. The absence of understanding allowed people to project magic upon phenomena. A spiritual experience could be explained by something otherworldly. Human intelligence could be described as sacred. To him, the revelations of science were magic. To others, science pulled back the curtain and revealed a lackluster world they didn't wish to live in.

CHAPTER 43

DERRICK

17 WEEKS AFTER THE MISCARRIAGE

January 25, 2018

Derrick almost believed that Amanda wasn't having an affair. Again. Her denial seemed sincere. Patrick Davis had given all indications of being forthright. Still, when she'd left the house this morning, he'd followed her. When he saw her pull into a motel parking lot, he wished he hadn't.

He idled across the street and watched as she sat in her car. Perhaps she was lost, consulting a map on her phone. *Please, let her be lost.* A silver Prius pulled into the spot next to hers. With something akin to panic, he watched Patrick Davis egress. Patrick stopped at Amanda's car and exchanged words through her window before entering the motel office alone.

Derrick's vision blurred. His hands trembled. He could barely breathe. Confronting them was not an option. He imagined getting out of his car, sprinting across the street, and—passing out. He saw himself, voice shaky: *What are you doing with my wife?* Their amusement as he collapsed into an unconscious heap before them.

Patrick exited the office and brandished a key. Amanda climbed out of her car and followed him to a room. Derrick wanted to leave, but he wasn't fit to drive. Patrick unlocked the door and disappeared inside with Amanda.

Four years ago, Derrick had applied for a gun permit. He'd gotten as far as registering for a training course when Amanda nixed the whole thing. She had just stopped taking the pill, and she refused to have a gun and a child in the same house. *If you want us to be safe, don't bring a deadly weapon into our home.* Amanda didn't know it, but she'd saved her life that day. Derrick wanted to shoot his way into that motel room and kill them both. But what if he couldn't kill himself afterward? What if he ran out of bullets or, worse, survived the self-inflicted gunshot wound? There would be a trial, Amanda's mother weeping quietly from the gallery. The world would see him as the bad guy. He was relieved not to have a gun.

He pictured what they were doing behind that door. He thought of Amanda's body, her naked thighs and breasts. He thought about touching them. He thought about Patrick Davis touching them. He drove home.

~

The beauty of the unblemished sky mocked him. God felt unreal, and he wondered if he was wrong about the faith pregnancy. Maybe she wasn't pregnant at all. Phantom pregnancy was real. And really, what was special about Amanda? She was a married woman who fucked other men.

Calvin, a fellow sales rep, liked to watch this video, a pack of hyenas taking down a wildebeest. *Love and loyalty,* Calvin said, *rely on unnatural, fragile conditions. This is the most real thing in the world. When you remove fantasies and idealism, when you remove everything, you're left with struggle. We envision the world as a Disney-built theme park. Really, it's violence and suffering and survival.*

Derrick liked Calvin but found him morbid. Now, he thought of the wildebeest. Just as Derrick prayed to God to save his marriage, the wildebeest probably prayed to have the hyena's teeth removed from its throat. And wish granted, the hyena extracted its teeth, only to let the blood and life drain out. He'd only just found God, and already, he seemed to be losing Him.

Now that he was home, he didn't want to be there. Amanda had chosen the house because of the spacious rooms and abundant natural light, but today, it felt claustrophobic. He turned on the television, but it was just noise. He turned it off. He stood in front of the window overlooking the backyard. Four years ago, he'd stood with Amanda in this very spot, minus the furnishings. *This is the house,* she'd told him.

She'd stopped taking the pill weeks before. They'd enjoyed condo living, but it was time for the next phase. She'd dragged him from sub-urb to suburb, looking for the community where they would raise their children. He'd had opinions about home styles and floor plans, but he'd acquiesced to her because she'd felt so strongly about it all. She'd spent hours scrolling through pictures online. She could cite school ratings and crime statistics. She'd dreamed about houses.

And now, the weight of the moment crushing his shoulders, he looked out the window and contemplated starting over. Weak, he leaned against the sofa arm for support. How many false starts would he endure on the singles scene? There were no guarantees in the unreg-ulated, wild world of dating.

Even if he managed to find the perfect woman, even if he fell in love with her and she with him, it wouldn't be the first time. How could he know that she wouldn't, out of the blue, confess to an affair? For weeks, he'd replayed memories, the early days with Amanda, looking for signs he'd missed, warnings that she would betray him. There weren't any. She said herself that she'd never imagined she would cheat. If she couldn't see it coming, how could he? How could he see it next time with the next perfect woman?

He felt shame, and perhaps this was the most painful aspect of it all, to know that he would take Amanda back if she walked through the door right now and apologized. In the weeks following her confession, he'd plotted a road map back for them. The first stop was a nightclub in the city that catered to thirtysomethings. It was exciting. For the first time in seven years, he gave himself license to have sex with someone who wasn't Amanda, and nearly every woman in the club was appealing. He met a flight attendant on layover. She had a fantastic body, and after several drinks and a few rounds on the dance floor, she invited him back to her hotel. For seven years, he'd resented monogamy and admiration from afar. But clearly, he wanted what he couldn't have, because he couldn't do this. The fantasy was nice, but he wanted Amanda. He wanted everything to be right between them. Revenge sex was a dead end on his road map to forgiveness. And that was frightening, because what if he did divorce Amanda? Was there any guarantee that he would ever again want another woman?

The second stop on the road map to forgiveness was an abortion clinic. He knew Amanda wanted a baby, but why not adopt? He could raise a child who wasn't biologically his, but he could not raise the child of a man who'd fucked his wife. What would he tell his friends and family? Would he share his debasement, or would he conceal the child's parentage? What would he tell the child? Would the child, for the rest of his or her life, provide Derrick's medical history at doctors' offices? And then there was the question, the one he couldn't bring himself to ask Amanda. He tried not to think about it, but it would always be there. Had she had the affair in hopes that this guy would succeed where Derrick had failed: In getting her pregnant?

He knew that ultimatums were dangerous. This child was her blood. He was not. He wouldn't bet the ranch on her choosing him.

Give it a chance, she'd pleaded. *If you do, you'll love the baby, and we'll do what feels right. We can get through it. And if you can't love the baby, I'll understand. I'll let you go. I won't ask anything of you.*

He knew she was trying to be reasonable, but it hurt that he was so dispensable in scenario number two. She wanted to fix their marriage, yes, but if he couldn't get over the small, inconsequential fact that another man had fathered her child, she would let him go. She wouldn't ask anything of him.

"Thanks a fucking lot," he said now as if she were standing before him, as if they could have the conversation again.

He walked to the kitchen and opened the medication drawer. He rifled through cold and flu pills and pain relief until he found temazepam. He twisted the safety cap. Good. At least a dozen pills. He grabbed an unopened bottle of rum from the pantry and headed back to his car.

He retrieved the envelope with Patrick Davis's address scrawled across the back from the glove compartment. He would be waiting when the good doctor came home.

CHAPTER 44

PATRICK

8 MONTHS AFTER THE ACCIDENT

January 25, 2018

Patrick couldn't believe they were doing this. "It seems wrong," he'd told her when she'd suggested it.

"It's far from wrong. We're righting a wrong. Living to the age of thirty-six without seeing *An Affair to Remember* is wrong."

"I can rent it," he'd suggested. "We can watch it at the same time. We can stay on the phone while we watch."

"I love technology, but I don't think the cell phone was ever meant to be a substitute for watching a movie with another human being. We'll rent a room. If you have any urges you haven't shared with me, I'm sure you can control them."

Patrick blushed, which embarrassed him further.

"God," she said, "I'm teasing you. I look like I'm seven months pregnant. I'm sure you can control yourself."

She looked beautiful, but Patrick said nothing. He nodded agreement to renting a room.

~

No double beds had been available, so Patrick turned down the spread on the king while Amanda logged in to her streaming account on the television. The room looked clean and there were no suspicious smells, which was all Patrick could ask for in a budget motel.

"Are you ready?" Amanda asked. She looked jubilant. She'd brought popcorn and chips and salsa. "When I was in college, I read that eating while watching television taps into our brains' pleasure centers, basically screwing us up. I told my grandmother, and you would've thought I was advocating burning Bibles. She told me she would unenroll me from my fancy university if I brought more crazy ideas home."

Patrick laughed.

"I learned not to mess with my grandmother's television snacks."

Patrick propped their pillows against the headboard, took off his shoes, and climbed into bed. Amanda followed his lead and cued up the movie.

"I have to warn you," she said, "I don't talk during movies, but I do pause them to talk. Basically, whenever a thought comes into my head. You're welcome to do the same." She pressed play.

"I couldn't watch this for three years after my grandmother died," she said during the credits. "I still miss her, but the memories are good."

Patrick wondered if his memories of Laura would ever be good. He doubted it. He forced himself to concentrate on the movie, which wasn't difficult. The dialogue was snappy, and he wondered what Cary Grant's character would've said in response to Amanda's comments about controlling his urges. Even now, with all the time in the world, Patrick couldn't think up a witty retort. Not one that he could deliver with confidence anyway. He was no Nickie Ferrante. Amanda, on the other hand, was more beautiful than Deborah Kerr. She was watching the screen, rapt, and he took the opportunity to study her profile. She turned to him and smiled. He turned back to the screen.

Several minutes later, she paused the movie. "The best scenes by far happen when Grant and Kerr are onscreen together. That's kind of a problem for the film once they leave the ship." She pressed play without a reply from him.

When Deborah Kerr's character became a music teacher, his mind wandered. Maybe it was the children's singing, but a particular memory wouldn't leave him alone.

He'd been standing over Laura's crib watching her sleep.

I have a confession to make, Marissa had whispered. He turned. He hadn't known she was there. *When I said I wasn't ready for a child, it wasn't really about my work. I knew we could hire a nanny to help. I was worried that I carried something within me that would lead me to abandon our child. Maybe I would use work as an excuse. I don't know. But standing here, looking at Laura, I would rather die than abandon her.*

Patrick had taken Marissa's hand.

I wonder if something happens to parents as their children get older.

What do you mean?

If my parents felt this way about me when I was a baby, I don't see how they left.

You're not your parents, he'd told her. *You're the most loyal person I know. Jen is lucky to have you as a sister. Laura is lucky to have you as an aunt. I'm lucky to have you as a wife. And when we have a child, he or she will be lucky to have you as a mother.*

Amanda paused the movie. "What are you thinking about?"

Patrick stammered. "I'm watching."

"I've watched you watch the movie," she said. "Where were you just now?"

He turned to look at her. Her eyes were beseeching. She wanted to know. "The kids and their singing is getting to me."

"You don't like it?"

"It's fine." He sighed. "I've told you a little about Laura."

"Your niece," Amanda said.

"Right. I guess you know she passed away."

She took his hand. "I suspected. I know you can't talk about it."

211

"I wanted children and Marissa wanted to wait, and I almost left her because of it."

"Why didn't you?"

"She asked me not to give up on her. And I loved her. Anyway, when we brought Laura home from the hospital, I worried that Marissa wouldn't bond with her. My worries were for nothing. They bonded almost immediately. Everything went beautifully. Laura was even a good sleeper until somewhere in her sixth month. She started waking multiple times during the night, every night. It didn't take long to get her back to sleep, but it took a toll on us. We had trouble getting back to sleep. Her crib was in our room, so we would both wake up when she cried. But we took turns getting up. One night, Marissa must have been exhausted, because she didn't stir when Laura cried. I got up twice in a row. The third time, I woke Marissa. I was drifting back to sleep when Marissa screamed."

They sat in silence, the movie paused, Amanda watching him. "What happened?" she finally asked, almost a whisper.

"When I got to them, they were at the bottom of the stairs. Marissa had a dislocated shoulder, and Laura had a—" He stopped talking. He couldn't bring himself to say *skull fracture*. He didn't have to. Amanda wrapped her arms around him. She stroked his back as she held him.

CHAPTER 45

PATRICK

1 DAY AFTER THE ACCIDENT

May 26, 2017

Patrick drove in silence, Marissa in the passenger seat. They were on their way to Dahlonega, Georgia, seventy miles to the north. Jen was in a mountain-bound rehab facility, doing the tedious work of putting her life on a better path. Patrick felt like a cruise missile, pointed at an unsuspecting target and carrying a payload that cared nothing for sanctity or beauty. Marissa had spoken to Jen's counselor, and he'd suggested they speak to Jen midmorning after yoga. *It's her favorite part of the day,* he'd explained.

Patrick didn't dare play music. His emotions were not within his control, and the wrong melody could very well send them off the road. He was thinking about the funeral. He'd never thought he would plan services for an infant.

"Would you prefer a funeral or a memorial service?"

"Neither," Marissa answered without hesitation.

He waited for her to say more. When she didn't, he asked, "Would you like to hear my preference?"

"I can't talk about this, Patrick," Marissa bit out.

He let it drop. After ten miles of silence, she said, "I can't share my grief. It's personal."

"I'd like to give her a proper goodbye."

"For what?" Marissa snapped. "It's too late to do anything for Laura. She's gone."

"I need to do something for her."

"It's not for her. It's for you."

"And I guess doing nothing is your way of honoring her?"

Marissa didn't respond. And then she cried, whimpers giving way to great sobs. He touched her shoulder. "I'm sorry." She continued to cry. He focused on driving.

~

They passed rows of cottages as the gravel road meandered through manicured lawns to a large house. He pulled into the lot and killed the engine. His legs were stiff when he stepped out of the car.

"Tell me how you want to do this," he said. Marissa looked like she was going to be sick. Her eyes were red from crying, her face washed out. "Do you want me to come in with you?"

She shook her head. "I'll do it alone. I don't know what to say."

He hugged her, buried his nose in her hair, fragrant with peach-scented conditioner. "You'll figure it out. There's no easy way to do it. Just let her know we're here for her. We can check her out today, and she can stay with us for as long as she needs."

Marissa nodded.

He checked his cell signal. Two bars. "Call me when you need me. I'll take a walk." He nodded at the sign for a nature trail.

~

The trail felt strange, almost otherworldly. He was surrounded by green, the basest signifier of life, and the sky was obscenely blue. And he had a feeling, deep in his core, that there was some way out of this. If he could just step outside everything, he would find a solution, a way to go back and beat Marissa out of bed. Or perhaps he could tell Marissa to let Laura cry it out. That would've made them all miserable, but Laura would be alive. He let his mind drift, and every thought crashed into one of two impenetrable walls: fantasy, where he could dream up a time-defying device but where he could never reside; and reality, where he was doomed to live in a world without Laura.

Even the sound of his phone's ringtone, intimately familiar, felt imagined, an affront to his new existence. Marissa was crying when he answered. "Can we please leave now?" she said.

"Sure. Is Jen coming with us?"

"Please, let's go."

He hurried back to the car. Marissa was standing beside the locked passenger door. She wasn't crying, but she looked beaten. He unlocked her door before taking his place in the driver's seat.

"Do you want to talk about it?"

"It was awful."

For a moment, Marissa told him, Jen had been happy to see her. Surprised but happy. Then Jen had sensed that something was wrong. *Is it Patrick?* she'd asked. Jen's counselor had given them the privacy of his office.

Marissa choked up and Patrick let the silence ride. They made their way past the cottages, and then he pointed them toward home.

"She blames me," Marissa said.

"She doesn't. She's in shock."

"'Laura was my ticket back.' She kept repeating that." Marissa closed her eyes and exhaled. "The look on her face. I'm going to have nightmares about it."

~

Patrick's sleep came in fits and starts that night, and he had broken dreams of Laura, the two of them trapped in a dark, windowless room. Marissa slept a quiet, drugged sleep. Dreamless, she reported. They were still lying in bed when Jen's counselor called. Jen was gone. She'd left rehab during the night.

CHAPTER 46

PATRICK

8 MONTHS AFTER THE ACCIDENT

January 26, 2018

It was early afternoon, and Patrick was listening to music on his phone, trying to think up an excuse to text Amanda. They'd watched *An Affair to Remember* the day before and had lunch together afterward, so maybe a text would be too much.

"Fifties?" Marissa asked.

He jumped. Fats Domino played with all the bluster tiny speakers could manage. He turned the volume down. "Nostalgia."

She smiled. "Nostalgia? Your parents were children."

"I would not want to live in a time before the internet, but you can't beat fifties music."

"We lived in a time before the internet," she said. "Most of our childhood. It wasn't so bad."

Now he smiled. "Remember looking things up in the encyclopedia? If it wasn't there, it wasn't anywhere. The internet is better."

"No argument here. Would you like to take a walk?"

The suggestion startled him. She hadn't suggested anything in so long. "Sure."

~

Their neighborhood was mature, the streets lined with oak trees as old as the houses. It was scenic, even more beautiful to Patrick when he walked hand in hand with Marissa.

"Life," she said, "is not what I expected."

He wondered, as he often did, if she was working up to ask for a divorce. He felt the familiar tightness in his chest.

"I didn't know it would be this hard."

"It's hard now," he agreed. "We have to get through it."

"I haven't been there for you."

He couldn't disagree. He could accept that they hadn't mourned together, but she'd denied him a memorial service for Laura. He would always regret not having a proper goodbye. "I don't blame you." He squeezed her hand.

"I used to tell myself that putting math before others wasn't selfish because I put it before my own needs. But really, math is a need for me."

"You've done something extraordinary," he said. "Or so I've heard."

"I've heard that, too, but they don't understand my work."

"Frederick doesn't understand it?"

She shook her head. "He sees the beauty in it, but he doesn't understand it. The physicists see potential applications, but they don't understand it either. They all appreciate it, but . . ."

"Do you understand it?" he asked.

She looked up at him, surprised. "Of course."

"What you're trying to do," he said, "I don't understand it."

"There are many facets of reality," she told him. "There's what we perceive with our senses. We know there's visible light because we see it, but what about the invisible spectrums: radio, infrared, ultraviolet. No one could imagine those until someone discovered them."

"How did that happen?" Patrick asked.

"How were they discovered?"

He nodded.

"William Herschel used a prism to split visible light. He was trying to measure the temperature of each color. When he measured the temperature next to the red light of the spectrum, where no detectable color existed, it was the hottest of all. He was measuring the temperature of infrared light."

"You're full of interesting facts," Patrick said.

She smiled. "I'm probing the structure of unseen realities through mathematics. I have no knowledge of these realities, so I listen to my intuition and follow each step to its logical conclusion."

"You have no idea where you're going, how you're going to—"

"Communicate with the dead," she finished. "No. It never occurred to me that it was possible until . . . I noticed something. Do you remember our first date?" she asked.

He nodded. He'd given her a prepared lecture on the state of the art in intuition problem-solving research.

"I wanted to know how we can suddenly notice things that have always been there. Now, I don't question it. I just follow where it leads. Tomorrow morning, when I wake up, I'm going to let it take me. I'm going to finish my work."

"And tonight?" he asked.

She grinned. "I was hoping my husband would take me to a nice restaurant. Afterward, we can come home and dance to fifties love songs, see where that leads."

∽

They dined at Lush. Marissa, uncharacteristically, told a story about Jen from their childhood. "She was fifteen, a year or so before my father left. We typically all went to the mall on Sunday afternoons, but Jen didn't want to go. Do you remember when there were bookstores in the mall?"

Patrick nodded. "And record stores."

"My parents allowed me to buy one book a week. Anyway, on that Sunday, when my parents and I got home, Jen was screaming, and Rigley was barking. We ran up the stairs. Rigley was standing at Jen's open bedroom door. Dog treats were scattered at his feet. If you knew Rigley, you would know that he didn't leave treats on the floor. Jen stood in the hallway, looking like a ghost.

"'What's in there?' my father said and stepped forward. Rigley turned to my father and gave him a look. You've seen pictures of Rigley, but you can't understand the ferocity of his looks." Rigley had been a big dog with intense pale-brown eyes and a long black coat laced with silver. "People asked me if he was part wolf. That day, he looked full wolf. My father stopped. He turned to Jen. She said nothing.

"'Rigley,' I said, 'sit.' Rigley relaxed at the sound of my voice. He truly was my dog. He sat, and our father passed by him into the bedroom."

"What did he find?" Patrick asked.

Marissa giggled. "A boy. Jen's boyfriend. He was standing on Jen's bed as if Rigley couldn't get to him up there. Rigley wouldn't let him out of the room, and he wouldn't let Jen in. Jen was grounded for a month, and she was so angry at Rigley. I told her that Rigley was trying to keep her safe, but she didn't believe it. 'He wanted to get me in trouble.'"

Patrick laughed. He felt ebullient, as if they were riding through this night on a beam of magic. He feared that an abrupt movement could break the spell, that he would awaken alone in their bed, Marissa working furiously in her office.

He wondered if, within this cocoon, on this night, it was safe to talk about Laura. He always wanted to talk about her, but only with someone who had known and loved her. Only with Marissa.

He was relieved when—before he could do something to ruin the evening, like bring up Laura—Marissa excused herself to go to the restroom. Instead of checking his phone while he waited, he allowed himself to think about Jen, dangerous territory on a lovely night.

~

Six days after Laura died, four days after Jen fled rehab, a body was found in an abandoned building. An overdose. Patrick went to the hospital while Marissa waited at home, clinging to a modicum of hope. *Maybe it isn't her,* Marissa said. *Maybe some woman stole Jen's ID.*

A clerk led Patrick to a conference room and handed him a manila envelope. "Take your time," she said. She slipped out of the room and pulled the door shut behind herself. The envelope felt too slight for the significance within.

Late one night, when they were still in graduate school, Patrick had asked Marissa to tell him her greatest fear. She hadn't hesitated. *That my sister will disappear. That I'll never know what happened to her.*

What would be better? he wondered now, the envelope hot in his hands.

He needed Jen to be alive. He would never tell Marissa—he would probably never tell anyone—that as he'd brought Laura home from the hospital, he'd hoped for Jen's death. He wanted to be Laura's father, and he wanted Marissa to be her mother, no ambiguity, no complications. Laura deserved a happy, amazing life, and he couldn't see that happening if Jen lived.

Now, as he pulled the photographs from the envelope, he couldn't bear the thought of Jen dead at forty-one.

~

"What?" Patrick asked. Marissa was staring at him between sips of wine.

"I was just thinking. You and I have had some good times. I let the math get in the way, but there were times when I didn't."

It sounded like a question. He nodded. "We've had some great times. And I always knew what I was getting with you. In graduate school, I was obsessed with Capgras syndrome. I haven't experienced that again, and I envy your passion."

"You shouldn't." She turned pensive. "If, in the future, I can't be here with you, I want you to walk away."

"What?" He took her hand. "Where did that come from?"

"I don't think I have a future. I've done terrible things."

He felt the spell cracking, and he wanted to patch it.

"We should go," she said and forced a smile. "I don't want to ruin the evening before we get started."

He flagged the waiter for the check.

~

Songs were short in the fifties, but Patrick had Marissa undressed before "In the Still of the Night" ended. By the last note of "Only You," they were in bed. He was startled by the feel of her, the softness, as if his memory couldn't adequately store the pleasure of contact with her skin. He delayed entering her because he knew he wouldn't last long, and he wanted this to last forever. He lost himself in her. And still, there was a part of his mind that played over their day. It played over their walk and dinner. Her words: *I want you to walk away.* This entire day, running into the night, felt like a goodbye.

CHAPTER 47

AMANDA

29 WEEKS PREGNANT

January 27, 2018

Detective Sebold: *I'm sorry for some of these questions. I only have one more that I hate to ask. Just for the sake of thoroughness: Are you romantically involved outside of your marriage?*

Amanda: *No.*

Interview at Amanda's residence, 9:45 p.m., Friday, January 26, 2018

~

Are you up?

A text message from Patrick. It was one thirty, Saturday morning. Amanda texted him back.

Against my will. No sleep in sight.

When she'd lived in the city, noisy foot traffic from the bars had occupied these hours. Now, she was propped in bed, in perfect silence, unable to concentrate on the magazine in her hand. They exchanged a few more texts before he called her.

"Sorry to get back to you so late. Marissa and I went out for dinner."

"Oh." Amanda had eaten cereal. Alone. She'd sent him three text messages.

"It was nice, but . . ." He trailed off. She didn't move to fill the silence. "It felt like a goodbye."

"I'm sorry. Are you okay?"

"I don't know. How are you?"

She didn't know if she should tell him, but how could she not? "Derrick is missing."

"Missing?"

She nodded, forgetting that he couldn't see her. "He hasn't been home since Thursday. I reported it a few hours ago."

"You have any idea where he is?"

"No. The detective doesn't suspect foul play. He's seen people disappear on purpose before. But he isn't ruling anything out."

"Why would Derrick disappear?"

She sighed. "I don't know." She herself had thought about disappearing. The prospect of ending their marriage felt so daunting at times that vanishing seemed preferable. But there were things she could never escape. Wherever she went, false pregnancy would follow. "He left his cell phone at home, which is unusual for him. The detective said people do that when they're trying to disappear. But I can't believe he wouldn't say goodbye to his parents. They're flying in this morning."

"Are you okay, Amanda?"

No, she wasn't okay. "The detective asked me a lot of questions. I wasn't completely honest."

"About what?"

Did he really have to ask? "Most missing persons cases are resolved within a few days."

"I'm coming over. You shouldn't be alone."

"No," she blurted before she could change her mind and ask him to hurry. What if Derrick came home and found them?

Her mind raced. Threats, practical and unlikely, loomed all around her. The floor caving beneath her weight. A house fire. A home invasion. "Can you stay on the phone until I fall asleep?"

~

Police were canvassing the neighborhood as Amanda met Derrick's parents at the airport. Lorraine embraced Amanda and held her for a long time. Henry gave Amanda an awkward hug. She started to lift Lorraine's suitcase to put it in the trunk, but Lorraine snapped at Henry to do it.

"We'll bring Derrick home," Lorraine told Amanda with conviction. She sat in the passenger seat. Henry was in the back. "And we're going to take care of you, minimize stress on the baby." She touched Amanda's belly. "If you need anything—I used to crave olives late at night—Henry will get it for you. Anytime."

Amanda thanked her. She didn't tell them that Derrick hadn't been making late-night runs to feed her.

An argument erupted because Lorraine wanted to meet with Detective Sebold straightaway. Henry felt that the detective could best serve Derrick by looking for him. "Not in front of Amanda," Lorraine finally barked, ending the disagreement. She called Detective Sebold, and he agreed to meet them at Amanda and Derrick's house.

Lorraine had written a to-do list on the plane, and she read it aloud as Amanda drove. She was going over it a third time as they pulled into the driveway. Amanda was assigned the sedentary task of calling hospitals and Derrick's friends and family. Lorraine and Henry would hit the streets, posting flyers far and wide. Lorraine would take point on media outreach.

Media. The word set Amanda's sympathetic nervous system afire. The media loved secrets. Amanda didn't want hers disturbed.

~

After a brief meeting with Detective Sebold, Lorraine and Henry left for the copy shop, and Amanda settled at the kitchen table to make phone calls. She started with hospitals. She was between calls when Meredith's name popped up on her caller ID.

"I'm coming to Atlanta," Meredith said the moment Amanda answered.

"You don't have to do that. Derrick's parents—"

"I'm sure they're wonderful company, but I'll see you tomorrow evening."

"I'd rather you didn't. It's just—"

"I caught Mom on the computer booking a plane ticket. It's either her or me."

"Any requests from the grocery store?" Amanda asked.

~

She'd worked her way through most of Derrick's many friends when she wondered who Derrick would call were the roles reversed. His list would be much shorter. As would be the conversations. *I don't know what Amanda has been up to over the past five months, much less the past three days.*

When she ran out of numbers to dial, she created a Facebook page to solicit information. She booted Derrick's computer and went through the files on his drive and his browsing history. She had his Windows password because she'd set it up for him, but she had to guess at the one he used for his email. After two failed attempts, she tried the Windows password. It worked. She'd warned him against using the same password for everything, but he hadn't listened. She accessed his social media and credit card accounts. She didn't find anything of interest.

~

The police issued a press release asking the public for help. Derrick's parents offered a $20,000 reward to anyone with information leading to his safe return. Lorraine looked exhausted after a second day of handing out flyers.

"Do you mind if I look through Derrick's things?" Lorraine asked. She was convinced that foul play was involved, but she was equally certain that Derrick was alive. She didn't ask Amanda's opinion.

"Of course." Amanda led Lorraine to their bedroom. "The bottom two drawers are his," she said, showing Lorraine to the dresser. "This closet is mostly his."

"Thank you." Lorraine looked as if she might collapse with gratitude. Amanda did not, in her own estimation, measure up to this woman. Lorraine was focused on Derrick, on bringing him home. Amanda was afraid. Much of the time, she didn't even know what she was afraid of. A good wife would be worried sick about her husband. It would never occur to a good wife that perhaps things were working out for the best. "I just feel that there must be a clue here," Lorraine said.

Amanda nodded. She'd looked through his belongings. She hadn't found a thing. She was turning to leave when Lorraine said, "I'm sorry."

"Why?" Amanda asked.

"Because I've been wondering. When Derrick didn't come home Thursday night, why didn't you call anyone? Are the two of you having problems?"

Even in Derrick's absence, being the one to tell his mother that they were barely married didn't feel right to Amanda. "When he didn't come home, I thought maybe he was traveling for work, that I'd forgotten. My brain lately."

"You didn't try calling him?" Lorraine persisted.

"He left his phone here. I fell asleep waiting to hear from him."

Lorraine didn't seem quite satisfied. But she didn't ask more questions, so Amanda left her to her search.

~

Meredith arrived as Amanda, Lorraine, and Henry were finishing dinner. Amanda had cooked, over Lorraine's objections, because she was running out of constructive things to do. None of them were hungry. "I made a root vegetable potpie," she told Meredith.

"I ate on the road." Meredith turned to Lorraine and hugged the older woman. "I've been praying for him."

Lorraine nodded without speaking.

"Grab your bag," Amanda said and led Meredith to a guest room. Amanda had already inflated the mattress.

"I don't think she likes me." Meredith dropped her bag on the floor.

"She's upset. And she'll never forgive you for what you said at Christmas dinner." Amanda smiled.

Meredith shrugged. "I didn't know he would go missing."

Amanda lay down on the air mattress, and Meredith joined her. They stared up at the ceiling.

"I feel like I'm still in a moving car," Meredith said.

"I feel like a whale," Amanda replied.

They lay in silence.

"What do you think happened to him?" Meredith asked.

"I don't know."

"Where would he go?"

"Japan maybe. He lived in Tokyo for a year. He speaks the language. And his brother is there. But I don't know. The man I married might have gone there, but I don't really know him anymore. He could be selling Bibles out of his trunk in some country town for all I know."

"Would anyone want to hurt him? Was he into something?"

"He was into church," Amanda answered. "You know about that. Remember the doctor I mentioned, the one who's been helping me informally?"

Meredith nodded. "Patrick."

"Right. Derrick 'accidentally'"—Amanda made air quotes—"opened my email and found some messages we exchanged. He went to Patrick's house to confront him."

Meredith sat up. "When was this? What happened?"

"Almost a month ago. Right after Christmas. Nothing happened. They talked. Patrick said it was cordial."

"Still," Meredith said, "that's some bold shit. Do you think Patrick did something to him?"

"No," Amanda said quickly. "I can't imagine that. Ralph showed up out of the blue last week. Well, it wasn't out of the blue. He'd left some voice mails. But then he just rang the doorbell. It was minutes after Derrick left, as if Ralph had been watching the house." She recounted her conversation with Ralph, his threat to speak with Derrick. Meredith chuckled. "What?" Amanda asked.

"Nothing. Sorry. It's just, this is stuff that should be happening to me." She placed her hand on Amanda's belly. "Except for this. This is all you."

"Thanks," Amanda said wryly and swatted her hand away.

"Do you think Derrick and Ralph crossed paths and—"

"God, I hope not."

"Did you tell the police about Patrick and Ralph?"

Amanda shook her head.

CHAPTER 48

PATRICK

8 MONTHS AFTER THE ACCIDENT

January 30, 2018

Amanda tapped the window, and Patrick unlocked the door. She climbed into the passenger seat. "It's getting cold out there," she said, rubbing her hands together.

He was parked in front of a Chinese restaurant. She'd called and told him she was picking up takeout for her family. She'd asked if he could meet to talk for a few minutes.

She leaned back, closed her eyes, and exhaled slowly. "Thank you for coming."

"Of course. Are you okay?"

"I don't know." Her eyes remained closed, as if she were trying to sleep. "I just wanted to see you."

"Are there any leads in the case?"

She opened her eyes and looked at him. "Nothing. Things are getting contentious between the detective and Derrick's mother. She's convinced there was foul play."

"How are you holding up?"

"I know this sounds horrible, but can we talk about anything else? Tell me a funny story from your childhood."

Patrick smiled. "Yeah, because my childhood was a barrel of laughs."

"Something funny must have happened."

Patrick considered it.

Amanda regarded him. "Are you telling me your childhood was humorless? When did you learn to laugh?"

Patrick continued to think. He smiled. "Christmas. I was eleven or twelve years old, and a raccoon got into our house. My brother and I were opening gifts when my mother screamed, an ear-piercing howl of terror. A raccoon the size of a small cat was in our Christmas tree. My mother told my father to get it.

"'Calm down, Chrissy,' my father said. Everyone but him called her Christina. 'How am I supposed to get that raccoon out of there?'

"'I don't know,' my mother screamed. 'Just get it. Now.'

"My father liked Christmas, so he was mellow. 'I'll call someone to trap him tomorrow. They can release him back to the wild. In the meantime, boys, get your stuff. We'll shut the door and let the raccoon have the room.'

"My mother didn't like it, but she agreed that it would be difficult to find someone to come out on Christmas Day. My brother and I gathered our gifts and vacated the living room."

"Did the raccoon stay in the tree?" Amanda asked.

"I don't know. My father was the only one who went in there. He took the raccoon water and bread and peanut butter and apples. He spent most of Christmas Day in that room with the raccoon. When morning came, he refused to call animal control because it was a Saturday. 'I'm not paying weekend prices,' he told my mother.

"On Tuesday, my mother threatened to move out if he didn't call animal control to take the raccoon away. Still, he wouldn't do it. Finally, my mother asked him if he thought the raccoon liked living in our Christmas tree. 'He's probably scared, Todd. He needs to go home.'

"'Yeah,' my brother said, 'that raccoon probably has a wife and kids.'

"My father wouldn't make the call, but he let my mother do it. The animal control guy showed up with a live trap and asked where the raccoon was. My father started to tell him but choked up. I thought he was going to burst into tears right there. He stormed off to his bedroom and shut the door."

Amanda waited.

"That's the story," Patrick said.

"That's a funny story from your childhood? What was the funny part?"

"My father choked up. He could barely speak."

"Okay."

"I guess you had to be there. My brother and I laughed about it for years."

Amanda said nothing.

"You put me on the spot. I'm not a comedian."

Amanda smiled. "You're very cute. That was a good story. Thank you. Why didn't your father get a pet?"

Patrick shrugged. "My dad didn't make much small talk."

Amanda checked the time. "I'd better go. I'm glad you came. I feel better now that I've seen you."

He imagined leaning forward and kissing her. It was a crazy thought that he quickly dismissed. "Call me anytime."

She smiled and touched his forearm. And then she was gone.

~

Patrick found Marissa where he'd left her: in her study working. He didn't disturb her. He needed to talk to someone, and as he settled on the living room sofa, he found himself dialing his mother. He was crestfallen when she didn't answer, and he hung up without leaving a message. The aloneness had burrowed inside of him, deep into his chest. He was turning on the television for company when the phone rang. His mother.

"Sorry," she said, "I was sitting on the porch drinking lemonade."

"I still forget that it's afternoon there."

"Your timing is perfect. You were on my mind. Are you still thinking about coming to visit?"

He hadn't thought about that in a while. He couldn't leave now, not after promising to help Amanda. "I've met someone, Mom."

She didn't respond immediately. "What do you mean, you've met someone?"

"It's not what it sounds like. We're only friends. But she makes me believe that there might be a life for me after . . ." He didn't finish. There was no tidy word or phrase to sum it up. Amanda was proof that, maybe, there could be life after Marissa. And there was a truth that he hadn't wanted to admit even to himself. "I think I'm falling in love with her."

His mother sighed. "That can be a trap, Patrick. New relationships are always exciting."

"I know. But there's nothing for me in this old life. Sometimes I think I'm living in a wasteland and I just need to move on."

"It's been eight months. Marissa lost her niece and her sister in the span of a week. Give her time to work through it."

"I would give her years if I thought it would help. I'm grieving too. I know she loved Jen and Laura. I know she blames herself for their deaths. I know she's having a hard time, but she won't let me help her. She won't let anyone help her. And she doesn't care what I'm going through. When Laura was hospitalized, Marissa could barely look at her. I put everything on hold. I sat with her. I held her. I felt every agonizing scream from her mouth. No one loved Laura like I did."

"You're a good man, Patrick, and I'm so proud of that. You're strong enough not to walk away from this. If you don't try to fix your marriage, what makes you think the next relationship will work? Give up now, and you've already quit on the next one."

"I've tried to fix my marriage. You have no idea."

"Rob and Sandra are separating. Did you know that?"

"When did that happen?" Patrick asked.

"They've been talking about it for a few months."

Patrick told his mother about the call he'd gotten from Rob a couple of months ago. "He beat me up for not telling him about Laura, even though I did tell him about Laura. But he didn't mention any problems with Sandra."

"You told him your niece died. He didn't know that Laura was practically your daughter, or that Marissa was carrying her when . . ." She didn't finish.

"Well, I didn't know that he and Sandra are separating."

"I guess that makes it all okay."

"Nothing is okay. I expected my marriage to work because I'm not Dad. I didn't know how much would be required of me."

"You're nothing like your father, and I'm grateful for that. If you or your brother turned out like him . . ." She trailed off. "It's hard enough for me to live with myself now."

"We're all fucked up, though, aren't we?" Patrick said.

"Maybe. I'd like for you and Rob to visit me. I think we could all use each other right now."

Patrick didn't respond. He couldn't imagine being away from Amanda. "Mom."

"Yes, honey."

"Do you remember when the raccoon got in our Christmas tree?"

"Who do you think cleaned up the little presents it left behind?"

"Why didn't Dad get a pet?"

"Your father didn't want a pet. When he was a young boy, before he became fluent in the language of violence, his father made him shoot, skin, and eat a raccoon. He never got over it."

234

CHAPTER 49

AMANDA

30 WEEKS PREGNANT

Baby's medulla oblongata, a structure in the brainstem, is mature enough to direct breathing. His hypothalamus can regulate body temperature.

—Your Best Pregnancy

February 1, 2018

Detective Sebold: *Have there been any recent changes in Derrick's behavior?*
    Amanda: *He's never been religious, but he joined a rather extreme church last year. He'd been going for months before he mentioned it to me.*
Detective Sebold: *Extreme?*
Amanda: *Faith healings. That sort of thing.*
Interview at Amanda's residence, 9:45 p.m., Friday, January 26, 2018

～

Amanda couldn't sleep. She booted her computer and logged in to Derrick's email account. When she'd checked it five days before, she'd looked only at messages from the last two weeks. Now, she expanded her search. From the looks of it, he never deleted anything. Most of his emails, unread, were notices from pharmaceutical sales associations. He seemed to conduct his personal correspondence through LinkedIn.

She logged in to his LinkedIn account and scrolled through the messages. She wanted to see what he'd been writing around the time she'd confessed her affair. Her search for clues, she realized, had turned into snooping, but she was pretty sure he'd been snooping when he'd stumbled upon her email exchanges with Patrick.

The tenor of his messages remained unchanged through their domestic turmoil. The day after she'd confessed her affair, he'd congratulated an acquaintance on five years with Pfizer and asked after the man's children. She read a few more messages. Humdrum networking.

She returned to his email account and navigated back several months. A message received in September, two weeks after she'd confessed her affair, caught her attention. The message, titled *New Reply*, was from deceptiveher.com to the email username drj1981. Derrick's email address didn't appear in the recipient line, so she assumed that messages to drj1981 were being forwarded to his account. His middle name was Ronald and he'd been born in 1981, so she also assumed that drj1981 was his alias.

There is a new reply to your post: Trojan Son. It included a link to the reply. Amanda's fingers tingled with the anticipation of discovery. Before she clicked the link, she checked to see if Derrick's generic password would log her in to the drj1981 email account. It did. He had twenty-seven unread messages. All of them were from deceptiveher. com, notifications that someone had responded to his post. She clicked on a link to the post.

A crude message board loaded. *Where men can be honest about feminine deceit.*

~

Trojan Son, posted by drj1981, September 2, 2017

I was overjoyed when my wife of five years told me she was pregnant with our first child. Shortly into her second trimester, I learned that she was having an affair with her boss.

What the hell? Amanda thought.

She ended the affair and we worked through it, but she didn't know if the child was mine. I demanded a paternity test, but she seduced me out of it. The child, a boy, was so sweet that I chose to forget her betrayal and assume the role of father. Our generic baby son grew slowly into the spitting image of my wife. We never talked about it, but I looked for clues that he was mine. Not an easy task.

He turned thirteen last year, and our relationship grew uneasy. He was defiant. He pushed boundaries. When I raised my belt, he threw his fist. I found a journal beneath his bed. He was devising plots to kill me. POISON HIS FOOD, he wrote at the top of one page. STAB HIM IN HIS SLEEP, read another. Underneath these methodologies, he listed pros and cons. Stabbing is painful—Pro. I might only wound him—Con.

I purchased a paternity test. I collected a swab from my cheek and hair from his brush. I waited. I needed to know if he was my son. One week later, he stabbed his mother while she slept. She was on my side of the bed because I'd spilled beer on her side. Instead of changing the sheets, I lay down a couple of towels and told her to sleep in my place.

Her screams woke me and paralyzed our son. He dropped the knife and cowered on the floor. "I didn't mean to, Mommy," he repeated, an infantile chant. She died in the ambulance. On the day of her funeral, I received the paternity results. He wasn't mine. He was an innocent boy born with the instinct to finish his father's work. But he was just a boy. That was our undoing.

Amanda scrolled down to the comments.

Banger52 wrote: You are saint for raising his kid. Your wife had it coming.

MadMan wrote: You should nipped this in the bud and treat her to a abortion.

Evictor wrote: We have no rights. Even if he wanted the kid, she could abort. But he's an asshole for even suggesting she abort a kid that she wants.

MadMan wrote: You have to smart. Push the bitch down stairs. Belly first. Works everytime.

Amanda stopped reading. She was trembling. She staggered through the dark hallway and into the guest room. She shook Meredith awake.

"Did they find Derrick?" Meredith asked groggily.

"No. I need to show you something."

Meredith got up slowly, and Amanda dragged her through the hall.

"Drj1981?" Meredith asked.

"Derrick."

Meredith read. She stopped after a few moments and looked up. "Are you fucking serious?"

"Keep reading."

She did.

"This is disgusting," Meredith finally said.

"I didn't get past the fourth comment."

"Derrick wrote this?"

"It appears so." She told Meredith how she'd found it.

"Did you find anything else?"

"I haven't looked. I don't think I can."

As if speaking to herself, Meredith said, "He fantasized that your child plotted to kill him and in the process killed you. He was the intended target, but you paid the price."

"I'm not sure it's worthy of analysis," Amanda replied.

"There's a lot that doesn't make sense to me," Meredith said. "He insisted that you have an abortion. You two fought over it. And then, when you miscarried, he fell apart. He became a religious zealot and concocted a faith pregnancy. Why?"

"What about me?" Amanda asked. "What do you think of me?"

Meredith touched her hand. "I think you were devastated by infertility. You got pregnant, and then you had a miscarriage."

Amanda closed her eyes against the tears. Meredith reached out and wiped one away with her finger. "I don't think you understand the pain I caused in our marriage. He wrote this a couple of weeks after I told him I was pregnant."

"I don't care. You had an affair, and that was wrong, and you're sorry. Derrick can forgive you or not. He can leave. But he can't post sick fantasies in which your son murders you. You don't deserve that. If Derrick hadn't disappeared and you found this, what would you say to him?"

Amanda considered it. "I don't think there would be anything to say. I would know finally that our marriage is over."

"Exactly."

Meredith had never been married, had never really been in a long-term relationship. She couldn't understand betrayal, the ugliness of it. But maybe she had a point. Amanda had to forgive herself. She'd done something terrible, but she hadn't forfeited her right to human dignity. She smiled at her sister. "I'll work on it."

"That's the spirit. Let's start by hacking this website. We'll shut it down and expose these creeps."

"Do you know how to hack a website?"

"No. You're the one with the computer science degree."

"I must have been sick during that lesson."

"Can't you figure it out?"

"Not tonight. Besides, it's a crime."

"This misogynistic website is a crime. We have to do something."

Amanda found the site's web host, and they filed a complaint.

"This makes me so angry," Meredith said. "I want to do more."

"I want hot chocolate."

They bundled up and sat on the porch in the cold morning air, sipping hot chocolate. They compared childhoods, and Amanda was surprised at how little she knew about Meredith's upbringing. "You left for college when I was five," Meredith pointed out. When a glimpse of the sun appeared in the east, Amanda retired to bed, and Meredith went for a run.

~

"I have news," Lorraine said cheerfully when Amanda entered the kitchen. The three of them, Meredith at one end of the table, Henry and Lorraine at the other, were eating submarine sandwiches. Amanda couldn't remember the last time she'd slept through breakfast.

"Maybe we should offer her something to eat," Henry said.

"Of course."

Amanda sat while Lorraine unwrapped a sandwich and placed it in front of her. "What's the news?"

"Channel Two agreed to run a segment on Derrick." Amanda felt movement in her belly. It could've been her condition. It could've been the rush of anxiety. "They want to interview you." Lorraine's voice faded as blood pulsed past Amanda's eardrums.

"It's the pregnancy angle," Henry said. "There's so much competition for media time, and they get missing person stories every day."

"We might get one of the national outlets to pick it up," Lorraine said.

"Stop it!" Amanda shouted, every secret she held pressing in on her.

Lorraine stared, her eyes hard. And then they softened. "Oh, honey. I know this is difficult. But Derrick is alive. If he wasn't, I would feel it. We're going to bring him home in time for the baby. He will be at the hospital, holding your hand and urging you to push."

"They can't interview me."

"Why not?" Lorraine asked.

Henry cleared his throat. "You're the reason they agreed to the story."

"I'm not pregnant," she blurted.

"What?" Lorraine asked.

Amanda sucked in a breath to hold back tears.

"She isn't pregnant," Meredith repeated. "She miscarried several weeks ago. The symptoms of her pregnancy are ongoing."

Lorraine gasped.

"When did you miscarry?" Henry asked.

Amanda answered. "Four months ago."

"Derrick never mentioned—"

Lorraine cut him off. "Did Derrick know?"

"Of course," Meredith said.

"That isn't true," Lorraine spit.

"I don't understand," Henry said. "If you miscarried four months ago, why are you still—"

"We'll go to the doctor tomorrow," Lorraine told them. "I want to see an ultrasound."

"Are you for real?" Meredith asked.

"We're talking about my grandchild."

Amanda stood. "There is no child. I'm not doing interviews." She left the sandwich on the table and fled to her bedroom.

Meredith knocked on the door a few moments later. "I don't often feel awkward, but being alone with them does it." She lay beside Amanda on the bed.

"Can you do me a favor?" Amanda asked.

"Favors are what I'm here for."

"The prenatal vitamins are in the kitchen drawer next to the sink. Bring me one."

Meredith hesitated. "Is it safe to take them when you're not—"

"Just get it," Amanda pleaded. "I'm four hours overdue."

"Okay. While I do that, you get dressed. We're going to the movies."

~

It was dark outside when Amanda woke. Meredith was asleep beside her. They'd gone to see *Pitch Perfect 3*. Amanda had crawled into bed as soon as they'd gotten home, despite the last vestiges of sunlight streaming through the window. Now, she had to pee. She flossed and brushed while she was in the bathroom and changed into a nightgown.

"What time is it?" Meredith asked as Amanda returned to bed.

"Two thirty. Go back to sleep."

"Henry and Lorraine left."

"Where did they go?"

"I don't know. They didn't say a word. I was sitting in the living room, and they walked right past me with their suitcases. They didn't even apologize for blocking the television. I had to lock the door behind them."

"Oh." They were angry. They probably blamed her. They probably believed they could get Derrick back if she just agreed to a television interview.

"Do you mind that I slept here?"

"No, I'm glad you did. It isn't easy waking up alone. It isn't easy waking up at all."

"This is much more comfortable than the air mattress." Meredith rolled onto her stomach.

"I miss that," Amanda said.

"What?"

"Sleeping on my stomach. And speaking of missing things, shouldn't you be in school? Sorry, but I just thought about it."

"I'm on hiatus. I need to change my major."

Amanda turned to look at Meredith. "You're halfway through your senior year."

"That's a problem," Meredith conceded. "A lot of my anthropology friends graduated last year. They work in offices now."

"I worked in an office."

"Yeah, for like a hundred K a year," Meredith scoffed. "Their pay is shit."

"A hundred K before my bonus," Amanda clarified.

"I don't expect to be Indiana Jones, but if I'm going to work in an office, I want to get paid. I'd like to retire by forty."

"I'm five years from forty, and I can't even see retirement. If you make what I made, you would probably have to save and invest half of your salary."

"I could do that. What percentage of my salary would I have to save if I make thirty-five thousand a year?"

"All of it." Amanda laughed. "Switching majors probably isn't a good idea. But there's always grad school. You could study computer science. I could teach you to code."

"That could be fun."

Amanda smiled. "Coding is more than fun. It's power."

"Speaking of money," Meredith said, "are you okay? Mom says you haven't worked in a while, and she told me to tell you—".

"I'm fine. For now. Derrick and I are both savers. He made enough money to keep us afloat." She tried not to think about the loss of Derrick's income. Without anything coming in, their savings would go fast. "Honestly, I miss working. I have a friend who got into remote freelance work because she wanted to move to Mexico. She's doing well. I've been thinking about giving her a call."

"You should. And if you need money in the meantime, Mom can help."

"I'm fine. But I'd like to do some freelance projects."

"I'm not marrying Brian."

"What? Why?"

Meredith yawned. "Maybe you don't want to hear my problems right now."

"I do," Amanda told her. "I don't want to hear my problems right now."

"I want to live a memorable life," Meredith said.

"Okay."

"I heard about this memory study on a podcast. Older adults tend to remember the details of their lives up through college. Their memories after that become generic. People remember the details of their wedding and their children's births and a divorce if that happens, but everything else bleeds together. Probably because life becomes monotonous. I want to remember my whole life."

"You can't live a memorable life with Brian?"

"Brian doesn't believe in saving money. He has this theory about diminishing returns on life. A trip to Brazil when you're twenty-five is worth more than the same trip when you're forty. He wants to maximize his youth."

"And you're set on retiring before forty?"

"I don't want to spend my whole life working."

"You could find a job that you like."

"I like freedom," Meredith said. "So does Brian. We just don't agree on how to get there."

"For what it's worth, I think you have plenty of time to get married. And I don't think your plan is a bad one. If you want to meet with my financial adviser while you're here, I can arrange that. You'll need to be smart about investing."

Meredith smiled. "I'd like that." She yawned again.

"Go to sleep," Amanda told her, though she knew it would take at least an hour to lull herself back. She wasn't looking forward to the day, because first thing, she would call her mother and tell her about the false pregnancy. Her secret was getting exposure, and she wanted her mother to hear it from her first.

As Meredith's breathing settled into that of light sleep, Amanda wondered what was on the other side of all this.

CHAPTER 50

PATRICK

8 MONTHS AFTER THE ACCIDENT

February 2, 2018

It made Patrick nervous. And still, he continued. He started with the most innocuous search: *Missing Man Atlanta*. Several articles about a man who had been killed by a prostitute were returned. Nothing on what he was looking for. Next, he tried *Derrick Jackson*, only to see his screen fill with results for prominent Derrick Jacksons. He tried *Derrick Jackson Atlanta* and found the man's LinkedIn profile. Patrick had never seen his smile, but he immediately recognized the man who'd confronted him in his kitchen. Finally, he went for it: *Derrick Jackson Missing Atlanta*. He found a Facebook page offering $20,000 for information leading to Derrick's safe return. It surprised Patrick that a man could disappear without any journalistic trace.

He cleared his search history before closing the browser. Pointless, he knew. If anyone looked, really looked, they would find his queries. He didn't know enough about computers to erase the evidence. He could ask Amanda—

He jumped when his phone rang. *Relax,* he told himself. It wasn't the Georgia Bureau of Investigation calling to interrogate him about his internet searches. It was Rob. He answered, grateful for the distraction.

"What's new?" Rob asked.

Nothing Patrick wanted to talk about. "Do you remember the Christmas of the raccoon?"

"When Dad broke down in tears." Rob chuckled. "That was classic."

"Right?" Patrick didn't remember tears, but he wouldn't ruin Rob's memory.

"What made you think of that? I laugh every time I see a Christmas tree."

"A friend asked for a funny memory from my childhood. Do you know why Dad loved that raccoon?"

"Love?" Rob asked. "Is that how you remember it? He kept the raccoon hostage for four days. The poor guy was scared to come out of the tree."

"He made it peanut butter sandwiches. Did Dad ever make you a sandwich?"

"I would've demanded a food taster."

Patrick told Rob about their grandfather forcing their father to kill and eat a raccoon.

"Huh," Rob said. "I've never thought about the depravity required to shape Dad's psyche."

They'd never met their father's parents, and he'd never talked about them.

"I remember thinking he didn't have parents," Patrick said.

"A soulless monster? I thought that a distinct possibility."

Patrick laughed.

"I've missed you, Patrick."

"I've missed you too, Rob."

"Whoa. Don't get soft on me."

"What? You said it first."

"I said it like a man greeting his dog after returning from war. You said it like a toddler reunited with his pacifier."

"Whatever."

"I'm not trying to hurt your feelings, little brother. I just want to maintain healthy boundaries. How is Marissa?"

Patrick hesitated. What could he say? They'd had that night together—the one he thought of as her goodbye. And nothing since. He wouldn't compare Marissa to a drug addict, at least not aloud, but it was the best analogy. She was like the guy in the dorm at the end of the hall who smoked weed every day. He typically made it to class and delivered passable performances, not great but good enough. And then you saw him at a party one Saturday snorting cocaine. Then it was every Friday and Saturday, but he was in control. You shook his hand and wished him well at graduation. He had a job lined up. And then ten years later, you saw him at the park. He was unkempt and wearing too many clothes. He was alternately high and sick. There was no neutral place in which he could exist.

"Not good," he told Rob. "She doesn't have a neutral place. She's lost in math or she's lost."

"Do you talk?"

"No." He didn't want to talk about Marissa. "Mom told me about you and Sandra."

Rob scoffed. "Of course. That woman would spread my grocery list around town if I shared it with her."

"I thought we were supposed to talk about our problems."

"My marriage is ending and it's my fault. Happy? I've talked about it. There's nothing more to say."

"You don't have any feelings about it?"

"When I want to feel something, I listen to soft rock. Life isn't about feelings."

"Right. You're a surgeon."

"I'm the best goddamn liver-transplant surgeon alive. It isn't because I read poetry in the OR."

"It certainly isn't your looks. Or intelligence. Or humility. Have you told Julie?" Julie was Rob's fifteen-year-old daughter.

"Julie isn't talking to me, so I haven't told her anything. Sandra and I were supposed to go to New Zealand for our anniversary next week. I transferred my airline ticket to Sandra's best friend. Now, Julie is angry that I'm going to be home. Sandra's sister was supposed to stay with her."

"Will you and Julie do anything special?"

"Besides developing strategies for never being in the same room together? I was thinking I'd come visit you. I've cleared my schedule for two weeks, and Sandra's sister has already agreed to stay with Julie."

"Sounds like fun," Patrick said. "We can reminisce about our childhood."

CHAPTER 51

AMANDA

31 WEEKS PREGNANT

Activity in the thalamus and associated subcortical brain structures shows coordination, raising the possibility of consciousness.

—Your Best Pregnancy

February 5, 2018

Detective Sebold: *When are you due?*
    Amanda: *Mid-April.*
Detective Sebold: *Was Derrick excited about the baby?*
    Amanda: *It was a contentious issue.*
Interview at Amanda's residence, 9:45 p.m., Friday, January 26, 2018

~

The day after Derrick's parents left, a journalist from Channel 2 called Amanda's cell phone. *I hope you don't mind. Your in-laws gave me your number.* Amanda minded. The journalist was polite and not at all pushy, but the unexpected intrusion left Amanda edgy.

Four days later, when the doorbell rang, Amanda woke with a start.

"I'm on it," Meredith said, passing through the living room, where Amanda sat dazed in the recliner.

After a brief exchange at the door, Meredith led an older gentleman into the room. He wore a black trench coat with khaki slacks. He removed his hat to reveal a headful of white hair.

"Don't get up," he told Amanda.

She hadn't planned to. Getting up or down weren't actions she took lightly. He extended his hand, and she shook it.

"I'm Gerald Mathews." He pulled a card from his jacket pocket. *Private Investigator.* "Do you mind if I sit?"

"No," Amanda said. He was already standing in her living room. He took off his coat and laid it over the arm of the couch. He sat down beside it, and Meredith sat at the other end.

"I was hired by Mr. and Mrs. Jackson," he told her.

As if sensing Amanda's panic, Meredith gave her a reassuring look. "I told Gerald that we would listen to his questions. And answer any that are relevant to finding Derrick."

He smiled and said, "She drives a hard bargain." He opened his notebook and pulled a pen from his pocket. "Do you mind if we start with your pregnancy?"

"She isn't pregnant," Meredith told him.

"Do you feel pregnant?" he asked Amanda.

"I don't see how that will bring Derrick home," Meredith said.

"Can you provide a note from your doctor?" Gerald asked. "Just to clarify the status of your—"

"She *is not* pregnant. Does that clarify the status?"

"They just want to know—"

"Are you investigating me or Derrick's disappearance?" Amanda asked.

Gerald hesitated. "Can you tell me about Derrick's mood on the day he disappeared? Anything out of the ordinary?"

"I've been over this with the police." If they couldn't do anything with it, she doubted this detective could.

"Mr. and Mrs. Jackson don't think the police are doing all they can to find Derrick."

"I didn't notice anything out of the ordinary. He was working from home that morning. That's unusual for him but not unheard of." She rubbed her temples, sensing the beginning of a headache.

Meredith caught her eye. "We should wrap this up. The only time she can sleep is during the day."

"Of course. I just have one more question." Gerald jotted a note. "You quit your job suddenly. Do you mind telling me about that?"

Amanda's headache threatened to turn into a migraine. Would Gerald talk to her old coworkers?

Meredith stood. "You should come back another time. She's tired, and honestly, she doesn't need the stress."

Gerald remained seated. He looked at Amanda. Amanda looked at Meredith. Meredith pulled her cell phone from her pocket. "Let's call Detective Sebold. You can tell him that he isn't doing his job. And then you can explain why you're refusing to leave her home."

Gerald stood. "I'm sorry," he told Amanda and shook her hand. "But you should know that I'm one of the good guys. I want to bring your husband home."

"Please do," Amanda told him. "If I think of anything that might help, I'll call you." She patted the arm of the recliner, where his card sat.

"I appreciate that." He removed another card from his pocket and handed it to Meredith. "Call me if you ever need a job." He smiled, and Meredith shook his hand.

"I hate confrontation," Amanda said when he was gone. Meredith returned to the couch. "I think you enjoy it."

"I enjoy sticking up for my sister."

"Forget learning to code. You should go to law school."

"You think?"

"There are a lot of people who need sticking up for."

Meredith smiled at that. "Maybe."

Amanda stood. "I'm going to lie down."

"I'll keep you company." Meredith followed her up the stairs.

"Talk to me about something light and fun," Amanda said, the two of them lying side by side.

Meredith was quiet for a long while. "When do I get to meet Patrick?"

"Why on earth would you want to meet him?"

"I won't embarrass you by answering that."

"His brother is coming in from out of town."

"Your sister is in town. Let's go out for dinner."

"How would that look? Derrick's parents just hired a private investigator."

"We can have them here for dinner. The investigator must have better things to do than stake out your house."

"For the record," Amanda said, "Patrick is not light or fun."

CHAPTER 52

PATRICK

8 MONTHS AFTER THE ACCIDENT

February 7, 2018

From: Patrick Davis
To: Amanda Jackson
Subject: RE: Unusual Conditions

People with body integrity identity disorder wish to be disabled. They may feel that a limb doesn't belong to them or that they should be paralyzed. In extreme cases, they may seek amputation or surgical bisection of their spinal cord. It's a psychological disorder that often starts in childhood, with no effective treatments. The condition has been correlated with irregularities in right parietal lobe activity but cause and effect isn't understood. The strong psychological desire to be disabled could cause the irregularities or the irregularities could cause the desire.

~

Patrick listened, unsure if he'd been dreaming. The room was dark, and he was in bed alone. He heard it again. A cat? He got up and put on his slippers. The light in Marissa's office was on. He approached slowly. She lay on the couch, wearing jeans and a blouse. She was crying.

"Marissa," he said. And then he realized she was sleeping. He sat in a chair and watched her. Her cries were soft and tearless. He considered waking her. She was having a bad dream. Was reality better? Once awake, she would retreat immediately into math. Perhaps that was what she needed. He didn't know. He never seemed to know anymore. He sat motionless.

He stared at her. There was so much history there. He could summon in his memory a dozen variations of her face. Abandon as she laughed. Glee as she danced. Concentration as she thought. Annoyance when she was interrupted. Guilt following an argument. Ecstasy as she climaxed. Neutrality as she sipped coffee. Anger when she was offended. Tiredness after work. Love as she held Laura. Relief when Jen turned up after a long absence. Despair when she learned that her sister was dead. He knew this woman. And yet, he had no idea how to help her.

He checked the time on his phone. It was a little after 4:00 a.m. Rob's plane was scheduled to arrive in three and a half hours. He'd told Marissa that Rob was coming, but he hadn't made plans with her. Instead, he and Rob were meeting Amanda and her sister for dinner tomorrow night.

What was he doing?

Or rather: What could he do differently?

Dinner plans with Marissa weren't possible. She was taking her meals in her study and had become prickly about interruptions. Besides, he wanted to check on Amanda. He'd barely spoken to her since the night in his car outside the restaurant.

He thought about getting up and doing something. Exhaustion won out. Marissa's cries subsided and her face relaxed. Her lips parted and she snored lightly. As the sun began its rise and light trickled through the window, he got up and dressed to meet Rob at the airport.

~

"How is the job search coming?" Rob asked. He sat in the passenger seat of Patrick's Prius. Patrick had met him curbside at the airport.

"I'll let you know when I start."

"How do you pay your mortgage? I can see you get your clothes from a shelter. And you're saving money with the budget haircut. Is this piece-of-crap car paid for?"

"My wife actually makes good money?" Patrick said. "And I hear there's a lucrative prize in her future."

"I feel a lot like Frank right now."

"Frank?" Patrick asked.

"Frank. His son graduated college last fall. Still doesn't have a job. Frank wants to light a fire under the boy, but his wife won't let him."

"Are we talking a literal fire?" Patrick asked. "Because Frank could be a psychopath, which means you two have a lot in common."

"Frank wonders if he failed his son somehow. I wonder if I failed you."

"Honestly, I've been in a fog. But I feel myself coming back. I've been thinking about what I want to do next. That's progress. Anything else you'd like to discuss? Why don't you tell me why your wife and daughter hate you?"

Rob didn't reply.

"Okay. I'll assume it's for the same reason I hate you. You're just so damn good at inspiring it."

When Rob still didn't respond, Patrick said, "Fine, we won't talk about it." He reiterated Marissa's obsession with work. He didn't want Rob to be surprised. "Watch your jokes," Patrick warned.

"Me? I'd never make fun of Marissa. I'm like the big-brained kid on the playground. I only pick on people less intelligent than me. You're my favorite target. I don't dare battle wits with Marissa."

"Smart man." Patrick told Rob about Amanda. He didn't want any surprises there either.

Rob whistled. "Recap. Your wife is spending every waking hour building a mathematical telephone that will connect her to the dead. Your girlfriend, who isn't pregnant, gives every outward appearance of being seven months pregnant? Are you the common link here? Are you making these women crazy?"

"Not funny." Bearing insults was part of the Davis legacy, but that one pierced the armor.

Rob placed a hand on Patrick's knee. "I'm sorry. That was low, even for me." Rob could be an asshole. He could also be sincere.

"She isn't my girlfriend. She reached out to me because she thought I could help her understand pseudocyesis. Somehow, we just started talking about everything. She means a lot to me. And her husband is missing."

"Whoa. What?"

"He vanished two weeks ago."

"And you thought you would just slip that in? Vanished as in hiking the Appalachian Trail with his Argentine mistress or vanished as in his wife poisoned him and recruited her idiot boyfriend to dispose of the body?"

Patrick sighed. "The police don't suspect foul play."

"What does Amanda suspect?"

"She thinks he ran off to start a new life."

"And what do you suspect?"

"If there was foul play, Amanda doesn't have any knowledge of it."

Rob fixed him with a look. Patrick kept his eyes on the road.

"You need to be careful, little bro."

Patrick nodded. "I've been googling her husband, looking for news online."

"Don't police look at that kind of shit?"

"Probably. But I keep doing it anyway. There's nothing online about him, not a peep outside of the Facebook page Amanda set up."

"And you've told me everything you know about this?"

Patrick hesitated. Then he nodded.

"Okay. You're not a reckless guy." They rode in silence. "When is the last time you played miniature golf?"

"It's been a while."

Rob pulled out his phone. "I'll find an indoor course. Loser buys breakfast."

~

Patrick hated losing to Rob. Always had. And still, he lost by three strokes. A reminder that Rob was the better athlete.

"Don't worry about breakfast," Rob said as they finished their meal at Dulce Cafe. "I got you."

"No," Patrick said and pulled out a card. "I'm good. Marissa will pay the bill."

For as long as Patrick could remember, Rob had found ways to best him. That hadn't changed. Another thing that hadn't changed was the security Patrick felt in his presence. They didn't talk about meaningful things easily, but everything important existed in the energy between them. Having a common enemy meant they hadn't fought as children. When Rob went to college, Patrick, only fifteen, followed. Many of Patrick's weekends began with a bus ride and were spent sleeping on Rob's dormitory floor. Rob's roommate didn't mind. Patrick and Rob never talked about why he spent the weekends there. They both knew. They didn't have to talk about everything. It was possible that he would never know what had gone wrong in Rob's marriage. Patrick didn't need to know. Rob was his brother.

CHAPTER 53

MARISSA

8 MONTHS AFTER THE ACCIDENT

February 7, 2018

Inspiration was the fun part of the mathematical process, ideas raging like wildfire. Unfortunately, Marissa spent most of her time, as she was now, bogged down by the hard work of organizing ideas into something coherent. She was constructing a proof, and the rap on the door, jarring, irritated her. She turned, annoyed, and then grinned involuntarily. "What are you doing here?"

"Patrick said you were busy, but I told him you could spare a few minutes for Rob."

She stood and hugged him. "Is this a thing," she asked, "referring to yourself in the third person?"

"It suits Rob."

She laughed. "Have a seat. How long are you here?"

Rob sat on the couch. She swiveled her chair to face him. "Two weeks. Patrick didn't tell you?"

Marissa searched her memory. There was something. "Maybe," she said sheepishly.

Rob waved a hand. "Don't worry. I don't listen to a thing he says either. Sandra kicked me out of the house, so you can remove her from your Christmas card list."

"What? What happened?"

"Her heart has grown cold over the years. I've had something to do with that. It's for the best. Have you managed to talk to any dead people yet?"

Marissa guffawed. It could be hard to stay on balance around Rob. "Not yet," she replied. "Either it will happen soon, or it won't happen at all."

"Keep me posted. I've been trying to read *War and Peace* for the better part of a year. I have some questions for Leo."

"I don't think it will work that way."

"Oh well. Maybe I'll buy the CliffsNotes. How are you holding up, all things considered?"

She paused. The truth was, she was dangling by a thread. "Do you ever open up a patient and realize things are so bad that the best thing you can do is close her up again?"

Rob nodded. "It happens."

"That's where I am. I just want to get through this without causing any more damage."

"Get through what?" he asked.

She shrugged. The effort to make herself understood was too much. She needed the energy for math. "Thanks for stopping in to say hello," she told him. "I'll see you around." She swiveled her chair back to her desk. She picked up her pencil and searched for the thought he'd interrupted. He sat for a few moments before standing and quietly leaving. She located the thought, and she was off.

CHAPTER 54

AMANDA

31 WEEKS PREGNANT

February 8, 2018

Detective Sebold: *Derrick's mother visited the precinct to tell me that you're faking a false pregnancy. Can you tell me anything about that?*
   Amanda: *I can't talk about my pregnancy.*
   Interview at Amanda's residence, 6:30 p.m., Friday, February 2, 2018

~

"How many outfits are you going to try on?" Meredith asked.
   "How many have I tried?"
   "Four."
   "Four it is. I'm going with the green dress. First instincts and all." She took off the black sweaterdress. The problem was she looked pregnant no matter what she wore. And of course, Meredith was stunning in her maroon dress.
   "I'm obsessed with your green dress. Why are you so nervous?"
   Amanda shrugged. She didn't tell Meredith that she did this every time she saw Patrick. Even if he was oblivious, she wanted to look good.

"And there they are," Meredith said when the doorbell rang. "I'll get it."

Amanda followed.

"You must be Meredith," Patrick said when she opened the door.

A tall man with sandy-blond hair stood behind Patrick. He stepped forward and handed Meredith a bottle of wine. "He picked it out," Rob said and patted Patrick on the shoulder. They looked nothing alike. Rob was reminiscent of a soap opera actor when he smiled. "I'm Rob." He hugged Meredith and then Amanda.

Patrick didn't typically greet Amanda with a hug, but he followed his brother's lead.

"Thank you for coming," she whispered in Patrick's ear. And then made introductions.

"I didn't see anyone out there," Rob said, pointing over his shoulder. "Do you think the police are watching the house?"

Patrick winced. Amanda stared at Rob for a few beats before Meredith said, "There's nothing to see here."

Rob appraised Amanda and Meredith in turn. "I disagree."

"Have a seat in the living room," Amanda said and showed them the way. Corn chips and salsa were already on the coffee table. "Help yourselves. We'll eat soon."

"You have a beautiful home," Patrick said.

Amanda wondered if being here made him think of Derrick. His presence here made her think of Derrick.

Rob sat on the couch and popped a chip in his mouth.

"I'll open the wine," Meredith said. Amanda followed her into the kitchen. "Patrick is what I expected."

"How's that?" Amanda asked.

"When you talk about him, he seems kind of nerdy. He has that good-looking nerd thing going. His brother—wow."

Amanda didn't reply. She put the salad in bowls. Meredith had said she would handle dinner, which turned out to mean she would find a food-delivery service.

"We'll start with a pear-and-pecan salad," Amanda announced as she placed the food on the table. Rob dipped and ate a final chip before standing to join them.

"Delicious," Patrick said when he tasted the salad.

Rob nodded and said, "I don't want anyone to feel awkward," which in Amanda's experience meant that something awkward was about to be said. "There are elephants stomping all over this room, and I see no reason not to acknowledge them. My wife is in New Zealand right now with her best friend. I'm supposed to be with her for our anniversary, but I didn't feel like it since she asked me to move out of the house by the end of the month. I'm visiting this guy because my daughter wants me in the house even less than my wife." He parted his hands in a there-you-have-it gesture. "No one has to say anything. I just want you all to know that we're family and anything can be discussed at this table."

Silence.

"Thank you for not being awkward," Patrick said.

"You're welcome."

"How was your flight?" Amanda asked Rob.

"Uneventful. Every time I'm in the air, I wait for a flight attendant to get on the speaker and say, 'Is there a doctor on board?' It never happens."

"Most people would consider that a good thing," Patrick said.

"You would," Rob retorted. "What would you do? Talk the medical emergency away? 'I know you're having chest pains,'" Rob mocked, "'but how does that make you feel?'"

Amanda and Meredith looked at each other.

"You're a surgeon?" Meredith asked.

"Yes," Patrick responded. "Some poor passenger will have heartburn, and this guy will cut his chest open. That's not a flight you want to be on."

Amanda excused herself to the kitchen. "Sweet potato, fennel, and eggplant lasagna," she announced upon her return and placed the platter on the table.

"It looks wonderful," Patrick said.

"Just like the picture online," Meredith assured them. Amanda sat down while Patrick served everyone's plate.

"This guy is putting me on a diet," Rob remarked and helped himself to more.

"I have an idea," Meredith said. "A game of sorts." She looked at Rob and Patrick. "And it isn't because you two aren't great conversationalists. Let's each tell a funny, maybe slightly embarrassing story about our sibling."

"Ooh, I like this game." Rob rubbed his hands together. "Me first."

Meredith smiled. "Go for it. Just nothing mean. You can make him blush, but don't humiliate each other."

"This guy does just fine at humiliating himself," Rob said. "My story isn't mean. Just maybe a little sad. Like my brother."

Amanda felt apprehensive. This didn't seem like a good idea.

"Patrick was fourteen, and he had his first girlfriend," Rob began. Patrick groaned.

"That's right. I'm telling that story. What was her name?"

"It was a long time ago," Patrick said.

"Just tell me her name so I can tell the story."

"Phyllis."

"Right," Rob said, "Phyllis. She was a nice girl, maybe a little wild for Patrick, a bad influence. Anyway, Phyllis's mother caught Patrick, Phyllis, and another teen couple in her basement. At two in the morning. She called our father and demanded that he pick Patrick up. Our parents didn't know that Patrick was out, and the old man was beyond pissed. Our mother was worried that he would kill Patrick. I mean that literally. Our father could go overboard with discipline. So our mother told our father that she would handle Patrick's punishment."

Patrick scoffed.

"'You'd better get creative,' our father told her. 'That boy needs a lesson to remember.'"

"She got creative," Patrick said.

"She bought one of those wearable signs, the kind that goes over your head. You have a large piece of cardboard in front and one in the back. On the front, she wrote: *I am abstinent because . . .* On the back: *Abstinence is the only way to prevent pregnancy and STDs.* She made him wear it to the mall on a Saturday afternoon. All of the kids from our school hung out there." Rob laughed.

"I think I would've preferred a beating," Patrick said. "I didn't have the courage to ask for one."

"Mom could be abusive too."

"The difference," Patrick said, "is that Mom didn't enjoy it."

"Correct me if I'm wrong," Rob said, "but you were abstinent long after wearing that sign."

Patrick nodded. "I didn't have another girlfriend for a few years. I wasn't great with girls before the sign."

"Poor Patrick." Amanda leaned over and touched his arm. "You don't have any problem with girls now."

Meredith and Rob looked at each other. "On that note," Meredith said, "would you like to respond, Patrick? Do you have a story?"

"How do I choose?" He smiled. "My story is about Rob, a girl, and a triathlon."

Rob leaned back in his seat with exaggerated frustration. "I'm a world-class surgeon," he quipped, "and still, I have to hear about the triathlon."

"What was the girl's name?" Patrick asked.

"Heather Ayers."

"Right. Pretty girl. Rob was a senior in high school, and Heather transferred in midyear. Rob asked her out, and she told him she was busy training for a triathlon. Rob, who even then thought he was God's gift to women, said, 'That's perfect because I stay in triathlon shape year-round. I'm always training.' Rob must not have known what a triathlon was, because he couldn't swim."

"I chose not to swim," Rob corrected.

"If you dropped Rob in seven feet of water, he would've chosen to drown. Let me tell the story."

Rob nodded, chastened.

"Heather was doing the triathlon for charity. It was Olympic distance: a mile swim, a twenty-five-mile bike ride, and a six-mile run. To Rob's credit, he was a good runner and a decent cyclist. They met up on the weekends to train. Meanwhile, after school, Rob and I would go to the Y, where I tried to teach him to swim. He must've really liked Heather, and I must have really liked him, because it was like teaching a frog to fly."

Rob nodded. "I did like Heather."

"After a few weeks, he could make it across the pool without stopping. He looked more like a drowning man than a swimmer, but he could move forward in a relatively straight line. A week before the triathlon, he and I ditched school to go to Lake Lanier. I was terrified that he would drown and pull me under with him, but he managed to swim a mile and a half. He was ready for race day.

"It was a Saturday morning and still dark outside when our mother woke me. Rob rode with Heather, so we didn't have to be there as early as the participants, but our mother wanted to see him enter the water. Our father slept in, which was fine because he didn't miss much.

"The sun was just beginning to rise when the swimmers entered the water. It was a horde of people, and we had no hope of spotting Rob, so we positioned ourselves near the bike racks. We wouldn't miss his transition. Our mother checked every face as the elite competitors emerged. 'He'll be a while,' I told her knowingly. 'He'll hold his own on the bike and kill them on the run.'

"'Go, Heather,' our mother cheered. I hadn't seen her emerge from the water, but there she was, climbing onto the bike. She'd made good time, along with a steady stream of competitors. The stream slowed to a trickle, and soon there were only a few bikes left. My mother and I looked toward the water. We couldn't see much from where we stood.

"'I thought you taught him to swim?' our mother said to me. 'I did the best I could,' I told her. 'It's like teaching a horse to add.' We watched a few more competitors trickle in, until finally, only Rob's bike was left on the rack.

"'Maybe you should go in after him?' our mother said. 'I don't have a wet suit,' I told her. The water was freezing."

"I would've hated for you to be cold," Rob interjected.

"We waited. And finally, Rob trudged up the beach, head down."

"'Go, Rob,' our mother cheered. 'I don't think he's racing,' I whispered. He looked distraught. 'Where is the car?' he asked tersely when he saw us. He wouldn't tell us what happened. We got in the car and drove in silence until he finally felt up to talking.

"When the race started, he'd nudged his way to the front. He knew his swim time wouldn't be good, but he didn't want to be last out of the water. He got in and he felt fine. A lot of people were passing him, but he focused on moving forward. He was halfway to the first buoy when someone kicked him in the nose. He sucked in water and panicked and started grabbing at other swimmers. Eventually, he was pulled into a boat for his and the other racers' safety."

"Heartbreaking," Meredith said. "Did you get the girl?"

Rob shook his head. "This was no romantic comedy."

"That lasagna didn't stand a chance," Amanda commented. Only sauce was left on the platter. "Should I get dessert, or do we want to let that settle?"

"I want to tell my story," Meredith said. "Then dessert." She looked thoughtfully at Amanda. Amanda returned her gaze with trepidation. "When I was five, I was kidnapped while Amanda was babysitting me."

"Kidnapped?" Rob asked.

"True story."

Amanda put her face in her hands.

"Our mother was on her first date since our father's death. He died shortly after I was born. Amanda had her boyfriend over, even though she wasn't supposed to. I know this because she promised me cookies if I didn't tell Mom. She'd received her acceptance letter from Emory University that day and decided to break up with her boyfriend. He was staying in Raleigh to work for his father's construction company. He offered to try the long-distance thing, but she didn't want that. Then he offered to look for a job in Atlanta, but she didn't want that either. Amanda put on a video and parked me in front of the television while they talked in the kitchen."

"Stellar babysitter," Rob said.

"Right?" Meredith smiled at Amanda. Amanda feigned annoyance. "I didn't know what they were talking about at the time, but I remember that they were both upset. Amanda was crying, and she went to the bathroom. Her boyfriend—I guess he was her ex by then—picked me up and said, 'Let's go out for ice cream.' I wasn't going to argue with that. He put me in the front seat of his car. I remember feeling very adult. I was still in a car seat back then. And we left."

"Where did he take you?" Patrick asked.

"First, we went to my favorite ice cream parlor. Then he took me to a carnival. I don't think that was planned. I spotted a Ferris wheel from the expressway, and he was like, 'You want to go there?' And meanwhile, Amanda was frantic. She had no idea where we'd gone. Instead of calling the police, she drove over to his place. Where else did you go?" Meredith asked her.

"Everywhere I could think of. I even drove around the mall parking lot looking for his car."

"Finally," Meredith said, "Amanda went to the restaurant to get our mom."

"She should have had a cell phone," Amanda said.

"Who had a cell phone in 2000?" Meredith replied.

"You're right. I shouldn't have broken up with Albert while I was babysitting you."

"His reaction was a bit extreme," Rob said. "Maybe you couldn't foresee that."

"Our mother is on her first date in over twenty years. She's nervous, but she thinks it's going well. And then Amanda barges in and tells her I'm missing. She calls the police.

"Meanwhile, across town, I'm having a blast at the carnival. I remember getting tired and kind of wanting to go home but not wanting to ask. We were on a teacup ride when it just stopped. A police officer asked me my name and took me home. It was an exciting night."

"For you maybe," Amanda said. "Our mother was furious. She told me I couldn't go to Emory. It took her a week to change her mind."

"What happened to Albert?" Patrick asked.

"We didn't keep in touch," Amanda said. "He pleaded no contest to the kidnapping charges, and he got probation. I haven't heard anything about him since. Can I tell my story now? I think I have everyone beat."

"Go for it," Meredith said. She was the only one who didn't show nerves in the hot seat.

"Actually, my story is so good that I want everyone to hear it over dessert." She went into the kitchen and retrieved the chocolate mousse from the refrigerator. Once it was served, she said, "Meredith can be very strong willed and combative. It cost her high school boyfriend dearly."

Meredith laughed. "I see where this is going."

"It was four years ago, Meredith's senior year. Her best friend got pregnant and made the very difficult decision to have an abortion. The father didn't know she was pregnant, so Meredith drove her to the clinic, waited with her, and then took her home.

"The next day, our mother confronted Meredith. 'Who are you having sex with?' Meredith didn't know what she was talking about. 'I just got a phone call from a pro-life activist. Your car was at an abortion clinic yesterday. They ran your plates.' Meredith asked if that was legal. Our mother didn't care to discuss the law.

"Meredith could have cleared everything up, but she chose to lecture our mother. 'I have the right to an abortion. I don't need permission, and I don't have to inform anyone.'

"'You live in my house,' our mother told her. 'You should talk to me about these things.'

"'Would you have told me that I can't get an abortion?' Meredith asked.

"'No,' our mother said. 'We would've talked it through, and if that's what you wanted, I would have taken you to the clinic.'

"Meredith was combative. 'I don't have to talk it through. It's my choice.'

"Our mother felt powerless, and you can understand why. She did the only thing she could. She called Tim's mother—Tim was Meredith's boyfriend at the time—and asked her if she knew about the abortion. She didn't, of course.

"Our mother didn't know Tim's parents well. She didn't know that they were staunchly pro-life."

"Antichoice," Meredith corrected.

Amanda nodded. "I don't know what transpired between Tim and his parents, but they took his car and donated it to a pro-life"—she glanced at Meredith—"antichoice organization."

"Tim was so angry with me," Meredith said. "It turned out he was antichoice, too, so screw him. But he loved that car. It was a Mustang.

His parents bought it for him, and he spent a year fixing it up. Every time he had an extra dollar, he put it into that car. That Mustang was my competition."

"You won," Rob said.

Meredith grinned.

"Did his parents find out the truth?" Patrick asked.

Meredith nodded. "I told my mother that I didn't get an abortion. Then I told Tim's parents. They still looked at me like I was an accessory to murder. So did Tim. Everyone was just angry with everyone. I haven't heard from Tim, but as far as I know, his parents didn't replace the car."

Rob shook his head. "You were an expensive girlfriend," he said appreciatively.

Meredith smiled at him. "I still am."

~

"This was a lot of fun," Rob said and hugged Amanda. "We should do it again."

They'd talked over wine and then water long after the chocolate mousse was gone. For those few hours, Amanda hadn't felt like the nonpregnant, pregnant wife of a missing man. She hadn't thought about Detective Sebold or the private investigator. "I'd like that," Amanda said. As she watched the brothers climb into Patrick's car, she wondered if the police were watching the house.

CHAPTER 55

AMANDA

32 WEEKS PREGNANT

Baby sleeps about twenty-two hours per day. Her pupils dilate and contract in response to light.

—Your Best Pregnancy

February 12, 2018

Detective Sebold: *I've been doing this a long time, and I don't see any evidence of foul play. People have the right to disappear, and I make it a point to keep out of people's lives when no crime has been committed. But I'll tell you what keeps me up at night. Missing something. My gut tells me there are important things you aren't telling me.*
    Interview at Amanda's residence, 6:30 p.m., Friday, February 2, 2018

～

Amanda led Meredith to a closet in the basement. "There it is, at the bottom." She pointed to a cardboard box, caving beneath the weight of several identical boxes.

"This better be a good book," Meredith said as she stepped forward to free the bottom box. The night before, they'd had a long conversation about what it meant to be educated. Meredith had complained that her knowledge of Africa was fundamentally Eurocentric. *I know what Europeans did in Africa, but I couldn't tell you a thing outside of the European experience.*

"You'll like it," Amanda assured her, supervising her sister's labor. It was one of Derrick's books. He'd read it and passed it on to Amanda. Meredith pulled the box from the closet and sat down on the floor to open it. "I wish I could do that." Meredith looked up at her. "Sit on the floor," Amanda clarified.

Meredith smiled and removed books from the box. "There," Amanda said. Of course it was at the bottom: *An African History of Africa*. When Meredith pulled out the book, a clear baggie holding white pills fell to the floor.

"What are these?" Meredith handed the baggie to Amanda.

Amanda studied the pills. "I have no idea."

"You want to tell me something?" Meredith asked. "A story about you, Derrick, books, and designer drugs."

"Derrick was a pharmaceutical sales rep," Amanda said dismissively. "Is," she corrected herself. "He *is* a pharmaceutical sales rep."

"Is that how pharmaceutical companies sell pills nowadays? In unmarked baggies?"

Meredith was joking. She laughed. But dread settled over Amanda. Derrick handled a lot of pharmaceutical samples, always in well-branded packaging. What could the baggie be if not illicit?

"What are you thinking?" Meredith asked, seeming to have caught her mood.

"I'm thinking that Derrick did not use drugs. And I'm thinking it would explain a lot if he did."

She was thinking other things but couldn't give voice to them. What if he used drugs to cope with the pain of her affair? He'd gotten drunk the night she'd told him. What if the drugs explained the religion and faith pregnancy and everything else she blamed him for? What if drugs had something to do with his disappearance? What if she'd noticed in time to help him? What if he was . . .

Meredith stood and took the baggie from Amanda's hand. She removed one of the pills and held it in the direct light of the lamp. "G 5008," she read. She placed the pill back in the baggie and pulled out her cell phone.

"You're looking it up?" Amanda asked.

Meredith didn't respond. She sat down in a chair as if she'd been punched.

"What?" Amanda asked. She'd heard about opioids on the news. Outside of that, she didn't know what kinds of illicit drugs people used.

Meredith had tears in her eyes as she handed Amanda her phone. She'd pulled up a web page for G 5008, misoprostol. The first thing Amanda saw was a warning at the top of the page: *Do not take this medication if you think that you may be pregnant.*

~

Amanda called Ben Talbot's office. He'd been Derrick's college room-mate and was now his primary physician.

"Talbot Group. How may I help you?" the receptionist asked cheerfully.

"I need an appointment with Dr. Talbot today." It was a few minutes before noon.

"Are you a current patient?"

"No."

"I don't see anything for today," the receptionist said. "I can work you in the day after tomorrow?"

"Can you give Dr. Talbot a message for me? My name is Amanda Jackson. Tell him I need to see him today."

Ben called her within the hour. He told her to come in at two.

~

Ben walked around the desk to hug her. "Any word on Derrick?"

"Nothing." She sat in a chair as he returned to his seat.

"I've been worried sick," he said.

She removed the plastic baggie from her purse and put it on his desk. "These pills were hidden in Derrick's things."

He picked up the baggie and studied it.

"Misoprostol," she told him. *Uses: (1) to prevent stomach ulcers; (2) in combination with mifepristone to terminate pregnancy.*

"You found them like this, in the bag?"

She nodded. "I miscarried nineteen weeks ago."

Ben didn't hide his confusion as he glanced at her belly.

"Pseudocyesis," she blurted, wanting this conversation to be over.

He didn't reply.

"Did you treat Derrick for ulcers?"

"Amanda, I—"

"Derrick never mentioned ulcers to me. I assume, if you'd prescribed these, they would be in a prescription bottle."

"Given his job, he probably had all kinds of pills on hand."

"I don't want to believe he gave me these, Ben. Can you think of a reason that a pharmaceutical sales rep would have misoprostol hidden in an unlabeled plastic baggie? Just tell me if you treated him for ulcers."

Ben shook his head. "I've never prescribed misoprostol for any patient."

CHAPTER 56

PATRICK

8 MONTHS AFTER THE ACCIDENT

February 12, 2018

Amanda was waiting at the coffee shop when Patrick arrived. She'd called and asked to meet. Sans smile, she countered his greeting with a quip about tardiness.

"You did suggest the time," she accused.

He ordered green tea and sat across from her.

"I'm sorry," she said. "Thank you for coming."

"Of course. What's going on?"

"I have a question."

"I can probably turn your question into ten questions."

She ignored his stab at humor. "Misoprostol. Do you think it could cause pseudocyesis?"

He hadn't heard her say *pseudocyesis* since she'd told him it sounded terminal. "Is that a drug?"

She sighed impatiently. The back of his neck tingled, the feeling he'd gotten during the early days of his residency, when he'd been expected to know everything despite being a year out of medical school. He used his phone to search online.

"Stomach ulcers," he mumbled, scanning the page. And then he looked up at her. "Abortion?"

"What do you think?"

He spent several minutes scanning various websites about the drug. "I don't see anything that would suggest any psychotropic effects. Honestly, I don't know."

She stared at him, eyes aglow, a side of her he'd never seen. "There's a pattern here. You never know anything. You're full of knowledge, but you don't stand behind any of it. 'The evidence suggests,'" she mocked. "'It seems likely that. To the best of our understanding. Insofar as we know.' Are all neuroscientists so irresolute, or is that a personal failing you bring to the profession?"

He was flabbergasted. And silent.

"Even this you can't answer," she taunted, her lips turning up in a small humorless smile, clearly frustrated.

"The brain is complex," he sputtered. "Just fifteen years ago—"

"Computers are complex. Neural networks are complex."

He chuckled, and her face flushed. He'd thought she was joking. Neural networks were constructed by engineers. The brain was the product of millions of years of barely understood evolution. Her eyes, completely lacking in mirth, made plain that she wasn't joking. He raised his hands in surrender, hoping to diffuse—whatever this was.

"Most serious neuroscientists are cautious. We don't want to make exaggerated claims, and unfortunately, there's a lot we don't know. You'll occasionally see a neuroscientist on television who throws caution out the window, but—"

"Forget caution. Why don't you know anything?"

"We know a lot. The brain is incredibly difficult to study. We—"

"You know what this reminds me of?"

"I can't wait to hear."

"The spermists versus the ovists."

"Okay."

"Spermists believed that a fully formed human existed within a sperm cell. That little human would travel to an egg, enter, and then grow. Ovists believed that a fully formed human existed within the egg. The little human would wait for sperm to arrive, a sort of fertilizer.

"Neither side had good reason to believe what they did. They didn't have the proper tools to discover the truth, but they had to believe something, I guess. And then microscopy improved, and they were both proved wrong. My question to you: Were spermists and ovists wasting their time spinning theories? They could've been growing food or something. Their generation just wasn't meant to know. Knowledge belongs to those with the proper tools. Maybe your generation isn't meant to know."

"I should be growing food?" he asked.

"I'd better go. I haven't been sleeping, and I don't feel well."

"Why did you ask about misoprostol?"

The conversation was apparently over, because she stood and left.

He wondered what their exchange looked like to an observer. He was a participant, and he had no idea what happened. He sipped his tea. When his phone rang, he thought it was Amanda calling to apologize.

Scam Likely, read the caller display.

⁓

Patrick joined Rob on the sofa, in front of a sports network. "How was your date?" Rob asked.

"It wasn't a date." He recounted the conversation with Amanda.

Rob laughed. "Welcome to my world. Just multiply by two. Wife and daughter. But in Amanda's defense, little brother, it sounds like she wittingly or unwittingly took an abortion drug."

"You think?" Patrick asked.

"Maybe she was asking for a friend from her pseudocyesis support group. Yeah, dummy, I think."

CHAPTER 57

AMANDA

32 WEEKS PREGNANT

February 12, 2018

Detective Sebold: *I've been over Derrick's financial records. Would you mind if I take a peek at yours?*

    Amanda: *What are you looking for?*

    Detective Sebold: *Just making sure I'm not missing anything.*

    Interview at Amanda's residence, 6:30 p.m., Friday, February 2, 2018

～

Amanda lay in bed, Meredith beside her, rubbing her belly.

    "If he resurfaces," Amanda said, "those pills are going to the police." She'd put them in the back of the bathroom drawer, where she wouldn't see them and they wouldn't be disturbed.

    "You should do that anyway."

    "So I can answer more questions about my condition? When I tell people I'm not pregnant, the first thing they do is glance at my belly. It makes me wish I could disappear. Besides, what would the police do? Try harder to find Derrick?"

Meredith didn't reply.

"I knew I shouldn't sleep with Ralph. I knew it would end badly. And here I am."

"Your determination to take responsibility for Derrick's actions is wearing me out."

"Maybe it's better if he's dead. If he comes back, there will be a trial. I don't want that." Amanda couldn't imagine that. Talking about everything they'd been through—everything she'd done—in open court.

"I'll be at your side if that happens," Meredith said.

"I keep having these crazy thoughts of calling Ralph and saying, 'He murdered our baby!'"

"Why would you do that?"

"I wouldn't. Just crazy thoughts." The tears came again, and Amanda wondered if she would ever run dry. "I should've left when I found out I was pregnant. I put my baby in danger."

"You couldn't know," Meredith said, soothing Amanda with her touch. "How could you know?" They lay together, two tearful sisters.

Amanda wiped her eyes. "I should apologize to Patrick." She picked up her phone. "I was awful to him."

"I think he'll understand."

Amanda didn't want to talk, so she sent Patrick a text. She apologized and told him she'd found misoprostol hidden in a plastic baggie among Derrick's things.

CHAPTER 58

AMANDA

32 WEEKS PREGNANT

February 16, 2018

The house felt desolate. Derrick had been gone for three weeks, but his presence lingered. His favorite mug was in the cabinet. His coats hung in the foyer closet. He hadn't shared her bed for a long time, but still, she slept on the right side because he'd once slept on the left. Meredith was out, and Amanda thought she'd catch up on reading. Restlessness made that impossible. She tried to pace, but her calf cramped.

She called Patrick, relieved when he answered on the second ring.

"I'm craving something sweet, but I totally understand if you're busy with Rob."

"Actually," Patrick said, "I'm not. Rob went out."

"Great." She hadn't seen Patrick since she'd told him he should be growing food.

~

Amanda apologized again. They sipped hot ciders at a coffee shop near Amanda's house. "I don't want you to stop talking to me about neuroscience."

"It's fine," he said. Again.

She didn't believe him, but she wouldn't push the issue. "Tell me about an unusual disorder."

"Amanda, we haven't talked about the misoprostol."

She closed her eyes, pushing down the anguish and fury that thoughts of misoprostol elicited. "There's nothing to say."

"Nothing?"

"I just fucking hate men right now." Amanda's eyes went wide. "Not you. I mean, you're definitely a man, but I like you."

Patrick smiled. "It's fine."

"Ralph came by my house yesterday, unannounced. In one breath, he told me that he cares about me and threatened legal action." She touched her swollen belly. "These men who supposedly love me seem more interested in controlling me. But I think Ralph might be gone for good. Thanks to Meredith." She recounted the episode to Patrick.

∼

Amanda had offered to provide Ralph with her medical records, just to get rid of him. Meredith, who was sitting in the living room with them, despite Ralph's request to talk to Amanda alone, objected.

"Just the record of the miscarriage," Amanda clarified.

"First of all," Meredith said, "it's none of his business. Second, if you provide proof of the miscarriage, he'll want to see your diagnosis. Let's just agree now that he won't get an inch or a yard."

"Are you a lawyer?" Ralph asked Meredith.

"Worse. I'm her sister. Did you know that her husband is missing?"

Ralph looked at Amanda.

"Derrick went missing a couple of weeks ago," Meredith continued. "Maybe there was foul play; maybe there wasn't. But I find your behavior suspicious. Maybe I'll tell the detective that you're demanding a paternity test."

"What is this?" Ralph asked Amanda.

"It's exactly what I told you," Meredith said before Amanda could respond.

"Your husband is missing?"

"We don't know if he's alive," Meredith said. "Maybe you know something about it."

~

Amanda sipped her cider and smiled at Patrick. "Ralph couldn't get out of there fast enough."

"Meredith is a good sister," Patrick said.

"The best. How is Marissa?"

Patrick hesitated. "Remember finals in college? Multiple big tests on the same day. Your grades on the line. Imagine if a noncollege friend stopped by your dorm room during finals week."

"I'd want her to leave immediately," Amanda said.

"Marissa exists perpetually in finals week. I'm giving her space."

Amanda nodded. She'd been hearing that story since she'd met Patrick. "What is Rob doing tonight?"

"He went to a movie."

"What movie? Why didn't you go?"

"*Maze Runner*, supposedly. I offered, but he said he likes to go to the movies alone. I suspect he's watching *Fifty Shades Freed*." Patrick laughed. "He would never admit that."

"Is he into those?"

Patrick shrugged. "You never know."

"Huh," Amanda said thoughtfully. "What did you and Rob do Wednesday night?"

"Wednesday? Rob met up with a friend from medical school. A guy he hadn't seen in years."

"And last night?"

"We grilled. In the cold. Why?"

"He's with Meredith," Amanda said suddenly.

"What? No." Patrick looked confused.

"Meredith went out Wednesday night, supposedly to see a friend from high school. Tonight, she's supposedly at a nightclub."

"You think they're together?"

"Meredith and I watched movies last night. What do you think?"

"How did they even get in touch?"

"They must have exchanged numbers last week."

Patrick pulled out his cell phone.

"What are you doing?"

"Calling Rob." He dialed and put the phone to his ear. "Straight to voice mail."

"What did you expect?"

"It's probably a coincidence."

"Let's hope so. How old is Rob?"

"Forty. I don't think he would—" Patrick stopped midsentence, as if reconsidering.

"I'm not jumping to conclusions," Amanda said. "I don't even want to think about it until I know for sure. I'll ask Meredith tonight."

"Would she tell you the truth?"

Amanda shrugged. "Not thinking about it. Not jumping to conclusions."

CHAPTER 59

PATRICK

8 MONTHS AFTER THE ACCIDENT

February 17, 2018

Patrick was nodding off on the sofa. He felt like a television dad, awaiting the return of an errant adolescent. It was a few minutes after midnight when Rob used his key to enter the front door. Rob moved gingerly through the darkness.

"Are you looking for your curfew?" Patrick asked, still in his television-dad role. "Because you missed it a few hours ago."

"What are you doing up?"

"Couldn't sleep. I've been watching videos on my phone." He turned on the lamp. "How was the movie?"

"Solid B-plus."

"Did Meredith like it?"

Rob grinned. He sat down on the other end of the couch and faced Patrick. "She doesn't want Amanda to know. I didn't want to hand you a secret."

"Amanda figured it out. Were you with her on Wednesday?"

Rob nodded. "I guess I didn't want you to know either."

"You're old enough to be her father."

"I know," Rob said, chastened. "She's seven years older than Julie."

"That was going to be my next point."

"I used to think getting old was something you did. I didn't realize it just happens to you."

"What are you doing, Rob? How did you and Meredith even get in contact?"

"She slipped me her number after dinner. I know. I didn't have to use it. But look at her."

Patrick shrugged. "What you do is your business, but I don't want you to mess things up with Amanda. It's a complication we don't need."

"Look, I'm sorry. I came here to spend time with you, not to start a fling and embarrass you. I need to fix my life."

"What happened to your family, Rob?"

He sighed. "Julie 'overheard' her mother say I've been unfaithful." He emphasized *overheard* with air quotes.

"Were you?"

Rob nodded.

"Do you love Sandra?"

"I don't think so. Things went wrong for us long ago. It was all my fault, but I spent a lot of time blaming her."

"It can't all be your fault," Patrick said. "There are two people in your marriage."

"It can all be my fault. And it is. I went through this phase during my surgical residency. Things were just hard, and I thought I needed to be with someone who understood it. Sandra taught kindergarten. She didn't know what it was like to lose a patient or to suck up to narcissistic surgeons all day. I had an affair with a colleague, and I fell in love with her. Sandra never knew. I was at the hospital all the time, and after that, having affairs was easy. I never fell in love with another woman, but I did what I did."

"What happened with the one you fell in love with? Why did it end?"

"She was in a car accident, traumatic brain injury. Never recovered. She lives with her brother and his family in Pittsburgh. I visit once a year."

Patrick was astonished. "You never told me that."

"Julie was four at the time. It wasn't something I talked about. What would you have said? To give up my wife and daughter to take care of Pam?"

Patrick shook his head. "I don't know what I would have said. I just thought we were closer than that."

"That's why you told me you were raising Laura as your own?"

Patrick shrugged. "Good point."

"It isn't difficult being a surgeon. Not for me. Becoming a surgeon was hell. I thought Sandra wasn't enough for me. If I could've made it through that patch a faithful man, I really think things would be different. I might still love my wife. She might still love me."

"What does Julie have to say about it all?"

"Nothing. If she's sitting in a room and I walk in, she leaves. She told Sandra I'm an awful father. She has no idea what an awful father is. I wish Dad had affairs, if it would've kept him out of the house more."

"You don't think he did?"

"I don't know what he did. I never knew the man."

They sat in silence.

"Are you glad you went to see him before he died?" Rob asked.

Patrick considered it. "I am. He was alone in the end."

"His charming personality wouldn't have anything to do with that."

"I wanted to know if there was ever the possibility that he could have been something other than what he was."

"And?" Rob asked.

"I think so. I saw a different side of him. He didn't apologize, but he wanted to know how I turned out. He asked about you. I told him you're an asshole."

"That seems to be the consensus," Rob said. "Fair or not. One night, when I couldn't sleep, I googled 'awful fathers.' After I scrolled past Darth Vader and Al Bundy, I found story after story about abusive fathers. Julie speaks four languages fluently. Do you know why?"

Patrick shrugged.

"Because I pay thirty grand a year to send her to an international school. I wish Dad were still alive so I could send her to stay with him for the summer. That would give her some perspective."

"Do you really want Julie to set the bar so low? Would you want her to marry a man like you?"

"Whoa, Patrick, don't pull your punches. If you need to make a point, just say what you mean."

"Answer the question."

Rob sighed. "When Julie was two, everything was Dada this, Dada that. I don't know why. Sandra did everything for her. I practically lived at the hospital, but when I was home, Julie loved me with a startling ferocity. If she fell, she would run to me: 'Dada. Dada.' I would kiss her knee, and that would make everything better. It annoyed Sandra, but I loved it. When she got older, she wanted to know everything about how the human body works. 'How does the heart know how fast to beat? How is food digested?' I would get out of surgery and have a message to call home to answer one of Julie's questions. I felt like I was in med school again, all the questions she asked. Then she decided she wanted to be a surgeon. I never thought about Julie marrying a man like me. I thought she would grow up and become me.

"Now, she wants to be a social activist. I didn't even know that was a job. Add my daughter to the casualties of climate change. I've spent hundreds of thousands of dollars educating her, and she wants to be a social activist."

"There are worse ambitions. And worse consequences of climate change."

"I asked myself what I would do if she came to me and said she wanted to be a psychiatrist."

Patrick smiled. "I thought you were going to say *stripper*."

"No. I would be devastated, of course. But ultimately, I would pay for her to go to medical school and read books by Freud."

"Sleeping with women young enough to be her sister won't help your relationship."

"I guess it won't. Problem is, I don't know what will."

"Start by keeping the lines of communication open. You have to keep talking to her."

"It's hard. Especially since she used to love me. I can't bear the way she looks at me."

"You have to. One day, when she's no longer a teenager and the hormones have leveled and her prefrontal cortex is fully developed, she's going to think of you. She'll think you're a jerk for cheating on her mom, but don't let her think you're a jerk for abandoning her. Let her hate you. Embrace her as she hates you. Be there for every moment of it."

"I don't know how to talk to her."

"Figure it out. Even as we get older, we make choices that define who we are. Your relationship with Julie twenty years from now could hinge on the choices you make today. Call her in the morning. Tell her you love her."

"I didn't cheat on Julie. It shouldn't be this hard."

"Stick with 'I love you.'"

Rob laughed. "Will do. Have you ever had an affair?"

Patrick shook his head. He started to say he'd never wanted to, but then he thought of Amanda.

Rob smiled. "Really. You haven't slept with Amanda?"

"Amanda told me tonight that she hates men. She hurried to say that doesn't include me."

Rob laughed. "The friend zone."

Patrick nodded. "It stung. But it shouldn't have. I'm married."

"It stung because you want to sleep with her."

"If Laura were alive," Patrick said, "I would never want her to wonder if there was ever the possibility that I could have been a different man."

Rob considered that. "Fair enough. You didn't tell me how bad things are with Marissa."

"I thought I did."

"Maybe I had to see for myself. What are you going to do?"

Patrick shook his head. He honestly didn't know.

"She needs you to reach her," Rob said. "What she's doing isn't good for her. You can't wait this out. You need to do something."

"You don't think I've tried? She won't talk about her sister or Laura. She won't talk about us. Hell, most days she won't talk at all."

"If she won't talk to you," Rob said, "find someone she will talk to. Do something."

"The surgeon's motto."

"If you were bleeding out right now, it might be an opportune moment to talk about the purpose of life and the meaning of death, but you wouldn't want me to do that. You would want me to take life-preserving action. Even if it failed. You would want action."

~

When Patrick awoke the following morning, he found Rob sitting at the kitchen table, staring out the window. He didn't turn when Patrick entered. "Is there a woman sunbathing out there?" Patrick asked.

"What?" Rob turned. He looked stricken.

"What's wrong with you?"

"I called Julie. I got her voice mail three times before she answered. She didn't even say hello. She said, 'What do you want?' I told her I love her."

Patrick sat down across from him. "What did she say?"

"She cried. She couldn't say anything. She managed to tell me she loved me, too, before we hung up."

"Sounds like a start," Patrick said.

"Huh. Maybe you psychiatrists do know something."

CHAPTER 60

AMANDA

32 WEEKS PREGNANT

February 18, 2018

Amanda sat in the recliner waiting for Meredith to wake up. She needed to talk, and she was contemplating blasting music when, shortly after ten thirty, Meredith staggered downstairs. "Patrick asked me to go to Princeton with him."

Meredith paused, squinting as if still trying to adjust to the light.

Amanda pressed forward. "He's driving to New Jersey to meet with his wife's former mentor. They've exchanged emails, but Patrick wants to speak with him in person. He hopes that the man can get through to her. Apparently, Rob convinced him that he needs to do something."

Meredith plopped herself onto the couch. "Rob is probably right. Why does Patrick want you to go?"

"I don't know. For the ride."

Meredith was thoughtful. "I think you should do it."

"I'm not sure I can take all the sitting."

"He knows your condition. He's a doctor. I'm sure he'll make frequent stops."

"It's too weird. He's going on a quest to save his marriage. Why does he want me there?"

"I'm more concerned about you than him. You're sitting in this house dreading another visit from Detective Sebold. If you won't come back to Charlotte with me, get out of town for a few days. You deserve it."

"Maybe," Amanda said. "Are you sleeping with Rob?"

Meredith blinked. "That's an abrupt change in topic."

"It woke you up."

Meredith laughed. "I've been seeing him."

Amanda closed her eyes, trying not to show disapproval.

"You don't need to take care of me," Meredith said. "You need to take care of yourself, and part of that is letting me take care of you. I'm fine."

"I can't just say nothing when I think you're making bad choices."

"He's going back to Baltimore to get a divorce. I'm going back to Raleigh to finish school. Unless I need a liver transplant, I'll probably never see him again."

"This has nothing to do with our discussions about money?"

"All I want from a man right now is that he not mess with my money. I can make my own."

Amanda appraised her, happy that she was finally getting to know her sister. "I know you can. What you need to understand is that I remember when you were two years old. Sometimes when I think of you, I think of that little girl. I want you to be happy, and I want everything to go well for you. I know that I can't protect you, but I still want to try."

Meredith bent over the recliner and hugged her. "I love you, Amanda. I want to protect you too. But I don't want to miss out on opportunities for good sex."

Amanda laughed.

CHAPTER 61

AMANDA

33 WEEKS PREGNANT

Baby has fattened up. His arms and legs resemble sausages.

—Your Best Pregnancy

February 25, 2018

Amanda pushed the seat back for maximum leg room. The SUV Patrick had rented for the trip was spacious, but her left calf was like a spoiled child in need of coddling. He placed water in the cup holder next to her. "Stay hydrated," he said. "We'll stop every hour."

They had twenty-four hours of driving ahead, round trip, and she still questioned the wisdom of confining herself even to this luxurious seat. Patrick had promised to break the drive into four legs. They would stop in Greensboro, North Carolina, for the night and arrive in Princeton the following evening. His lunch meeting with John Wells was scheduled for the day after that. They would spend an additional night in Princeton before returning south via Tennessee. They began their journey with a playlist from Amanda's phone, but even that failed to keep her awake.

"Where are we?" Amanda asked groggily, surfacing from a nap.

"Anderson, South Carolina," Patrick replied cheerfully. They'd been on the road for two hours. "You slept through our first scheduled break. I didn't know if I should wake you."

"Never wake me." She smiled. "But I really have to pee."

They stopped at a rest area with manicured lawns, picnic benches, and tree-lined walking paths. "I could spend the day here," Amanda commented. They contented themselves with twenty minutes.

Amanda sipped water once they were back on the freeway. "I'm exhausted all the time. Did I warn you about that?"

"I downloaded some podcasts. Sleep as much as you want. I just like having you with me."

That made Amanda smile.

The motion of the car and the soft music were lulling her to sleep when he said, "You mentioned last week that you were tired of men trying to control you."

"Did I?"

"You did. And it stuck with me. I wonder if I'm trying to control Marissa." Amanda started to speak, but he continued. "Grief doesn't have to be logical. Why should she grieve in the way I want her to?"

"How do you want her to grieve?"

"I want her to accept that Jen and Laura are gone. I want her to process that and adjust to a future without them."

"How do you think her mentor can help?"

Patrick shrugged. "When Marissa couldn't stay at Princeton for her doctorate, John Wells convinced her that she could still be a mathematician. She respects him, and he seems to understand that there is more to life than math. He can urge her to seek treatment. I've seen medication make a tremendous difference."

"What about her math? Could that be impacted?"

Patrick nodded. "That's why it has to come from a mathematician. At the very least, psychotropics would inhibit her motivation. Her creativity could be impacted but not permanently. She just needs help getting through this patch."

"When I mentioned controlling men, I was talking about Derrick and Ralph. For them, loving me had nothing to do with my happiness. You're not like that. You care about Marissa's well-being. And you aren't coercive. You're a psychiatrist. You could probably get Marissa committed against her will. You haven't done that."

"I wouldn't," Patrick said. "But I doubt I could. The bar for commitment is high. For good reason."

"You get my point. I saw a documentary on the lobotomy last week. It made me so angry, and I couldn't help but think that sixty years ago, Derrick might've had me lobotomized. He could've taken me to the hospital, and I, a Black woman, wouldn't have stood a chance. Then off to some back alley for an illegal abortion."

"Psychiatry has a dark history," Patrick said.

"Humanity has a dark history. Certain groups just bear the brunt of it. That American doctor who performed thousands of lobotomies. Freeman."

"Walter Freeman."

"Right. Imagine if he got hold of Marissa. He would've jumped at the chance to crush her mathematical prowess. A lot of his victims were gay, an attempt to suppress homosexual behavior. The originator of the lobotomy won a Nobel Prize. I lost respect for the Nobel institution when I learned that."

"You don't assume that modern-day scientists are fully enlightened?"

"People panic over the prospect of superintelligent machines," Amanda said and yawned. "I'm more afraid of people." She closed her eyes. The sleepiness was like an illness. "Did I help?"

"Yes. Very much. Take a nap. We'll stop for lunch when you wake up."

~

Amanda and Patrick spent the night in a motel, she in room 49, he next door in 51. He picked up takeout, and they ate in Amanda's room. They ordered a movie, but Amanda fell asleep midway through. When she awoke, Patrick was gone. It was 2:00 a.m., and she was wide awake, so she did some work on a consulting project she'd picked up the week before.

~

She could've slept longer when her alarm went off at six, but she wanted to shower and wash her hair before another day on the road. Forty minutes later, she called Patrick, but he didn't answer. They hadn't pinned down a time to meet, just made vague plans to have breakfast at the diner across the street. She walked next door to his room and knocked. She thought she heard the television, but there was no response. She used the key card he'd left on her nightstand. *I'm notorious for locking myself out,* he'd told her. The light turned green, and she opened the door slowly and peeked inside.

A rap video blared from the television. He was shirtless, doing a ridiculous dance in front of the mirror. She watched him, mouth open, so distracted that when he turned and saw her, she'd forgotten that she was invading his privacy. He lunged for the shirt on his bed and fell, landing on his back on the floor. She rushed forward and, not knowing what else to do, picked up his shirt. His face was red, and she lost it. She covered her face with his shirt and laughed.

"I could've been a rapper," he called as she backed out of his room.

She returned to her own room and only then realized that she still had his shirt. She called Meredith. It rang twice before she answered.

"I'm in love with him."

"Who?" Meredith croaked.

"You know who."

"Yes, I'm kidding. I was asleep."

"I want to tell him to cancel the meeting with his wife's mentor. I want him to drive us somewhere warm. I want to sit in the sun with him on the beach. And then I think about shopping for a maternity swimsuit, and I'm like, no thank you."

Meredith laughed. "Slow down, okay. Slow way down."

"What do you mean?"

"Let it play out. Things are super complicated with his wife. Just let it play out."

"I shouldn't seduce him with my pregnant body?"

"You joke," Meredith said, "but there's an entire genre of porn that stars pregnant women."

"Ew. I didn't need to know that."

"I'm just saying. But no, absolutely no sex."

"He's married, and I'm on a road trip with him. I don't know how I got here."

"I do. I also know he feels the same way about you. But you need to let him figure that out. I don't know what Patrick has told you, but Rob doesn't think his marriage is going to make it."

"I feel terrible for his wife," Amanda said. "But I want to be happy. With her husband. Is that horrible?"

"It's human."

"Did Patrick say anything to Rob about me?" Amanda held her breath as she waited.

"I don't think so. Rob asked me if the two of you were sleeping together."

She exhaled. She'd hoped for insight into Patrick's feelings.

"You need a good friend right now," Meredith said. "So does Patrick. Be there for each other. And be patient. No pregnant sex."

Amanda sighed. "You are wise. Did you know that?"

"That's why you called me, right?"

Amanda had called her because there was no one else she could tell. *Wise* wasn't a word she associated with her sister. Maybe she needed to reassess her assumptions. "I called you," she said, "because I needed a friend who isn't Patrick."

CHAPTER 62

PATRICK

9 MONTHS AFTER THE ACCIDENT

February 27, 2018

Patrick met John Wells at an Italian restaurant near Princeton's campus. John was tall and broad shouldered and had the handshake of a wrestler. "It's nice to meet you," Patrick said and resisted the urge to dunk his tortured hand in ice water.

"I brought Marissa here when she was an undergraduate," John said as they settled at a table. "We try to meet here when she's in town." John nodded to the menu. "I recommend the eggplant parmesan."

Patrick took his advice, and John selected the wine, a half bottle.

He told Patrick about the first time he'd met Marissa. He'd been a graduate student visiting his sister. One of her neighbors had had a cookout, and he'd ended up talking to Marissa because he was bad at small talk with adults. And he'd never met an eleven-year-old who was interested in what he did.

"She had an interest, but I had no idea how far she would take it. I was thrilled when she came to Princeton as an undergraduate. She worked in my lab. I and another professor, Dmitri Kazakov, competed over her. She was my favorite student."

"She speaks very highly of you," Patrick said. The combination of bread and olive oil was superb.

"I've followed her career more closely than those of my former doctoral students. Before she left Princeton, she asked me if she would be able to come back as a professor. I told her the truth: probably not. She would have to do something extraordinary. Even then, the right person would have to recognize it. When you're not at a top-tier university, your work, even great work, can be ignored. I read everything she published, looking for the extraordinary thing that could bring her back."

Their food arrived, two identical plates of eggplant parmesan.

"She was a star at Halford," Patrick said. "What did you think of her work?"

John hesitated. "It was solid. As good as most of the stuff coming out of the top-tier universities. I saw hints of brilliance, but ultimately, her work was conventional. I don't want to say she lacked creativity, but she never strayed far from the canon."

"Have you seen her current work?" Patrick asked. The food was excellent, but nerves dampened his hunger.

John nodded and paused to chew his food. "Nothing conventional about it. Are you a ballet enthusiast, Patrick?"

Patrick shook his head.

"Well, as you can imagine, dancers have differing levels of skill. Some are exquisite, but they're still doing ballet. Marissa is a ballerina who is no longer doing ballet. She's doing something far more beautiful and complex than anything we've seen. It's dance but nothing we recognize."

Patrick knew his wife was brilliant. He didn't need metaphors. "Marissa is delusional. She isn't in touch with reality. If a brilliant grad student applied to work in your lab and told you she wanted to communicate with the dead, would you accept her?"

"Frankly, if she were doing math at Marissa's level, I would."

"I love the mathematician in Marissa, but she's so much more than that to me," Patrick said. "Can you understand that?"

"I care a great deal about Marissa. I sat at this very table with her fifteen years ago. She wanted to be great. I told her to put her family first." John sighed as if the memory hurt. "I was struggling at the time, going through a divorce, barely seeing my children. At that moment, at that time, I regretted not putting my family first. Maybe I believed I was a man who could put his family first. Now, I see my folly. My children are nearly grown, and I barely know them. I've remarried to a woman who understands my passion for math. I'm happy. Maybe family doesn't—shouldn't—come first for people like Marissa and me.

"Marissa gave up a lot for her sister. More than I ever did for anyone. And still, here we are. If I could go back in time, I would tell Marissa to stay at Princeton. She belongs here. I would tell her that nothing is more important than her talent. I would tell her that because I care about her."

Their plates, half-finished despite the premium quality of the food, sat between them.

"Have you considered," John asked, "that Marissa is working through her sister's death in her own way?"

Patrick had considered that. He found it disingenuous. If Marissa had spent months building a phone of plastic and wires to communicate with her dead sister, then everyone would readily accept the obvious. But she'd chosen a method of communication that produced special math. And they acted as if special math were evidence of sanity. He wanted to lash out at this man, another mathematician with no regard for Marissa's emotional well-being.

As if sensing his thoughts, John said, "I know what you're looking for. I'm sorry I can't give it to you. But I want to help you understand something. Life is short. For all of us. The history of math is long. Archimedes approximated the value of pi over two thousand years ago. Newton labored three hundred years ago and Gauss a mere two hundred. They're all gone, but they have one thing in common: those of us living today are still using the principles they wrangled from thin air. Five hundred years from now, a thousand years from now, no one will give a thought to the turmoil in our personal lives. Marissa's work will be remembered."

~

Amanda was at the hotel finishing up her consulting project. She informed Patrick via text that she was a couple of hours from completion. He explored downtown Princeton on foot until he was driven indoors—his clothes no match for the northern cold. He settled on a mom-and-pop coffee shop and ordered a hot chocolate. He placed his phone on the table in case Amanda finished up early. He would ask her out to dinner and a movie.

CHAPTER 63

AMANDA

34 WEEKS PREGNANT

Baby can track movement as her eyes continue to develop.

—Your Best Pregnancy

February 28, 2018

They set off for Roanoke, Virginia, after a quiet, leisurely breakfast. Quiet because they barely spoke. She was peeved by his reticence, his refusal to talk about the meeting with John Wells. It hadn't gone well—she'd inferred that much—but when she pressed for details, he shut down.

He'd been distracted the night before. He'd asked her out for dinner and a movie. She'd agreed to dinner but hadn't wanted to waste money on a movie ticket. She wouldn't have stayed awake past the opening credits.

Now, as they entered Maryland, she was seething. She'd shared so many intimate details of her life with him. She closed her eyes for another nap but then said, "Why did you bring me here?"

He glanced at her. "What do you mean?"

"Why did you bring me? You're on a mission to save your marriage. Why am I here?"

He focused on the road.

When, after a few moments, he didn't reply, she said: "You've lost the ability to answer simple questions?"

"I'm trying to figure out where this is coming from."

"Where do you think it's coming from?" He was making her angrier. "What do you want, Patrick? Are you capable of saying what you want?"

He slowed and pulled the SUV onto the side of the road. Cars whizzed by them on the left.

She sat up. "What is wrong with you?"

He put the SUV in park, took off his seat belt, and kissed her. Her body responded before her mind registered what was happening. She closed her eyes and kissed him back and drank in the taste of him, the feel of his tongue on hers. And then he stopped. He settled back into his seat, fastened the belt, signaled, and pulled back onto the road.

Amanda's body, pregnant and not pregnant, felt foreign to her, but she recognized desire. She didn't know what sex would be like, but she wanted him inside of her. She listened to the hum of the engine, the soft whir of the heater.

"Okay," she finally said, the spot where they'd kissed far behind them, "you know what you want."

"I know what I want," he affirmed.

~

She didn't remember falling asleep. "We'll stop in five miles," he told her when she awoke.

"I'd rather you get me to my hotel room," she said, the feel of him still lingering.

"In due time."

He signaled to exit the freeway. Moments later he pulled up to a bed-and-breakfast.

"Is this us?" she asked.

He nodded.

"When did you plan this?"

"While you were napping. Do you approve?"

"You're a sneak," she said.

"Is one room okay? We can still go to a hotel."

She felt a pang of anxiety, fear that her body wouldn't work. She thought about sharing her fear with him, but that could qualify as too much information. She could text Meredith for advice. But there were two things wrong with that. One, Meredith had been firm in her sentiment that sex was a bad idea. Two, Meredith was a child. She wasn't going to seek sex advice from a child. She was on her own. She climbed out of the car.

"I think you should get our bags," she told him.

CHAPTER 64

MARISSA

9 MONTHS AFTER THE ACCIDENT

March 7, 2018

Defeat.

There was no other word for it.

Marissa had come a long way in the eight months since she'd first examined the many-worlds interpretation of quantum mechanics. The theory promised the existence of universes where Laura hadn't died, even universes where Jen had never experimented with drugs. The failure of wave functions to collapse at the quantum level meant that every possible outcome—the choice to have coffee, tea, or juice with breakfast—led to a split where each was realized in a different world. Bizarre, but so much about the universe was bizarre.

From there, she'd turned to string theory and an investigation of the fundamental building blocks of matter. Two days ago, she'd been startled by a discovery in her equations: all universes occupied the same position in space. She'd once envisioned universes crowding each other like so many bubbles in a solution. She now understood that universes were separated by the fundamental properties of their matter, specifically the combination of frequencies assumed by the finite number of strings that comprised a given universe. All matter was composed of strings; all strings were identical save for the frequencies at which they vibrated.

The implications were thrilling. She could model each universe as a vector where each entry in the vector represented a string belonging to that universe. Each string in turn was represented by a real number: the frequency of its vibration. Matter and energy in a modeled universe could be formed from linear combinations of the vector. She could model herself as a vector composed of strings from the universe she inhabited. If she changed the frequency of just one type of string within her body/vector, she would find herself in a different universe. The smaller the change, the more likely she was to land in a universe similar to her own, a universe where Laura had been born but hadn't died.

The model of herself captured far more complexity, requiring not only frequencies of strings but also their counts and positions. The computer was Marissa's least favorite tool. One of her early break-throughs had been a transformation that compressed the representation of high-dimensional vectors without losing essential properties. Even so, she didn't have enough notebook paper to transcribe a vector from her model. Forget about performing the computations by hand. She logged in to the math servers at Halford and used a linear algebra library to build and manipulate her models. Running programs without first reserving time was a violation of the rules, but she would apologize later. If it came to that. She worked assiduously, impatient with the computer's processing time, even as the shape of something, a wall, emerged.

She was working in the realm of the theoretical, and one—not minor—practical obstacle had been apparent from the start. She had no physical way of manipulating the strings that comprised her body. Researchers routinely worked at the nanoscale, but for her purposes they would need to go far smaller. Certainly, it wasn't an impossibility, but it would require time and resources to get there.

As she studied the behavior of her model, a second, more discouraging problem emerged—the real-life ramifications of transition from one universe to another. She could do it, but she would no longer be herself.

In the moments before Laura had died, there was a version of Marissa who'd decided to rock Laura instead of attempting to carry her to the kitchen. That decision had split into its own universe where Laura thrived, its matter composed of its own unique combination of vibrating strings. If the current, grieving Marissa managed to change the vibrations of her own strings to match those of that coveted universe, then she would become the Marissa who'd never attempted to take Laura downstairs. There would be no grand reunion. The past ten months as she'd experienced them would be gone—the person she'd become in that time ceasing to exist. She would be as oblivious to her fortune as was that other, blessed Marissa.

It was a fundamental structure of time, and she was coming to see that no probing would get her around it. Time moved incessantly in one direction. As desperately as she tried, it was impossible to connect in a meaningful way to the past because she was no longer the person who'd experienced that past. She'd moved forward, and her existence could only be realized in the present.

Defeat.

CHAPTER 65

PATRICK

9 MONTHS AFTER THE ACCIDENT

March 8, 2018

Detective Sebold: *Thank you for talking to me. I just have a few questions about your relationship with Amanda Jackson. Did you know her husband?*
  Patrick: *Indirectly.*
  Interview at Patrick's residence, 7:00 p.m., Thursday, March 8, 2018

~

Patrick hadn't been surprised when Detective Sebold, dressed in plain clothes, knocked at his door. A line from some movie he'd seen—*What took you so long?*—flashed in his mind as the detective introduced himself and gave Patrick a look at his badge. The anxiety had been simmering beneath the surface for a while, but by now, Patrick was nearly immune. He was becoming a master at compartmentalization.

He'd learned that lies reproduced. The first was innocent. Patrick had told Marissa he was driving to New Jersey to see a neuroscientist friend.

Why not fly? she'd asked.

Because he was taking Amanda with him, a second lie was born. *I want to make a few stops. Just for myself.* The lies could've multiplied, but Marissa, eager to get back to her math, hadn't questioned him further. Then he'd kissed Amanda, and everything had changed.

The thought of sleeping in the bed he'd shared with Marissa made Patrick nauseous, so his first night home, he slept on the couch. The following morning, he stuffed his guilt in a pack, shouldered it, and returned to Amanda. They made love in her bed. Their lovemaking was gentle and considerate, and what they lacked in adventurousness, they made up for in frequency.

Patrick cooked for her. He experimented with new cuisines, eschewing anything in his repertoire. Any meal he'd ever shared with Marissa was off limits. He could believe sometimes that he was two different people. It was important that he not let those strangers meet. He returned home every night, and he took care of Marissa. As much as she let him. He stocked the refrigerator and cleaned the bathrooms. He secured the locks at night and brewed coffee in the morning. He let her focus on math.

CHAPTER 66

MARISSA

9 MONTHS AFTER THE ACCIDENT

March 20, 2018

Marissa hadn't looked at her models in nearly two weeks, but two questions nagged at her, one mathematical, the other philosophical.

When she'd modeled her transition between two universes, a fifth constant vector had been required to make the math work. Generating the constant was tricky, requiring sophisticated algebra she'd spent the better part of a month developing. By the time she'd managed to reliably get good results, she'd had no idea what the constant vector represented. She knew only that it didn't change during the transition. What did it capture? She abhorred unexplained terms in her equations.

The math was convincing: changing the strings that composed her body to match the frequencies of the strings of another universe would meld her with the Marissa of that universe. On a philosophical note: Why should that be? Conversely, when a decision split the universe, she ended up in two different places. And yet, she was the same person. How could that be?

Could her philosophical question be related to her mathematical one—that unexplained constant?

She drove to a nature preserve in North Georgia, mostly to avoid the temptation to turn to her computer models or pencil and paper. Sometimes, uninterrupted thought was all she needed.

The weather was beginning to warm—the first hints of the coming summer—but she barely perceived anything of the physical world. She walked the trail, her attention turned inward.

What was she? Who was she?

A thought experiment: If she lopped off her hand and left it on this trail, would that change who she was? She'd be short a hand, and certainly that would change her life, but did it change what, who, she was? If she returned for the hand a week later, could she even know for certain that it belonged to her? Decayed and picked clean, it would no longer look like her hand. Of course, she could submit it to a DNA test. That would prove conclusively that it was her hand. But what if she had an identical twin and that twin performed the same experiment next to her? Even DNA couldn't tell them whose hand it was. DNA, she reasoned, held the plan for her body, but it didn't define who she was.

She'd known identical triplets in graduate school. One was a smidge thinner than the others, another a smidge taller. One was studying mathematics, another law, and the third worked for a bank. One had a temper. Or at least, only one had openly displayed his temper. Identical DNA. Different people.

If Marissa believed anything at her core, it was that the universe was ordered. It wouldn't confuse identical triplets even as it split. They were, after all, governed by the same principles as the rest of us. If one triplet stopped eating, the others would not lose weight. Their distinct tastes and temperaments remained constant. Those things didn't flow fluidly between them.

What connected Marissa in this universe to the Marissa in the coveted universe? They were separated by both time and matter. Some form of bookkeeping had to be at play. It couldn't be her DNA. Identical twins were proof of that. It couldn't be the cells of her body. They were a product of her DNA. Most of them had a life cycle separate from her own, influenced by her environment. What was the essence that made her Marissa?

Three years ago, when she and Patrick had still done things for fun, they'd spent a summer reading about consciousness. They'd joked that their reading vacation was a journey as fascinating as a visit to the pyramids of Giza. And much cheaper.

The first challenge was to understand what the conscious mind was. What was subjective experience? Her conscious mind perceived her body, but it was not her body. She referred to her consciousness as *I*. Her consciousness experienced red when she glimpsed an apple. It experienced happiness when she was touched and anger when she was dismissed. When she loved who another person was, she loved their consciousness. But what was it?

Marissa and Patrick were both materialists, but Patrick was more open than she to dualistic ideas. As a staunch materialist, she insisted that consciousness could be purely ascribed to the activity of neurons. She was optimistic about consciousness research where Patrick was reserved, a part of him holding the dualistic view that even a complete description of the brain might not explain consciousness, as if some part of consciousness might exist apart from the neurons that composed the brain.

She found some of the research haunting. There was a famous study that probed the existence of free will. Subjects were told to make a choice to push one of two buttons and were asked to record when the choice was made. The study found that activity in the motor cortex was predictive of subjects' eventual decision, suggesting the choice originated outside the conscious mind. The study, replicated many times over, was far from conclusive and had no shortage of detractors in the neuroscience community, but it gave Marissa a philosophical framework for separating consciousness and free will.

Marissa felt like she made decisions—or more specifically, like her conscious mind made decisions. And yet, there were instances in which decisions were clearly made outside her conscious thought.

She paused to read a sign: PLEASE STAY ON THE TRAIL. She stared at the sign, blue with white lettering. She could let her vision go out of focus. She could direct her thoughts inward. But if she looked at the sign, she could not help but to resolve the lines into letters, the letters into words, and the words into a sentence. She couldn't see green where the sign reflected blue. Not only was her conscious mind powerless to control her perception, it seemed irrelevant to her perception, as if it existed only to experience what it was given. She continued to walk.

If my unconscious mind can do so much, what is my conscious mind for?

If Patrick were here, he might say: *Your unconscious mind reads the sign. Perhaps it's up to your conscious mind to decide if you will heed the warning.*

Maybe. That feels right. But how can I know that the decision to heed or not heed the warning isn't given to my conscious mind like so much else?

She could imagine his smile. *I can think of three clever experiments off the top of my head. But I'll never tell. I don't do consciousness research.*

She hated the taste of baked beans. She loved the sweetness of mango. She didn't know why. Was it possible for her to eat baked beans and taste mango? She didn't think so. She could probably be conditioned to like baked beans and hate mango, but that didn't feel like a choice. Why couldn't her conscious mind, at the very least, choose what it found pleasing?

In some sense, it seemed to her that consciousness was not the driver but rather along for the ride. Perhaps her unconscious mind made decisions and let her conscious mind take credit for them. That wasn't contrary to the notion of free will. Her unconscious mind was just as much a part of her as her conscious mind. The morning before, she'd awakened and eaten three squares of chocolate, her self-imposed

313

daily limit. Somehow, after lunch, she'd found herself in the pantry eating another three squares. Whether she blamed her conscious mind or her unconscious mind, it was her hand inserting chocolate into her mouth. She was the culprit.

Patrick had given her a paper on blindsight that summer. Blindsight. The word alone evoked mystery. It occurred in people who were blind because of damage to their primary visual cortices. Their eyes worked, but their conscious minds saw nothing. In the paper, a toy car was placed in a subject's visual field. Of course, the subject couldn't see it. But when asked to point to the car, the subject did so successfully. His conscious mind couldn't see the car. His unconscious mind could not only see it but could tell his conscious mind where to point.

Marissa had always felt as if her conscious mind was all there was. Clearly, there was more to the story. And it begged the question: Outside of experiencing her life and acting as her identity, what did consciousness do?

By the time she reached her car, her legs exhausted by the day's elevation gain and loss, an idea was tugging at her. The materialist in her—the believer that consciousness arose wholly from neural activity—resisted the notion. The mathematician in Marissa, however, held nothing above logic. And it just didn't make sense that she would have a meaningful physical connection with Marissas in other universes. Unless. It required every bit of her self-control to obey the speed limit—within ten miles per hour—as she drove home, her mind on that mysterious constant.

∼

Still in her hiking boots, she wrote a program to disprove her hypothesis. Her program contained one million iterations. On each iteration, it generated two random universes, two models of herself (one in each universe), and the constant that would allow her vector representations to transition between universes. If her mystery constant represented what she thought it represented, she would find that it had a consistent property over every iteration. She was looking for a counterexample: one iteration where the constant lacked the property but still worked. Then she would know that her hunch was wrong.

She wouldn't allow herself to fantasize about being right. No. Not until she had sufficient evidence. The letdown of being wrong would be too much.

~

She showered while the Halford servers chugged through a mind-blowing number of calculations. As she toweled off, she heard Patrick come in and settle in the living room. He was coming home late these days. And sleeping on the couch. Before she could wonder at the implications of that, her mind returned to the constant. She wanted with all her being to be right. Which was why she had to do everything possible to prove herself wrong. The idea was so exquisite. She didn't want to fall victim to wishful thinking.

She had to stop thinking about it. She had to stop her mind from floating into the clouds. Television? There was nothing she wanted to see on television. That was the problem: mathematics was her best distraction.

~

After several eternities of pacing her office, the strenuous hike forgotten, the computer program returned. She couldn't look at it. Despite the fretful waiting, she couldn't face it. There were two possibilities: the program had halted because a counterexample had been found, or the program had reached the end of its million iterations without a counterexample. In the case of the former, she would walk away from the constant and accept its mystery. The case of the latter was almost beyond imagining.

She held her breath as she read the program's output. Her head bowed with relief.

She knew what the constant represented. A million iterations without a counterexample didn't make a proof, but she knew good math when she saw it. She was doing good math. And her mind reeled as she followed the result to its logical conclusion.

∼

The constant vector represented a universe. In every example, it was a linear combination of the other two universes as well as the two Marissas—meaning it shared a commonality with them all. This property, she understood, was the link that connected the Marissa in one universe with the Marissa in another: consciousness.

Marissa's consciousness was not something that belonged solely to her. It wasn't even something that existed within her. It existed in a separate universe, and it was shared by every Marissa across dimensions. That the Universe of Consciousness remained constant took on a new beauty for Marissa. Even when Marissa left Universe Y to enter Universe Z, a signature of her consciousness remained behind. The Universe of Consciousness was still a linear combination of Universe Y as if to say: Marissa was here.

She would never again see Jen's smile or feel her embrace. But Jen—the being she'd fallen in love with—hadn't gone anywhere. Her consciousness—the essence of her—continued to exist. It was real, and it was physically possible to pinpoint its location.

Like all universes, the Universe of Consciousness existed in the same space as the others, differentiated by the combination of its strings. In a sense, her materialistic instincts had been correct. Consciousness was made up of matter and energy, as was everything else in every

316

other universe. Theoretically, if Marissa changed the strings of her being to match the strings of the Universe of Consciousness, she would become her consciousness, and she could interact directly with Jen's consciousness.

It was beyond anything Marissa had imagined.

She would need help—a team of physicists and engineers. The practical obstacle of manipulating strings remained. But she didn't think there would be any shortage of help. Not after she shared her models.

She lay down on the couch, suddenly exhausted. She would talk to her sister again.

CHAPTER 67

PATRICK

9 MONTHS AFTER THE ACCIDENT

March 11–24, 2018

Detective Sebold: *You married, Patrick?*
Patrick: *Yes.*
Detective Sebold: *Happily?*
Patrick: *We have our challenges. We're working on it.*
Interview at Patrick's residence, 7:00 p.m., Thursday, March 8, 2018

~

Amanda's headaches grew more common as she moved deeper into the third trimester, and on those nights, they skipped sex and lay in the dark, listening to classical music, waiting for the baby to move. The more of her body she sacrificed, the more she longed for a child. They read the pregnancy blogs together because Patrick thought it was important and Amanda couldn't bear it alone.

At thirty-five weeks, Baby is processing more and more complex sounds. His body movements may change in response to music.

Amanda worked nearly full-time on consulting projects, and Patrick spent his days in her living room studying entrepreneurship. He had an idea, a mobile application that psychiatric patients could use to monitor their mental health between doctor's visits. He asked Amanda questions about machine learning, and she patiently explained how it might be used to detect declines in health before they became symptomatic. He was carrying on an affair, something he'd never imagined he would do. And yet, he felt like he was returning to himself. He didn't reflect on that. Not thinking was his coping mechanism.

Absence of forethought had gotten him here. Even now, he remembered their first kiss with trepidation. What if she hadn't reciprocated? What if she'd railed against him for violating their friendship? It could have been an awkward drive home. But he hadn't considered the ramifications. He'd just kissed her, and now, he was standing on a ledge, agitated crocodiles to his left, venomous snakes to his right.

He only pondered the precariousness of his life in the early-morning hours when he couldn't sleep. When that happened, he texted Amanda, and often, she was awake also. He distracted himself with her voice. They talked on the phone until one of them fell to fitful sleep.

At thirty-six weeks, Baby's immune system is prepared to mount a defense against a hostile world.

In an unguarded moment, Amanda told him she missed guilt-free sex. He knew she was referring to Marissa. "You want an uncomplicated life," he said.

"I want that more than anything."

And still, her belly grew. *At thirty-seven weeks, Baby is gaining three to four ounces a week.*

Strangers grew bolder in commenting on her pregnancy. She accepted congratulations with a false smile and grew wary of her time in public. They stayed in more, and she treated him to an education in classic cinema. They learned to play chess together. The future never made it into their conversations.

"I'm sorry I can't tell you why this is happening," Patrick told her one evening, his hand resting on her belly.

She sighed. Her smile seemed forced. "It's okay. You're the smartest neuroscientist I know. Don't ask me how many neuroscientists I know."

Patrick met with Susan Lattimore, a nurse-midwife and the wife of a neuroscientist friend. "Do you think Amanda will experience labor?" she asked him.

He shrugged. "I hope so. Her symptoms seem to be progressing on schedule. But there's no guarantee. This has lasted for years in some women." If labor came, Susan agreed to oversee it at the birthing center where she worked.

In nine days—thirty-nine weeks pregnant—Baby will be full term, all systems prepared for life.

Patrick was content if he didn't think. For someone who was naturally reflective, he found it surprisingly easy.

CHAPTER 68

MARISSA

10 MONTHS AFTER THE ACCIDENT

March 26, 2018

It wasn't so much a dream as a revelation in the dead of night. Marissa awakened, her heart racing. It was dark, and she had no idea how long she'd slept. She asked the digital assistant on her phone for the time: 3:15 a.m.

She'd finished writing a paper on the Universe of Consciousness four hours before. Her intention was to read over it again in the morning before sending it to a few colleagues.

That would never happen.

Repercussions exploded in her mind, dire and terrifying in their scope.

It was theoretically possible for her to interact directly with a consciousness—just as she interacted with people all the time. She was certain of that. And if she could interact with a consciousness, she could destroy it—just as she could murder a fellow human being. What were the ramifications of that?

Weapons of mass destruction gave humankind the power to destroy the earth. But only within one dimension. Without doubt, ruined dimensions existed, their earths wrecked by nuclear weapons. The destruction of a consciousness would reverberate through every dimension in which the person existed. It might be used to destroy a Hitler, and Marissa wouldn't have a problem with that, but who could stop the wrong person from abusing that power? What if a Hitler held that capability in his hands?

She fumbled for the lights and booted her laptop. Hands trembling, she logged in to the Halford math servers and deleted her models.

She paced.

In the event they were recovered, could anyone reverse engineer what she'd learned?

She spent an hour convincing herself that her theoretical work could not be deduced from the vectors and transformations she'd stored on the server.

She had to destroy her paper, her notebooks, anything with any reference to her work. She considered the proofs she'd already shared with Frederick Peters. He'd been sharing them indiscriminately with other mathematicians, she knew. She'd received an email from someone at Carnegie Mellon who'd found a minor mistake in one of her proofs. He'd just wanted her to know so she could fix it. Frederick had shared her writings with a few experimental physicists who believed they could build on her work in quantum mechanics. A computer scientist at Duke had emailed to tell her that her vector transformations could be applied to massive data sets to make formerly intractable learning problems solvable.

She couldn't take any of it back. That knowledge was in the world. Was it enough? How much harm had she done? It would take a major leap from her early work (now being studied by the physicists) to the realization that all universes existed within the same space. She would never speak of that truth and hope that it was a long time before someone in some universe discovered it.

Was there a Marissa somewhere who was choosing at that moment to push forward, determined to interact with Jen's consciousness? The many-worlds interpretation said yes. Or maybe not. Only the possible happened. Was it possible that there was a Marissa somewhere who would risk this? She didn't believe there was. Destroying her work wasn't a choice. It was the only thing she could do.

CHAPTER 69

PATRICK

10 MONTHS AFTER THE ACCIDENT

March 29, 2018

Detective Sebold: *Derrick Jackson has been missing for a month, and you took a road trip with his wife. Can you explain that to me?*
Patrick: *That trip was about me saving my marriage. Amanda was with me as a friend.*
Detective Sebold: *Did it save your marriage?*
Interview at Patrick's residence, 7:00 p.m., Thursday, March 8, 2018

∽

"Why have you been sleeping on the couch?"

Patrick hadn't realized he was awake until Marissa spoke. When he opened his eyes, she was standing over him. She stepped back and sat heavily in the recliner.

He sat up and pulled the covers onto his lap. Marissa's eyes were dreamy, a sure tell that she was approaching intoxication.

"What's that?" He motioned to the glass in her hand. She never drank while she was working.

"Vodka. Now you." Ice cubes clanked as she sipped.

"Now me what?" His thoughts were sluggish.

"Answer my question. I'm drinking vodka because the math is gone. I've reached the end. There's nothing left to do. Why have you been sleeping on the couch?"

He shook his head. "What time is it?" Not quite nine, judging by the quality of the light streaming through the windows.

"Eight thirty. That's two questions I've answered to your zero. Maybe I don't want to know."

He winced. He was vulnerable, and her words, like a blunt weapon, could harm.

"I love you, Patrick." Her voice trembled.

He felt nauseous. She'd barely spoken a sentence to him in two months.

"I love you too." He could cling to that truth.

"Do you love her?"

"Who?" He was a little boy, chocolate from a forbidden bar smeared on his cheek. If he refused to acknowledge reality, perhaps she would accept the unbelievable.

She raised her eyebrows. He looked away as she finished the glass.

"I saw her, you know. I saw the two of you. In the park."

His heart raced. A cardiac event?

Marissa laughed. "You look like you're facing a firing squad. It's okay. The two of you looked good together. If I didn't know better, I could believe that she was pregnant and that you were the father."

He tried to hold Marissa's gaze, but her face blurred. Everything went out of focus.

"I'm not accusing you of having an affair," she continued. "I'm just saying, if you love her, maybe that's not a bad thing."

He stood. "I have to use the bathroom." He needed a moment to think.

Marissa stood also. "I need another drink. I'll pour you one. We should talk, Patrick."

He didn't respond. He shut the bathroom door and stood in front of the mirror. He expected to see a ghost, a shadow of the man he'd been, but a substantial form stared back at him, the same face he saw every morning. He was not the man he'd thought he was. And then he was on his knees, gripping the sides of the toilet bowl. His stomach heaved, sending everything up in a rush. He wished he could separate himself from this pathetic man, who at this very moment should be speaking to his wife. He spit into the toilet bowl. He stood unsteadily and rinsed his mouth in the sink.

~

Marissa was sitting in the recliner, a new drink in her hand. The drink she'd made for him sat on the coffee table in front of the couch. She hadn't bothered with a coaster. Was this what the end of a marriage looked like?

He sat but didn't pick up his drink. His hand would tremble. He didn't think he could keep it down anyway. If he had a syringe, he would've injected the alcohol directly into his bloodstream.

"I didn't just happen to see you at the park," Marissa said. "I followed you there. I watched you walk with her. I watched the two of you talk. I watched you picnic. Do you know what struck me?"

He shook his head.

"The silences. You enjoyed talking to each other, but you were comfortable with the silences. That told me everything I needed to know."

"Why did you follow me?" His voice was hoarse. He'd thought she was completely absorbed by her math. He hadn't known she thought of him at all.

She shrugged. "Curiosity." They stared at each other when she didn't elaborate. And then she said, "I don't blame you. I grieved without you.

The only place I found peace was within mathematics, and I couldn't take you there. So I left you behind. I was wrong to do that, but I wasn't oblivious to it. People, especially you, cut me slack because I'm a mathematician. I get away with things because everyone assumes I don't know any better. But I knew that you were hurting. And I let you hurt alone. I don't blame you for anything, but I can't stay married to you."

He flinched. He opened his mouth to ask why, but nothing came out.

She answered anyway. "I know what happened to Derrick Jackson."

CHAPTER 70

AMANDA

38 WEEKS PREGNANT

Baby's brain is growing and forming new connections at an astonishing rate, preparing her to absorb and process the vast amount of information that awaits her in the outside world.

—Your Best Pregnancy

March 29, 2018

Patrick's phone rang and went to voice mail. "Damn it!" Amanda hung up. The contractions had started a couple of hours ago, but now they were coming regularly. They'd woken her, though she hadn't known what they were at first. She had so much trouble getting comfortable lately that anything could wake her. She'd taken a shower, and only after that had she realized what was happening. She didn't want to go to the birthing center without Patrick. She didn't want to do any of this without him. She called his cell phone again.

"Patrick's phone," a woman said. "This is Marissa."

Amanda didn't breathe.

"Hello?"

She considered hanging up. But certainly, she was in Patrick's contacts. Marissa already knew who was calling. "I'm sorry to call," she said hesitantly.

"Don't be. It's no problem at all," Marissa said kindly. "Here's Patrick."

"I'm sorry to call," Amanda repeated when Patrick came on the line. "I'm in labor."

"Now?" he asked, as if she'd chosen an inconvenient time.

"Now," she said.

"How far apart are the contractions?"

"Five minutes. Should I go to the birthing center?"

"Yes. Go. Susan set everything up for you."

"Will you meet me there?"

He hesitated. "I can't."

And then Marissa was on the line again. "Patrick will pick you up in fifteen minutes. Good luck, Amanda. With everything." She hung up before Amanda could respond.

The magnitude of the day was beginning to settle over her. For months, she'd hoped that her false pregnancy would spontaneously resolve itself, that she would awaken with her old body. Labor was the second-best outcome. It was scary but maybe the only way out. This ordeal, she had to believe, was coming to an end.

And then, as she sat in the window waiting for Patrick, she wondered if Derrick had been right, if she was going to deliver a healthy baby today. Maybe it wasn't a faith pregnancy but a medical blunder. She'd read a story about a man who'd been diagnosed with terminal pancreatic cancer. A year later, after he'd quit his job and spent his life savings, doctors realized he had nonfatal pancreatitis.

Another contraction hit, starting in her back and pulsing forward. The pain wasn't bad, not unbearable, but it was enough to know that something real was happening. Like billions of women before her, she was in labor. She just hoped that things would work out for her.

~

"You don't have to drive so fast," Amanda said. "I promise not to give birth in your car."

"Don't make jokes. You're in labor."

She resisted the impulse to snap at him. She'd thought his presence would be comforting, but something was off. He could barely look at her. It had to do with Marissa answering his phone, she knew. She couldn't deal with that right now. She didn't want to know what Marissa knew. She wanted to get through labor, and then she could deal with anything.

~

Delores, the midwife assistant, offered nitrous oxide for the pain. Amanda refused. This experience had been the most difficult of her life, and her instincts told her that the only way to the other side was through a grand rush of pain. And it came. Patrick held her hand as the contractions worsened. Susan positioned her legs as the room—Susan, Delores, Patrick, and Amanda—waited for what would come.

Amanda felt hot as her innards contracted and she pushed, moving something along. But she didn't feel anything move, just cramps so painful that she silently prayed for it to be over. She waited for Derrick's faith to seize her.

"It's okay," Patrick said. "You're doing good."

Only then did she realize she was crying. She didn't believe in anything. Instead of finding faith, she found herself stripped. She'd once believed, by virtue of being a woman, that she could get pregnant. She'd believed in the man she'd chosen to marry, the man who'd chosen her. He'd never been violent, and yet, his act, the misoprostol, had been as violent as anything she could imagine. Perhaps the treachery of her own body was worst of all. She'd miscarried, and yet, here she was—pushing.

She lost track of time as exhaustion clouded her thoughts and the pain grew sharper. She was asking for nitrous oxide, or at least she thought she was, when the worst of it gripped her. And then it subsided, slowly. She lay panting, her body finished. Three faces stared down at her with concern as she listened for the wail of a baby.

"Is she okay?" Amanda asked into the silence.

CHAPTER 71

MARISSA

10 MONTHS AFTER THE ACCIDENT

March 29, 2018

Nothing could escape the gravitational pull of a black hole. Once the event horizon was crossed, all paths led to the center, the singularity, where individuality was sacrificed to oneness. Marissa didn't know when she'd intersected the event horizon. It could've been the chance meeting with John Wells and her premature introduction to Fermat's last theorem. Or it might've happened upon the eve of her mother's resolution to leave without a glance back. Or perhaps it had been on an ordinary day, the only disturbance a young woman's innocent experimentation with a street drug. Or maybe Marissa had been born into an event horizon, each push from the womb carrying her closer to the singularity.

Anything but empty, the abundance of mass compacted at the center of a black hole exerted an inexorable pull. The mass tugging on Marissa had been collecting for a long while: the loss of her parents, the death of her dog, the loss of her sister, the death of her daughter, the death of her sister, the loss of her husband, the destruction of her work.

Marissa could feel herself tearing apart, the bits of her joining the mass of misery as she neared the center. Jen would never hear the words

Marissa longed to say. Laura would never feel the comfort Marissa hungered to give. She missed them, and more than anything, she wanted them to know it.

Marissa hadn't, as a scholar, been called to take an oath. If she had, she imagined it would say: *I swear to unflinchingly seek out truth and to freely share that truth so that others may build upon it.*

Destroying her work had been a violation of her instincts, an act of self-mutilation. A waking hour didn't pass without regret, a little voice asking if she'd done the right thing. She'd anticipated remorse, and that was why she'd been so thorough. Every piece of paper had been shredded, her hard drive dismantled, the dry-erase paint on her office walls scrubbed clean. There was nothing left. Her memory held the broad strokes, but the details born of meticulous toil were gone. She didn't know if she could replicate her results if she tried.

She sat at her desk now, experiencing a rare moment of peace. There was nothing left to fight for, nothing left to fear. The staggering debt of the guilt she carried would soon be paid. It was over. Patrick was with Amanda, and she could believe that there was not another living thing in the house. Silly, she knew. Life was everywhere, even where she couldn't sense it.

She slid the desk drawer open and reached in. A twinge of panic shot up her wrist as her fingers brushed the back of the drawer. Her blind search grew frantic. And then she relaxed as her fingers settled on the smooth glass of a cell phone. She pressed the power button. Dead. Not a surprise. She hadn't used it in ten months. She'd told Patrick it was lost, and he'd gotten her a new one.

She attached the charger and waited a few seconds before powering it on. She scrolled to the picture gallery and hesitated. Reluctantly, she opened the app. She didn't have to scroll far to find the image she was thinking of. Jen sat on the couch, three-day-old Laura in her arms. It was the day after they'd brought Laura home from the hospital. Marissa remembered looking at the two of them and thinking that Jen was finally going to do it. The love in Jen's eyes as she'd looked down at Laura had convinced Marissa that the drugs were behind them. She'd grabbed her phone to capture the moment.

The future, even when it was close, could be hopelessly obscured. She thought of an evening twenty years ago, the night before she'd left for Princeton. She'd been excited in previous weeks, but on that night, her bags packed for an early-morning departure, she'd been nothing but scared. And sad.

"What will happen if I'm miserable there?" she'd asked Jen. They were sitting on the back porch, sharing a smoothie and waiting for a breeze.

"You won't be miserable there."

"What if I don't make any friends?"

"You'll make friends." Jen's confidence matched Marissa's doubts.

Marissa decided on a direct approach. "Will I be able to come home if I want?"

Jen laughed. "That's why it's called *home*. Of course you can come home."

Marissa had felt like crying, and Jen had taken her hand. "The best thing about the word *sister*," she'd said, "is that it's a permanent title. You can stop being friends with someone. You can stop being married to someone. You can never stop being my sister. You're the one person I know I'll still talk to when I'm old."

Marissa powered off the phone and put it back in the drawer. She'd reached the end of the line. She retrieved a pen and paper to write Patrick a note. She owed him that. *Husband,* she began. And then, dazed, she stared at the paper. She felt nothing, and yet, beneath the numbness was so much that she didn't know how to put it into words. She'd made so many mistakes over the years. So many misread situations and miscalculations about the future. She'd failed everyone who relied on her. Had she failed herself by destroying her work? Had she failed Jen? Had she failed Laura? She didn't know. The weight of it was beyond words.

CHAPTER 72

PATRICK

10 MONTHS AFTER THE ACCIDENT

March 29, 2018

Detective Sebold: *You seem like a good listener, Patrick, so I'll unload my problems. Everything I've heard leads me to believe Derrick walked away. But what do I do with the possibility of a love triangle, that there was a confrontation, and maybe it was an accident, but Derrick didn't make it through?*
Interview at Patrick's residence, 7:00 p.m., Thursday, March 8, 2018

∼

"Are you sure you don't want to come in?" Amanda asked. "I can't imagine being alone tonight."

"I know. I'm sorry. I have to get home. I'll call you in an hour or so."

Amanda took his hand. "Thank you for everything, Patrick." She kissed his cheek.

A goodbye? He had a distinct feeling of déjà vu, and it made him feel sick.

"Of course." He squeezed her hand. "Just take it easy tonight. I'll call you."

She smiled as if she didn't believe him. "You've been a good friend." He wanted to reassure her, but he couldn't think. He called Marissa as soon as Amanda was out of the car. The call went to voice mail.

~

He drove fast, as fast as he'd driven Amanda to the birthing center. This time, if he was pulled over, he wouldn't have a woman in labor to point to. But his luck held. He didn't cross paths with any police. He pulled into the driveway.

"No," he said as the garage door opened. "No, no, no." Marissa's car was gone. The panic he'd been holding at bay was moving into his throat.

He called her name as he stepped into the kitchen. No response. The house was quiet, and it felt different, awful, a personal hell.

"Marissa!" He ran up the stairs and called her name again. She wasn't there. He knew where she'd gone even before he saw the note on their bed. He couldn't read the words from where he stood, but he stared at it for a long while, motionless. And then he picked up his laptop, the closest object of any worth, and hurled it against the wall. He sat down on their bed. And he cried.

CHAPTER 73

AMANDA

POSTPREGNANCY

March 29, 2018

Amanda looked at herself in the mirror. Her breasts were swollen, but her abdomen had flattened somewhat. She still looked pregnant, but as if she'd traveled back in time. Given everything, she couldn't rule out that she'd stepped twenty weeks back into her false pregnancy, but she didn't believe that to be the case. She no longer felt pregnant. She felt alone. Alone was something she hadn't felt in a long time. It was over.

She was exhausted and achy, and her eyes were red from the conversation with her mother. She'd called to tell her mother that she was flying to Charlotte in the morning. She'd found an affordable connecting flight despite the short notice. Her mother hadn't asked why she was coming. She just wanted to know what time to meet her. When Amanda tried to answer, she was overcome with sobs. She couldn't control it, and it made her mother cry. "I can stay on the phone for as long as you need me," her mother said. "We can talk until morning, until you get on the plane."

Amanda wanted her mother more than anything at that moment, but she didn't want to talk. She didn't want to say that she realized, truly understood for the first time, that she might never have a baby. She didn't want to tell her mother that she'd fallen in love with a married man who was in love with his wife. Her thoughts were all over the place. She wondered if Patrick no longer found her interesting now that she'd delivered her phantom baby. He'd gotten a front-row ticket to the show. He'd seen her phantom pregnancy transform her body, and he'd seen her false labor. And he'd left before the credits finished rolling. Nothing more to see. But who could she blame? How many women before her had stood naked in front of bathroom mirrors, eyes red, utterly alone because they'd built their lives around married men? It wasn't an original story. And yet, it was her story. Patrick was at home with his wife. Where else did she expect him to be?

She hadn't been in the nursery since Derrick had surprised her with it, hadn't even opened the door. She stepped inside now, a portal to the past. She traced her finger along the smooth wooden edge of the crib. She sat in the rocking chair, meant for cuddling an infant—her infant. Meant for a different time, different people. She inhaled the scent of newness. And when she walked out, she pulled the door closed. She said goodbye.

She didn't want to think. There were sleeping pills in her medicine cabinet, sedatives Derrick kept just in case. She would pack her bag, set her alarm, reserve a Lyft ride to the airport, and then take a couple of pills. As tired as she was, she would probably sleep through the flight.

~

Thirty minutes later, she had the pills in her right hand, a glass of water in her left. The doorbell rang. She put the pills on the kitchen table. The last unexpected visitor she'd had was Ralph. A lot had happened since then.

~

"I was on my way to bed." Amanda didn't hide her annoyance. "Why didn't you just call?"

Patrick stood on her porch, looking the way she felt. Beaten down. He shrugged. He didn't move to enter her home. She hadn't invited him in. "I need to talk to you," he finally said.

She closed her eyes. She wanted those pills. "You don't. Really. You helped me. You don't owe me anything else."

"The police are going to contact you at any minute," he said. "I need to talk to you before they do."

CHAPTER 74

MARISSA

7 MONTHS AFTER THE ACCIDENT

December 31, 2017

Marissa ignored the doorbell. She didn't want to break her train of thought, but alas, the knocking was persistent. She imagined a car accident, a broken stranger pounding with the last of her strength. She peeked through the living room window. A man wearing a dark suit and tie stood on the porch. She opened the door.

"Marissa Davis?" the man asked. He was handsome, midthirties. Clearly not an accident victim. A process server?

"Yes," Marissa answered warily. She couldn't imagine who would sue her, but you never knew.

"Your husband, Patrick, is with my wife. I think they're having an affair."

She stared at the man, stunned. She tried to remember if Patrick had told her where he was going. "You are?"

"Sorry. Derrick Jackson." He extended his hand. "My wife is Amanda Jackson."

She shook his hand. *Amanda Jackson.* The name was familiar. An academic? No. "Does she have pseudocyesis?"

The man raised an eyebrow. "She thinks she does. But no."

Marissa considered that. A pregnant woman who believed she wasn't pregnant. Confusing.

"May I come in?" Derrick asked.

The man didn't seem dangerous, but wasn't that the talent of a certain type of dangerous man? She stepped aside.

"Thank you," he said and entered. "I'll be brief."

~

Marissa sat alone at the kitchen table. Derrick had been gone for an hour, and still, she couldn't focus. Patrick and Amanda, according to Derrick, were spending most days together. Marissa hadn't noticed Patrick's absences. Was that possible? She looked at the date on her phone: December 31. She barely remembered Christmas.

In all their time together, Marissa had never worried about Patrick cheating on her. She wasn't above jealousy, but with Patrick, there was no cause. Of course, things had been different lately. She was different.

Perhaps he had been spending his days with another woman. She couldn't blame him. Laura was like his daughter. She'd killed Laura and left him to grieve alone. If Amanda Jackson was what he needed, she wouldn't protest. She understood need. Right now, she needed math.

~

Derrick appeared again, unannounced, the following week. Marissa wasn't happy to see him, but she smiled. "Let me guess. My husband is with your wife."

He nodded and stepped inside. He wore a dark suit and tie. "But I came here to tell you that God has a message for you from your sister."

She waited for a laugh, his acknowledgment of the joke. His eyes were serious. "What?" she asked.

"I'm sorry if my words startled you. If someone said something like that to me three months ago, I would've asked them to leave my home. I was raised in the church, but like many adults, I didn't think about God until I needed Him. When that happened, I needed Him desperately. And once I accepted Him, I learned that there are two realities: one with God and one without. I could exist in either, but only one would allow me to live."

Marissa was intrigued by his concept of different realities. She used math to probe new realities. The language of mathematics had no term for God, so she did not seek him, but for months now, she'd been obsessed with probing the unseen and untouchable.

"A message from my sister?" she asked softly.

"Do you pray, Marissa?"

She shook her head. She hadn't been raised in the church. She didn't know how to pray.

"You need God," he told her. "And God needs you."

Marissa considered that. Was she probing God through math without realizing it? Did God need for her to make a breakthrough, to show others?

"Is it possible to pray through mathematics?" she asked him.

"We pray with our hearts. If math is in your heart, God put it there to praise Him. If you don't mind, I would like to pray with you. What God has to say, He will say only to you. If you receive His message, you will speak to your sister again."

Marissa's heart raced. She led him to the living room. He knelt before the sofa, and she followed his lead. Hand in hand, they prayed.

～

Marissa felt as if she were bathed in a warm glow when Derrick left. After praying, she'd heated leftover spaghetti, prepared by Patrick, and they'd sat at her kitchen table and talked about God. Marissa, neither a believer nor a disbeliever, had never given much thought to God. She respected the dearth of evidence.

When she returned to her office, to the equations on the walls, she expected the warm feeling to translate into progress. She expected communion with math. In short, she expected God to deliver on his promise.

And yet, nothing happened. There were problems in some of her equations, and the fixes eluded her. She struggled in silence against both her frustration and the difficulty of the task before her. She lost days. On the fourth, she discovered a major error she'd made weeks before. Good to know, but a fix wasn't obvious.

She was blocked. The math just wasn't there. And finally, she did what she'd always done when this happened. She took a break. Three days, she told herself. She wouldn't look at math for three days. Unless something big came to her.

It did not.

She was on the third day of her forced break, in the middle of a crossword puzzle, when Derrick knocked at her door. She would give him her phone number, she decided. His tendency to turn up unannounced irked her.

He invited himself in. "How have you been?" he asked and removed his coat.

"Not good." She led him to the living room. She told him that her math was blocked. She blamed herself for focusing on God.

"It isn't about the math," he told her. "It's about your faith. Math doesn't have the power to give you what you want. Only God has that power."

"So I ask him to speak to my sister, and he'll make it happen? Like magic?"

Derrick smiled. "It isn't magic. It's faith."

"And I don't have to do anything?"

"Faith is no small feat."

343

"Why does God care about my faith?"

"Will you pray with me?"

"How did you know my sister died?"

"God told me—"

"How did you first learn that my sister died? I would hope that a believer in God wouldn't lie to me."

Derrick looked sheepish. "I found her obituary when I googled you."

Marissa shook her head. She silently cursed Patrick for insisting on obituaries. She wanted Derrick to leave.

"The message from God was real. I wouldn't lie to you." He leaned forward to kiss her.

She jumped back. "What the fuck?"

"I'm sorry."

"Is that why you told me bullshit about my sister? To—"

"No." He put his hands up defensively.

"Is Patrick even having an affair with your wife?"

"I think so. Everything I told you is true. I just thought . . ." He didn't finish.

She took a deep breath to calm her temper. "It's okay," she said, "but I think you should go."

"Please," he said. She could hear the repentance in his voice. "Can we just pretend that didn't happen?"

"We can," Marissa said. "We should. But you have to go." She walked him to the door. Giving him her number was out of the question.

CHAPTER 75

MARISSA

8 MONTHS AFTER THE ACCIDENT

January 25, 2018

Finally. Something. Marissa returned home with an inkling that the math could be back. Nothing solid. But as she'd walked the sidewalks of her neighborhood, Beethoven's Seventh coaxing her unconscious, she'd had an idea—a nugget she could offer up as an invitation, an entreaty.

Hunger guided her to the refrigerator, but she didn't have time for food. She was cautiously eager. She searched for juice, something with glucose, just to get her through. Apple would suffice.

She closed the fridge and felt an unnerving chill, a draft. She turned to find the window open.

"Patrick?"

He hadn't been home when she'd left for a walk. And the window certainly hadn't been open. The sun was just beginning to set, and the waning quality of light blended eerily with the stillness. She listened. Nothing.

She pulled her cell phone from her pocket and dialed 911. She held her thumb inches from the call icon as she stepped quietly through the house. There! Fingers trembling, she tapped the screen. A man sprawled on her couch.

She hung up before the call went through. It was Derrick.

"What the fuck?" Her voice was a decibel below a scream. She didn't put the phone away.

His eyes were glazed when he opened them. He sat up slowly, with effort.

"What the fuck is wrong with you?" She thought of the day they'd prayed together. Had she led him on? She didn't think so. But he'd tried to kiss her.

"Everything." That one word, thick with intoxication.

"You should leave." She considered calling the police. She hadn't told Patrick about his visits, but she could. She had nothing to hide.

"You weren't supposed to find me."

"You're on my couch."

"I'm waiting for your husband. They got a room at the Beltway Motel."

"Who?"

"Amanda and your husband."

"So why are you here?"

He pulled a prescription bottle from his pocket. She approached for a closer look. Alcohol fumes emanated from him. Her entire body was trembling now. *Temazepam.* His name was on the bottle. *Take for insomnia as needed.* "How much did you take?"

"All of it."

She didn't know what that meant. Had the bottle been full? Half-full?

"Why?"

"Your husband should know what he's doing. He's ruined my wife." Derrick giggled. "I mean, my life."

"Okay." She stepped back. "You're clearly in pain."

"Ding, ding, ding."

"Do you have a friend I can call?" She didn't mean to imply that she wasn't his friend. But she wasn't his friend.

"You can call your husband."

Marissa sat in the chair facing him. "You don't want to be here when Patrick gets home." She didn't want him to be here when Patrick got home. Sure, Patrick could help to get him out of their living room, but the episode would force a conversation she didn't wish to have. "I'll drive you home," she said and stood. "Let me help you up."

She extended a hand, and to her relief, he complied. Mostly. She had to pull with her full strength. She left him leaning unsteadily against the couch while she retrieved her purse from the kitchen.

"Lean on me," she said, offering her shoulder. "I'll help you to the car." The two of them staggered through the kitchen and into the garage, Marissa bearing more weight than was comfortable. She was winded by the time they reached her car. "You can lie down in the back." She opened the door and he crawled/fell inside. She walked around to the other side and, hands beneath his shoulders, pulled. She hoped he would sober up a bit during the ride to his house. Getting him out of the car would be a challenge.

She opened the garage door, and there, in her driveway, sat his car.

"Fuck," she muttered. How was she going to explain that to Patrick? Derrick's eyes were closed now, his legs folded awkwardly in the back seat. "Wake up." She nudged him. "Change of plans."

"My plan," he slurred, "is for your husband to leave my wife the fuck alone."

"I'll probably regret asking," Marissa said, "but why are you so fixated on my husband? Isn't your wife the one you have a problem with?"

"My wife went to your husband for help. He's manipulating her, telling her she isn't pregnant. If he would leave her alone, we could fix things. Instead, he's taking advantage of our difficulties."

"Right," Marissa said. "Well, you've conjured up a brilliant plan. You need to dig deep for this, champ. We need to get you out of the car."

Ten minutes later, Marissa was sweating despite the cold, and Derrick was in the back seat of his own car. She sat in the driver's seat and realized she didn't have his keys. "Jesus." She turned to him. "Car keys." His movements were agonizingly slow, but he managed to find them in the third pocket he checked.

She adjusted the seat and rearview mirror. "What's your address?"

He didn't respond. She shook his shoulder. He moaned. His breathing seemed shallow. "Derrick." She tapped his face. It felt cool. Had he overdosed? She touched her own cheek. Was she any warmer? It was cold outside. She wasn't a physician. She needed Patrick—a nonoption.

"Derrick." She slapped him. His eyes opened. "I'm taking you to the hospital."

"No, no, no."

"You can send Patrick the bill."

Derrick laughed. "That's good."

She used her GPS to search for the nearest hospital. She wanted to drop him off and get back home. She had work to do.

～

She turned on the headlights as she made a left onto Ponce de Leon. The area was in transition, the poor being pushed farther and farther out to make way for the affluent.

"Are you okay back there?" She hadn't heard a peep in a while. She listened. Engine humming. Tires on asphalt. And then an abrupt sob. "Derrick?"

"You and me," he said, "we're alike."

"How's that?"

"We're consumed with guilt."

She really wanted to finish this good deed and be done with him. "For someone who doesn't know me, you have a lot to say about me."

"My wife has told me some things. She's—"

"Having an affair with my husband. I got it."

"I don't deserve her."

Marissa didn't respond. What could she say? He needed medical attention.

"I gave her an abortion drug."

Marissa's eyes left the road as she gazed at the rearview mirror. She couldn't see his face, sprawled as he was in the back seat. "What?"

"She doesn't know. I just—"

"Why?"

"She was pregnant."

Marissa turned back to the road as the silence stretched. She wondered if he'd passed out again. His voice startled her.

"I did it. But it wasn't me. Not the Derrick she married. It was her. She created something in me, and it's like I watched it happen. I carried the pills for days. I almost threw them away a hundred times. But I did it. For her. She couldn't see what she was throwing away. I mixed the drug into a drink. And I sat with her and we had a romantic dinner, and I had to pretend that everything was great. When we went to bed, I put more of the crushed pills on my fingers, and I had to make love to her." He began to cry again. "It was as bad for me as it was—"

"Stop talking." Marissa's voice was quiet. Nothing like the scream roiling beneath the surface. Listening to this man sob. What was she supposed to do with this information? She didn't know Amanda. And somehow, she felt as if she did. The GPS instructed her to turn right, and she nearly missed it. She didn't know where she was. She was in a strange car. Dilapidated buildings lined the dark road. And this monstrous man—

A woman, walking on the sidewalk, caught her eye. *Jen?* Her heart raced. It was impossible, and yet, she stopped the car.

"Where are we?" Derrick was struggling to sit up.

Marissa opened the car door slowly. She was afraid that a sudden move, an unintended noise, could shatter the vision. The street was quiet, nothing but the buzz of the idling engine, the warning beep of an open door. The woman, Jen, continued, oblivious. She cut through overgrown grass toward what looked like a former corner store, boards where windows might've been. Marissa followed, slowly, silently, terrified of spooking her. A man emerged from the building, and Marissa paused, straining to hear the woman's voice as they exchanged words. Neither of them knew she was there. And suddenly, the woman turned and was walking toward her. Marissa recognized the strung-out look in the woman's eyes, but it wasn't Jen. Same height and build.

Her sister was gone.

As she watched the woman walk away, she imagined herself running to catch her, coaxing her into the front seat of Derrick's car. She could buy her a meal, convince her to get clean before it was too late.

Jen had been there. In the flesh. For years. Marissa had wanted nothing more than to take the drugs away. Take Jen's hunger away. Even the math, even her life, Marissa would have given it all to save Jen. But Marissa's will, her desperation, had meant nothing in the face of Jen's addiction. "I tried, Jen." Marissa didn't know if she'd spoken aloud, but the man was watching her now. His gaze turned to the idling car. Marissa couldn't breathe. She couldn't imagine that she would ever feel okay again. The pain. She wondered if Amanda felt it when she saw pregnant women, glowing with expectation. She wondered if Patrick felt it when he saw babies pushed in strollers. If Jen were alive, would she feel it every time she heard the name Laura? Would anything ever—

Math was all she had.

"You looking for something, lady?" The man's tone wasn't unfriendly. He approached slowly.

Marissa felt as if she were dreaming. She wanted to wake up. "Do you have something for pain?"

The man smiled. "That's why I'm here. I take the pain away." He was close now. Marissa had never seen a drug dealer. There was nothing striking about him, and she realized that probably she had seen them before and not known. "Hydros," he said. She returned to the car, where Derrick was passed out. She retrieved her purse and paid the dealer in cash.

~

She drove past the hospital, the GPS insistent that her destination was on the left. It demanded a U-turn, but Marissa continued.

"Where are we?" Derrick asked as she pulled into a MARTA station parking lot. She drove to the back, to a patch of asphalt untouched by streetlights. Derrick managed ungracefully to sit up. He looked out the window. "You know I'm a married man, right?"

"I know." Marissa killed the engine.

"Does your husband know?"

"My husband is a better man than you'll ever be." More quietly, she said, "He's a better person than I'll ever be." She got out of the car and opened the back door. "You're probably right about one thing," she told Derrick. "You and I are alike."

"How so?"

"You're asking me? You said it." She climbed into the back seat.

CHAPTER 76

PATRICK

10 MONTHS AFTER THE ACCIDENT

March 29, 2018

Amanda was expressionless as Patrick spoke. She mindlessly picked at the cushion of the overstuffed chair, several feet from where he'd settled on the sofa.

"Marissa sat with him in the back seat. She gave him the hydrocodone she'd bought from the dealer. And then she left him, keys in the ignition."

"Was he alive?" Amanda's voice was strangely devoid of emotion.

"She doesn't know. He wasn't moving."

Patrick stood. He couldn't sit any longer. His legs wobbly, he leaned against the sofa arm for support.

"Why?" Amanda asked.

Patrick shrugged. "She tried to describe the moment to me. He'd given you an abortion drug." Patrick considered the downside of telling Amanda what he suspected. But right now, Amanda deserved the truth. All of it. "She wanted you and me to be together. She didn't want Derrick to stand in the way of that."

Amanda gasped, as if struck.

"Today, while I was with you, she went to the police." He'd begged her not to. "I don't know what she told them." He glanced at his watch: nine fifteen. "Is telling them." He sat. He had a favor to ask, and he didn't know if Amanda would throw him out of her house for it. "I told Marissa not to tell the police about the hydrocodone."

Amanda stared at him for a long while. He couldn't read her. "Why did you tell me?"

He didn't respond. Why had he told her? He hadn't meant to. He'd just known that if he didn't tell her now, it would be a secret that he would have to carry forever.

"You want the police to think he committed suicide," Amanda said.

Patrick nodded. Marissa had found him, panicked, and left him in his car at the MARTA station.

Derrick *had* committed suicide, after all. Who was to say the hydrocodone killed him?

Amanda seemed to mull it over. "She doesn't know that he's dead," she said quietly, almost to herself. "He might've woken up and driven to Mexico."

"Or someone might have stolen his car and disposed of—" Why was he offering Amanda that image? "Marissa wants to go to prison. The night of the accident. Laura." He paused. "Marissa took a sleeping pill before bed. She didn't tell anyone, not even me. Not until today. She wanted to be able to get up with Laura and then go right back to sleep."

"No one could tell she was intoxicated?" Amanda asked.

"Apparently not. The police interviewed us, but there was no toxicology screen."

"If no one could tell, it probably wasn't the pill."

"That's what I told her, but—"

"You never mentioned the hydrocodone to me," Amanda said. "We've all suffered enough."

~

They lay in bed, Patrick holding Amanda, a now-familiar ritual. Amanda fell asleep quickly, but Patrick was less fortunate. He spent most of the night watching her, listening to her exhalations, and feeling the weight of her body against his. He got up once in the night for a glass of water and noticed two pills on the kitchen table. He sat down and pulled Marissa's letter from his pocket.

> Husband,
> I told you I would wait, but I've gone to the police. I have nothing to wait for. I'll never see Jen or Laura again. For a long time, I refused to face reality, and now, I can't live in it. Math holds nothing for me, and frankly, neither does life. I can't imagine eating dinner or going to bed or getting out of bed or taking a shower or brushing my teeth. I'm prepared for whatever will come. It can't be worse than what has passed.
>
> I've failed you and I'm sorry. If I could have handled my grief in any other way, I would have. Please understand that. I responded the only way I could. Even now, I am doing the only thing I can. Life doesn't feel like a series of choices as much as a series of guided steps. Derrick has people who love him, who still hope that he will come home. They deserve to know what happened. I never thought I could hide this forever.

I love you, and I always will. I want so much for you to rediscover life. I'm grateful that you found me when I needed you. And I'm grateful that Amanda found you when you needed her. Keep her close. You've given me so much, and now, I want to give you something: my blessing. Whatever you and Amanda have built, friendship or romance, I bless it. Remember me as I was, before I lost my way. And let me go.

Love,

Marissa

Reading her words was physically painful, and yet, he read the letter through three times. He couldn't imagine life without her. He thought of Amanda sleeping upstairs. He couldn't think anymore. He returned to Amanda's bed and resumed his vigilance over her sleeping form until, finally, sleep claimed him.

~

He awoke alone, to sunlight. He turned over. Big mistake. His head ached, and when he thought of Marissa, his heart raced. He listened for running water or the television downstairs, but all was quiet. He climbed from the bed and started to call out for Amanda but didn't want to risk disturbing a private moment—meditation or prayer.

He stepped quietly through the house, peeking into rooms he'd never seen. Two were bare, even of furniture, and another was a beautifully decorated nursery. He recalled Amanda's words: *I want to find a crowbar and destroy the fucking thing.* When she'd said that, he hadn't imagined the labor, the attention to detail. The paint still smelled fresh, probably because the door had stayed closed. Large multicolored block letters plastered the wall above the bookshelf: *Hooray!* Derrick had created something truly magnificent, a gesture of optimism. Patrick backed out, pulling the door shut.

He called her name when he got to the bottom of the stairs. Nothing. He moved through the kitchen to check the garage. Her car was there. Maybe she'd gone for a walk. He reached for his cell phone and started to dial when he saw the note on the kitchen table where the pills had been. It was long, handwritten, more words than were required to tell him that she needed fresh air. He slumped into the chair. He knew, even before he read it. Amanda was gone.

EPILOGUE I

PATRICK

1 YEAR LATER

Marissa is one year into a thirty-month sentence, the calculated time with good behavior, after pleading guilty to concealing the death of another person. Until recently, she refused to put Patrick on her visitation list. And then she did, so here he is. And still, he worries that she won't see him.

The door buzzes, and he walks into a large room with small tables arranged cafeteria-style. A guard instructs him to have a seat, so he does. Other visitors spread out, claiming tables. A female inmate is led into the room. Not Marissa. He watches the door. Two more inmates enter and find their visitors, and then she's there. Marissa. He hasn't seen her in nine months, since her sentencing. She wears khaki overalls. She's lost weight, but besides that, she looks like the woman he proposed to. She spots him, and despite herself, she smiles. He knows this woman. She told herself she wouldn't smile.

He stands. The guard was clear on the no-physical-contact rule. It hurts that he can't hug her. He returns her smile, and they both sit. He doesn't know what to say. He should've prepared. Asking an inmate how she's doing seems clueless. And Marissa is no help. She could never be counted on to help with small talk.

"Being here," he says, "reminds me of the day you sucked me into your revenge plot against Melvin Young."

She laughs. "You were so scared."

He nods and smiles. It had taken him a month to calm down. He was scared, but there was also something thrilling in it. Two weeks before Melvin's birthday, while he was at work, Patrick and Marissa broke into his apartment and hid two dozen raw eggs: in the backs of cabinets and cluttered drawers, in the pockets of winter clothes, in the bottoms of boxes, beneath couch cushions and the mattress. *Don't be afraid to crack a few,* Marissa said. It was her last act of vengeance against her sister's abuser. Patrick was honored to be a part of it.

"How are you doing?" he asks. "Considering."

She's thoughtful, as if she no longer believes in the culturally accepted stock response. "I'm at peace."

"You look good."

She smirks. "I teach a literacy class. When they learned I was a teacher . . ."

He smiles at that. Marissa never thought of herself as a teacher. If a student was anything less than brilliant, there wasn't a lot Marissa could or would do for her.

"I'm surprised too," she says. "It's changed my perspective. I really am a teacher here."

"No math?"

"No one has shown an interest in math. Reading makes more sense here. How are you? You look good." She glances at his arms. "You've been working out."

"I just finished a stint as a visiting lecturer at a little college in Colorado, in the middle of nowhere. I taught an introductory neuro-science course and did a lot of hiking and swimming."

"Did you enjoy it?"

"I needed it. It feels good to be back in the city, but I needed to be there. Julie visited me for two weeks during the summer. She taught me how to kayak. She's an impressive young woman. She wants to study political science at Georgetown."

"I'm glad," Marissa says. "She's a smart girl. Rob must be horrified."

"They're working through it. She wants to visit her aunt Marissa. She told me to tell you she loves you."

Marissa smiles. "Tell her I love her. I'll be out soon. She can visit then. I'll take her out to dinner."

"My mother wants you to visit her in Hawaii when you get out."

"I know," Marissa says. "We've exchanged letters."

"Will you go?"

Marissa shakes her head. "I want to keep in touch with your mother. I love her, but I can't pick up where I left off." She's thoughtful for a long while, and then: "People are saying that my math will transform the world, but I don't care about any of that. I learned one thing from it."

Patrick leans forward.

"The only way to live meaningfully is to forge new connections. As much as we want what we had in our past, we can only experience the present. Rigley was a great dog. I loved him so much. But the only way I can experience the joy he and I shared is to bond with a new dog. New connections don't erase the past. They allow us to appreciate it. I finally understand that.

"When I look back now, I realize that I own the good moments. I had a happy childhood before my parents left. Their leaving doesn't change that. I had good times with Jen before the drugs. Nothing can take that away. Our marriage." Her voice cracks, and she pauses. "We loved each other, and you made me happy. If I made you half as happy as you made me, our marriage was a success. Even if it wasn't forever."

Patrick starts to reach across the table but catches himself before taking her hand.

"A good moment," she says, "is a good moment."

Patrick forces a smile. "We had a lot of good moments. Go see my mother. Forge new connections with her that have nothing to do with me. You're allowed that. Have you been thinking about your future? After this?"

"Others have. Mathematicians from around the world actually want to work with me. They write me letters. Frederick Peters has been petitioning for some type of work release." Marissa shrugs. "I think I'm finished with math. We had a good thing. But . . . new connections, right?"

Patrick smiles. "Right."

An awkward silence settles between them. For once, Marissa steps in. "What are you going to do next?"

"Start a business. I've always wanted to, and it's time."

"That's great. Are you still thinking about psychiatric software?"

"I think so. I just need someone to handle software development."

"I'm sure you can find someone."

"I already have someone in mind."

She hesitates and then asks, "Was Amanda with you in Colorado?" He shakes his head.

She sighs. "I really wanted things to work out for you two." She means it. And it doesn't hurt him. "Do you still speak to her?"

"No. I made her a promise. I won't speak to her until I can keep it."

∼

The breeze is cool, so Patrick wanders until he finds a bench bathed in sunlight. He thought it would be hard to walk away from the prison, Marissa behind the gates, but saying goodbye was cathartic. He wanted her to know that he would always have her back, but he needed to say goodbye.

It's nearly noon, and Patrick hasn't eaten. He doesn't even consider it. Too much anxiety. Amanda's letter, the one she left for him on her kitchen table a year ago, is in his pocket. He's nearly memorized it, and still, he pulls it out to read.

∼

Dearest Patrick,

I love you. I'm in love with you. But I can't stay. So much beauty exists between us. I can't imagine giving up what we have, but I don't know how to build atop the ruins. We were wanderers, feeling our way through darkness, when we stumbled upon each other. You were my light, my guide to the other side. I don't want to leave, but I need to walk alone. I need to rebuild.

This isn't goodbye. This isn't me ending what we have. This is me going in search of the woman who can love you, who you, I hope, can love. Take a year. If we're meant to be, meet me at noon on March 29th at the Earth Goddess. My grandmother told me that everything happens for a reason. I don't know if I believe that, but perhaps "An Affair to Remember" meant something for us. If after a year, I feel that I can be the woman you deserve, I will wait for you at the Earth Goddess. Until then, take care of yourself. And promise me one thing: at the end of the year, if you're still in love with Marissa, if you still wish things were different so that you could be with her, don't come.

Yours always,

Amanda

P.S. If you want to see me, but you miss our date somehow (God forbid you're hit by a car), don't be an idiot. You have my number.

P.P.S. I want you to know. This is the most painful thing I've ever done.

EPILOGUE II

AMANDA

1 YEAR LATER

One year ago, Amanda gave birth to a phantom. She gave birth to an ending and a beginning. She gave birth to her freedom. Her mind had locked her body in a prison of false pregnancy, and equally enigmatically, it let her go. But really, that was her old way of thinking about it: trapped, imprisoned. Now, from the other side, she sees it as a long goodbye. She never knew the life she created—never had the opportunity to celebrate it—but she needed time to say goodbye. She needed to know that she would never waver in defense of her child. Even if it cost her everything.

Standing on the canopy walk above the woodlands, she catches sight of the Earth Goddess, and it takes her breath away. The goddess's face and hand are verdant with life, her hair vibrant waves of red, yellow, green, and purple. The view stirs something in her. Faith. Or something like faith. Standing before this glorious vision, she believes that the Earth Goddess has the power to bring Patrick back to her. She didn't know of the Earth Goddess's existence when she was trying to conceive, but she believes, somehow, that this deity might have given her a child had Amanda honored her properly. She closes her eyes now and asks for happiness.

She lingers on the walkway above the forest floor, savoring the moment, the possibilities. Right now, it's possible that she will walk to the Cascades Garden and find Patrick waiting for her. In fifteen minutes, that possibility won't exist. It will have either happened or not happened. She wants it to happen.

She makes her way slowly toward her future. Because she will have a future, with or without him. It will just be better with him.

She told her mother about the misoprostol, the abortion drug, but not about the hydrocodone, the drug that may or may not have killed Derrick. And she moved back into her old room. Her mother made three solo trips to Atlanta. One to pack up Amanda's house. Another to sell and donate Amanda's belongings. And a final trip to sell Amanda's house. When Amanda left the letter for Patrick and locked the door behind herself, she knew that she would never return. She didn't want anything from the house, not her clothes or dishes or art. The clothes belonged to a woman who pushed herself preternaturally hard to have a baby. The dishes belonged to a woman who betrayed her husband. The art belonged to a woman who couldn't cope, who paid with her mental and physical health. And the nursery. It belonged to a couple who would never have use for it.

She interviewed for a few data scientist positions in Raleigh, but she'd grown accustomed to working from home and making her own hours. There was plenty of well-paying consulting work, and when she wanted to lose herself in it, she accepted more contracts. When she wanted free time to spend with her mother or her sister or by herself, she became picky about the work she accepted. She volunteered at a youth center in Raleigh, teaching robotics to underprivileged girls. It felt good. She learned that mothering wasn't limited to those who give birth.

Meredith was accepted to law school, and Amanda envies her youth. She's full of big plans and idealism, and though she lives on a strict budget, Amanda predicts that there is no early retirement in her future. *There will always be people to stick up for,* Amanda told her. But just in case, Amanda helps her with tuition. *Nothing delays retirement like student loans.*

When Amanda felt up to it, she reached out to Cecile, Sara, Rani, and Jana from BPI. She'd left rumors in the wake of her sudden resignation, but her friends didn't hold a grudge. She made a trip back to Atlanta for a girls' night out, and she felt that she'd reclaimed part of her life. She called Beverly, her oldest friend. It was awkward at first, but as the conversation stretched, the six-month gulf between them contracted. Beverly cried when Amanda told her about Derrick, mostly because Beverly hadn't been there for any of it. They spent a week in Jamaica, just the two of them, their friendship convalescing in the warm, clear Caribbean waters.

Amanda feels shaky and occasionally good. She's on the mend, learning the merits of diminished expectations. She once thought she could banish Derrick from her thoughts, but there is too much history. A restaurant, a conversation, the weather—almost anything can spark memories of him. When she remembers the tender moments, and there were plenty, the realization of his death chills her to the core. His body hasn't been found, but she knows that he would never abandon his parents. He's gone.

Accepting that she didn't have to forget Derrick was a turning point. She can carry it all with her, and she will be okay. Growing older is a process of accumulating the good and the bad.

If Patrick doesn't show, she can carry him too.

She descends to the forest floor and walks along the curving trail, the same path she once walked with Patrick. She didn't love him yet then, but maybe a seed had been planted. She doesn't know. She enters the Cascades Garden, and Patrick stands when he sees her. *Play it cool,*

Meredith advised. But she doesn't play it cool. She grins. She runs, and then she's in his arms. Bad things will happen, she knows. There will be days so dark that the existence of light won't seem possible. But this moment—Patrick squeezing her as if he's been waiting his whole life for this, the Earth Goddess pouring water into the fountain—is perfect. She's happy.

The End

ACKNOWLEDGMENTS

The difference between this manuscript being published and not is my wonderful agent, Sarah Bedingfield. Your enthusiasm for this book made my day, and your editorial acumen made the book better. Your grace carried us through tough revisions, and your steadiness kept me focused when I questioned my vision. You are a champion in every sense of the word, and it has been an honor to take this journey with you.

I couldn't ask for a finer editor than Tiffany Shelton. I loved our long talks, bandying about ideas, your keen instincts ensuring we settled on the right ones. From the beginning, you got what I was trying to do, and you helped me to do it better. I am supremely fortunate that my manuscript landed in your capable hands. Many thanks to Carmen Johnson and to Tiffany's team at Little A: Emma Reh, Merideth Mulroney, Kristin Lunghamer, Erin Calligan Mooney, and Sarah Shaw. RaeChell Garrett, Riam Griswold, and Bill Siever, thank you for making the book better.

Thank you to Courtney Paganelli for the careful read and thoughtful notes, and for stepping in to guide me while Sarah greeted and then introduced her beautiful son to the world.

For early encouragement, thanks to Yvonne Chang, Khaliq Perry, Versie Mitchell, Tracey Weaver, and Gloria Nadeau. Hannah Wood, thank you for the sage advice and for saving me from a bad title.

For support in my other career (the one that kept the lights on while I wrote), I owe a debt to Sam Starcher, Sim Harbert, Michael

Matthews, Sean Thomas, Ai-Ping Hu, Maithilee Kunda, Agata Rozga, Kaya de Barbaro, General Ronald Johnson, Raj Vuchatu, Bill Robbins, Dave Penticuff, Lacey Greenway, Michael Roybal, Pankaj Singh, Reem Fareed, Rashmi Kasam, and Alex Furer.

Labarron Roberts, fire lieutenant, I could thank you for being a hero. Craig Miller, I could thank you for your example of seizing the moment. Instead, I'll thank you both for the hours we spent talking about our hopes and passions. You didn't have to read a word of my writing to know what I was writing about. I hope you felt as encouraged by me as I did by you. Khaliq, that goes for you too.

Miles Larason, I was touched by your life. I'll be forever grateful that we talked shortly before my daughter was born. You shared your experience of your daughter's birth, and your words of wisdom prepared me for mine. You are loved and will be forever missed.

The books of my childhood shaped my passions, and those earliest ones were passed down to me from my sister Tracee. On road trips and airplane rides, you suggested that we take turns reading to each other. I'm lucky for those moments and to have you as a sister. If there were a fancy prize for best aunt, I would nominate you.

My wife's siblings are a great argument against having an only child. Carrie and Hal, thank you for making me a part of your family.

Scott, Brent, and Dylan, you all have big dreams, and I look forward to watching you accomplish them.

My father taught me that I could be anything I could imagine. When I told you I wanted to follow in your footsteps and become a doctor, you gave me a medical thriller by Robin Cook. I devoured one medical novel after another and somewhere along the way imagined that I could write fiction. Thank you for that conversation we had twenty years ago about the patient you saw during your obstetrics residency. Amanda was born on that day. It took me a long time to get to know her.

My mother was my first and best teacher. Learning is one of the great pleasures of my life, and I owe that to your patient tutelage. I can never repay you for being the best mother I could ask for. Without you, none of this would be possible. You instilled in me a love of reading, and even today, you're my favorite person to share books with. As a grandmother to an irrepressible little girl, you are unsurpassed.

My wife and the love of my life, Melissa. In our early days, you asked me to write you a romance novel. Alas, I lack the talents of a romance novelist, but I possess a passion for our life together. Everything comes late to us, and we haven't seen the best yet. Together, we are writing our life, and I'd say it belongs squarely in the romance genre. Thank you for always encouraging me to write, even when my writing is dark and even when it has made our lives difficult.

To my daughter, Ashley Lynne Mae. My singular pride is being your father. You amaze me every day and make me wish I could slow the passage of time. As you move through your fourth year, I glimpse the contours of the amazing person you are becoming. But please—just to show there is mercy in the world—stop growing up so fast!

In memory of my paternal grandparents, C. J. and Geraldine Washington, and my maternal grandparents, Maurice and Edith Jones. Papa, thank you for thinking of me and leaving something behind. Nona, thank you for being the origin of believing in dreams and encouraging me to write. I'm sorry I didn't finish this soon enough. Granddad, thank you for being a role model and for believing in me even when we couldn't see eye to eye. I regret that I was slow in receiving your wisdom, but at last, I am honored to pass it down. Grandma, thank you for showing me what's important and for always being there. I miss talking to you. I wish you all could read this book, but I take comfort in knowing that you infuse my writing. I wish you all could know my daughter, but I will settle for the not-insubstantial gift that she will know you.

ABOUT THE AUTHOR

Photo © 2021 Atlanta Headshots® / Foster & Associates

C. J. Washington is a data scientist and writer. He has a master's degree in computer science from the Georgia Institute of Technology and lives in Atlanta, Georgia, with his wife and daughter. *The Intangible* is his first novel.